Coming Back to the City is **Anuradha Kumar**'s eighth novel. Her first novel, *Letters for Paul*, was published by Mapinlit in 2006, while some of her other novels have been published by Hachette India: *It Takes a Murder* (2013) and two works of historical fiction written under the pseudonym of Adity Kay: *Emperor Chandragupta* (2016) and *Emperor Vikramaditya* (2019). She also writes for younger readers, and has contributed often to Scroll.in, *Economic and Political Weekly*, thewire.in, theaerogram.com, and other places. She has a Master's in Fine Arts (Writing) from Vermont College of Fine Arts, and has degrees in management (human resources) from the Xavier School of Management, XLRI School of Business, and history from Delhi University. She was awarded twice (2004, 2010) for her stories by the Commonwealth Foundation, and has received other awards from *The Little Magazine* and Hindu-Goodbooks.in. Anuradha presently lives in New Jersey, having lived in Maryland, Singapore and several other places in India before this.

Coming Back to the City

Mumbai Stories

ANURADHA KUMAR

SPEAKING
TIGER

SPEAKING TIGER
4381/4, Ansari Road, Daryaganj
New Delhi 110002

First published in paperback by Speaking Tiger 2019

Copyright © Anuradha Kumar 2019

ISBN: 978-93-89231-53-3
eISBN: 978-93-89231-52-6

10 9 8 7 6 5 4 3 2 1

The moral right of the author has been asserted.

For
Maithreyi and Krishna Raj; Ajay and Devyani

'But a city is more than a place in space,
it is a drama in time.'
—Patrick Geddes

'The whole city was richer because he was in it,
and every street, and turn of a road held the
possibility of his appearance.'
—Attia Hosain,
Sunlight on a Broken Column

Contents

Pooja: The Language of Longing

'She's from Amrika, your new tenant, Pooja. A gori.'

Ghatge Sahib hung up abruptly, like he always did. Pooja was relieved. A new tenant would scotch those rumours about the room once and for all. Whispered stories that the room was haunted had gathered pace barely hours after the old woman's body—the ticket-checker's mother—was discovered. Soon everyone in this crumbling, seventy-year-old building— the Jupiter Mills Chawl—believed them. Neighbours mentioned to Pooja things they had seen or heard: footsteps and vague sounds of the radio; bursts of song interrupted by advertisement jingles and an announcer's staccato voice.

Many of the old workers' families who had once lived in the chawl had already moved out. Several had lost their jobs as the textile mills slowly shut down. A few others were opting for a scheme which would give them apartments in the city's distant suburbs of Goregaon and Borivali, in return for the rooms they owned in the chawls. There were several chawls that still peppered this central part of the city; a part the government said was in need for urgent redevelopment, like any other modern city. This promised a real bonanza for real-estate barons but there were a few, like Jupiter Mills, which were still holding out. Five years earlier, the old lady's son, the ticket-checker, had leased a room but had not turned up since the funeral. Now everyone knew the truth about him as well—he had never been a ticket-checker, nor had he ever worked for the railways.

Housing in Mumbai was expensive and rents in this central part of the city had quadrupled in recent years, as high-rises and malls rose in the place of old buildings that had already been demolished. Any vacant space, any unoccupied room, always had too many takers. Pooja waited for the rumours to subside but there were always jealous neighbours. The two rooms, one which Pooja and Mahesh lived in, and the other they rented out, had actually come to Mahesh from his father, who had once been a millworker. Mahesh hadn't thought of leaving yet because Ghatge Sahib, whom he worked for, hadn't said anything. As for Pooja, she did think the rumours might have easily been scotched by a token puja to propitiate the dead woman's spirit. But, as Pooja always told herself bitterly, when had the gods ever been appeased by the prayers of a childless woman?

The ticket-checker never came back, nor did he repay the arrears he owed. It took Pooja the better part of two days to scrub stains off the floor and sponge the windows, and then the room was ready again. It hadn't taken Ghatge Sahib more than a month to find them a new tenant. As Mahesh told her later that night, awe and worship in his voice, Ghatge Sahib could always be counted on. Ghatge Sahib wasn't just the leader of the textile mill union, he was *their* leader, their mai-baap, the man who knew the politicians, the builders, the man who could always get things done.

Pooja liked the thought of their new tenant being American. A foreigner wouldn't ask her all those questions about her marriage, her childlessness. Instead, being American, the new tenant might even need help. And then, Pooja thought, she might learn things from her: their kind of food and some English too. Provided, of course, the new tenant had the time. Ghatge Sahib had mentioned that she was here to do research on the city's old chawls. Renting a room in a chawl would also give the new tenant a flavour of how life was lived in one.

A flavour, as Pooja soon understood, that had Maria spending most mornings in her room. Every time Pooja walked towards it with the tray of food—for the room came with a fully functioning air conditioner and three meals a day—or with the stainless-steel tray bearing the masala chai Maria had come to love, Pooja would find Maria waiting by the door, wide smile in place, holding out things she'd discovered in the room. Maria's research work often took her out into the city, to its mills where she met the workers. Still, at times, Pooja found it unsettling to come upon Maria during the day.

That afternoon Maria was there, leaning against the door, elbows pressed against its green louvres, feet tapping the floor in rhythm. Dressed in her usual manner: jeans, a thin T-shirt and, as Pooja noticed right away, no bra. As she neared, Maria assumed a more languid pose. A hand flicked over her red-brown curls, she rubbed the freckles on her neck so they turned an angry red.

'Here's what I found today.' Maria held out a photograph before fanning herself with it. The thin cotton of her shirt showed the clear outline of a nipple.

Pooja tossed an alarmed look around and waved her hand in quick warning. *No*, she pointed to Maria's breasts. *No, this is India. Behave.*

If a woman took risks like these, anyone could sneak in. Didn't she read the papers to know of things that happened to women? Mumbai was no different from others, not any more. Pooja knew this from Mahesh's furious rants about the outsiders who were flooding the city.

Pooja looked among all Maria's scattered paraphernalia, found the mirrored dupatta Maria was fond of and tossed it her way.

'Really? One needs this?' Maria rolled her eyes. She looked down at the dupatta and then she remembered the photo and held it out. Her fingers touched Pooja's and lingered there a little. Pooja didn't seem to notice the caress. 'Tell me, who's this? Your daughter?'

Pooja stared; she had hidden the photo away for it drew attention for the wrong reasons. That one happy day she now hated because of all the innocuous questions the photo invited.

In the photo, standing between Pooja and Mahesh, was a girl with tight plaits, wearing a bright smile. It was clear she wasn't their daughter, still people were curious, and from that one question would follow all the others, tinged with pity and a certain accusation. Isn't it time you had a child of your own? How many years have you been married?

Only Mahesh and she knew this: that the girl had been crying, minutes before the photo was taken, in the photo studio at the Essel Amusement Park. Mahesh and Pooja had done their best to make her smile, make her forget the fact that she was lost. They had cheered her up and it was Mahesh who had alerted the police.

But Maria had questions of her own, all different, like Maria herself. 'Who is she? I don't see her around.' Pooja wanted to make herself understood, even if her token English, the way she spoke it, made things difficult.

'Girl, we...meet in park once.'

'Oh, a friend.'

Maria pressed her finger on the photo, traced the outline of the man's face and moved on to other matters. 'Ma-hesh?' Pooja giggled. It was the way Maria broke the word up. 'Love?' Maria then said, pointing to Mahesh in the picture and then her heart. Pooja was okay going along with the miming. She just hoped she wouldn't laugh too soon. Talking in gestures soon reduced one to a state of silly helplessness. Love Mahesh? Pooja wasn't sure what Maria wanted to hear.

Pooja fasted for Mahesh, prayed to the gods for his good health and long life. She waited up for him and accepted most of his decisions. Her life was tied irrevocably to his.

'Love?' Pooja let herself blush. It was easier to pander to what Maria wanted to see and hear. Then Pooja said, 'He is good man.'

Maria laughed. 'That's cute,' she said and then reached out to touch Pooja's hand in the strange tickle-inducing way she had. 'Love,' she said, softer now, looking at the picture and to Pooja's amazement, when Maria looked up, there were tears in her eyes. She was missing someone.

'All right,' Pooja managed to say, tiring of this strangeness, of Maria's sudden changes in behaviour, and thinking of all her chores left undone. Then the siren announcing the change of shift blew out from the last mill and Pooja knew she had to rush. She had only an idea of whom Maria was missing. A woman with short dark hair and a narrow, too-thin pointed face. Just as Pooja reached the door, Maria called for her again, 'The photo, don't you want it?'

Pooja laughed, waving her hand, 'Late...I go now.'

In the bus, some hours later, Pooja turned her mind to other things. From the recent episode of *MasterChef India*, she had had a new idea for dinner: rice that wouldn't be too spicy for Maria. Maybe, Pooja thought, she could add saffron and sprinkle raisins at the end. She was always working out new ways of cooking food, and for the most part, her culinary efforts had been well received. Mahesh barely noticed what he was eating most times. He had been keeping very late hours the last few months, but Ghatge Sahib, the ticket-checker, his mother and now Maria had had nothing to complain of yet. Just last week, Pooja had received a new order to supply lunch boxes to the bank that had just opened in one of the renovated mill complexes.

Now the bus climbed over the bridge and Pooja watched the exhausted trains below it, waiting for passengers. The afternoon city was sluggish around her. Cabs lined the roadside, some empty, in others the drivers waited.

She passed the brownstone buildings with the old shops on the first floor. New Modern Textiles had some new fabrics strung up on hangers under the awning that stretched over the narrow sidewalk. Pooja rested her elbow on the window, glancing idly into every shop and restaurant. The Udupi café with its afternoon customers now stopping for a paan in the shop outside, the cycle shop with its shutters half-downed and the afternoon light on the rows of orderly metallic wheels made them glisten and buzz, and there was the luggage store just after. Her eyes drooped in the afternoon heat.

That day she was to help the Sisters of St Joseph's bake cakes at the convent in Mahim and Pooja had already decided that it would be her last day there. The new order for the bank, which would begin the next month would take up more of her time. Moreover, the Sisters were beginning to get curious about her, and offering their brand of instant solace.

'Listen to Jesus. Hold him in your heart. He helps everyone, child,' Lisamma, a thick-lipped, thick-waisted nun, told her that day. Her hands were nice and warm and when she patted Pooja's shoulders, her piety rolled dough-like over Pooja.

Lisamma always mistook Pooja's fatigue for sadness, for she was tired by the end of it all: the churning and stirring of the batter, the placing of the trays in the oven that made one flinch when the heat rushed up like an angry storm, then the arranging of the cupcakes into neat numbered boxes. Pooja could not even bask in the lemony fragrance of all that she had conjured up. Sometimes it was fine to let people think what they wanted.

It was around seven when Pooja finished but that was all right, for neither Mahesh nor Maria would be back soon.

'Nobody's home yet,' she told herself, and her pace slowed automatically. She wanted to stop by the flower women with their jasmine braids, to linger by the vegetable stalls for prices dropped a bit by evening. There were other women shopping too, some nagging their children with a shrill insistence. There was someone twisting her child's ear for having wandered off. Then Pooja saw someone she recognized, threading her way towards her, past the line of the vegetable vendors, their goods displayed on sacks by the roadside. The woman lived in the same chawl as she did. Pooja saw the way the woman's eyes ran over her shimmering red sari, the bangles that always matched. The woman looked tired, her sari was frayed, but she had children and that allowed her that certain disdainful expression as she caught Pooja's eye.

'Pooja, arre, long time!'

'Yes.' Pooja smiled, now looking with deliberate interest at the vegetable stalls.

'Looking very smart, Pooja.' The woman fingered Pooja's sari, assured herself it was inexpensive chiffon, and went on. 'Is there something to celebrate?'

Pooja knew what the woman was getting at. She smiled her tight smile, pulled her bag closer and said she had to rush.

'You're always in a rush, Pooja; big family to cook for, right?'

Pooja patted the woman on the shoulder and sidled around her. She wanted to remember something about the woman, but she couldn't. And so, she couldn't ask her anything in turn. It was a childless woman whose life was an open book, her shame a matter of public display. Pooja took quicker steps homeward, keen to leave the woman and the whole day behind her now.

Once home, she filled a plate of rice and curry, ran down the stairs quickly to put it out for the mongrel who had made the chawl his home. He'd come by soon. She returned to thoughts for dinner. It had been a chore but this last year had become something else, something she gladly thought of, when she wasn't tormented by the fact of her childless state.

After everything had blown over with the ticket-checker and his mother, with Mahesh's increasing busyness, Pooja had been on her own, finding comfort in all that she cooked up. Small solaces that filled her with secret happiness. Just like her sadness remained unshared, she didn't mind not having to share her happiness either. Tomato rice, eggplant fritters, a raw jackfruit curry. She could leave the methi paratha for later. *Five years had gone by and she was still childless.*

Five years, and everyone, not just the woman in the street, hoped to remind her of this. As if Pooja needed reminding.

Five years, and Pooja remembered a day from that time. The last time she was ever asked her opinion about anything. She wondered if the gods in her village, those small stone ones sitting in their wayside shrines under the tree, or even the big Ganesha sitting with his curved elephant trunk in the village's main temple, had known even then that she was accursed. That her dead mother's spirit which had seemed to guide her since the previous year had somehow vanished for a few hours when it mattered, gone instead for a dip in the river. That the women who had gotten her married, had been moved by her pitiable state, and she, for her part, had said yes to everything, to almost everything, not realizing the sadness that lay ahead. But that day she hadn't been thinking all that. It just happened to be an unusually hot day and Pooja had been glad to make her way up the winding road to the big white house with its red-tiled roof.

It was the afternoon she met Gauri Tai, and by the end of the day, her marriage had been decided. It had been a Wednesday, and mid-week being the busiest time, it was the time her father managed their small tea stall by the bus stand, leaving her free for a few hours. It was a village, but ideally located, close to the highway that connected Mumbai and Goa.

Pooja waited in the small balcony at the back of the house in the company of the blue and yellow budgerigars. She knew the story from her mother: someone who wanted to set up a hotel further south in Goa had visited the Ghatges and the birds were a present. That time, the Ghatges' daughter, whom Pooja knew as the forever ill child, had still been alive. Then the budgerigars in the front porch would always cheer her up. Pooja would see her too; the times she came up to deliver something her mother had cooked specially for the girl. Gauri Tai was in Mumbai often with her husband, leaving the girl in the care of an old ayah. The girl would swing by herself on that hot porch, smiling dreamily at the chattering budgerigars. When she died, the budgerigars were moved to the small balcony and now they hopped towards Pooja, beaks knocking against the iron grilles, still chirping incessantly in the manner she remembered.

It was a big sad house, enlivened only by the small chirping birds. After a while, Pooja rose to get the birds some water. Empty bottle caps lay strewn in a corner and she filled them from a basin. Then she dipped her finger in the water and pushed it in through the grills for the birds. She felt a certain thrill in the way they stabbed her finger repeatedly with their beaks. It prepared her for what lay ahead.

She had had only a dim idea why she had been called. Her father, his body racked with coughing, had said it was time she got married. It was just a year since her mother died.

'They are powerful people, it's good they are concerned for you. They knew your mother.'

Pooja had, of course, thought about marriage. Her friends were all married now. They came back often to their natal homes to have their babies. Their mothers would fuss over them and the thought filled Pooja with a hollowness. But she couldn't cry while her father was here. The emptiness left by her mother had only deepened over time; all their tears only dipped into an unseen well. She knew leaving the village would mean leaving her father too. But when someone like Gauri Tai called you, you didn't refuse.

Gauri Tai looked up briefly as Pooja entered. She was with two other women and strewn around them was the paraphernalia of pickle-making. Pooja saw them looking up at her, taking in the jasmine braided into her hair, and the skirt she wore, now short enough to rise over her ankles. They stared longer than she felt comfortable. One of the women then drew in her breath and Pooja lowered her eyes. The first impression, she understood, had not been one of disapproval.

She saw the cauliflowers and the pieces of unripe mango on the cloth at the centre of the covered veranda. In some relief, Pooja obediently took her place, patting the florets dry and stretching them out on the cloth. After a long silence, Gauri Tai spoke.

'How are things, Pooja? Finished school?'

Gauri Tai knew she had stopped school the year she had turned fourteen, so without waiting for an answer she asked after Pooja's father.

'He's in the shop.'

On cue, one of the women looked up, 'Too hard for him to be managing it now...'

Pooja did not look up. She knew what would follow: the quick exchanges of looks between them, the unspoken signals, how the conversation would proceed from there. Gauri Tai stirred the spice mixture into the hot oil. The mustard spluttered, a flame flickered onto the floor, and as she reached out to stab it out with a quick finger, Gauri Tai gestured with her spatula. That cut short the niceties drastically.

'Ghatge Sahib is here, and there's Mahesh. Mahesh Patil. You know he's worked with him for a long time.'

Pooja's hand stilled, she did not look up. Gauri Tai spoke in a more conciliatory tone. 'He has bright prospects.'

Then another woman chimed in, 'It's better for you if he has no family. No mother-in-law.'

As the laughter broke, Pooja placed the dried mango pieces on the dry cloth in neat order. They were taking an interest in her life, and all she had to do was to look suitably grateful. The women had gone on talking almost as if she wasn't there.

'Yes, and Mahesh is hard-working, and will go far.'

'There is no way her father is going to get her married. He's always...'

Hush, hush, for then they would remember her too, and rein in their conversation.

'You will like him. He's a good man.'

'Don't make him work too hard.' the women giggled.

'Yes, work hard at having fun.'

'The babies can come later.'

Gauri Tai rose, washed her hands in the pan next to her, and then turned her head, intending to tell Pooja she could go now. But it was the girl's tear-stained face that made her stop. Pooja could hardly get the words out. Gauri Tai stepped over the drying florets to come up to Pooja, held her by the shoulders gently and then lifted her chin up.

'Don't worry, he's a good man.' But there was an uncertain note in her voice, as if she wondered if she had been convincing enough.

Pooja said instead, 'I believe you, Tai.'

But Gauri Tai bent to ask her, 'Tell me then. I mean it.'

'My father?'

'He will be okay.'

'I can't leave...'

'Don't worry. We are all there for you.' She brushed Pooja's hair away from her forehead and held her in a gentle embrace.

Five years had gone by since then. She hadn't been

comforted that way ever again. And like everyone else, Gauri Tai too, might have lost all her old kindness.

He's a good man. That was what her father said too. His expression told her he was neither happy nor sad about her marriage. He had become quieter since her mother died. Pooja spent more time in the shop but made little effort in trying to get him to talk. She saved her energies now to stop him from drinking too much.

Her mother's presence had been the only thing that stopped him. Pooja was embarrassed and now even frightened to ask for her father at the liquor stall. At the end of every evening, she downed the shutters and hated the slow walk to the stall, its halogen lights hanging over low brown walls which turned the blue canopy a ghastly green. From some way off, her eyes would search for her father, moving down the row of benches, hoping he wasn't the one lolling under the table. As she broke into a last helpless run towards him, she would remember what her mother had often told her. A woman running presents the most ungainly sight ever.

Mahesh had gone about the marriage with a brisk precision. He had stiffened with a certain pride when Gauri Tai led Ghatge Sahib up to them. With Mahesh, Pooja too had bent to touch his feet and, as Ghatge's hand rested on her shoulder in an exaggerated paternal fashion, he had proceeded to tell her how much he relied on Mahesh. Her new husband had looked abashed, then smiled in a way that made him look vulnerable.

The night of their wedding Mahesh had told her how devoted he was to the Ghatges. Pooja read in his devotion a certain desperation. There were few jobs already, Mahesh was saying, and the people from outside were taking them away. Most politicians only pandered to them, little knowing how difficult life was in the city. Survival took money. And it'd be a chore to set up and run a house. Children could always come later. 'We must give ourselves time.'

He had touched her face gently and told her then that she was lovely; just looking at her made him feel considerably less lonely. 'Mumbai is a big city, but you are not to be scared.' But five years had gone since then and he no longer spoke to her this way.

Days and years later, she would always remember that moment. Just as she would his silences, the way he had described sex to her, telling her he would understand if she wanted time, the way he kissed her forehead after the first time, his obliviousness to her surprise when she realized it had taken less time than his description of the entire thing, the way he'd kiss her the same way always. He was a good man, she believed. Not like the men whose misdeeds filled the pages of the city's newspapers, the ones who raped little children, or beat up their wives. He was even unlike her neighbours, and Pooja knew those responsible for the stifled screams, the thuds of flesh hitting a wall that sometimes sounded very close and always made her hold her own screams back.

That evening, long after dinner had been prepared, she received that one call from Mahesh. A hurried one, telling her not to worry, he would be late. Maria neither called nor texted, Pooja knew she would be late. In that quietness, she thought of Maria's airy American voice, her frequent high-pitched exclamations, and especially her way of saying 'cool.'

She liked that word and tried it out now. People came in from the station lugging bags of vegetables. Pooja said cool, and the word slipped out onto the burnished road, cooled by the night. Someone came in on a scooter. Its light flashed coolly along the walls, lit up the face on a movie poster. Somewhere a pressure cooker whistled, and a utensil fell from someone's hand. Then, in the lull that fell, Pooja heard the drummers playing in the late-night café. It was drawing in a different kind of clientele and that seemed to worry some of the people in the chawl. There had been cases of drunken boys pissing against the walls. And as always, everyone waited for Ghatge Sahib to do something. Pooja suspected, however, that Ghatge didn't really want to do anything about it. He had, perhaps even got a cut out of the business proceeds, but she would never air her suspicions aloud.

Now she stayed out on the balcony long after the night got cooler. In some apartments, there was now a dim blue glow; she knew then that the prime-time serial was on. She leaned against the column in the long veranda. She closed her eyes momentarily and when she opened them again, the blueness had only spread in an eerie, even glow. Pooja felt the chill on her neck. And did not turn around. The room wasn't haunted. The old woman, after all, had been too nice for her spirit to turn into something malignant.

Pooja shivered, finding solace in the light on in her own rooms. The old lady had been dead in the days her son had doused the room over and over with room freshener, lit incense sticks as he tried to hide the evidence and plan his own getaway. He'd rush by more frequently towards the bathroom, bedpan in hand. It smells too much, he'd explain with a taut smile. They had had no idea of his elaborate plan.

For a week that had been his story. The room did smell nice and fresh and one day there he was, dapper and fresh in a new suit. He had folded his hands in a namaste and said he had a new job, he'd return late that night. But it was around midnight that the police came. Two constables who said they had received an anonymous call. And that was how the dead body came to light. The ticket-checker had preserved it very well. It turned out there was no one by his name who worked for the railways. He had been collecting money from ticketless passengers on false pretexts.

Now in the darkness, looking up at the sky, she saw a plane. It was, for that moment, trapped in the square between two high buildings. But the plane would break free while she never would. She thought of the old lady's dying face and her mother's constant stillness. What was it that they waited for if not death? But for her mother death had come too soon. Pooja drew in her breath, and then knew she was sobbing, not really sure what had made her cry.

Pooja waited in the veranda as the last of her sobs died away. She scraped her bangles against the rails, and waited for the welcome sound of one breaking, scratching her till the blood ran.

She took a last look around her rooms. She cleared up again. She lit the incense sticks before the altar and saw that the food was still warm. Pooja tore a piece of paper out of a notebook, pulled out an old English newspaper and began painstakingly copying out words at random. Words that at first made no sense. Words that horrified her, once she read them aloud. Words that made her feel that the city was a universe unto itself, with people living lives so very different from her own. Words that gave her the feeling that, despite everything, the world was bigger than she imagined, while she was being thrust into a smallness she did not want.

Then she wrote the sentences she always did as she practised her English.

He is a good man.

He is a very good man.

I am good. I am bad.

She wrote a word she had picked up and wrote it again and again.

Awkward.

It was a strange word. She had no idea what it meant. It had a kind of stumbling sound to it.

Pooja had almost dozed off over the newspaper on the

floor when her cell phone rang. Her voice was sleepy, almost glazed. Was it morning already? Then she had to rush to the tube well. She strained to hear Mahesh's snore next to her, a sound almost familiar to her every morning, but the voice that came into her ear was different. A heavy baritone, but now so gentle that she could feel the words brushing against her ears. The way it had done on the day she had been married. She knew then that Mahesh wasn't home, and it was almost eleven at night.

'Gauri? Sleeping?'

She felt her heart catch. Ghatge's voice sounded overfamiliar. 'Yes, it's late.'

'Mahesh is on his way home. He makes you stay up late for him.'

He spoke in a low drawl, then laughed, and it came too soft against her ear. She could imagine him stretched on his low leather sofa, watching something on his huge flat screen TV.

'Your Gauri Tai will be here soon for a visit. Make her the special something you make always. Though you haven't made it for me in a while.'

Ghatge Sahib paused. Almost as if he expected Pooja to say something. She was unsure, knowing small talk at such hours wasn't quite the proper thing. 'Pooja, hello. Are you there?'

'Yes. Yes.' She pulled a chair loud across the floor and it made a distinct scraping sound. It'd make Richard and his mother, who lived just a floor below, look up in consternation.

Ghatge asked, almost mildly, 'Is someone there?'

This time her answer was breathless and quick, 'Yes, Maria Madam.'

'Oh.' Ghatge Sahib sounded hesitant and then disbelieving. Pooja played around with the chair. She made it knock against the table in desperation. 'Gauri Tai will be happy to see you,' his voice was now confused, drifting away.

'I will too. It's been ages since I saw her.' She turned her face away to say, 'Yes, Madam, coming.'

To Ghatge she said in a deliberate undertone, 'The new madam next door. She has nightmares. She thinks the room has a ghost.'

He was laughing as he hung up. Pooja felt her own laughter rising too. It was surprising how easily he had fallen for it. She could never be sure about Ghatge Sahib. There was the way he looked at her. Perhaps he hadn't made a move yet because of Mahesh, or because of Gauri Tai, or even because she, Pooja, came with bad luck.

The varying sounds of darkness faded around her—the last traffic, footsteps, a baby crying—and then one last truth came to Pooja with certainty. It was far better being here than in the village. Tomorrow, she would cook up a sumptuous breakfast, follow it up with a lip-smacking lunch too. In time, she would supply meals to ever more people, at a fixed price, a fixed menu for every day. She would then have the entire city, or most of it, eating out of her hand. What she did would then matter more than what she was—and did that really matter? Pooja frowned in confusion—she had no answer and she gave herself up to welcome sleep.

Neera Joshi's Unfinished Book

Neera Joshi's cell phone rang in the afternoon. Perhaps it was the bai telling her she could not come that evening. Neera sighed and stared at the instrument, its charger plugged into the wall. If the bai wasn't coming, she would have to make do with bread and the leftover coriander chutney for dinner. Or she could have a banana later. It couldn't be that clueless American researcher, Maria, either, for she always emailed. Neera leaned back again on the rocking chair. The bai would tell her later that she had tried to call. It was time, Neera thought, she engaged someone who provided more regular meal services. Not that she needed much but, at her age, one needed to eat healthy.

The phone was a shiny grey instrument, the sun glinting on the silver around its screen. Its trilling—for Neera always had the volume turned up high—filled every empty corner of her apartment. Neera noted the stain of old oil on the floor, the corridor leading in and the wind chime caught in the curtain folds. She looked at the diamond-shaped chimes, swaying and twirling, and it was a while before Neera realized that the phone was now silent. Memory kept things alive, long after everything else had gone. Then, almost as if she willed it, the phone rang again and Neera answered. The bai never tried more than once, so it had to be a wrong number.

The light came in from the high window, and Neera, leaning forward to lift her phone from the low table, saw herself in an old photo. She had aged but she knew there was none of that middle-aged spread about her. The silver in her hair gave her features a certain delicacy, she thought. Then she heard her name in a soft, pleasant, voice, one just like the television announcers but this one had a certain hesitation in it.

'Neera Joshi?'

'Yes.' Neera matched her voice to the one in her ears. The voice at the other end identified herself as Raina. She was from *City Magazine* that wanted to interview her.

'What for?'

There was a silence. She had been called difficult before and now Neera felt a sudden regret. In that short silence, as the voice that had called itself Raina disappeared, Neera wanted to pull it back towards her again. She cleared her throat. 'I didn't quite understand...'

The girl said, still in the same unchanged tone, that *City Magazine* wanted to do a feature on her and other women who had made the city.

'Made the city?' Neera asked. 'You could say we unmade it in many ways.' She couldn't help it, the tall buildings that stared down at her own, cast shadows on her reflected face. It was the city that made you, never the other way around. She heard the girl's reassuring 'no' at the other end. It was that which made Neera agree. There had been no apologetic giggle on the girl's part, no overexplaining.

The next afternoon, Neera took a taxi to Ghatge's office to meet Raina. Not too long ago, the textile mill union had its meetings here too. The short ride from Sewree to Parel took, depending on the traffic, anything from ten to forty-five minutes. But the afternoon sun was gentle, the high-rises blocked the sea breeze and left darkened zigzag stripes on the road below. The cars took up too much space everywhere, even the roads could not hold them. Neera gave up the taxi once it took the last turn to the union office, and only moments later rued her decision. A blue sedan came lurching on the sidewalk as it tried to thread its way through the jammed road, forcing Neera to dig her way through the queue of people waiting for a bus or a taxi.

The two of them were waiting for her in Ghatge's office. It was cool inside; Neera barely heard the hum of the new air conditioner. The refrigerated breeze on her bare arms felt blissful. It reminded her of long-ago walks on the Marine Drive, or along the Gateway and the Taj Hotel. She had been with someone then; someone always at the edge of her memory, who slipped in at moments like this. The memory came back to her with a sweet pang.

'It's nice of you to meet us.' Raina was in jeans and a kurti, her hair was tied back firmly, and her features appeared sharp and clear. She pointed to the young man with her and introduced him as Jeet. He lifted his camera to his forehead, in a gesture both obsequious and cheeky.

Raina smiled, almost as if to reassure her about what lay ahead and Neera did too, allowing herself to relax, swivelling a little on the leather chair. From the windows, she saw life unfolding by habit all around her in the chawls of the millworkers. A new high-rise called the Marathon now rose just where the chawl building gave way. Neera could see the taller, more imposing gate of the new building and the driveway that ran for almost a mile before ending at an impressive lobby complete with a Roman fountain. When construction had begun, the Marathon, at twenty-five floors, was one of the tallest in the city but, three years later, it was already a dwarf, adding to the ugly acne on the city's face.

Everywhere she saw the aggressive new jostling out the old. At the other end of the crossing, where the old mill showroom had once been, was the new pub. The tea stall where the workers and union members had gathered still stood. The old storehouse where the old union office had kept its records was now marked with a brown nondescript door, with the heavy lock on it. Scooters and bikes were parked haphazardly around but even two decades ago, it had been a plain ordinary building, just as overgrown with weeds as now.

Jeet, training his camera on Neera, made her do several things. He made her face the window, walk to the door, stand against the shelves with all the recent files, then asked her to sit at the table. He was polite though, even when he asked Raina to help Neera arrange her sari a bit differently around herself. Raina's fingers were cool around her neck as she rearranged the pleats on Neera's sari.

'Too many photos,' Neera finally murmured. Raina smiled in her languid friendly way, saying photos spoke more than words did these days. 'It will make the readers read about you. Seeing is believing, right?'

Raina nodded at the photo when Jeet held out his camera towards her, and then began, in an offhand way. 'All this needs explaining.' Raina's hands waved, indicating the office and the world outside. 'What happened and how? And for a long while you were involved with the union politics and leading the workers' struggle, weren't you, Neeraji?'

'Yes, a long time ago.' Neera's words came slow. She pointed to the old shed across the road, with its metal door and the chain lock. 'That was the old office; this is a far plusher place.' She wondered if this was what she really wanted to say. Her eyes met Raina's briefly before she went on. 'The union leaders are different now. Maybe you need someone who can better manage things...or to talk to the people above, the politicians. The workers, the people, don't figure anywhere.'

She rose to look out of the window. Neera knew now why she had agreed to meet the journalists. There was something in the girl's voice, something precise and to the point. She wasn't one for playing around with emotions. Haltingly, Neera told them then, bits that came to her easily, about the story of the union in the city, the twists and turns the struggle had taken. The movement the workers had led, that had fought for a new state more than four decades ago, had been disbanded soon after the state had come into being. That, Neera still believed, was a mistake by the left parties, for then the Native People's Party had simply swamped everything, taken all credit for itself. The workers had lost their identity, their sense of pride and now all they had left was a narrower and more constricted sense of themselves. It left nothing but hatred for those who were different.

Raina went on to ask her about present-day issues, things at least some journalists were still familiar with: the issue with the mill land, the workers' compensation and if they were being given a fair share in the planned new housing constructions. Neera shrugged, then took a chance. She asked Raina if she would like to go around the chawls, see things for herself. The girl readily agreed, ignoring the silent message in Jeet's eyes.

'Some of this ought to be preserved,' Neera was pointing to the greying four-storey buildings on the other side of the road that abutted the wall. Almost every window was differently coloured, with a creeper clinging to the wall, drooping over the ledges. The red tiles on the roof were now blackened in places. No matter what the season, pigeons and gulls clustered on the tiles.

They walked out in that late afternoon, crossing the road to where the chawl was. The ground floor stood a foot higher from the ground, lined with columns and a veranda that led to the rooms inside. The rooms on every floor were alike in every way, but every occupant, no matter how temporary, took care to do things just that bit differently. Doors were painted in various colours, some floors had a flower pattern in front, drawn in coloured powder, and water vessels and buckets stood outside every room. They walked up the short flight of steps, ducked under the cloth awning, the clotheslines and felt the touch of the creepers on their faces.

As they neared, someone came rushing down the staircase, and because her smile was directed at both of them, Neera guessed Pooja knew the other girl. 'Nice to see you here, Tai,' she said to Neera while Raina murmured, somewhat distractedly, 'Always so busy.' Pooja tossed a smile back in acknowledgement, 'Just like you, Raina Didi.' They looked at Pooja walking quickly away, then at each other. Pooja had that effect and Neera wondered if Raina had seen what she had. The quiet darkness on Pooja's face, dismissed by the quick smile. 'She does a lot of work. The women always do.' Neera's voice trailed off.

'It'd be a pity...' she sighed again. 'A pity if they didn't get the compensation they truly deserve if the builders have their way and this land all goes...'

The women were beginning to understand, Neera thought. They knew things happened one at a time. But the men wanted too much at once: a good apartment, preferably with a sea view, a job and then not just a job, but a proper government one. For the men still liked doing nothing much and ordering everyone around. Hadn't they learnt by now—too much radical change was just impossible? So much blood had already been shed in the name of revolution. You took it little by little and that was enough.

She would never have dared to air all her thoughts aloud when younger. But no matter what, as even educated women like herself knew, women had never had a voice. And Neera laughed softly instead when Raina asked her about the labour strikes nearly four decades ago, and what the women had done then. Neera pointed toward the old paani puri stall. It was lucky now to be frequented by celebrities, especially since *Time Out* magazine had that feature on its owner, a man with an impressive moustache, who had once had a bit role in a Bollywood film. 'On the other side now hidden behind that motor showroom is the alley that led to the station,' Neera said. 'This was where we hid when the police charged at the striking workers.'

Later, they stopped for coffee (Neera for lime juice) in the café on the first floor of the mall, one of the first to come up once the mill land began to be auctioned. They sat on high stools on a wobbly circular table that looked out into the square. It was the place newspapers now called High Street, though the taxi-drivers, old and new, still used the old name for it, Phoenix Mills. That somehow reassured Neera. The café had glass-fronted walls, and a patio, now empty and unoccupied in the heat.

'Tell me about your book,' Raina broke in, and Neera smiled. Something about the afternoon made her feel that she could consider that question innocuous. Besides Raina had poise; she reminded Neera of herself once. 'Every time I begin I wonder if I should make it fictional. I am not sure if it's too early to reveal truths.' Raina pointed to her phone and said all this was now off the record.

Neera brushed it away, 'Nothing I say matters. Probably nothing of what I write will matter too.'

There was a silence. Neera looked down at her glass, and the varnished table only confirmed what she knew: Raina was glaring at Jeet who stood outside, nonchalantly smoking. It was time for them to go, and something made Neera say the words, 'All the leaders, most of them, have gone now.'

'People you may not even know...' she said, her voice trailed away.

'Ramakrishna Desai...' It was the first time in years Neera had heard his name aloud, and she held herself still, not wishing to look Raina's way. Of all things, she had not expected Raina to mention Bhau this way. Was this what growing old meant?

That one's instincts would fail one day; that the knowledge about human nature that one had gathered over the years was nothing but sham and had conspired to deceive all this time. But Raina was speaking as she looked down at the photos on her camera phone.

'My mother knew him too.' When Raina said that, Neera knew what she should have known all along. In the girl's face, she saw her mother. Raina was thinner, and her hair was shorter. But there was the shape of the face, the straight nose, the even look in her eyes, the way she held herself, a bit disdainful and still shy.

'And what is your mother's name?' Neera asked, trying to keep the tremor in her voice away.

'Mohini.'

Neera sighed, she should have guessed as much. The other questions that came to her seemed redundant now. In the girl's face, Neera read a hesitation before it disappeared. 'What was her name before marriage?'

'I should remember,' Raina's voice was lame as she searched for her words. 'Though I should know.' Her poise had slipped and Neera felt her voice had gone a long way away. Neera talked some more instead.

'There was a gym here,' waving to indicate something beyond the chawl. 'And now the boys play cricket there when it doesn't rain. There used to be a dais in one corner.' She looked, a flattened palm shading her eyes, and she could still make out that empty flagstaff, in that vacant space between two buildings. She saw Raina looked tired. It had been a day crowded with memories and new information. As for Jeet, he had the photos to develop.

Raina had promised to call, and so Neera waited. She remembered the time she had waited in a similar way. All she had to show for it was that immense unceasing throbbing in her temples, the frequent walk to the windows at home or where she worked, just in case he, Bhau, came by. She sat by the window like before, but now comforted by the old creaking familiarity of her old rocking chair, ringed by her bookshelves. From her high floor, Neera could see a good way out, as far as the new flyover which skirted the salt pans. Around her stretched skeletal frameworks of buildings promising to rise higher than her own. There were some things one just could not stop. Ten years ago, following the attack in New York, there had been proposals to cap the high-rises coming up in Mumbai in case something similar happened. But then just as quietly, such plans all died away.

She looked through the windows again and leaned forward as something caught her eye. Far away by the salt pans, in the light of the setting sun, she noted a series of red and pink dots. The flamingoes were back.

Sewree, right down to where the swamps began, was where Bhau and she had spent some evenings together. They would take a taxi to the Dockyard Road station and walk to the very end of the pier where, by late evening, things would fall very quiet. The last boat to Mora had already left and usually there were a couple or two sitting on the green benches, or resting against each other, tenderly holding hands, their bags secure by their feet.

One evening, as they looked at the colours dimming on the flamingoes, and the sun, too, drifted away from the sea, Bhau had said in the dreamy slow voice she heard rarely that it would be a nice idea for them to sail away to Goa. She had loved the smile on his face. 'What would everyone say... Ramakrishna Desai and his friend...?'

'Girlfriend...' he had said, his arm on her shoulder, she leaning on him. It was the first time she had heard someone use the word. The thrill that had run through her—for the first time, Neera felt truly feminine. She felt it was all right that she belonged to someone, and all this, despite the fact that he was a married man.

She had first met Bhau—everyone referred to the leader as 'older brother'—when Raina perhaps hadn't even been born. And she, Neera, might have been just as old as Raina now was. It was the early 1960s. As a young reporter, Neera was part of a meeting called to commemorate the twenty-two people who had been killed in police firing on unarmed demonstrators, protesting for a new state. She followed the thousands marching with a sense of purpose towards Dadar beach, shouting slogans, promising to keep the struggle alive. Neera looked at the posters of the martyrs, and those of the leaders of the movement. She had not known anything about Bhau then, except the name the newspapers called him by, Ramakrishna Desai.

On the day of the protest march, when Neera first saw Bhau, he was standing at the dais looking out at a sea of people. A lean square face, a thin smile that made his eyes crinkle up behind his glasses, and his hair, black streaked with grey, brushed back. Some among the crowd wore white Gandhi caps, others held up newspapers, for it was beginning to get hot. Beyond them and the dais stretched the sea, framed by palm trees. Despite the agitation in the air, the evenness of the waves rolling in and the somnolent trees watching over things left a soothing effect. The marchers fell silent as they found their places on the rough mats spread out on the sand and even the policemen lowered their batons. In that silence, Neera even made out the sound of a microphone clicking as someone checked it one final time. She heard the wind caught in it, like someone invisible whistling and looking up, she saw the clouds drift by.

She remembered the moment Bhau first spoke. He raised his hands, fisting them together, and the voices of the people rose in unison.

Then Bhau spread his palms wide one final time and a hush fell. Neera felt the sound falling like a hollow drum into a deep well. His voice filled her ears. He spoke in measured tones, his voice even gravel, sounding close. There he was on the dais, saying the creation of the new state would benefit everyone, not just workers but all those who belonged to it. It would be a state united by language, culture and history. The listening audience loudly cheered him. He raised his hands again asking for silence before he had read out the names of the martyrs, all twenty-two of them. They did not, he said, pausing at the right moment, die in vain. In that quiet, his voice had an impact, and as she breathed in the smell of salt, sand and the human sweat around her, she knew the souls of the martyred men too would find peace.

Balwant Patil
Sahas Chiplunkar
Gerald Menezes
Ali Mohammad…

The workers' movement had involved people from everywhere. It had cut across religion and even region, drawing in Maratha Hindu workers from the Konkan, the Bohra Muslims from the inner, drier regions of Maharashtra and the East Indian Catholics. That was the first report Neera had written for the magazine and it pleased her editor. She knew then what she wanted to write about. She began spending half a day at the Times of India, riffling through old issues in its archives. She read up more about Bhau. His rise through the ranks, his escape from Moscow as Stalin's madness became apparent, and the West, sated with its World War victory, had simply let Stalin be. As Neera read in one of Bhau's interviews, he had journeyed through Siberia via Mongolia in the company of an American journalist who wanted to visit Nepal. That American had been a man who hated the commies and yet it was he, Bhau said, who saved his life. That was the reason he couldn't ever be severe against those he disagreed with.

Neera wrote to Bhau for an interview. She had tried to find a number but was told by Shiva, the peon who ran errands for her magazine, that Bhau stayed in a chawl, with two rooms to himself, just like an ordinary worker. One could leave messages for him at the phone booth outside, or he, Shiva, could take it for him. Days passed this way and every morning Shiva would appear only to disappoint Neera with his noncommittal replies. 'I did give it to him and he even saw it. But...'

'So is he going to give me an interview...?'

Shiva shrugged and looked helpless. 'I can't keep waiting for him, I have other work as well.'

She took to tipping Shiva then, so it became an informal arrangement between them. He would come by her table every second day and she would give him some money.

But as Bhau gave no answer and proved hard to get, she worked out places where he could find him. There were the grounds next to the chawl where the workers wrestled and were taught martial arts. It was a way, Bhau had said somewhere, to build their strength, for workers were warriors in every sense. It also helped build camaraderie among them. Neera also knew the hospital where Bhau had been a daily visitor for an entire week to ensure that the workers who were fasting for their demands were looked after. She had gone there hoping to find him and had seen his wife instead. Maushi was what they called her. Neera had even seen the reverential look on Shiva's face when he confirmed this for her. His father had been a millworker who had been laid off, despite the union's persistent attempts to reinstate him. The union had even failed to get Shiva a job. He had been lucky to find employment in the magazine, and yet he and almost everyone else looked up to the union. 'It is our family,' Shiva said. Neera would remember that when barely five years later, he proved quite a turncoat.

In the archives, Neera found a clipping that dated back to 1942; it told her of Bhau's first love. She had looked at the grainy black and white photo and, at first, felt no envy. The Quit India Movement had just been declared against the British, as the latter had chosen to go to war without the consent of the Indian leaders. That prompted a crackdown, and Bhau and Maushi, both young workers and still in their teens, had hidden in the marshy swamps off Sewri. At nights, soon as the search was called off, they would wade to the fishing villages along the banks. It was on one such night that Maushi's parents had found them, and the scandal of finding their daughter hiding in the company of a boy near her own age could only be assuaged when Bhau assured them with no hesitation that they intended to get married. Neera had tried to match the pale, delicate-looking girl with the matronly bespectacled woman she now remembered seated behind him on the dais, but it was hard. In her dedication to the cause, or even Bhau, Maushi had not been kind to herself.

After her article had appeared, Neera had sent a clipping of it to Bhau with Shiva, repeating her request again. The war with China had ended, and the Cuban Missile Crisis too had seen a welcome resolution; didn't this mean the dawn of new hope? There would be no more wars but a new era of cooperation. She had written that note on a day in late November, watching from her window the crowds drift out from the movie theatre. People doing ordinary things, and he had finally deigned to reply, though Shiva had said he had laughed when he had read her note.

That had been the beginning of a secret exchange with him. Neera wrote to Bhau who would reply some days later, with Shiva the go-between. The happiest moment of her existence came one New Year's Eve. She sensed it would be something special for the evening held promise. The moon was still in the sky, and the breeze came in silent. Everything seemed joyful, the clinking of glasses and the sound of laughter in the restaurants, the people who came out of Regal Cinema, the boys playing their pipes, and, in the chawls, they had already strung up the old man on every roof, dressed in rags, and stuffed with cotton. He would be burnt at midnight.

Her editor always had a New Year's Eve party in the magazine's office on the sixth floor of a building that overlooked the customs houses and the Irani café that always closed too early, no matter the time of year. As the night advanced, the sounds of revelry outside only grew. If Neera leaned out, she could hear the singing, and the unmusical trumpeting on the seafront. On the road, only a few restaurants were open, their lights soft and comforting, the doormen standing like sentinels watching another year pass. The luxury hotels were filling up, however, for the rich never had to work the next day. Up on the sixth floor, where her magazine had its office, the party had just begun. Bhau came in late, with another associate. He was clad in a kurta and carrying a long cloth bag. It was just before the navy ships in the harbour blew their horns as the year changed. It was 1966, another war with Pakistan had ended, President Johnson in the US had signed new legislation, the riots in East Pakistan had stopped. The world seemed made again and she felt a whole new person.

Looking out of the window, Neera had felt a distinct sense of exhilaration. Even the stars were like faraway fireworks. When she turned around, Bhau's eyes were on her face and there was that smile. 'Finally,' she said. He smiled, his eyes crinkling up, 'Finally, but not an interview.' They sat on the ledge, and she smelled the sweet liquor on his lips, and much later, they walked to the editor's house as the last fireworks died away. The editor stayed in a two-room place just behind the Taj Hotel. There was still a crowd outside the kebab stall, and there were three youths, rich and evidently drunk, leaning against their cars parked by the sidewalk. Bhau casually put his arm around her shoulder as they passed.

There were others too who had gathered in the apartment. The night grew still, the last cars drove away and everyone spoke drunkenly of politics, Edith Piaf, Maria Callas and Ravi Shankar. Neera insisted on serving them tea, and longed to get Bhau's attention. But she ignored his teasing smile as she handed around the cups. There was the sound of the sea, hissing and swirling against the rocks, the sonorous sirens of the ships, the last trotting horses as the Victorias took lone lovers out for a drive, and then at last, there were only the lights of the hotel. There was a timelessness as things passed into the new year. Neera remembered waking up to a new morning, a new year, with him on the rocking chair. Everyone else was scattered around them, some sleeping on the carpet, someone on the dining table, and she, on the rocking chair with him.

She remembered how late in the night he had held her, laughing into her ears, putting away her hairpins on the table, running his fingers through her long dark hair. He smelt of ink and cigarettes. That morning, she had not looked at anyone as she got up hurriedly. It wasn't that she was embarrassed, but she wanted to keep those moments to herself. Later, the editor would leave an envelope on her table. It had her hairpins and for a long time, that evidence gave him reason to tease her. Her editor hadn't been a bad sort.

Later that week she met Bhau in a hotel in the shady alleys of Colaba that one reached through narrow lanes bypassing vendors with their carts. Through the green louvred windows, Neera smelt the drying fish, heard the shouts and the broken conversation of the dock workers, of crates being unloaded. She would forever associate these with love. There was another hotel near Dadar station that he knew about, and then a film director's flat in Bandra that overlooked the sea, the old fort, and a famous actor's bungalow, and she considered herself the luckiest girl. They met once every week, then once every fortnight and it was by the time she got to meeting him once a month, that she began to be afraid.

But there was a new prime minister in the country, a woman who refused to be bossed around, America too, had a new president, and Vietnam was a mess. But it was a time everyone sensed freedom, everyone marched for equality and what was theirs by right. The past was giving way yet Neera clung to Bhau. She thought he didn't pay her as much attention as before and she longed for that crinkled-up smile, the smell of the city on him. It had seeped into her being. The feel of his hands against her in a crowded street, his hand on her shoulder urging her forward, his lips on the crook of her neck. She was herself only when she was with him, only when thinking of him, and the euphoria drove her on.

She wrote more stories about Bhau. There was a new organization in place now, one that promised to work for the millworkers. The early phase of the struggle was over, Bhau said. Perhaps she lived in a bubble and was naive. Or that Bhau was far too magnanimous, and devoted to ideals, that compromised with no one, not even himself. For how else could he have missed linking the dots? For that new party was calling itself the Native People's Party, and it claimed all the credit for the workers' struggle. And this city could not hold two parties, especially one that wanted power at all costs. There was a war in the city's streets, but one in her heart too and she missed everything else.

Neera lived for the days she heard from Bhau. She reported on the visits of labour delegations, the events in China, the famine whose knowledge had been suppressed. She also sent Bhau a teary note, telling him of her sadness the day Martin Luther King was killed.

When he did not reply, she panicked. She wanted to save their love. It meant no harm, she imagined herself telling him. She could live with his being married. She had hung around outside his chawl, leaning across the balcony, impatient and longing. She studied the blue painted railings, saw how in some places the colour had already run. She stuck her toe through the rusting metal, patterned in the form of circles. From these minutes spent waiting, Neera now forever remembered the patterns. Flowers that alternated with shells, and sometimes she thought she caught a winking eye too.

Bhau's niece opened the door a couple of times. 'No one home,' the niece had told Neera.

'And what are you doing?'

'Studying,' the niece would reply morosely. Even years later, this niece, Sneha, who ran a radiology clinic, looked much the same. She still had that outraged expression, her habit of standing arms akimbo when talking to anyone. The radiology clinic was on the first floor of the building that ran like a ring around the chawl. It had first been a night school for the workers and then it held typing classes. There was a south Indian restaurant next to it, and not too far away the cybercafé, and the branded clothes shop. The clinic now had a more impressive signboard, discounts were offered for sonograms and Neera wondered why that was necessary. The niece now wrote and campaigned against women being coerced into such procedures and the abortions that resulted simply because sons were preferred. Some of that earlier combativeness, Neera always thought, had indeed helped Sneha.

Neera had little idea of how much time she spent looking out for Bhau. Her desperation made her blind to what was happening around her till one day, her editor called for her.

'You will not write about him. There is no point,' he said flatly, not looking her in the eye.

Her spirits sank but she gave nothing away. Did her editor mean love had no point? But he was a kind-hearted man who would die in a year's time. 'It won't help,' he said, looking down at his papers, effectively dismissing her from his presence. 'That movement is all doomed. You see, my dear, they are not violent enough.'

As she turned away, furious, he said, 'I do mean what I say, Neera. I'd like you to report on the music festival.'

For all her efforts at following Bhau, she was late to the scene when the union office was attacked, its glass panes shattered by a crowd pelting stones that had vanished as soon as a few policemen appeared. But before that, the doors had been broken down, and the files lay all scattered. She picked up a file before she rushed to Bhau. But there were others too, making her hesitate, and then she saw him looking bewildered. He picked up his glasses, and she saw he was running his hands through his hair, looking flustered. He had the utterly lost look of a boy who has been bullied but whose naïveté wins him no sympathy. Then Bhau turned and saw her. In that one split second, she knew what her sinking heart had always known. For he would refuse to speak to her again.

Her editor refused to give space to the attack on the union office. It was some disgruntled workers, he said, that's what the police are saying. This, for her too, was the beginning of the end. She handed in her resignation. In the days she spent at home in Malabar Hill, she saw the men when they turned up at her home. They wore the white Gandhi cap like every worker but they had the red vermilion marks like an angry arrow on their foreheads. The men from the Native People's Party were demanding funds and jobs for their men and even her father would cave in.

Neera still inveigled to meet Bhau; for her, the longing for him would never be assuaged though in time its intensity would dim. Her father was one of the patrons of Mithibai College and she had gone to a function in his stead. She had seen Bhau right away but his attention had already been claimed. There was Mohini, a lecturer, and Neera knew her as the wife of a businessman, a younger acquaintance of her father's. Bhau was looking down at Mohini as Neera approached, smiling in the way she remembered. She had walked within his eyesight, even jostled into Mohini. Then when Bhau turned to smile at her, nothing seemed to have changed in him. Neera could only say with a trembling voice, that she had something important to tell him. Her father wanted her to be married.

There was a circle of girls around him, and Mohini looked on, an expression of shrewd curiosity on her face. Neera had tried to pull Bhau away, then hissed into his face that she would never get married, not if she could help it. This time Bhau nodded, told her he indeed had heard something, that he had not known where to reach her since she no longer worked for the magazine. This was where Mohini chimed in, 'Marriage is at best a compromise,' she had said. Neera did not know then that she taught sociology.

Bhau had then thrown his head back and laughed heartily in the way he had. A man not bound by the tragedies of the past or even the failures that seemed increasingly apparent. It was a time when, in her insecurity, Neera hated all women. It was that one moment when she had hated him too. Then a photographer had appeared, juggling his camera and his tripod, and she and Mohini had flanked Bhau on either side as they waited. Neera had seen the flash almost signalling an end of sorts and she knew she had to walk out then.

Almost five years to the time they had gone to see the flamingos and Neera knew she was silly to remember such things, she was waiting for him again. She parked her car in a small lane that ran by the chawls and asked one of the urchins to keep an eye on it. The fragrance from the nursery plants reached her as she walked to the restaurant on the other side, hoping to catch a glimpse of Bhau, for a chance to run up to him. She wanted her past back. Neera waited till the streetlights came on, she saw the women gathering up the clothes from every balcony, and then there were the three men, with foreheads vermilion-marked, and Gandhi-capped, who appeared, leaning against the wall, almost as if they were guarding the lane.

Something about them was familiar. But there were too many men like that now, marking themselves that way. It was an evening when the rain fell slowly. She saw the glimmering lights caught like teardrops in the puddles. When the signal turned green, a wave of umbrellas passed, bobbing and swaying. She hoped she would not miss seeing him.

She had asked for another cup of tea, her third, and had just glanced up from the evening paper when Bhau appeared. His kurta flapped gently along his knees as he walked down the stairs of his chawl. Neera remembered his easy grace, the smile around his lips, the way his hair rose brush-like. She had forgotten he could walk fast, and she began running to him, as the rain came down. She saw the crowds gathered at the signal, and knew in a few moments they would rush in. Her feet could not keep pace with the lightness in her heart. She saw only him, not the men who followed some distance away. And when she stepped aside to avoid a puddle, she heard the shots.

There was something in the way a car screeched to a halt by her. The man in her sight fell, his glasses rose high, caught the orange streetlight and fell in a thousand splinters to the wet earth. She heard the delicate falling of glass, then the drops of blood and the scream. A woman rushed out of the chawl, and soon there was a crowd. Somehow, she heard her voice, away from the crowd, knowing what she had to do. 'Take him to hospital.' Two men were holding up Bhau, but he was already turning cold, and she smelt the metallic blood.

She rushed him to hospital, flagging down a taxi, forgetting her own parked car. His head rested on her neck in the way she remembered, his blood soaked her too, his last breaths drifted over her. She remembered looking out, through the taxi window, and in the passing streetlights saw his blood splattered on her clothes. It reminded her of the flamingoes, pink against the greying salt pans. They waited for long moments at the traffic signal, before she leaned forward and asked the driver to drive on faster. But he was brought in declared dead.

Raina wrote to Neera after a long time. Some of the photos Jeet had taken were enclosed in an envelope. Neera saw herself looking beautiful. Raina was apologetic in her note. Some of the photos had not been used, and she hoped that was all right with Neera. Neera didn't mind in the least. If Raina were here, and if they met again at the café, she would tell Raina how her own editor, for all his integrity and faith in a journalist's work, had asked her not to report on Bhau. Yet she had, and had lost everything for doing so.

So many things you do for love. Neera had that sadness in her eyes as she looked out of the window and after she had wallowed in her sadness long enough, she turned again to the photos, and the letter. This time she went over things slowly. There was another photo with a post-it attached. Neera liked Raina's handwriting. It was curved and loopy, evidently Raina was someone who spent time on her thoughts. *Here's a photo I found in my mother's album, shows her, with you and Bhau. Maybe you'd like to see it too.* Neera recognized the photo instantly. There he was, his arm about the other woman's shoulder but his eyes were looking down at her, Neera. Bhau was smiling at her, in a way that deceived no one. It was just a moment later, after the camera had recorded its flash that she had looked up, and found Bhau gazing at the photographer. All she had seen then was his jaw creased, his lips tight and a thoughtful expression in his face, before Mohini had pulled him away, asking him to meet someone.

It's always like this in real life, Neera thought, the real moment isn't what is ever remembered. She wondered if things would have been different if she had seen this photo before. Her love story did not matter to anyone but her. The book, she knew, would now never be finished.

Dr Joshi: Eyewitness to Murder

The window caught the craggy half of Dr Joshi's face, his chin jutting like a peninsula, the light clear on the scar that ran close to his ear. The dust motes and his silver hair formed small rainbows in places. He had stepped into a prism. It was afternoon and for a few minutes there was a lull in the traffic below.

He saw figures behind the darkened windows on the other side of the road. A flash of someone on the terrace. A man appeared fleetingly behind one of the columns along the arcade, before the doctor realized it wasn't what he thought. The dark colonnaded building had long gone. There was a glass-fronted one in its place now. That glassiness had now turned his world askew. The views of his past were mingling with those of the present. Sometimes, in the middle of a painting, Dr Joshi did find himself lost. People he had seen long ago appeared just as they had been, loitering on the streets below. Shops he was certain that had been demolished when roads were being widened all over the city were somehow still there with their thriving crowds. In the last decade, things had changed too fast. His memory simply hadn't kept up.

It was bad, especially at night. For it never got truly dark, the stars vanished; instead, a burnished purple and orange took their place. The billboard flashed, the sky itself became a mirror, playing the myriad colours back, swirling through his glasses, making his head swim. So he had taken to improvising, imagining things, making them up. His canvasses now had wild sweeps. Critics and buyers called them 'abstractions'. Some even called his style 'experimental'. *City Magazine* had gone overboard and called him 'wildly prolific' in his productive late years.

Dr Joshi didn't know whether to be happy about that or not. His hands now trembled more than earlier, but he couldn't give up painting. Of late he had found himself lacking patients. He wondered if all the changes in the city, the new buildings, the new roads, even the new names on old roads, would make his clinic only a memory. There were the new hospitals and some of his old patients were losing faith in him, his old-fashioned habit of just letting them talk. The way their faces changed, the expressions that words could never hide, told him many things.

Dr Joshi placed his palms on the glass and stared back at himself. His hands were gnarled and had their own story, like the myriad lanes running through the city. There were times he realized he felt more tired than before; too tired to paint, or to talk, and sometimes if his will faltered, too tired to check his email. But at that thought, the fatigue on his face lightened visibly. The email was now a habit, a late development. Now moving his palm one last time across the glass, he stretched, walked back towards his table, and flopped down on his swivel chair. The screen caught his face again.

As he logged in, Dr Joshi wondered whom, of all the people who often turned up in his inbox, he would meet now. The many ghosts in his life, as he called his email correspondents. Then he sighed, for there was a mail from Joyce; yes, the artist Maria had talked about. Then there was one from his agent too, telling him that another painting had been sold.

Dr Joshi remembered this one well, the painting called 'The Woman at Dawn'. He had caught the young woman one morning. It was the night after he had just finished another painting. The one of the prostitute, a woman with a young-old, sad-happy face he had seen standing by the road leading up to the Mahalakshmi temple.

That early morning the buckets were already lined up by the tube well. As a bus rolled by, he felt them quiver, an odd sound hitting his ears. He heard faint drum notes and the glass panes shivered before the bus passed. It was just then that the young woman bent towards her bucket, and the rising sun burst through a gap in the buildings to catch her face. He quickly stepped under an awning. It wasn't that he recognized her but that he was certain now of her strange beauty. The sun grazed her face, burnt her forehead, and as she lifted a hand, a strand of hair came undone. He imagined the shadow it left on her cheek, and when she lowered her eyes, he imagined silver dew on her lashes.

His painting of her had streaks of gentle colours, with half her face in orange. 'It looks like she carries the sky herself,' emailed one of his prospective buyers. Dr Joshi wished he could title his works better but he had never written anything. Anything apart from prescriptions. What no one knew was that she had featured in another of his paintings. And that the other painting was one of his secrets.

It was a year or so ago. The young woman had first come to his clinic with that man in tow. Dr Joshi knew Mahesh all right, though it did give the doctor a considerable start to realize he was married to her. The doctor frowned, for he never quite knew what Mahesh did, except that he was now almost a right-hand man to that goon politician Ghatge. Dr Joshi watched the couple emerge from the shadows towards his table. There was a certain way the woman with Mahesh bent her head that caught his attention. But he felt that undercurrent too, something distinct and unstated between them.

They were not looking at each other. She was quiet but

there was much that was pent up in her. Mahesh looked awkward, there was something in his sheepishness when he would be otherwise aggressive. They were both locked in, yet it was Mahesh who seemed afraid. A fear of looking at something right in the face. His face, the doctor noted, was turned slightly away from his wife's. He knew then that he'd never get an answer from him.

'Mahesh?' Dr Joshi was hesitant, but Mahesh misunderstood the doubt in his question and smiled. 'Hello, Doctor, I got the Mrs to see you.'

It broke Dr Joshi's heart then to see how helpless Mahesh looked. But he kept an eye on the changing expressions on the woman's face. The caution had given way to a slight interest as she took in the doctor's room.

'But I can see she is unwell. If she rests...' Her hands on his table were wrinkled and thin, and a bangle end had chipped, leaving those scratch marks on her skin. Her eyes now flashed up to meet the doctor's and he held her gaze, before deliberately picking up his glasses. Their thick lenses helped mute the intensity of his gaze somewhat, but he saw for himself the sadness on her face which vanished on a closer look. Then Mahesh, his voice raised as if he had read his thoughts, interrupted.

'Some medicine to make her strong?' Mahesh asked, before he laughed, almost embarrassed, 'Her friends...who know more, advised this.'

'Eh?' Dr Joshi sounded abrupt, as if someone had intruded into his reverie. 'But I am not one of those herbal doctors or homeopaths...' He looked at her mildly as he spoke, expecting surprise in her eyes. People expected to be treated even if their ailments remained undetected. But there was an acceptance and even a challenge in her expression. Her eyes were luminous and deep, the vein ran blue in her forehead, and there was the strained way she held her lips. He lit the other lamp on his table and it only made her fragility stand out.

'Doctor,' she spoke up then, her voice clear. She would not even acknowledge her husband's look of gratitude as she took over the conversation. She gestured with her hands, 'We have been married for four years now...' She looked too deliberately casual, but her eyes, her hands, did not stray towards her husband, seeking his support.

'That long already?' He asked, eyebrows playfully raised. Couples got so flustered these days and it was something that simply needed time, at first. But his absent-minded gaze gave nothing away.

Dr Joshi sighed. 'I understand.' He was studying her face. There was something there, some secret she was hiding from her husband. And Mahesh had never even learnt to trust his own shadow. Dr Joshi was sketching her already in his mind. 'You should give it time, but who am I to argue? I could say you should get to know each other better, enjoy this time together, rather than worry about children. This is already a country with a big population, you know.'

Mahesh laughed at that and she let herself smile too. It wasn't what the doctor intended to say and it certainly wasn't what she wanted to hear.

It was late. He had been sitting on the window ledge with his whisky, thinking about her. At least he had got them talking. She was a woman with her secrets, some she didn't know herself. But he remembered she had smiled and Mahesh had laughed. Some of his totally serious utterances had that effect. At least the momentary bonhomie would help more than any of these new-fangled interventions. That night he sketched her in charcoal. Tomorrow, he would complete it. 'Woman, Untitled'.

But he never saw them again, not at his clinic. Perhaps they had chosen to consult other doctors with their more impressive degrees and machines. Those who would monitor their systems, record everything, produce reams of data. As if this knowledge was proof of all that was correct in their diagnosis.

For instance, there was Sneha Desai's sonogram clinic that drew many. She was supposed to be good, so very good that she knew how to make a girl child vanish. But he caught himself. It was never good to speak ill of someone, especially someone whose uncle he had once known. A man shot down in cold blood. Dr Joshi's wayward thoughts returned to Sneha Desai. She was practical and for a doctor that was important these days. She told her clients just what they wanted to hear. She could tell at a glance what was wrong and then she would recommend them to bigger doctors in the huge private hospitals the city now had. Her patients now were the city's rich, even the very important and busy sought her out. She had different hours for them as well, for at night, as the doctor well knew, parking in the narrow roads of Parel was infinitely easier.

Perhaps Mahesh and his wife had consulted her. But the doctor wasn't overly curious. He had those two paintings of the young woman—and he now knew her name, Pooja—and paintings had their own secrets. That morning, the time he had watched her at the tube well, the sadness on her face was apparent. She was caught in the wrong moment, or perhaps she was waiting. And that, the doctor knew, was always the wrong thing to do. He knew a thing or two about waiting and the price one paid for leaving things too long.

Dr Joshi often wondered about Mahesh though. Mahesh seemed to have made some mess of himself, getting in with that man Ghatge, an ambitious man who manipulated everyone. Now that Ghatge was such a powerful man, there were many who said he manipulated in good ways too.

Mahesh had been working in a garage when the doctor

had run into him last. The don who headed one half of the
city's smuggling mafia and owned several of its hotels had
insisted that the doctor accompany him in his new Impala for
an early morning joyride. Dr Joshi couldn't very well refuse.
The don in this case was one of his main benefactors. He had
helped find many buyers for Dr Joshi's paintings. The car's
horn rose and fell like a siren. That and its speed helped it run
clear of the many traffic signals, and they raced from the city's
centre, past the defunct cigarette factory towards the south.
The towers on Nariman Point appeared like swaying palms
before the doctor's eyes, for he sat right behind the driver, and
thought he took one too many excruciating turns.

He was lulled to sleep, however, and only jerked awake
to the sound of a loud pop, and a painful screech. They had
stopped at a signal and as other cars caught up, the driver
turned sheepishly, and in a trembling voice admitted to the
don that there had been a puncture. The car lurched its way to
a petrol pump. The young mechanics recognized the car and
its owner and stood to attention, as the don heaved himself
out and ordered his driver to emerge. A crowd gathered as the
don beat his driver with the butt end of his revolver.

The doctor saw the sunlight dipping and dancing on the
car's windshield. He had not stepped out of the car and so
did not know just when Mahesh had come forward to help
with the tyre. But he had that swimming sensation in his head,
unable to keep pace with the don's hand that lifted and came
down time and again in a merciless frenzy. As the doctor leant
his head tiredly against the cool tinted glass of the window,
his eyes found Mahesh, squatting on his knees, only a foot
or so away, gritting his teeth as he worked the jack, looking
studiously away from the don and his driver.

Mahesh was a lean, short man with a thin moustache and
a fixed look in his eyes as he rolled the tyre into place. But a
speck of blood that landed in a neat flick on the car window

alerted the doctor to the fact that the driver was severely bleeding from the nose. The doctor emerged from the car, slamming the door behind him, and that caught the don's attention. The doctor coughed once, and then repeatedly, hoping to disperse the crowd around them. Then he ordered some ice, and the coughing overtook him again. 'The smells,' he said, pulling an old torn handkerchief out. 'I can't stand it.'

The don's hands were still raised in mid-air as if he would simply disregard the interruption, but Mahesh broke in just then. He smiled ingratiatingly, pointing to the tyre that he had fixed up quickly. There was another rush of steps and the garage owner now came forward, insisting there would be no charge. The don had graced his garage with his mere presence. But the latter, in new magnanimity, shoved a wad of notes into Mahesh's pocket. 'Good work,' he said, patting Mahesh on the chest, right over his pocket.

The driver was sniffling as he still knelt on the ground. He was doubled over, holding the cloth grubby and damp with ice over his face, and his swollen eyes. The doctor knew the car would never be driven now. Another short discussion followed. It was nine and the traffic was already heavy on the roads. The Impala, still wearing its marigold garland, had to be protected at all costs and only a tow truck could evade the envy of other cars. And it was Mahesh who drove the tow truck, and the don, easing himself next to the driver's seat, presented a pathetic figure. His safari suit was all crumpled, and the sunglasses did little to hide his misery. He complained of the lack of space and the absent air conditioning. The doctor for his part said he would take a taxi home. But even he was not let off easily. The other boys working in the garage were commanded to flag a taxi down and the doctor sent home in it free of charge.

Mahesh had made his way up steadily. He became indispensable in the manner of all henchmen. Sometimes the doctor would see him everywhere, as he did, when he caught Mahesh canvassing for votes during the elections. He managed several phone booths, then it was the cybercafé and by then he had firmly attached himself to Ghatge, who too, had worked his way steadily up. Ghatge was a man who straddled every world efficiently—of business and politics and the need to keep the workers happy—and Dr Joshi no longer knew where the margins between good and bad, clean and corrupt, really were.

It had been a long time but Dr Joshi had remained wary of Ghatge. Dr Joshi knew that Ghatge's men were everywhere, shadowing him, and giving Ghatge a detailed report of just what Dr Joshi was up to. A report that was also passed onto Ghatge's bosses. The doctor had known this, had felt shadowy figures trail him, for there was something, he, Dr Joshi, had seen once, that had been and remained, important for them.

Critics noted the muted darkness in Dr Joshi's recent paintings of the city. He ignored the glitzy malls, the swanky showrooms that had now appeared in the first floors of old respectable buildings. He chose instead the city's narrow lanes where old houses still jostled for space and held their secrets. He looked up at the louvred windows and studied doors with their heavy locks. He stood by porches and soot-stained walls. He lingered where weeds rose high out of old warehouse windows. He chatted with the decrepit, the unwanted, who for a time had made a home there and he painted all this.

The degradation and decay of the city was all around him, but there was some light still in his paintings. A flash of lightning that could turn the city purple. Where he lived on the third floor, a place that doubled as home and office, the light entered in myriad ways. A light turned on at a high window would make a darkened patch of floor below smile. The swish of a car's headlights, as it came down the flyover; the flashing colours from the billboard opposite, the blaze that came as a construction worker opposite lit up his last cigarette for the night. Dr Joshi felt alone, especially in these light-filled moments.

His eyes moved around his small room till he came to the closet with its sliding doors. One could miss it, for he had placed an old iron clotheshorse in front of it. That closet held his secrets: the paintings he had resolved to forever keep hidden. That of the young woman, and another, totally different, for it showed up evil, stark and unadorned, a face totally devoid of any measure of goodness.

The doctor had had no idea it would be the day of the shooting. But it was at that restaurant, at that corner table, hidden away behind a pillar, where he had been sketching Neera in secret that he had seen that other face, one that had seared itself into his mind. Neera, he knew, was here because of Bhau, and Dr Joshi had followed her, though he didn't want Neera to know that. He didn't want the disdainful look on her face to spoil things. His love was a lost cause. It wasn't his looks, the fact that their families knew each other, or even his teasing that they, Neera and he, were naturally matched for they both had the same last name, but that she had lost her heart irrevocably to Ramakrishna Desai. With love as stubborn and undaunted as Neera's, Dr Joshi knew he had little chance.

The three men had walked into the restaurant, and into Dr Joshi's thoughts only moments later. The doctor heard them place their orders in a far too perfunctory way. Their eyes had a way of straying outside every few seconds. And there was one moment when, looking up, he sensed the utter stillness about them. It was especially so about one of them. The other two had their eyes on the newspaper, riffling its pages in no order. But not this one. He toyed with his glass, looked up to size himself up in the mirrors that ran across one entire wall of the restaurant and then smiled as he patted himself on the hip.

The doctor knew then he had to get him down on paper. The thought had taken him over so completely that he strained to hide his excitement. His hands shook as he pulled out his wallet to pay. But he heard first the clatter of coins that fell off the plate, onto the table, as the man, his quarry, left. His two companions followed seconds later, leaving behind an unexpected quiet. The doctor had no recollection when the stillness ended, but he felt it on his back as he walked out as well, down the steps, and began threading his way past the crowds. The rhythmic slap of footfalls rose and fell around him and soon it was subsumed by an unquiet, unfamiliar jostling. It wasn't the usual urgency of crowds walking home. Instead, the human mass around him appeared desperate to move on, arms and limbs threshing out to extricate themselves. Then the hiss the doctor heard; that only later, when thinking over things, he understood must have grown out of shock, after those shots were fired; the sounds that had first registered in his ears as that of a firecracker. The doctor had turned to see the crowds converging around a fallen man. Just for a moment, the crowd had parted, and he had seen Neera.

Dr Joshi made the connections then. The men he had seen in the restaurant and the murder they intended to commit. Dr Joshi had not known what else to think. He found a corner bench but when he felt it shaking under him, he realized he was trembling and all he could then do was walk home.

The face of that one man in the restaurant was still stark in his mind, and he had barely sketched an outline when he heard the stomping on the stairs, then the scream of the woman downstairs. Instinctively, the doctor had hurled the thick paper into the closet. There it would stay even after it was finished. Where it still was. When the front door burst open, he was wiping his hands on the curtain and it looked as if he had just come from the bathroom. The doctor had found himself face to face with Ghatge for the first time.

'Sorry to interrupt.' The other man lifted his hand almost in a mock salute, but it was only to brush his hair. 'But there has been...an incident.' Ghatge's eyes were fixed intently on him, despite the smile. 'Someone...Ramakrishna Desai has been killed.' The doctor gripped the door hard and stared at Ghatge, unwilling to believe his words. For he wondered at his own surprise. He had seen Neera reach for the falling man, and yet the final connections had eluded him. The face of the murderer was all he had in mind.

He could still see that man, dressed in nondescript black trousers and a blue shirt. There had been something on his face; the doctor recognized now for what it was: pure evil. The man was stocky and short, yet with a certain power coursing through him. There he had been, leaning on the table, fingers rearranging his hair as he studied himself in the mirror; and then he had smiled. That slight twist of his lips, his hair, the way he kept rearranging it, fascinated the doctor. The doctor could now tell it was this man who had fired those fatal shots, the man who had killed Ramakrishna Desai.

Ghatge, never taking his eyes off the doctor, reached for the swivel chair at the other end of the table. He was a tall man, and the room already looked considerably shrunken. Ghatge swung himself around in the chair once, toyed with the pen stand, then having rubbed his fingers on the table, and looking with distaste at the paint that came off on his fingers, asked the doctor if he had seen anything.

'What?' The doctor took off his glasses and put them back on again. He willed his hands not to tremble. But Ghatge threw his head back into a guffaw that turned hoarse towards the end. 'No, I came home.'

Ghatge shrugged away that answer. He looked around the room, his eyes lingering on the paintings. 'Then I am sorry to bring bad news. I know you were a friend of Desai's, and of his girlfriend too. But you see, we know you were there. We hope you will help with the investigations.'

'I was just having tea there,' the doctor said in a measured voice, and then looking up at the old wall clock, its metallic pendulum catching the light of the chandelier, he said, 'It's six already, time for me to see my patients.'

Almost on cue, his first patients were there, as the doctor knew they would be. At the door, shuffling their feet for attention, he saw the man with the persistent cough and the woman constantly by his side. Ghatge and his men saw them too and the doctor noticed the invisible signal that was passed. *There must be no scene.*

'All right, Doctor, but remember the police will be here to ask.'

He scratched his forehead. 'I have patients to see.'

That year, as investigations into Ramakrishna Desai's murder gathered pace, and some men were arrested only to be soon let off for want of evidence, the doctor found himself constantly visited by one of Ghatge's many henchmen. Every time it was a different set of people, which just told Dr Joshi that Ghatge had now come to wield considerable clout. Most times his men delivered their threats in an obscure way.

Then one evening Mahesh too, turned up, offering the doctor a pamphlet listing all the benefits and discounts one could get from long distance calls placed through the phone booth he now managed. This was a hint just like all the others. The painting remained hidden away, in a secluded space in the doctor's bedroom where he painted it, till he thought it was done. The light that came from an overhead window proved just right. It lit his subject's eyes in a strange life-like manner though Dr Joshi could never look the man in the eye. Nor could he have painted it any other way. Long after he was done with it, when the painting ceased to obsess him, he still retained his old precautions.

It must have been some uncanny intuition that made him do this. For there was soon another evening Ghatge's men had burst in through the door with no warning. The doctor had heard their steps, and he emerged once again just in time. In the front room was another unfinished canvas still on its easel. It was a still life, one he had just begun, after a vase of marigold flowers in the chawl window opposite, had caught his eye. The slight appearance of colour against the wall's grey drabness was something he was finding hard to capture, and then the door had been flung open with little preliminaries. The intruding light from the corridor had slashed a neon line across the flowers. The doctor stared, unable to look away till he was yanked rudely back by the shoulder. You could never tell the moment death chose to look you in the face, he remembered thinking, as he found the gun pointed straight at him.

The next moment, the man lifted his hand and laughed. 'Those flowers look nice. The boss will like it.' The others with him chuckled appreciatively too.

Dr Joshi heard the click as his intruder turned his gun away. The man played with it then, flipping it over and catching it just in time, and the doctor tried not to look terrified. The men laughed again, sensing the doctor's fear as they circled him. Theirs was the laughter of hyenas and Dr Joshi knew that unless the leader among them gave any indication, he would not be harmed.

Once they had tired of this game, they looked at all his paintings, shuffling those he had stacked against the wall, fingering none too gently the ones on their easels, moving the thin paper covering away carelessly in places while the man who had first threatened him perched himself on the table and watched them with some indulgence. When the boredom struck him too, he raised his arm, but before he could aim for the chandelier, the doctor broke in.

'I implore you, Sir, if that light breaks, its shards will scatter and all this, all this, all this.' His outstretched hands indicated all the paintings scattered across the room. The man leaned wearily back, and rubbing hands over his eyes, mouthed a tired command to his men. 'Leave his stuff alone.' That made one of his men about to step into the inner room stop short.

Men who worked in evil often got tired with all the evil they did. It was then they could be unexpectedly helpful. That night would be the longest the doctor would ever remember, one that turned his life somewhat. The men took him with them, and they drove to Bandra to the Hotel Sea Rock, going to seed with its peeling façade, worn carpets, the smell of a tired city and the sea washing against it, bringing back the dirt time and again, everywhere. Dr Joshi allowed himself to be swept along once he knew they wouldn't do him harm. On the contrary, proximity to such evil, now that it was muted, excited him.

With the four men trailing him, he was led to a hotel room by a bellhop with a deadpan expression on his face. The doctor had no idea that an impromptu meeting had been called. As he was directed to a plush sofa by the window from where the sea sounded very near and looked blacker than night, he recognized the man sitting opposite—one of the city's leading textile mill owners. By the time the night was over, his paintings had begun to sell, more than ever before, at prices he'd never have imagined.

But there was a flipside to this new fame. Dr Joshi became testy with the phone calls that interrupted his sessions with his patients or when he was deep in a painting, and after a while he made his protests clear. But to his amazement, his complaints were accepted unhesitatingly by the businessman, his many friends, and the ganglords, and the more his paintings sold, the more industrialists and ganglords figured among his acquaintances. They were all connected in some way or another and they all seemed to understand his artistic genius.

If he told them he only painted when the fancy struck him, that he was never inspired by someone who formally sat for him, they accepted with no compunction. He once said that he hunted down his models and when that evoked puzzlement, he had explained. 'It's like you hunt down your victims too.' That had led to some uproarious laughter, and the industrialist wiping tears away from his eyes, had finally said, 'You are a killer, Doctor.' But the calls dwindled, and they worked out a way to fax Dr Joshi a buyer's details. A part of a corner shop that doubled up as a travel agency was requisitioned as a front office, and a boy came over every evening to deliver the fax messages especially to him.

Sometimes the doctor would come across one of his paintings that had sold well but he felt only a strange detachment. He would see his own creations at restaurants and hotels and tell himself they were not his any more. The ones he valued were those hidden away in his closet. His bank statements startled the doctor as well. He would look at the statements that arrived by mail every month and then return to his paintings, and his patients.

The website though was another matter altogether. One evening, among his usual visitors was a frightened young man who had been dragged along. The doctor was told that a new website would be developed so his paintings could reach a wider audience.

But the website came to exert a strange fascination on the doctor. He saw his paintings turn into smaller thumbnail images, filling up a page, fascinating him like a frequently changing puzzle. People with different sounding names, from places he knew he'd never visit, wrote to him, and some even bought his paintings. He began a correspondence with some of them and began a kind of parallel life. It was as if he knew some of these people: from their names, their way of talking on email so he could almost picture them. As the city disintegrated around him, he found refuge of a kind in these people he never met. Every week there was someone new. From all these names that conjured up magic places, secret lives, he was free to create things anew—a whole new world peopled by ghosts.

The stranded ship off Bandra in one of his paintings had ghostly passengers, except that you couldn't see them. There was a tightrope walker you could see in still another painting, one who had walked the city's twin towers, the Imperial Towers in Tardeo. One of his correspondents, a venture capitalist from California, had told him about a similar stunt in Chicago and the doctor knew he had to paint one for his city, too. There was an Indian hotelier in Italy who wanted a painting showing Bandra in the 1960s and Dr Joshi had obliged.

But it gave the doctor a considerable jolt when there was the chance of such ghosts becoming real. That all the formless, shapeless people, those he could give life to, could have a separate real life of their own, was something the doctor found hard to fathom. And he always wished he had never acceded to Maria's request.

Maria had come to him one evening, complaining of slight fever and breathlessness. Her hair fell in waves but her glasses were blurred, and there was that wobbliness in her lips. Dr Joshi offered her a chair and later Maria would tell Pooja of how gallant Dr Joshi had been.

There was the smell of the cramped room that was all on Maria, and something else too. Someone else's unhappiness that made her skin look pale, that set her hands all aquiver on his table. The will and the spirit were so clearly divided. She was lovely in her mid-thirties, and greedy for life, but life was eating her up. Dr Joshi wondered how he could help her.

'You are the first doctor who doesn't have a queue.' He laughed at her joke and made one in turn: that ever since he had used a paintbrush to check temperature, his patients didn't trust him. But she looked serious and so he had to explain. 'I did have patients. But now you see, the illnesses have changed. Or rather they don't believe my explanations.'

Her eyes were now on his paintings and Dr Joshi read the admiration in Maria's eyes before she turned her eyes away, as if she couldn't help it. He leaned forward and took her wrist between his fingers. Her hands were clammy and cold and he knew from its faint beat that something was missing. Her heart was not there. But it was only in her second consultation with him that Maria brought up the subject of Joyce, her friend in America. Maria had done her hair differently this time, arranged it carefully around her ears. She wanted to be looked at, the doctor realized. She had her secrets to share. Her eyes had a more inward look, and that was what made him ask. 'Have you had distressing news?'

A tic appeared on Maria's forehead and though she shook her head repeatedly, she admitted 'The friend I stay with...' she began, before she finished with a rush, 'I just hope she's all right.'

Her face was a mass of conflicting emotions. But there was that distracted look again, a sweeping gaze that took in all his paintings. 'I'd have wanted my friend, Joyce, to see all this. She's back home in Maryland, and it's she who should have been here, not me.'

There she had said it, almost all of it, the doctor realized. Her heart was caught in different places, in different people and it had given Maria considerable relief to unburden herself—in a strange land, for the first time. Dr Joshi noticed how the tic slowed and then eased, and relief at his understanding flooded Maria's face. Dr Joshi leaned back and waited for her to speak more. There was nothing he could do to help otherwise.

'She loves to paint,' Dr Joshi could still hear Maria's words in his ears as, some hours later, he looked at Joyce's email.

There was Maria, but he could also hear Joyce's strangled, high-pitched voice in the words she had typed, almost as if one was trying to shout the other down. 'She paints goddesses of a kind, in all their hidden power. The Indian goddesses are the most fascinating of all.'

'She is much influenced by the Calcutta School.' It's old guard, the doctor thought but he hadn't told Maria this, not right away. 'She is keen to get to know the Indian art scene and if she could exhibit in certain galleries.'

He had promised Maria, in his offhand way, to put Joyce in touch with people who could help. But right from the time Joyce wrote to him, a day after Maria's visit, that task looked difficult. There was an intensity about Joyce that he felt singed by. To Joyce, it seemed, the things Maria had mentioned were not what mattered really, at least that was not how Joyce sounded to the doctor. A couple of emails later, it was clear to Dr Joshi what it was Joyce was so anxious to learn about.

It wasn't about art, nor about ambition. With Joyce, it was all suspicion and jealousy. And the doctor knew a thing or two about jealousy. He had converted it into art, but then jealousy had made him a coward. It wasn't just fear that had made him hide away the portrait of Ramakrishna Desai's killer. He had wanted his own secret, one he suspected Neera tormented herself over; for Ramakrishna Desai's death remained, even forty years after its occurrence, one of the city's unsolved mysteries.

He read Joyce's last sentences, and understood the ugly power jealousy wielded. It changed the self utterly and completely. He could now imagine Joyce pushing her hair away from her face as she read his every word, thinking up her own reply. She was frowning hard as she wrote the second paragraph in her email—her emails were always chatty and convoluted—and those last lines were always about Maria. The doctor noted how progressively the mention of Maria moved up, from second to the first paragraph and then Joyce's emails became more inquisitional. She was polite, but her words were sharper, more staccato, and manipulative.

She wanted to know every single detail; things the doctor knew she was aware of already from Maria's emails but it was as if she wanted him to confirm them for her, or even to give into what she suspected. *The food is good, isn't it? Maria was telling me her landlady is excellent,* Joyce wrote once. Sometimes she would try and make a joke of things, but the doctor already knew, Joyce was too brittle a person. *We should sponsor the woman here. She has been so helpful to Maria, but you never know, people like her would just overstay.* But it was not for Dr Joshi to confirm if Maria had indeed lost her heart and perhaps her head too.

For a month, Joyce emailed him almost regularly. Emails that weren't much about paintings, his or even hers, but more about Maria. *It's been almost two days I haven't heard from her*—she had sounded plaintive.

It did make Dr Joshi suspect Joyce's artistic credentials. A true artist, Dr Joshi thought, as he considered his own solitude, didn't really bother too much about relationships. On the other hand—his brush made a stroke thicker than he wanted, to his irritation—a true artist needed someone as a sounding board always. Who was the truer artist then: the loner or the wilful parasite?

Curious, but not keen on a philosophical answer, Dr Joshi emailed in his own turn. He asked Suhel to check up on Joyce. Suhel was more than just a ghost friend, he was someone the doctor had known once, but they had lost touch with each other. Suhel had grown up in Mumbai but had left, soon after his mother's death, and now owned a medical research company in Maryland. It was Suhel who had written in first, only some months ago at the doctor's website but they had not dwelled on the old times. There was an initial stiltedness between them as if both feared the other would bring the past up. Suhel had also picked up a certain American breeziness— Dr Joshi winced on being addressed as 'Hey Doc'—it was a manner that forestalled deep exchange in any sense. But this time, Suhel had written back soon enough about Joyce.

She teaches in an art class. And I have seen her work. Well, quite pretentious but promising.

A few days later, Maria let him know about Joyce's plans. Maria's face was unusually pale as she did so, her words came out quick and there was that withdrawal in her eyes. 'She has plans to visit India,' she said. Dr Joshi was taken by surprise. Maria seemed incoherent, in a dazed way, and he had to ask her to repeat herself.

All Dr Joshi knew then was that he had to get away. He could not handle in person the terrible intensity he sensed in Joyce's emails. He longed to tell Maria this but the expression on Maria's face made Dr Joshi diffident.

He blamed himself for having pre-empted Joyce in some way. She had asked him for his number, suggesting she could better explain herself on the phone, but Dr Joshi had prevaricated. A phone number was the easiest thing to find out these days. Entire phone directories had now been uploaded onto the internet and maps readily gave away everything. No wonder he held stubbornly to his secrets and memories.

He would take up a long-standing invite from his industrialist friend, the one who worked closely with the city's mafia on so many things; and who had proved an unintended benefactor to Dr Joshi in many ways. In the industrialist's farmhouse in Panchgani, up in the hills, a four-hour drive from Mumbai, the doctor knew he could vanish for a few days, without a trace, and not even the maid who came in daily would have an idea. But the doctor had to get some things sorted out first, ease himself out of some long-held secrets.

There was that painting in his closet. Not of the young woman—there was still something unfinished about it—but of that other man, whose identity would always be a secret. That was how Dr Joshi had labelled it; inking carefully on the back of the canvas, a title: 'Killer, Name Unknown'. He had hidden it away for too long. Now he had to return it to its rightful owner: the woman he had desisted from visiting so long, the woman who deserved to know the truth behind Ramakrishna Desai's murder.

That evening Dr Joshi took a taxi to Neera's apartment. He knew she had moved only recently, to this apartment in a complex right on the Eastern Express Highway, close to the Sewri mudflats.

Neera, it's me. Pankaj Joshi. He saw her face, grainy and speckled through the interactive screen. *Something urgent.* His voice must have cracked, and she waved a hand in the nonchalant way he remembered. 'No need to shout. I can see and hear you clearly.'

In the light of the corridor Dr Joshi caught for a moment Neera Joshi's luminous younger self and realized that just like before, he had little idea of how to begin a conversation. 'I had to return this.' He looked silly saying that with little preamble, holding out the canvas in its neat wrapping.

His hands were vague and fluttering, and she smiled. 'I thought we had reached the age when nothing bothered us, but you are as stiff as before.'

'The painting,' he began again. Then, once inside the small living room, with its shelves, rocking chair and the curved bamboo chairs, he unveiled it, slowly. He felt himself very nervous then. He didn't want time to catch up with Neera too fast, slap her hard with old truths across the face. 'This picture is actually yours.' He averted his eyes, and felt the tightness in his heart. She looked at him, sighed, as if dismissing those memories. Dr Joshi heard the tap running, and then someone he recognized came with a glass of water, a smile on her lips.

It was the woman of his paintings, the one he knew formally as Mahesh's wife. He was so unprepared for this, he had no idea what to say next. Dr Joshi heard the clink, as her bangles slid down to her wrist. She was thinner than he remembered. It seemed to him that the two paintings of her had fused together to create a new haunted look on her face. When he looked back at Neera, she had her head against the rocking chair, her face turned away from his.

'Pankaj,' she said as Pooja left, her gentle presence gliding across the room. 'D'Souza died long ago. He was no good. He lost his life during the riots…twenty years ago'

'You mean…' but the words did not come, for everything seemed unnecessary then. D'Souza had met a violent death after all.

'No one remembers,' she said, looking at him evenly now. 'No one does and if you guard your memories this way, they just die on you.' He knew her answer covered all the questions he hadn't yet thought of and those he would never ask. She smiled, and his hands no longer trembled. 'It still has its value, you know. You could sell it off.'

He shook his head, sensing her mockery. But Bhau, the man who came between them, was long dead, killed by a man who too was dead and even thinking all this seemed an inane thing to do. But to give in to the present was to invite a new tension. Neera stared at him, then looked down at the painting now unfurled on the divan. Dr Joshi knew she, too, was thinking things over. 'All right, I did think of something. And your paintings make millions too.'

She said it offhandedly. He raised his eyebrows but did not contradict her. Nothing it seemed would ever ruffle her. He envied Ramakrishna Desai, who could unsettle Neera so very easily that she had never let love happen to her again. Then with a start, he saw him, Bhau, framed on the mantelpiece, in a photo, with Neera and someone else.

'That's a nice photo,' he said, automatically. They were both looking at the photo and her voice was low and dream-like as she spoke next. He strained to hear her. 'Pooja did mention she had been to you. The artist doctor, she called you.'

'I wasn't much help,' he said as they heard the tap running in the kitchen again and Neera nodded towards the sound. 'There is something I want to do for her.'

She was her old decisive self again, always the one with the ideas—all they had to do was follow suit. 'There's just too much pressure on every woman to have a child.'

The sound of Pooja's bangles in the distance made a kind of slow music, and Neera's words moved in accompaniment to that. 'That is just what I tell them too,' the doctor said.

'No, no. I am saying that for a married woman, it gets too much. When it's not necessary,' Neera sounded impatient now.

Dr Joshi went blank, she was making her arguments too fast. It was like those weeks and months the time after Bhau's death, when she had argued for the millworkers, and he could hear her voice lost in the dark lanes, floating over the narrow by lanes, telling them never to give up.

'She would like to have a child. All women do. But you know how things are. All those advances in science, IVF treatment and all, are very expensive. But we could work something out, for her? With your painting?'

He found himself agreeing to everything Neera suggested and it was an hour or so later, that he walked out, the painting still with him as Neera had insisted. She didn't trust the newfangled houses. 'There could be water leakages. And I always think one of the planes will knock against us.' His hands rested one last time on Neera's shoulder and felt her fragility. Against the grey light of the passageway, her wrinkles looked more pronounced, and he realized how terribly tired he was.

Maria Figures Things Out

'At first it sounded like a cat and then it hit me. It was a woman crying.'

'Stand in one place and just speak into the phone!' Joyce yelled.

Maria jerked the phone away, rubbing her ear where it tingled. She moved nearer the window, looked down at the road and imagined Joyce in Baltimore, her nose pressed to the bay window, the frown etching two clear lines on her narrow forehead.

'Your voice has gone nasal. Is it a Mumbai thing?'

Maria smiled; Joyce's sarcasm at times masked concern. It was two days since they had last spoken and the affection now came easily. Maria moved her hands away from the thin window bars, the green peeling in places to show rust. Outside, she could already hear the traffic building up.

'Are you still there?'

'Yes. One second.'

Maria pushed the window latches in more securely. Now only the sound of construction remained, a dim undying hum that Maria heard even in her sleep. There was also the sound of bangles but she'd never tell Joyce about this. Through a slit in the louvres she saw a crane with a worker rising high against the scaffolds. A flash of fire and a shower of pebbles fell in rhythm. The soot-coated chimneys and the slanting roofs of the textile mill stared dourly and forbiddingly back.

Mumbai stretched all around her and she was right in the heart of the city where the textile mills once threaded the city's prosperity. But like the Jupiter Mills in front of her eyes, every other mill was now defunct or closing. The chawls where the workers lived still hummed with life but Maria knew these were doomed too. The land around her held riches and only those in real estate knew the exact millions of its value.

'Sorry, the traffic is just too loud.'

'You were telling me about her.'

She could imagine Joyce tossing her hair back in the impatient way she had. Maria began again, 'So you know how it is, we have to queue for the bathroom. But I found it locked and there was that cat instead.'

Joyce made a strangled giggling sound. Maria knew she had Joyce's full attention. But a cat couldn't have just got in. The bathroom always had someone in it and other times it was kept carefully bolted. Someone had to have put a cat in there. The very thought had made Maria's head reel. She had leaned over the balcony railings, looking to call, even holler for help. She had thought of calling the police. Or even the SPCA, the Society for the Prevention of Cruelty to Animals. And then the sound came again, someone mewling softly in pain that would never go away.

It was nine then, she told Joyce. A stillness like gold lay over the long veranda that stretched between Maria's rented rooms in the chawl to the bathroom at the other end. The men's washing hung over the railings. Puddles of water lingered in places where the old floor had sunk, the curry leaf plant gleamed in some sunlit joy, its stem sinuous on the railing. On some doors were heavy brass locks, the rooms emptied for the day. The empty wrought iron chairs scattered on the landing rocked with remembered weight.

Maria did not tell Joyce how long she had waited, holding her breath. She told Joyce instead that, just as she was about to knock, there was that soft crying again. A sound like a low moan, so soft yet insistent that it seeped into her bones, turning her blood cold. Then the soft jingling of bangles, just once. Maria knew then it was Pooja.

'So how long was she crying? Did you research that too?'

The next moment Joyce said sorry and then, 'So it was her. Why don't you just say that?'

Maria titled her head back, seeing the crack of sky where the buildings gave way. She thought about Pooja, all the questions she wanted to ask her, feeling her own pulse rise, imagining Pooja's shy smile. A smile that appeared shy only because Pooja didn't want anyone to see inside her. Yet Maria did understand, just as she now understood the reasons for Joyce's sniffing, the way she said before she hung up. 'I need to go. Call later, love you.'

Joyce's last words were erratic and broken and maybe she didn't hear Maria's last pleading, now fervent and almost teary. Maria never wanted to end a conversation this way.

'Wait. One second more. Don't go. All right, hugs, darling and love you.'

Perhaps Joyce had seen something amiss in her painting and she had to set it right that very moment. Maria knew she should be relieved. It hinted at some normalcy returning between them. There was that canvas Joyce had ripped up when Maria had finally told her that she could not put off her Mumbai trip any more. That time Joyce had slashed the trees and the women too, all with a paper cutter. Maria's study grant had at long last been approved, but Joyce's own, to study the cave paintings at Ajanta hadn't come through. Maria had put off her visit for long as she possibly could but grants never came at the same time. Sometimes Joyce just refused to understand.

Maria squatted on her upturned bucket as she waited outside the bathroom door. Later, she would remember every second of that still, long wait, when images, thoughts, wishes, desires, longings hurtled through her. The old aluminium bucket's sharp rigid ends bit through her pyjamas and made her wince. She ran fingers through her tangled red-brown hair, for she still hadn't found a good salon. The crying, soft and continuous, only continued. It mingled with the metallic sound of mug striking bucket, its bubbling dip into water, and the stream of falling water muting then, the thin rhythmic jangle of bangles. Maria had heard Pooja crying at night but never this time of morning. Maria thought of Pooja's husband, whom Maria rarely saw, for he left early in the morning and returned late, just when she, Maria, was drifting off to sleep. She'd know from the way the floor trembled just outside on the corridor, the sharpness of door bolts sliding open and the furtive murmurs of conversation between husband and wife. A few moments later, the windows would close too. Sometimes, later in the night, she'd hear them open. The latticed green window, brushing the one that was hers, right next to it, and she wondered if Pooja ever slept.

Sometimes, if she stood a little sideways at her own window, Maria could catch a glimpse into the room next door, the one Pooja and her husband Mahesh lived in. In the mirror affixed to the wall by the window—where Maria could see herself, her too angular face, her always tangled hair, and her hips that already showed some signs of middle-age thickness— she'd often see Pooja at work. Pooja, her arm stretched over the kitchen counter, or squatting as she mopped the floor, her bangles always musical, giving away her mood. They sounded quick and deliberate as she stirred something, muffled as she kneaded the dough, and then quiet and very slow as she raised them time and again to stifle her sobs. Sometimes the bangles caught against the metal bars and everything would fall quiet, even Pooja herself.

At last Maria's wait outside the bathroom was rewarded.

The latch moved back, there was the sound of a pail striking the wooden door and Pooja stepped out. Only to stop a moment later as she spotted Maria. She became so still that Maria felt the curry leaf plant near her wriggle further into the rusty blue railing. Pooja tried to walk away quickly, her right foot grazing the floor, her anklet rising and falling with the move. Maria noted the furtiveness on Pooja's face and reached to stop her. *Wait.*

Pooja warded her away. A broken bangle edge struck Maria sharp on the skin. A needle-like pain followed the streaky white that appeared on Maria's wrist, the sound of Pooja's quickening steps, her rushing into the open door of the room she lived in. Banging it so firmly shut behind her that its echoes resounded in Maria's ears, just like Joyce's yelling only a few minutes earlier.

Maria lifted her wrist to her lips and sucked. It helped mask the tears too. A tiny bit of the bangle lay on the floor. It caught the sunlight and gleamed mockingly. The door opened and Pooja was there again, smiling. She was pushing a strand of damp hair behind her ear, and her green eyes glowed in the way Maria now knew, for Pooja smiled only to hide something.

Office? Pooja asked, using that one word. That was how they spoke and understood each other. Pooja, with a searching look on her face spoke first, her gestures usually shaping the word for her.

Not gone?

Maria especially liked the way her hands moved, when the green bangles slid down to her elbow, in musical obedience. Maria pointed at her watch and made a face, rolling her eyes. *They never come on time.*

The eyes flashed again in laughter and Pooja pointed to the train tracks just across the road, behind the high wall. The train decided such matters. The 9.13 just went by and the blinds shook. The workers' union office officially opened at nine but Maria always found it closed then. A cleaner would turn up only a good hour later, dust the tables and chairs, and Maria had always had to wait at least an hour more before someone more important came by. Ghatge Sahib, as he was called by everyone, the union leader and rising political star, with, as rumours went, a secret interest in real estate too, sometimes turned up as well, but he was never one for answering Maria's questions in a straightforward manner.

Tea? Pooja made a gesture.

Yes, Maria smiled. Pooja left her door open, and Maria, not waiting for another smiling invite, walked in.

It was a neatly arranged front room, only a little bigger than the kitchen back home. There was a bigger room behind it. Maria looked around curiously, to describe it to Joyce later. The kitchen itself was in a corner, a rack holding steel utensils over the small stove; in another corner, just behind the wooden almirah, the low bed with its cushions that doubled up as a sofa in the morning. Maria saw the two buckets of water, yellow and blue, covered with cardboard. Every morning these joined the other buckets in a line before the municipal tube well and Pooja brought them in one at a time. If Ghatge was a leader, why didn't he do something about them, about the water supply, for instance? Maria knew she couldn't ask Pooja that right away. She didn't have the right gestures for it, it would confuse Pooja no end. And everything, even this friendship with her, was just too new.

Pooja dipped a small pan into the bucket, rubbed away with her heel a drop or two that had spilled and then squatted on her haunches before the stove. Maria, sitting on the window ledge watching all this, felt clumsy.

The half-done road below, like a stage set, was now experiencing a change of scene. In place of the buckets that had stood all night long in a queue before the municipal tube well, the children were thumping stumps into the hard, red earth to begin their morning game of cricket.

Maria leaned out for a better look but a new, different kind of smell made her turn. Pooja stood by the window, very near, her arm stretched as she yelled to the boys below. The bittersweet fragrance of her soap mingled with her bangles and Maria felt the soft, often washed sari against her skin. The boys laughed, looking up, their mockery clashing with Pooja's loud insistent voice that bordered on shrillness. Pooja was warning the boys off, pointing to her window, where the glass had cracked. Lines like a child's drawing of the sun's rays had spread, and the sun blinked, as it caught itself in a small crack.

Breaking things, these boys, Pooja said, her hands cutting across each other. Maria patted Pooja on the elbow, understandingly. It was getting late, Maria admitted. At the union office, there were still many files and old records to go through. Pooja rushed back to the stove.

At the union office, Maria noticed Ghatge was with someone but he rose as she entered. She had described his oily smile in detail to Joyce. *It's as if he's thinking something else all the time as he's looking at you.* He looked now at Maria with his unseeing eyes, the same all-knowing smile on, and she heard a chair's painful screech as someone rose to leave. Ghatge had on a sleeveless jacket over a short kurta that reached well above the knees. In recent days, he had taken to dressing himself more nattily. His photos appeared quite regularly in the newspapers, for his opinion as a representative of the millworkers was considered important.

Sit, Madam, please...one minute. Ghatge's moustache moved as he spoke, he straightened it between pauses. Maria pulled a chair towards the low square table, where the day's newspapers had been arranged. Ghatge's conversation with his other visitor was now in a distinctly low register. He was explaining her presence to the other man.

A boy came up with a tea tray. Balancing it on one hand, he carefully moved the table fan closer to her. The voices of the two men talking rose and fell as a rush of welcome air hit her, the papers fluttered in her hands. From the window, she could see again the spires and the red-tiled slanting roofs of the closed textile mills. Everywhere, men out of work lounged around the alleys and byways, and their children, when not in school, played cricket or simply crowded the streets. A few of the girls, she had been told, now worked as shop girls in the new malls. That was what most aspired to. Everything else, for them, the children of unemployed mill hands, seemed impractical and impossible. At last there was the sound of chairs being pushed away and Ghatge came towards her.

'Sorry, Madam. Head of local party wants share in mill land. He sent chamcha to find why I waiting.'

He continued after a significant pause, as if disappointed at Maria's careful incuriosity, 'But I can't say "yes". All people depend on me. They should get something. Decent money. Decent jobs.'

Maria looked through the green window bars. Always, the same set of men played cards on the charpai. Or they gossiped in small groups at the atta-chakki. Next door was the video parlour, its blue door marked with photographs of underdressed starlets and there, on a cane chair, with that glowering expression fixed on his face, was Mahesh, Pooja's husband. As she looked on, Mahesh got to his feet, kicked the chair on which he sat. It went sprawling to where a mongrel had been lounging under the awning that stretched over the video parlour. The mongrel yowled, turned tail and vanished. It made the men laugh. Then, with quick strides, Mahesh walked to a scooter parked nearby, revved it up and was gone.

Perhaps he had gone to follow up on yet another job, another shift, somewhere. That was what some of the millworkers now did. Either they didn't work or worked at too many things, just to keep things going.

'Well, no one seems interested in getting them a job,' she said lightly.

Ghatge spat into the bin, a burst of streaky red juice, 'Why they work as courier boy and security guard? They need good jobs. I am fighting for that.'

Maria changed the subject and asked after the old files. Ghatge tossed a vague look around, preened his moustache and gave her a sad look.

'The researcher is not here today. She has taken the files with her. But tell me, Madam, have you been having fun in our city?'

There was a glint in his eye as he smoothed his hair. Maria gave nothing away. One way or another Ghatge had delayed showing her the files. These files had every record and detail of the great textile strike, the infinite and more reasons why the workers' demands had remained unmet, and would remain so, no matter how many elections were held, how many leaders were elected, promising everything to the millworkers. Maria had learnt all this from Neera Joshi, who knew every detail about the millworker strikes.

Ghatge had just launched into an account of how he had been discovered by the leader of the Native People's Party, who saw the promise he had, the greatness that was written all over him, when Maria stood up abruptly. Ghatge stopped in full flow, his hand still on his forehead.

'Going already, Madam?' he asked, a steady glint in his eyes. She saw now how black they looked, and knew he was a man to be wary of.

'Yes, I forgot. I had an appointment.'

When Maria heard her phone ring, she fumbled in her bag to find it. For a septuagenarian, Maria thought, Neera had been quick. But it was Joyce instead and she proceeded to make a huge scene on the phone.

'You don't even recognize my voice,' Maria heard Joyce say before the phone fell abruptly silent.

Maria blamed herself, of course. She had not paused to check who had called and had allowed herself to sound puzzled. So the low huskiness she permitted herself with Joyce was missing. Mumbai did that to you. It absorbed you, engaged your senses in every way and your past became something you left behind.

Maria called back several times, but Joyce did not answer. Twice Maria was even cut off. Maria knew she sounded like a raving madwoman on the streets: hand held to an ear, yelling into the phone. The noise everywhere rushed at her like undying waves, and over all this, her own shrill voice rose high.

To get away from it all, she plunged into the nearest restaurant. Her eyes blinked in the darkness, from which a young smiling face emerged. It was the helper who doubled up as dishwasher and waiter, and he guided her to a table. The phone rang again as she sank back into the darkness with relief.

'Joyce, don't be angry.'

The voice that came now was broken in places. 'Hello, please,' said someone sounding very elderly. One look at the green dial confirmed her relief.

'Oh yes, Neeraji?'

She had to say it twice. That afternoon whoever she spoke to appeared strangely hard of hearing, but by the end of it all Maria was smiling again as she keyed in a message for Joyce. Neera had agreed to meet her the very next day at the protest march called in support of the textile workers.

When Joyce did reply, it was short and brutally truncated. *U go on and on abt Pooja.*

Maria knew then she had to look up her email to Joyce. Joyce held grudges but it was Joyce, Maria knew, she would have to go back to in Baltimore. It was late but the twenty-four-hour cybercafé was still open. Maria walked fast, past the shanties and the food joints. Families cooked meals on the pavement outside and Maria saw the blinking blue screens of televisions on inside as she hurried on.

On the main road, the sound of traffic dipped and rose in waves. Sounds that died away as Maria pulled the door of the cybercafé open and stepped inside. To her relief, her favourite cubicle stood empty and unoccupied. There was no one but the man who operated the café. A mix of relief and irritation swept through Maria once she knew for certain that Joyce had made a silly fuss over just one line in her email.

Maria couldn't stop laughing though, her eyes blurring over as she read the line again. *The softness of her melts in your mouth.* Maria was describing the dessert Pooja had made for dinner the night before.

'What a typo,' she said aloud, beginning to laugh. Perhaps Joyce would understand things too once she explained. Maybe she was just being difficult, and this too—a missed word that led to a mess up—would just become another thing on the list of things they would laugh over, later, and long after later too. Maria laughed hard, her head thrown back.

It was only after she crossed one building, as Maria gingerly tried not to step too close to the walls, that she heard the man following her. This was a part of the road where the high walls of the old mill looked down, and there was only a lone shop at the corner. Three streetlights did not work, the other two glowered at the puddles of orange light at their feet. Cabs and autos idled by the roadside. There was no one in them and no one around, for that short stretch. There were only the footsteps she heard behind her.

'I give you lift on my scooter.' It was the man from the cybercafé, his breath falling hard like distinct commas after every word.

'No. I do not need one.'

'I give you lift,' he repeated, coming closer, his voice insistent and low. His words mingled with the menace that flooded Maria's heart.

'I do not need a lift,' she said, turning once and then breaking into a slow run. But the walls on one side seemed higher than she remembered. Her screams would never rise beyond it. On the other side of the road, shops had downed their shutters. The man was a different person now. He wasn't deaf but her voice, her answers, simply had not registered. The mask of politeness was gone. The one look she had tossed behind her showed the glaring intensity in his eyes. Her heart hammered—she wanted to pound with her fists on the high wall. But all she could do was run. He had that smell she recognized, or perhaps it was her own raw fear, rising with every moment.

'I want to walk,' she said again, her voice strangled. She remembered all the things she had been told. Every city will reveal its real truths in the darkness, every city has its rules to be safe. She ran harder, her eyes on the road ahead. She did not want to stumble and fall. The light from her mobile phone, still in her hand, flashed on the buckets already placed in line. The light dotted the pavement as she ran, marking it grey and blue in places. She could not even stop to dial for help.

When a car emerged from inside the chawl in a jerk of sudden light, Maria ran headlong into its path. The headlights blazed into her face, the screech of tyres filled her head.

*He...help...*Maria hated the way she sounded. The door opened with a distinct click and Ghatge descended. His fingers brushed his moustache and he ran a hand over his hair.

'Arre, Madam, you are here! Everything okay?'

The man came up behind her. She leaned against Ghatge's car, gasping for breath. On the sidewalk, just where the car turned, she noticed now the sleeping bodies stirring to unwilling life. There had been people around but if she had stopped and screamed, would they have helped? Her thoughts whirred around in circles and refused to settle down into certainties. She could not say if the danger had passed or if she had become even more cornered. She bent her head, and did not notice when someone passed a bottle of water to her. But it dropped from her hands and rolled over under the car. The driver knelt on his haunches to look for it.

It gave him something to do, as Ghatge cleared his throat and spat. Then he began talking to the man who stood a little way off, rigid, an animal smell still on him. Ghatge spoke quickly. The trees and the high-rises loomed down on her. Everything was a witness yet they were oblivious to her. She jerked up as she heard other harsh sounds. Ghatge was slapping the other man, clean and hard on one cheek, then the other, and all over again. The driver turned away, somewhat unwillingly, and she heard the decisive slam of the car door.

Next, Maria heard a scratching sound by her feet. A balled-up figure at her knees, with his hands scrunched up. The man was asking for forgiveness. Maria yelped, moving back. Her arm struck the car but her former pursuer was now relentless in other ways. He stayed on his knees and wheedled, 'Sorry, Madam...sorry...'

'Chal, get out. Now,' said Ghatge. His eyes were glittering as he read her face and then shoved the man away with his foot. It was just like his tone with her.

'Madamji, come. I will take you home.'

The light of the street lamp turned his bald spot into a neat purple halo, and his gold watch glinted. 'Please come,' he said as she hesitated. 'In our country, we respect women. We hold them high on our heads. You people should write about that.'

The words came at Maria, intelligible and in a rush. For a

moment she thought he was reading the words from a nearby billboard. Then a slim, somewhat squat figure appeared in the darkness, and she bit back another scream. But it was his driver who had emerged again, to hold the door open for her. His moves, affected and very studied, added to her dread.

It wasn't my fault. It wasn't my fault, Maria was readying herself to say but Ghatge leaned closer as the door shut. She saw his face as the car grazed by a streetlight.

'Arre, Madam, I save you and you go, do things behind my back, eh?'

All that had been behind her back, trailing her for long agonizing seconds, had been that hungry, roving monster who hadn't taken 'no' for an answer. But Ghatge patted her on the shoulder, making her jump, before he laughed in that gentle sinister way he had.

'You talk to Neeraji, no? I get all the news, from everywhere.'

It was a short ride, the car stopped before the decrepit cigarette shop, now closed, from where she took the lane into the chawl building she stayed in.

'Next time, ask me only.' There was that glitter in Ghatge's eyes, and then he leaned out one last time. 'Good night, Miss Maria. Sweet dreams.'

She trembled long into the night; several times she half made up her mind to pack up and leave. She wanted to call Joyce and yet she couldn't. Maria knew she would have been raped, and perhaps left to her death. There were alleys between buildings that no one ventured into. Perhaps her death would have unsettled Ghatge. She wondered how the news about her email to Neera had reached him. She knew she had been careless at the restaurant, not keeping her voice low when Neera had called. Ghatge had his men everywhere.

As the night's darkness eased, Maria saw a fragment of a green bangle on another ledge only a window away. Part of it had embedded itself into the grainy cement. The green bangles that every married woman wore—it matched Pooja's eyes, Maria thought.

When Pooja came in with her tea the next morning, she smiled at the paper in Maria's hand. *Going?* She pointed at the article Maria had been reading. Pooja wiped her hands on her sari end, but nothing, not even Maria's long sleepless state, could erase what she saw: sharp red welts on Pooja's wrists. Maria felt the anger rise, directed at all men and then towards that boor who was Pooja's husband. She would have Pooja report him. She would take Pooja to the police station and complain about the man from the cybercafé. Pooja could be her interpreter.

Maria's breath choked up at the memories. She frowned as she thought of ways to explain it to Pooja. And there was Pooja wrinkling her nose up, then smiling. *So boring, always so much work.* Her bangles moved, indicating things behind her on the balcony: the washed clothes hanging on the line, the buckets she had already fetched.

The words came automatically to Maria. *Let's go out.* Maria moved her arm in a wide arc, taking in at one end, the black line where the sea stretched and then the other, where the train line ran. 'Come on.'

Pooja pursed up her lips, looked away and, to Maria's surprise, nodded. This was how it was all decided between them, with pointed gestures, ready laughter and conspiratorial glances. Perhaps her own sleepless night and those marks on Pooja's wrists had decided it for them. They would be companionable, Maria thought, no matter the differences between them. The train was crowded as it rushed in, people made slanting figures as they held onto the door, but Pooja pulled her through into the women's compartment. Maria's breasts brushed against other breasts, she smiled into other women's faces and she let the last few hours melt away. There would always be time to explain. She did not want Pooja's smile to vanish again.

At the far end of the coach, some eunuchs took up an entire row but made a place for them. They sang, played on their drums and when one of them pointed to Pooja's flat stomach, there followed much raucous teasing.

'You will have a son.'

There was great laughter. Some of them leaned forward and caressed Pooja on the face, Maria too. They blessed them both, promising them every happiness and then held out their hands. And it was only Maria who saw Pooja's tears when they got off three stops later. 'Oh, don't cry.'

Maria rummaged in her bag, taking her time. The truth had struck her so hard she couldn't find anything. She fumbled, stuttered, amazed at her own stupidity. She, who had always prided herself on being perceptive, had missed the obvious, the most blinding of truths. The inside of her bag smelt of many things, reminding her of Joyce and all her untidiness. And Pooja, her nose wrinkling in amusement at the tissue Maria finally held out, sniffed it in deeply. It was her childless state that was bothering her, Maria knew now. It was eating her up. Maria wished she had found out the truth some other way. She wished there was something she could say.

They had chaat at Opera House, where Maria tried asking her gently, pointing to her own cheeks. Pooja only shook her head. Up close to her, Maria saw clearly the folds in her cheeks from all the tears, and the scratch marks on her wrists. Her husband evidently blamed her too. Maria felt the heat of anger rise, but the afternoon had turned mellow, a surprise breeze touched it here and there. Low clouds drifted overhead and stayed over the city. Everyone was out, everyone with heads raised to the sky, delighted by the unexpected good weather.

They laughed as they rode an old Victoria carriage towards

the red-domed, grey-walled Taj Hotel. Maria laughed as Pooja haggled with the driver for the outrageous price he charged. 'Madam,' he tried to explain to Maria. 'It's for the experience, not the distance.'

'You better take care of the horse then.'

Maria pointed to his pony as Pooja nudged her away. Its mane was henna coloured like its owner's, but the animal was even more skeletal and stunted.

'Call it restroom,' she whispered when Pooja asked for the toilet. The bathroom in the Taj Hotel was as big as her room in the chawl, she told Maria, giggling. It was lit up with chandeliers and flower stands as big as buckets stood outside each stall. She saw Pooja's wistful face as the water ran just when she placed her fingers under the tap. They giggled through the thin wall between them as the automatic flush started up, once and then twice.

They took the stairs to the café where their table offered a wonderful view of the sea. Under the table, when Maria's feet played with Pooja's anklets, she didn't move away. Instead, Pooja was staring out at the sea, looking at a grey yacht, and the sun glimmered silver, its light bending and breaking over the unstill waters.

You have to pay so much for this? Pooja's wide eyes said it all.

Maria put her hand on hers, 'We will come here again.'

Pooja emptied three sachets of sugar into her tea, stirring loudly. Maria wrapped the three chocolate chip cookies, as big as bread slices, in a napkin. 'For the train back,' she winked, and as they sat watching Mumbai in the late afternoon, Maria asked again, 'Are you happy now?'

Pooja's eyes clouded over, and Maria only heard the jingle of bangles.

'Your husband...?'

Pooja gave her a quick look, then she looked away.

'Yes...he. Yes. Fine...'

But her face was all wooden, she was not even looking her way, and Maria understood. She still held Pooja's hand. 'Poor thing,' and she stroked it again and again. Pooja's fingers were uneven, not tapering like Joyce's. They were thin and bony, with weak arches. Maria thought her own hands looked grotesque and ugly in comparison.

'Come on, tell me...'

Pooja shook her head, and Maria searched for the right words to invite confidences. Once they were outside, they came across office executives out for a smoke. Dapper and flashy, they had an easy abruptness about themselves. The cabbies strolled by, leaning into each other as they exchanged jokes in their lunch hour. Schoolgirls walked past in pairs. Some turned to look at the two of them. They did make an incongruous pair, much as Maria wished otherwise. Maria knew she was the wrong age to be a friend; she was just wrong in every way. She struck her chin out and walked defiantly as if her pose would alter these truths in some way.

They walked towards the Gateway of India where the photographers with their Polaroids pursued them. Everywhere couples posed obligingly, with the brown stone edifice of the Gateway as the backdrop. 'Only one minute,' a photographer wheedled. His face was grey and he looked half-starved, and it was Maria who persuaded Pooja, a half-teasing note in her voice, 'Maybe just one then?'

The camera flashed a second later, but what Maria would always remember was the way they had stood, their arms around each other's waists, and she smiling as she tried to catch Pooja's eye.

'Do you want two copies?' the photographer asked.

Her copy would have to be hidden away forever, away from Joyce's eyes. Maria nodded, missing the feel of her arm around Pooja. Pooja was already placing her copy in her purse, and Maria only said, 'This makes us friends, right?'

In the train home, Maria saw she had a missed call but did not call Joyce back. An hour later, as they turned into the chawl gate, Pooja's feet trailed, and Maria, following her eyes, saw Pooja looking up at her husband who glowered at them from the veranda above.

Maria gestured, chopping the air around with her hands, 'Does he beat you?'

Pooja touched her stomach, her cheeks, and gestured to the empty air around them. Her face held an emptiness and Maria asked again, holding Pooja's wrists, her fingers across the scratch marks. 'You know, he could go to the doctor too?'

Pooja raised hands to her ears as if Maria had spoken some very unwelcome truths. 'No no, it's all right.' She said something in Marathi; a familiar name came up too. It was all broken, but Maria understood. *He has a job. He works for Ghatge Sahib. And Sahib takes care of us always.*

Maria saw through Ghatge now. Of course, that was it! They were all his people, Pooja too, and she would find her way through all this. But she, Maria, would never be part of it. Pooja's husband called out to her now, his voice hoarse and ragged.

Maria tried to explain. 'She was just taking me around. It was fun.'

He turned that angry red face to her but said nothing. Pooja nudged her elbow, stopping her from saying anything more. 'He came early today,' she said. 'I must go to him.'

But Maria held on to her wrist. She wanted to say something, but couldn't. 'Come,' she said, her fingers pressing hard on Pooja's wrist, but the rest of what Maria wanted to say died away. In Pooja's eyes, Maria saw the wild pleading look in her own eyes. Maria knew the man pursuing her must have looked the same way. She tried once more.

'Come away. Leave all this.' She put in a bit of the eunuchs' wheedling, cajoling tone, and then with a pleading look, she gave back to Pooja her own earnest shy smile. But Pooja broke free, she gestured to her husband a floor above and then ran. Maria heard the tinkling as a bangle broke and fell to the ground. She saw the red welts on Pooja's wrists and on her own fingers too.

Later that night, as Maria stood quietly by the window, she was certain she heard Pooja crying. Maria wanted to ask her if she was free again, the next day. They could perhaps take the ferry off the Gateway and go to the Elephanta Caves.

Maria heard the door slam once, and footsteps ran past. Then she must have drifted off to sleep. At first light, Maria saw the white car again near the gate and, straining her eyes, she saw Pooja too, joining the water line. She does work hard, Maria thought. It was a long time later that she saw Pooja return.

In the veranda, watching Pooja at the far end, hanging up the clothes on the line, Maria could see new scratches on her wrist. How could one break so many bangles in one night? But Pooja was not even looking at her.

Maria felt alone in a crowded city. She did not talk to anyone, not even Pooja, about what a total, utter, blissful fool she had been. The sides of her palms were red now, when she beat them against the wall. As red as the scratches on Pooja's wrist, red as the splotches of scattered paint on Joyce's torn-up canvases.

A fortnight later, when she was leaving, the white car was there at the gate once again. Ghatge had arranged for her ride to the airport. Her accounts would be settled over email, he had assured. There was no one to say farewell to. Pooja would never speak to her any more.

When Maria reached home a day and a half later, Joyce

was waiting at the airport. They patched things up over the next few days. And then Maria got an email from Neera. *What happened? That day we waited for you at the protest march. I do hope your trip was fun.*

When a woman wept softly and for too long, she sounded like a cat crying.

Wives and Other Beings

The reason she gave her husband wasn't really why Gauri Ghatge travelled to Mumbai for the first time in nearly a decade.

Everyone, her husband too, had wanted her there for the function. Ghatge was president of the labour union, and the new office, which now occupied the entire ground floor of what had once been the old textile mill's administrative block, had to be inaugurated. Now there was a guard sitting on a stool by the door. There were air conditioners at every window and potted plants stood wobbly on the ledges. In the blue painted hall inside were rows of tables and chairs and, arranged haphazardly along bookshelves, were files with dog-eared, spiralling ends of paper.

For Gauri, the function had unfolded in a haze of discomfort. The steel of the chair was hard under her, the weight of the marigold garland prickled her skin and her head buzzed every time Mahesh came into view. He seemed to run on batteries. He was in several places at the same time, doing far too many things at once. He pushed the media people around, he pulled the boys up for the sloppy way they served tea or passed the food trays around. He was there wherever Gauri looked, which meant she had less time to watch Pooja.

If Mahesh was the one who got things moving and running

smoothly in the office, did that mean he had no time for Pooja? For it was to size Pooja up, to put her in her place, that Gauri had come to Mumbai.

'He's concerned about everyone but she's pretty, you know.' Some women had just come back to the village from a wedding and they spoke in hushed tones. *Gauri Tai, you should not leave your husband alone for too long*—this was their conclusion.

Women would be women—they would gossip, spread malice; that was their way of making friends. Gauri knew this just as she knew Vidyadhar, her husband—Ghatge Sahib to everyone else—whose mind was always on the big things, the things which mattered, which made you famous. Even on their wedding night, he had seemed in a hurry to get it over with. Even in the moment that Gauri knew she had lost her virginity, she had looked up shyly, hoping to share it with him, even her pain, only to find him looking far away, a look of fixed concentration on his face.

But the women kept on with their gossip. It wasn't just that Pooja was pretty. She made very good food too—crunchy misal pav, the coconut fish curry made just the way their mothers had taught them, and even sabudana kichdi on the days everyone fasted. There were a lot of people Pooja now provided meals for. Outside her door there were always at least a dozen or so lunch boxes. Sometimes she delivered them herself to all the new offices now coming up in the old mill area.

When a woman praised another woman's cooking, Gauri knew there was something to worry about, especially when Pooja also provided Ghatge his three meals of the day. But what made Gauri make her mind up once and for all was what she heard from an older aunt who had just come back from the city. 'Your Sahib, he is busy but too much alone. Mahesh is a good boy, but a bit distracted. It's the air in the city. You never know what it can do.'

That whole week before her visit, Gauri remained tense. She had to decide on an auspicious time, she had to put her house in order, and then there were all the things to make for Vidyadhar, and for Mahesh and Pooja. She would take a sari for Pooja too. After all, this was her first visit after Pooja's marriage and she, as befitted her status as someone who had arranged Pooja's marriage with Mahesh, would be an honoured guest at their house.

Gauri muttered to herself as she made her preparations. It wasn't even a house but two small rooms in a chawl. How had things changed so quickly? Pooja had been a quiet girl who had suffered the misfortune of losing her mother early. That was why she invited bad luck. Life, after all, was a complicated map and had to be negotiated carefully. Mothers could tell how it could be done. But Pooja had no one, and it was she, Gauri, and others who had taken her under their wing. They knew the colours one had to wear on certain days, the days one had to fast, and the appropriate gods to be worshipped for every occasion.

The time Pooja lost her mother, Gauri had been busy, sending her first child off to university in Mangalore. One of her friends had taken over supervising Pooja. She was taught the things to make sure she got a good husband, and to ensure that he stayed good. It was Ghatge Sahib who had suggested Mahesh as a possible groom. Mahesh worked in Sahib's office in Mumbai, but he had roots in the village. He was hard-working and had no bad habits, at least not the kind people acquired in a city. What more could a girl want?

Pooja's father, relieved and grateful, had agreed readily, and Ghatge too came down from Mumbai for the marriage. Gauri found herself then busier than ever. In a marriage, there were many things, big and small, that demanded attention: the marigold garlands that were exchanged, the gifts for everyone, the order for every ritual had to be explained, for even priests could not be trusted entirely on such matters. Gauri had been relieved to note Ghatge's presence, though she rarely caught his eye.

The bride is very pretty, everyone said, once the silk curtain between groom and bride had been raised, and they had looked at each other for the first time as the auspicious moment dawned. There was a silence, then someone blew the conch shell, and the women exchanged pleased looks with each other, happy with what they had done for Pooja. But, now, it seemed to Gauri, a lot still remained.

Gauri found herself a comfortable seat in the late night bus from Chiplun. She had already seen the movie that was playing, and she found herself laughing long before the others. But there was a girl who was laughing hard too, someone way up in the front. A few more minutes into the film, Gauri heard her again, speaking in loud, demanding tones this time. Gauri craned her neck, and saw that it was a young woman in a sleeveless red shirt, and she was making a fuss about the air conditioning. She gave herself away as a city girl. Gauri closed her eyes to it all and turned away. True, it was hot, but the bus was full too. It was a seven-hour journey from Chiplun to the terminus in Dadar.

The movie moved into its second half as the lights in the bus were dimmed and some people settled down to sleep. Gauri muttered her usual prayers as she drifted off to sleep. She was jolted awake some time later by the shrill cry that broke through the sound of the television, over the gentle hum of the moving bus, and tore into her sleep. Gauri came to, first in darkness, and then in a blinding flash as the lights came on. For a long time, she did not know where she was. There

were voices, figures moving up and down, and then, through
a gap between flaying arms and jerking figures, she saw the
girl again. A moving, dancing figure in red, her hair swinging
loose, and she was shaking and moving malevolently. Gauri
heard words she had never heard used. All she could make out
was a litany, an unending torrent. The woman was speaking in
English; angry, raging words spoken in a voice that rose higher
with every note.

'How dare you? You did it. I caught you in the act.'

The tirade was directed at a man, now fumbling with his
shirt, gesturing abjectly with his hands, but the woman in the
red shirt was uncontrollable. She moved up and down and
with so much agitation that it took Gauri some moments to
realize that the bus wasn't moving at all and that it was pitch-
dark outside.

'I grabbed his hand. It was here.' The woman was pointing
at her red shirt.

'Madam, there was an insect.'

'Oho. And you think you saw it in all this darkness.
Really?'

Someone stood up just as Gauri craned her neck to follow
the exchange. Then more people rose in their seats, and the
wall of people turned everything grey in front of her. But the
voices carried, the woman's, and then Gauri heard others
speak up too and she knew clearly what had happened.

Gauri felt a pang of sympathy, then a wave of anger. No
place was safe any more. Her sense of justice rose in equal
measure. She nodded, and her nods kept pace with all her
righteous thoughts.

It's true. Women cannot ever be safe.

The guy deserves a thrashing.

Next, she heard the sounds of skin hitting skin, slaps like
a hammer hitting stone, and then the man's yelps. The woman
insisted that the police be called immediately and the tension

in the bus only grew. The only thing glowing and alive in that darkness, Gauri noticed, was the bus perched on the hill road like a night creature, glowering and dangerous. Then she saw more people standing up, moving up and down the aisle, some taking down things from the overhead shelves. Soon other voices raised themselves in a low grumble.

There were signs and gestures, and Gauri heard the words, in different voices. *How long must we wait?* Her phone rang— it was Mahesh, and she told him of the delay.

She drifted in and out of sleep as she waited and the bus did not move. A slow greyness crept into the morning. There were rough voices, voices edgy with fatigue, and the guilty man's voice rang out still, now hoarse with his protests and explanations. It sounded like someone had pressed the repeat button for a television show.

A few minutes later, Gauri realized the police were already there. There was their jeep parked alongside the road, blocking the road. There were vendors walking up and down past every window, holding up water and packets of peanut candy. Then her phone rang, and it was Ghatge. She heard the impatience in her husband's voice.

'Mahesh told me you are late.'

'Yes, an...incident...'

'Accident...?'

'No.' She struggled for words and then, in a lowered voice, said with a note of excitement, 'Someone hurt a woman and...'

'Oh, so it was an accident.'

'It's all right,' he said to Gauri's own 'It's all right' when she couldn't explain it all to him. 'Mahesh will wait for you...' With that he hung up. At least things in her own small world were all right.

There was still some jerkiness around her. The bus heaved and shook but did not move. She felt giddy and thought it was because of her broken sleep, or that she had not had her usual morning cup of tea. People were getting off the bus and she knew where they were heading off to. Gauri joined another woman and as they squatted, a thick bush hiding them from the world, the woman began in a companionable way. 'I wish she hadn't made such a fuss. The driver was giving the man another seat and some of the men beat him up. They forced him to say sorry too.'

Gauri nodded, feeling the relief as the pressure eased. 'We are already late.'

'My sons will go off to work now,' the other woman went on, 'and I have to take an autorickshaw.'

She prattled on about how the auto-drivers in Mumbai fleeced you, especially if you were not careful. By the time they went back, Gauri saw that the police constables were questioning the man, and she found herself promising her companion that she would have her dropped home.

When Gauri finally found herself alone with Mahesh in the car, she wasn't quite sure what to say to him. The heat sapped everything. The traffic was a stubborn, unmoving mule. The car droned, lurched, then halted, dozing for long minutes at a red signal. Twice, despite the patent disapproval on Mahesh's face, Gauri rolled down her window to cautiously throw out a few coins to some children begging on the street. Mumbai was even more terrible than she had imagined, and once again Gauri berated Pooja. It was she who had got her here. A woman who did not know her place.

She sniffed, and Mahesh at the wheel was apologetic. 'Just a little bit more, Tai.'

He kept saying that and by the time they reached the chawl, it was late morning. She felt dirty and smelly.

Then Gauri saw her, a woman smiling tentatively, running down the creaky wooden stairs to greet her. She stopped at the very end, smiling at Gauri as if that would make up for her breathlessness and for not being able to speak an immediate word of welcome. Yet she looked beautiful and so, for some moments, Gauri found that she could not quite recognize Pooja. She had also rimmed her eyes with kajal, and was draped in a shiny green sari when it was far too hot and a simple cotton one would have sufficed.

Pooja stood there waiting to be appreciated, but Gauri bent, her hands reaching for her suitcase.

'I've been waiting and waiting for you, Tai,' Pooja finally said. 'Let me carry it.'

'No, it's all right. I will.'

Mahesh came up and calmly, very deliberately, took it up the stairs.

There was a strangeness to the heat in the city. In the village, it was hot everywhere but here the heat stamped itself on you. It was like a ghoul that caught you by the nose and breathed hot air into your body until you just didn't want to move. Gauri lay there on the bed. Every time she tried to sleep, the loud honking outside stirred her awake. Yet she had to admit that it was a comfortable room. Pooja had put up dampened sheets all around the bed's four posts, over the mosquito net. The fan creaked rhythmically, urging her to get some sleep.

Gauri met Vidyadhar a few hours later, as the afternoon waned. She heard his footsteps first, but it took him a long time to appear. Mahesh and Pooja had two small rooms in the chawl; a big one that combined the sitting room and the kitchen, and there was this inner room, with its four-poster bed. But Gauri heard Pooja's voice and it fuelled her dismay, made her mutter under her breath. Instead of coming to see her, his wife, Vidyadhar was talking to some other woman. The other voice in her piped up immediately. *You have been married for twenty years. Hold yourself.* That other voice in her head made her drowsy again, and so when Vidyadhar finally came in, she found it difficult to look up at him.

He looked down at her and then looked away. They had not changed much in each other's eyes and relief was best expressed this way. Pooja hung around for a bit.

'Take her out to the city. Show her the things to see,' Gauri heard her husband tell Pooja. And the command lightened Gauri's heart. As a husband, he still knew his place. He was making sure his wife was looked after, that it was the responsibility of the younger woman of the house to do so. Pooja nodded in agreement and then turned away, closing the door behind her as she left. Gauri waited for her husband to say something, but he only sat in the old cane chair, looking away, thinking his thoughts, moving his fingers idly over his phone. Gauri shook her head, irritated by her own drowsiness.

'Maybe I just need to go to the temple,' she said aloud, finally.

He thought about it and then climbed into bed beside her, stretched out and belched. His phone rang and he answered laconically. 'Call later...'

Then he turned to her and asked about everyone in the village. Then, as she told him of the water crisis, of the dogs turning green because of the new chemical factory, and the relentless smoke that made everyone cough, he nodded. Then he climbed on top of her and, pushing her sari up, said, 'Yes, the government should do something.'

'Do something,' he repeated. Looking up, she saw the same fixed expression he had on their wedding day and every time they met afterwards. She smelt him in with the heat; it was hard for her to breathe and still harder when he had got off.

They were silent, it was just like the times when he visited her in the village. It made her happy and relieved—at least her husband was still interested in her. When she woke up, she noted to her consternation that it was the twilight hour. Gauri knew the rituals, the correct time for everything, and now she sat up hurriedly and did her hair. She was horrified at herself, and annoyed with Pooja for not waking her up.

'Isn't it the correct thing to let you rest?' Pooja answered but the teasing note in her voice subsided when Gauri arched an eyebrow in reply. The girl had indeed learnt to answer back. She had eaten a lot of the city's air.

Pooja took her out on some mornings after that. Gauri noticed how she no longer wore her sari the way the women of the village did. Pooja had taken to wrapping it neatly around herself and bringing one end around the shoulder. Pooja was quiet as they walked to the vendor stalls under the bridge, right to where the road led to the Parel railway station, but she haggled and bargained effectively with the vendors, using not an unnecessary word but all the right gestures. Gauri approved of this; it revealed her experience in running a house. There was the attention she gave to the vegetables, turning them over, holding them up against the light, and knowing how to pick out faults, even when they were carefully masked.

But Pooja wasn't doing anything about the many eyes on her. The vendor whose eyes lingered a moment longer than necessary on her face, the loitering men who came a little too close to ask pointless questions of the vendor. Gauri felt an irritation and then the same tired jealousy seeping into her. 'Cover up,' Gauri snapped in an undertone.

Pooja pulled her sari tighter around herself as the vendor hid his smirk. Later, once they were home, Pooja got out a stool for her. All the unused small bits of furniture had been pushed under the bed and Pooja wriggled in and out in no time, not a hair out of place. Seated on that stool, Gauri watched her in the small kitchen that took up just a corner in the main room. Pooja sat on her haunches, cleaning, dicing and slicing the vegetables neatly and cleanly. She knew how to run a house all right. The basil and the curry leaf plants were on the veranda outside and they looked well-watered. As the silence stretched, Pooja broke in to explain what Gauri already knew: that she made lunches for the men in the offices around, including Ghatge Sahib. She pointed to what Gauri had already seen: the rows of lunch boxes standing, waiting to be filled, all along the veranda. Gauri offered to crunch the coconut for her. She gently crushed the sour kokum so a thick syrup emerged, and nothing was wasted.

'Sahib will know it's all from your hands,' Pooja attempted to tease again but Gauri said nothing. If Pooja noticed she gave no hint. Pooja fetched the lunch boxes and placed a soft cotton cloth at the bottom of each for the chapattis and wiped away stray drops of dal along the rims. She was generous in her portions; Gauri could tell with her experienced eye that it wasn't a put on. There wasn't too much gravy, but also peas and potatoes in equal measure. Pooja put in chillies, lemon and pickle in separate sachets and finally, pulled the ends of the tiffins up tightly and neatly.

One afternoon, soon after the function at the union office, as Pooja grated the ginger for their tea, Gauri asked, 'Do you keep the fast for Ganesha every Thursday?'

She nodded.

Gauri went on, 'You are too thin. How long have you been married?'

She understood Pooja's hesitation right away. Gauri recognized the lowered eyes, the way Pooja bit her lips, pulled her sari around her shoulders. When she saw the vulnerability, Gauri seized her chance. 'Yes,' she went on without giving Pooja the chance to reply 'Of course I remember. We got you married.' She saw Pooja's still lowered eyes and that encouraged her. 'Our families helped your father. Five years after that seem so long. It's time for a child. What are you waiting for?'

The next afternoon, Gauri asked after her father. 'He is getting old. A grandson would make him happy, you know.' Pooja nodded in the way Gauri had learnt to recognize. Gauri stared into the hot sun and thought Mumbai was a very boring city. But at least she knew she had got under Pooja's skin.

The girl called the very evening Gauri had declared her intentions of taking the bus home the next day. It was Pooja who came up with Gauri's phone; she had left it on the kitchen table. 'Tai, call for you.' Gauri's surprise made her miss the open curiosity in Pooja's eyes. It increased when she heard the polite voice at the other end. The woman spoke in such dulcet tones that Gauri felt a coolness on her skin, she felt the city's heat disappear.

'Hello, Mrs Ghatge. I am glad to speak to you. I've been looking for you for so long.'

Nothing had prepared Gauri for the onslaught of politeness that now came over in wave after rolling wave through the telephone into her ears. The woman at the other end said 'please' and 'thank you' too many times. Then she called her *Tai*, before placing herself and her honour totally in Gauri's hands. Gauri found herself saying yes to everything. Yes, of course she remembered the man who had troubled her in the bus. She soothed the girl who had a sob in her voice. Yes, of course she understood. And yes, she would testify in her case.

'Will you be here on the twenty-fourth?'

'Yes,' Gauri found herself declaring, 'even if it is next month.'

The other voice now sounded so elated that Gauri too felt a sense of accomplishment. It was nearing Diwali, and a firecracker shot through the high-rises and made for the clouds.

Her husband's face, however, broke into a frown when he learnt of Gauri's plans. He harangued her with one question after another. As she had done with the girl, Gauri resorted to saying 'yes' to all that he said.

'Isn't this matter one big jhamela?'

'Yes,' Gauri nodded her reply, but she would still do it.

He snapped at her, and in front of Pooja too. 'The man she is complaining against is close to the local leader. I know him too. It's all false. All lies.'

Gauri frowned, looking straight at him, ignoring Pooja. 'Yes, but it is my duty.'

'Don't you see it could be a problem for me too? It will embarrass me?'

Gauri folded her arms around herself, looked at a spot over her husband and nodded. Yes. But the woman was also embarrassed.

Ghatge pursed his lips, turned around and made to walk out of the door. Past him, Gauri saw Pooja appear with a glass of water that she offered her husband. But Ghatge side-stepped her and walked away. The glass on its tray shook and Pooja held up a hurried hand. But Gauri was sure her husband had not even glanced at her once. Pooja looked hurt. It was this, despite her disagreement with Ghatge that brought Gauri Tai great elation.

'The girl is not worth it, Tai,' Pooja said, 'but you did the right thing.'

Gauri snapped at Pooja. 'You can't say right and wrong at the same time. There can be only one thing. Good and bad do not hold together.' She held Pooja's gaze and this time it was the girl who looked away.

Gauri left the next morning. It was Mahesh again who carried her suitcase down the stairs. Gauri watched Pooja run up, a flash of blue and green, the sound of her ringing anklets rising and falling like a faraway bird. She returned in no time. A married woman should not run that way, Gauri thought in some disapproval. But for now, she blessed her, as Pooja held forward the plate holding turmeric and vermilion, the colours that married women blessed each other with, each one praying for the other's long and fruitful married life. She felt her hand cool on Pooja's forehead, and saw her face reflected in Pooja's light green eyes. Gauri caught herself smiling, her hands lingering on Pooja's cheek.

She wondered now why she had come. She had nothing to fear from a childless woman. Such a woman drew everyone's pity, not a man's lust, certainly not her busy husband's.

'Bless you, my dear. May your marriage prosper and be fruitful.'

The girl from the bus called her in the bus, and again as soon as Gauri reached home, and then several times. Indeed, she never let up and even called her an hour before she boarded the bus back to Mumbai the very next week.

A few hours later, when she had the accident, Gauri knew she had invited bad luck on herself. It wasn't just that she had gone against her husband's wishes, but that she had let herself be convinced about a journey she clearly should never have undertaken in the first place.

The bus had ploughed into a field after the driver, new on the route, had turned to speak to a passenger just behind him. His moment of distraction had now left Gauri with a sprained ankle.

Ghatge, who had rushed to her as soon as he could, was immensely relieved. It wasn't a disaster and, by the standards of road accidents, almost routine. He knelt by his injured wife who lay on the grass where she had been helped off the bus. He also oversaw the shifting of some other passengers to the local hospital. This was how he had always been, and so Gauri didn't complain. She did protest at the way she had to be helped inside Ghatge's car, assisted by her husband and

Mahesh, her arms around their shoulders. Since the time of her son's birth, it was the first time she had been so physically close to another man besides her husband.

As Gauri stretched herself out in the back seat, her husband fitted himself next to her, almost at one corner. Mahesh who was driving, placed her luggage next to him. Gauri was certain of one thing: the accident would never have happened had that girl not forced Gauri to visit the city again.

'It's nobody's fault but that girl's,' Gauri said, once she heard the engine start. She briefly put her hand over her eyes as the sun came in fiercely through the window. 'Since that day nothing has been right. She meant evil.'

She felt Ghatge squirm in his seat. 'You are tired,' she heard him say. Then as she moaned in her pain, he cursed Mahesh, asking him to take the bends carefully. Mahesh scratched his ear and murmured his apologies.

On the highway, the afternoon sun kept pace with the car, turning the dry leaves on the trees brown. The red soil gleamed relentlessly, tiring the eyes. Spires of factories appeared, abandoned warehouses, and then villages struggling to hold onto the hillside.

Drive carefully, Gauri heard her husband say every now and then. The newspaper flapped loosely but his voice came as if from a distance, and she knew he was looking out of the window at the passing land, imagining things other than trees: resorts, hotels, even factories. Gauri never asked him to elaborate on such matters. He became different and he made the world, as she knew it, look different too.

'Perhaps I shouldn't have come to Mumbai at all,' she repeated a while later, when the outlines of the sooty Mumbai high-rises came into view. There were blue hills that, on close viewing, would become pockmarked by shanties. There was the dull brown smoke that came from other cars on the roads. Ghatge leaned over and rolled up her window. It embarrassed her. He had never seen her so immobile, not once.

She slouched lower on the car seat; it seemed too small for her now. Her sari covered her blouse decorously but she looked ungainly, not her usual stern held-in self. The flowers had all come undone from her braid and lay strewn on the leather seat between them. It gave everything a strange fragrance, and made her more garrulous than she intended to be.

She had had no intention of keeping her promise to visit Mumbai again, Gauri now said almost in a pleading tone to her husband. But the girl had called again and again. She had not followed the usual standard practice, Gauri went on still in that self-abnegating tone, and that was why she had invited such bad luck. The girl took up so much of her time, intruding into her routines, turning her vague assurances into promises that Gauri had let herself slip, forgetting to follow the rites and rituals that had helped her always face the unexpected and unannounced. She had not even gone down to the river last Saturday for a bath. And, worst of all, she had travelled on a Wednesday, the worst day of the week to do so.

It was then Ghatge did the strangest thing, one Gauri hoped Mahesh didn't catch through the rear-view mirror. As the car waited at yet another signal, he placed her ankle, swollen purple and loosely bound up in a soft blanket, on his lap. She felt awkward. Right next to them, a bus waited too, and people looked down from the windows. Then Ghatge placed his newspaper over her feet, shielding them from everyone's gaze, even his own.

Her toes were short and stubby. She remembered her toe rings and the way her husband had put them on her feet on their wedding day. Since then he had never properly looked at her toes, but here he was now, looking at them with great attention through the gap left by the newspaper. The nail polish had frayed, there was a thickness about her toes, but when his hands touched her and lingered on her skin, she felt a softness.

The traffic was building up as they neared the city. The waits at every signal grew longer. Then Gauri clearly heard her husband say something, words she had never heard him say before. 'I will get a Lamborghini.' The way he said it made Gauri turn to look at him. It was as if her husband had mentioned something brand new, something foreign and expensive. She caught Mahesh's eyes in the mirror, and she read curiosity, and excitement in his gaze. But a cold hand had gripped her heart. She hoped he didn't mean a woman. It would look ridiculous to ask for clarifications in front of Mahesh.

'What did you say?' she murmured softly instead, bringing a confiding note in her voice.

Ghatge was looking at his phone, and Gauri heard the popping of the text messages which arrived as connectivity improved. His fingers moved with a rapidity that astonished her, and he did manage a reply.

'You rest. It's the best car. And such a powerful engine.'

Her head jerked back in fatigue, but just then Mahesh spoke up, sounding enthusiastic in a way he had never been before, 'Mer...Merchedees car, Sahib. The new model is very good, Sahib...'

'You don't tell me what to get, and what to do, idiot,' snapped Ghatge, and she felt a stabbing pain in her toe as his hand grazed her none too gently.

Mahesh braked hard then, as if the answer had stunned him too. Gauri felt the pain return to her ankle.

When Gauri drifted awake from the short nap she had fallen into, the pain had eased and so had the thick haze in her head. Now she was aghast to see her feet on his lap. That girl had indeed made her do the unthinkable. Ghatge looked up from his phone, feeling her eyes on him, and she sighed. 'You were always right. She was a distraction in the bus. And it was not the man's fault if his hand slipped accidentally.'

He did not say anything more but his fingers were still on her toe rings. She felt comforted, though it did hurt when he moved his fingers a certain way. After a few hours at the hospital, where Gauri's ankle was placed in a firmer elastic wrap, she was driven to the chawl and Pooja was there to welcome her. Gauri would again have the same room as before. Between Ghatge and Pooja, they took her up the stairs, overriding her protests. She was still in pain but they seemed to be making a heroine out of her. She was not used to the attention, even from her husband.

The next day she saw her husband on television. Ghatge had not mentioned a word of this to her but, from his words, Gauri understood how carefully he had listened to her the previous day. Of course, Gauri heard him say, the bus incident was being blown out of proportion. What was being labelled as molestation was an accident. Though the man should have had more sense. Yes, Ghatge said, his wife knew about it. She had been a passenger in the bus too.

A woman reporter thrust a mike right into her husband's face. 'Do you agree with what your wife did?'

He took off his Gandhi cap. Its triangular flat top had fallen flat and he patted it into shape before putting it back on again. He chewed his lower lip in the way Gauri knew and she heard him say, 'Yes, I do. I like what Gauri did. A brave woman must stand up for other women.'

She glanced at Pooja who was staring reverentially at the television. Suddenly Gauri felt nothing was right in this world. A man calling his wife by name. A married woman staring unabashed at another man. 'Shameless girl,' she said instead, alarming Pooja. She pointed to the anchor who was now simpering up at her husband. She was so close to him; he could almost be looking down into her blouse. 'Look at the way she is dressed. And on television too.'

'I have to go. Tomorrow I shall return home. This is

enough,' she said to Pooja, an adamantine insistence in her voice. Pooja looked alarmed as Gauri repeated this over and over again, and she texted the same thing to Ghatge. He'd see it right there in front of the television cameras and take it as seriously as he had taken the reporter's question.

Gauri made her intentions clear to the girl when she called again. Gauri had made up her mind, and had practised how she would handle things this time. She knew the girl's wiles by now, the cajoling tone that would soon creep into her voice and Gauri had steeled herself to this. Her leg was encased in a tight brace and she felt its armour all around her. She chanted a silent prayer to Ganesha, as she heard the girl's voice in her ear. Her heart beat fast as the girl's attempts to cajole her to stay on picked up pace and Gauri had to think of Ganesha again. She thought of her narrow escape from the accident, her husband's face as he stared at her in the car. She thought of the priest's face and knew he had been right and she prayed again.

The next day, Gauri packed, and Pooja tried to help in any way she could. There weren't the usual tears, but Pooja lingered, stayed close by, or came back every so often from her other chores. Gauri knew that was important. Her waiting, her wasting time on trifles. If she had not cared, she would not have waited. 'You should not wait for me. It's time you make the food.'

Instead, Pooja bent over to touch her leg, running her hands over the brace and, when she looked up, Gauri saw the childlike mischief there. 'It's made my leg stronger,' Gauri said, trying to make light of things.

'Yes, now you can give the louts on the bus a kick.'

The Best and the Worst of Days

For a long time, Richard had not known that his habit of blinking had a name. As a child, the boys in his school called him 'Blinker'. But it became something of a problem when he found himself failing interviews. The previous week, Ghatge Sahib had mocked him in public by addressing Richard by that hated old name. Richard had found Ghatge's behaviour insulting in every way, especially when he and his mother still hadn't received his late father's dues. It was also becoming increasingly clear to Richard, though he didn't want to tell his mother this, that Ghatge Sahib had no interest in helping them in this matter.

One of Richard's interviewers, a man in a yellow polka-dotted tie and with a clipped accent, gave Richard the name for his condition.

Richard had applied for the position of a store manager for a new supermarket. He had just graduated, but then like before, he failed. Richard had come to believe that he lacked the required immodesty to sail through any interview. He just couldn't talk of his unique abilities for the job, he believed he had none, nothing at all. But this time, the interviewer had surprised him at the end. Clipping his pen back into his pocket, he had apologized, and then nodding offhandedly Richard's way, he had said, 'Listen…you might want to see a doctor for that.'

He indicated Richard's eyes, making him even more

conscious of blinking. 'It's called blepharospasm, and there is an easy cure, you know.' Richard blinked again, this time to ward off surprise tears. The man's tone had been strangely kind.

When Google confirmed for Richard, the fact that his strange habit had a name, it gave him relief of a kind. He now had a new, more valid, reason for his failures.

But Richard's oldest friends, Carl and Jeet, whom he met at the Five Gardens later that evening were scornful. 'That's just a fancy word for nothing.' It was only a name thought up by doctors or the medicine companies to make a profit, they said. Instead, they suggested, he must work more on his résumé. Richard knew his friends were only being kind. After all, his résumé did appear confusing. While studying to be a graduate, he had worked in a cybercafé, been a tutor, played the piano at the Portuguese Church some Sundays, and he had also worked in that firm with Jeet which processed student applications for universities abroad.

The truth also was that what he loved doing was not worth putting on a résumé. Richard liked to design small things from stuff lying around. He made figures out of old coconut shells, new paper lanterns out of old ones, the oddest of things out of e-waste. But this wasn't enough to get one a job. Richard was beginning to get worried. One either had money or a job. His anger against Ghatge had always been a hopeless cause. And, now, he also had an illness with a fancy name and no proven cure.

'You should not mind what Ghatge Sahib says,' was his mother's response when yet another meeting with Ghatge had yielded nothing. She shook her head, opening cupboards, turning the stove on and Richard heard her stirring the spoon as the tea boiled over. He sat stone-faced in the room, unwilling to go to the park or face anyone. The bamboo flute he had been working on rolled ineffectually on the floor. But, at his mother's words, he got to his feet, and despite the imploring look in her eyes, the way she held the saucepan in her hands, he walked out. Richard hated that look and her faith in Ghatge. He would never help them, and she still expected so much. She would never recognize the truth unless it hit her across her face, violently and bloodily, the way his father had done. She had looked the same when the news of his father's death had been thrust on them. That had been some years ago, and the memory made him feel more helpless.

Richard remembered sitting with his mother on the hard hospital bench. There was no one with them, or even around, though it was a crowded hospital. It was as if everyone knew what they were waiting for. When the gurney was wheeled up towards them, Richard could not believe that the man on it, trussed up in white, was his father—a raging, angry man, now forever immobile. Every time he had beaten his mother, Richard had felt terribly forlorn. Now there was his mother turning her soft, forsaken eyes towards him. As if life had left her too, as if the world was not hers to live in any more. Richard blinked and blinked again and still that vision of his terrified, helpless mother never left him.

What Richard remembered most was his father turning in wild inexplicable anger towards him. Richard no longer remembered what he had done that day—what he did remember was the force with which his father had held him. The tight pain which exploded from a knot in his forehead soon spiralled all over his body; then the knot brightened like a bulb and its yellow glare spread over him. Shafts of pain were swirling in his head, striking him all over, as his father, his face, dark and very close, hurled him time and again towards the wall. Behind him, Richard felt the wall and its hardness, that it held the same force as his father's blows. The reds and yellows mingled with black, lines zigzagged across each other, and the pain grew till it filled his whole world.

Richard had come to with a soothing cold compress on his head. He saw his mother's fearful eyes and there were other women too, craning their anxious necks towards him. There was a bump on her head that she kept touching, as if she had forgotten all else. Then one of the ladies, her sari end in her mouth said, 'He'll be fine, Rosie.'

The blepharophasm—though he had no name for it then—aggravated Richard more after this. It struck when his father took him to school. He blinked every time his father came near. His eyelids fluttered with little control as he tried hard to not feel his father beside him. The evenings were always the worst. Richard would hide under the bed till he was discovered and pulled out. He whimpered as his father bent over him, murderous intent clear on his face. When Richard wet his pants, he was humiliated, but also relieved, for his father's mockery and disgust would spare him a worse fate. As Richard grew older, he spent more time at the Five Gardens. He found things to do, using a blade and a paring knife to make things out of stuff that had been discarded. There were the other boys who turned up too. They were friends in a way, all with their own shameful secrets, and comfortable in this new solitude they found.

Richard had shed no tears when his father died. His mother, though, seemed weighed down with a sorrow Richard did not really want to understand. He preferred the emptiness that now reigned in their two rooms in the chawl.

A week after the funeral, Richard had been called to Ghatge's office. Ghatge did not mince words. He said that the relief amount his father had been getting would not accrue to his family. 'Accrue?' asked Richard.

Ghatge pulled out a file and read it. He then said, 'The retirement dues from Shakti Mills were only for your father, Gerard D'Souza. Not for his immediate kin.'

He looked at Richard then, the only time he ever had. 'Apart from the compensation for your father's job loss, it will all end here, for your mother and you, Blinker D'Souza. All right?'

Richard hated the man then—the one who claimed to be doing things for them. Ghatge did nothing. He might have explained all this during his father's lifetime. It made Richard believe the rumours. That Ghatge did indeed take money from everyone, especially the builders who had been eyeing the mill land for years now. The truth of this realization about Ghatge first angered Richard and then he was filled with disgust.

People were foolish to believe that anyone who was important, or wielded power, could be good, Richard realized. And he hated it most when his mother, in her soft whinnying voice, insisted he must defer to Ghatge. She believed Ghatge would still do something. Richard doubted the existence of goodness; of all things, he hated God more.

His anger would have lasted had he not heard Pooja crying, that first time and then many times after. She lived directly above them, and he hadn't ever really seen her crying. But he had learnt to listen for her. The window where she chose to weep was just above his own, and he could hear her if he crept over the bed and leaned on the ledge. He heard her anklets on the stairs or just overhead, in those moments when the open windows and utter silence coincided. The buckets screeched as Pooja pulled them across the floor. And he knew Pooja from her steps, quick at times, serious and somehow sad at others.

But Pooja got him all tongue-tied. She was married, and a married woman held secret knowledge boys like him could only speculate about. He remembered the day she had come to live in the rooms above theirs. His mother had blessed her with one of her special lemon cakes and everyone had teased Pooja as they did new brides. But it was over all too soon and now even his mother sniffed at her. She thinks too much of herself, his mother had once said. His mother had even offered to take Pooja to church, to believe in God's will, that he would bring her luck. But perhaps Pooja, his mother thought aloud, believed too much in this modern thing: that children could wait, or were not necessary in a marriage. 'Five years they've been married, and no child. Soon she won't be able to keep that man of hers.'

Richard did not tell his mother that Pooja could not be all that she said. Some nights, he heard Pooja at her window. From the clink of her bangles, Richard knew the moment she leaned against the bars. Then a harsher sound, as her bangles caught against the bars, and the metallic silence as she raised hands to her face, and the sniffles that sounded in between. Everything else was still, the streetlights, the nets where the boys played volleyball, even the buckets arranged in a line before the tube well outside.

Then he caught his thoughts, for the stillness he imagined was all deceptive. Nothing in this city ever was, and women were stranger still—his mother weeping over his father's death and Pooja with her tears for herself and, for the world, her smiles.

His mother told Richard one evening of the job she had found in Valsad; in a small factory that made towels. Something broke through his indifference then, not the fact that she had a job, but the way she said it. Her voice was calm and very matter of fact.

'What will you do there?'

At first a confused look appeared on her face, to be replaced by a glimpse of cunning—Richard couldn't quite explain it.

The next day, she volunteered more information on her own. 'My job has something to do with quality, to check the weave in every towel. Things like that.'

The change he noted in his mother a week or so later came as a surprise. It was a two-hour commute by train to Valsad both ways, but she looked fresh, even happy, on her return. Richard knew he should have been suspicious then; later he just didn't want to think about it.

The days he was alone, he found himself thinking more about Pooja, except that he didn't quite know what to think of her. Once he hung up a paper lantern on the balcony outside her rooms. When Pooja met him next by the stairs, she only laughed nervously, and a flush had spread over her face. It embarrassed Richard too. He didn't want his intentions so clearly understood. He fashioned a series of clay elephants and left them outside her door, close to her flowerpots. One afternoon she opened the door as soon as he came up, almost as if she had been waiting for him. This time he had designed a vase out of old discarded CDs. But Pooja shook her head firmly. 'No, no. You must stop.'

'Why?' Richard asked, willing his hands not to tremble. He looked down, hoping to still them in some way.

She must have seen his face. He caught for a moment a distorted version of himself in the old CDs, his eyes too large, his hair falling over his face, his face a narrow triangle and then he pulled out a handkerchief and sniffed. The soft cloth was gentle against his eyes. He did not want her to see his blepharospasm, even if he now had a name for it.

'Don't be upset.' Her words washed over him, soft and pleading, 'it just doesn't look good if you keep doing this.'

Perhaps she had tears in her eyes, and maybe her cheeks were flushed. Richard stepped back, abashed in turn. The next day Richard had gone to a doctor, the one who had his own paintings all over his consulting rooms. Dr Joshi had suggested some eye drops and the compounder had measured it all out in a small bottle. Richard had thought it would work. Then for days after that he practised before the mirror, staring at himself a long while, till the tears rolled down his face.

It was Carl, in his new job as a cameraman for a television company, who told Richard about the job. One evening, Carl had turned up at Five Gardens, catching Richard then working on a coconut shell.

'No one does Halloween here,' said Carl, clapping Richard on the back, dislodging the plastic cap on the coconut head. Richard shrugged. 'Maybe they will.'

'You could make this a business, have a website or something,' Carl's voice rolled over Richard, desultory like the late evening traffic. They had grown up together, all through the times the mills had abandoned them, and their families. Their fathers had lost their jobs and in turn, they had been left alone by their parents. When Carl and he were teenagers and bored with school, they would slip away many a time to Bandra Fort on an old scooter Carl had fixed up. They'd smoke pot and look at the lovers who came there in secret. Depending on the mood they were in, they'd either warn them about the policemen or just slip behind the rocks to watch the fun and the policemen gather money from the hapless couples. A few months later, they had graduated to taking photos, first of the fort, the Russian ship that had run aground in the sea close by, and then of the Sea Link as it came up, that impressive cantilever bridge that shortened the distance between Bandra and Worli. But Carl was now a cameraman and kept odd hours. Now he leaned sideways and pulled out the box where he always carried his business cards. It was one Richard had designed and Carl now held out a card for him.

'There could be something for you. Not exactly what you do, but then what the heck.'

The production company Carl worked for needed someone to design a set. Some rooms in a small apartment, where certain episodes of a serial were being shot, had to be done up. Richard did not know about the serial and Carl explained. 'It's quite a new concept. A young woman has left her in-laws and moved to this flat with her young son. This is where a confrontation will happen with the mother-in-law.' The flat, Carl said, was in Borivali and had to look like a middle-class Maharashtrian house.

When Richard looked doubtful, Carl reassured him, 'Just say you have some previous experience. They hardly check.' It was the crowded journey by train that he was going to hate, but he didn't want to tell Carl that.

A week later, Richard went to Carl's office to get the keys. The shooting would begin in the afternoon two days later and he had to get it ready by then. The guys in administration gave him the keys, and even a cheque to make improvements. It was all done with a careless trust that impressed Richard. The scrupulous accounting his mother and he had endured in recent years now embarrassed him. Everywhere around him, there was a crazed busyness. Richard felt that if it all stopped just then, they'd forget what they were busy about.

A locked-in untidiness hit Richard the moment he entered the flat. It was a small two-room place on the first floor. Richard went to open the windows, the ones in front that overlooked a patchy ground and a walkway but the pane knocked hard against the branch of a neem tree just outside and he let it be. He looked through its leaves at another apartment, saw the swing with its green and white awning and flowerpots on the balcony. It breathed life, unlike the one he was in. Through an open door, he read a certain cool comfort inside, despite the darkness.

Richard took in everything about the flat he was in and felt the first stirrings of excitement. He lifted the covers off the sofa, the low divan, the two ottomans and the beds. He checked the things left in the closets. It could look so very different, if the furniture were just rearranged and with some right material. He reminded himself almost at once. *It's not what you want, but what the serial wants. Don't make that mistake.*

Richard was still muttering that reprimand to himself as he walked over the rooms again and made notes. He rested for a while on the low divan, he took a shower, and then made notes again. The bittersweet smell of the neem tree filled the apartment and he breathed it in as he looked outside, through the latticed windows of the kitchen. It was as he made to move to the balcony when something in the flat opposite made him pause. His hand stilled on the latch. The branches shifted slightly, the leaves shook and through it all he saw again the walkway that led to the building opposite.

In the flat just opposite his, Richard saw the empty balcony now occupied by two people, one of them his mother. There she was, he saw, seated quite comfortably next to a man, considerably older than his father had been, on the low wide swing with its green and white awning. It moved with a certain regularity, and the man's grey hair fell across his forehead often. They were listening to something, perhaps to some music playing inside, for the man was tapping his hands on his knee, and his mother had her eyes closed.

It had to be his mother. The tilt of her head, the way she did her hair, the sari she wore convinced Richard, though he had never had a moment's doubt. It was his mother, looking at peace. And no matter how long he stared and how often he blinked, he could not wish it otherwise. Then she abruptly opened her eyes and looked around, almost as if she sensed something. In the silence, as the breeze now stilled, Richard heard the song, and the sound of a car scattering gravel on a road very close.

Richard took a step back into the darkness. The light

through the windows made patterns on the floor that dissolved and formed again. The man now took up a newspaper. Richard saw the careful way he plucked out the supplement and held it out for his mother and once again they were absorbed in this new task. Richard turned his attention to the man. His wavy grey hair now fell over his spectacles. Once he turned, leaning towards his mother to say something.

His own flat seemed emptier now. He felt all its past residents were looking through the window too, at the two of them. And like him, they did not know what to do. He felt the walls breathe, the branches move, and the sunlight break up. He heard the creak of the swing, the newspaper rustled in their hands, but the two people, companionable on the swing, stayed the same. Then his mother asked something for the man shook his head. But she still got up and then leaned across the railings to look across at the flat, right to where he was. He shrank back into the flat.

He then made himself busy. He used an old rusting knife on a discarded piece of carton to carve tiny animals. He wanted to pull down the curtains, not let anyone see what he had. But his hands stayed on the curtains and he now wondered if he could replace them with the ones inside the cupboard. It was hot and the newer shades of blue and yellow would suit the living room. The corner divan, low stools, and the flat table would all look different. Richard pulled out the portraits from the closet and held some up against the walls.

Then he heard something ring very close and realized it was his own phone. It thrummed loud in that emptiness. Someone from the company was calling, telling Richard he had to leave the keys in the office for they closed at six.

His mother returned late and so did he. It wasn't that he could not ask his mother about her lie, but he just didn't want to. The lie would not turn into the truth if he confronted her with what he had seen. And her truth was something he would never understand. He spent the next two days at the flat, pulling things out from closets, pushing others in. He redid, rearranged the furniture and followed his mother's new life as it unfolded before him on the balcony.

But he did try and ask Carl, in careful and oblique ways. 'Can two old people fall in love?'

Carl looked knowledgeable and then puzzled. 'It could happen, but it's unusual, especially in countries like ours.' But when Carl moved on to other things, like libido, and how this could be improved with medication, Richard hurried to change the subject.

He only knew that for most of the time, his mother and the man with her, just sat together quietly. He had no answer for that silence. It always took courage to let another person into your silence.

On the day of the shoot, the crew came around early. They fussed over small details. They stepped back and forth, pulled apart the curtains, drew them back again, moved the sofa around. The noise made some people gather outside but, in the flat opposite, the couple remained in their balcony. Richard wore a cap, afraid of being noticed.

When excited hisses, yells of recognition, and some prolonged whistling, could be heard, Richard knew that the stars, the two women actors of the serial, had arrived. The younger of them had had some success in the movies. With them was a chirpy young boy of seven or eight who had a role in the serial too. The crew made a fuss over him, calling him Vicky, ruffling his hair and announcing that he looked just as handsome as Hrithik Roshan.

The sunlight came in through the latticed windows and Richard heard the director explain, in a measured tone, the scene to the three actors. Vicky didn't have much to do, and he played with someone's cell phone. The paraphernalia of the shoot unfolded around Richard. There was the clank of tripods as equipment was set up, wires loped and trailed across the floor, chairs were pushed around randomly, people talked into their mobile phones and gesticulated to each other, the camera lights flashed, and the two woman actors began a conversation. They laughed often and kept interrupting each other. Only the occasional dips into silence made everyone self-conscious.

Richard's eyes strained to catch all that was happening on the balcony opposite. Every blink of his eye was like the final shutter of the camera. His mother had gathered the clothes up and she was folding them in a neat pile, while the older man was lying back. His eyes were closed, and his fingers tapped against the curved hands of the swing. The boy Vicky had wandered away and was now checking the fridge. 'Why is it empty?'

No one answered him and Richard shrugged, as he caught Vicky's eye. He had some scraps of coloured material left over from the curtains, and now he tore it into smaller strips, knotted some bits and clipped off some ends.

'Are you making a plane?'

Vicky drew nearer. Richard lifted his head, and saw that on the balcony opposite, his mother had returned with a watering can.

'Is that a fighter plane?'

For a moment Richard's mother's hand stilled before the flowerpot. Then she looked in their direction. Richard wasn't sure why, but he told the boy to duck. The grin spread on Vicky's face. He thought it was a game, for his eyes had followed Richard's. Vicky noticed the couple and he hopped and skipped his way into the balcony outside. Richard saw his mother smile as she caught Vicky's eye, and the latter ducked again. Richard froze at this surprise impromptu game. But the boy fell into it happily. He would lift his head over the railings, wait for them to catch his eye and then duck again. Now the older man on the swing laughed too. He waved to Vicky and Richard heard his mother laugh. He had never heard his mother's happy laughter before.

Richard tried to coerce Vicky back in, but the boy was stubborn. Then Richard held up the bird he had managed to fashion out of the stray cloth strips. He had stapled on a red beak, pleated together some ribbons to make a nice plume of feathers, and then wrapped a piece of yellow silk around some discarded cotton balls.

The boy looked sceptical. 'Do you think the bird will have space to fly anywhere?'

'Vicky Baba, don't trouble him.' That was when Richard spotted his nanny. A girl in her early teens but only a little taller than the boy. The shadows had eaten her up entirely and she emerged only now that Vicky was being so adamant. She had long hair she wore in a tight plait, and the bones on her face stuck out stark and delicate. The girl rummaged in a plastic bag and held out a snack bar. 'Do you want this, Baba?'

Vicky looked at her disdainfully. 'Can't you see I am busy?'

Richard looked at her in some sympathy but when she returned his gaze, he turned away. She would see his forever blinking eyes, then place him as someone weird. But instead, she looked embarrassed for having raised her voice and being noticed. There was a whirring noise, the sound of someone clapping, and Richard saw the flashing lights. Another voice asked for the curtains to be drawn and then called for Vicky. 'Ready with your lines, Vicky?'

The boy had the bird in his hand as he said his lines. The two women actors, however, fluffed theirs. They had both taken too long, haranguing the one make-up man they shared between them. For long minutes, as everyone waited, they had examined their faces in the mirror, though in reality they were checking each other out. The tension, then, hung thick in the air. The assistant director called for them again in some exasperation. But the second take went awry too, and Richard caught the snide remarks made in careful undertones.

'They always take too long.' Vicky said, and he added, looking at Richard. 'You wink with both eyes, don't you?' The boy and his nanny laughed but it wasn't mocking in any way.

'Yes, it happens,' the girl said in her soft clear voice. 'In my village, some people do that very often. It's funny but it does go away.' The girl clapped a hand over her mouth, cutting herself off abruptly. It was as if such impulsive behaviour was a tic of hers too.

The boy repeated his lines for the third take. He made the bird zoom up and down, as he spoke, and it made everyone laugh. They called him a totally spontaneous actor.

Vicky had only a small role and when it was over, he came away to where Richard and the nanny waited. He repeated his newly learnt lines again, and then again. The girl seemed amused and fascinated. Richard sidled by the door leading to the balcony while the girl sat on the low ledge, the rails against her back. The boy tried to make the bird fly and she laughed, warning him not to. Then Vicky threw the bird right back into the room and Richard was too late in reaching for it. The bird zoomed past him fast. As the girl lunged to catch it, she tripped over a wire. The camera shook and would have toppled over, but this time Richard caught it.

He saw the cameraman turn in dark irritation. 'It's all right. It was an accident.' Richard said quickly, and pulled the girl away, staring guardedly at the cameraman. Another voice piped in, and the cameraman returned to his work. Not wanting the girl to thank him or even look embarrassed the way she was prone to, Richard turned to warn Vicky. 'You ought to be careful, doing something like that.'

The bird's silken coat had come undone, but Richard

reassured Vicky he could easily make another one. Easy peasy, he said. He gathered together other cloth pieces, and began sniping off the odd ends quickly and then methodically. Vicky used the stapler with great enthusiasm and the girl watched, shy but with a great curiosity.

As the crew filmed the last scene for the day, with the two women caught in an argument, Vicky, by now tired, rested on the divan. Richard did look out occasionally, but the curtains were now drawn in the flat opposite. He did see someone through the netted curtains of the kitchen window. He saw too the outline of the man in the kitchen and the moment when the two outlines came far too close, forcing Richard to look away.

Inside, the din of the crew beginning to pack up unfolded, and he saw the girl arranging Vicky's things. She was also talking to someone on her phone, holding it in the crook of her neck. Then a fragrance drifted up, and something silky brushed past Richard's arm. The lead female actor had come up. She looked at him, then at the girl, tossed a casual smile at them. As Richard turned away, more in boredom than anything else, he caught the girl's surprised, distressed face in the mirror. He realized then what had just happened, that he had been too late once again. The bird he had fashioned had caught the actor's eye and she had picked it up from the table, with the same casualness she had bestowed on the two of them. Now they looked at her in shared consternation, but the actor was already on her way out. Richard saw her, laughing now at one of the cameramen who bowed theatrically and held the door open. 'Ma'am, after you.'

She must have heard Richard as he raised his voice in an 'excuse me' but her eyes flicked over him. She rearranged her dupatta over her shoulder, looked at herself in the oval mirror in the corridor and walked on. He called again after her, 'Madam'. She lingered by the door for some moments.

The crew lumbered with its equipment down and she bantered with them, asking why they always took so long over things, for she had to rush. Richard was nearer now, stepping over the wires and he thought the girl was following him too. *He had to get the bird back. He wanted to get it back.*

'It's okay, Sir,' The girl pushed an arm forward, hoping he would stop.

'It's my bird.'

It's not hers, he went on with gritted teeth. The men ahead made way for the actor as she continued her royal descent down.

'Mad-dam.' Richard stretched the word out, saw the simpering smile she gave someone, and he bounded down the stairs too, edging past the crew. He threaded his way past people, not thinking of anything else. The closer he came, he smelt her perfume, felt the fall of her dupatta as it brushed against the walls. Behind him, the girl spoke up again. Her voice sounded different to him. The situation had changed them both. 'It's all right,' he heard her say. She had obviously never raised her voice before, and Richard looking back, caught her flushed, fearful face. He knew then he had to get it back, before they came out of the building, in the full light of day. He could not risk being seen and that left him with very little time.

'Madam, I made that bird for her.'

He later remembered that that was what he did say. It made the actor stop at the very bottom and then he explained, deliberately very slowly, not taking his eyes away from her. 'You picked up something, a small bird that I made, for them.'

'Really?'

Her mocking gaze held his, but he did not look away. He felt instead a jostling around him. He was jerked forward and reached a hand out to grip the banister. 'Hey, what's happening?'

The scornful smile grew on the actor's face, as she saw the crowd gather. *This?* Her eyebrows arched. Her red clipped nails stole into her bag and she held the bird up gingerly. Already one of its feathers was falling off, its beak looked wobbly.

Richard said, 'I can fix that.'

'Well, I don't want it any more,' She tossed it high and he caught it, stepping on someone's toes who shouted furiously, 'Idiot, look where you step.'

Richard was yanked back sharply, pulled up by the collar and someone yelled very close to his ears. 'Don't you know how to behave?'

'Oh just leave him,' the actor's lazy drawl came up to where he was, and they let him go abruptly. His hands reached for the wall to steady himself. The sound of many footsteps rushing down the stairs was now deafening.

Phit phit, blink blink, they called after him, the hurtful words that came so easily. He looked back at them defiant, and he took a step up, wanting to get away at the same time.

As the last of the crew trooped out, and vans drew up outside, Richard felt the sharp coldness around him. Behind the slap of their retreating shoes was the dust and all the world's stillness. The floor throbbed with several hundred memories. He pushed his hair back, looked down at the bird and then he heard quick short steps very near. It was Vicky and a bit behind, there was the girl. 'You are not hurt?' the boy asked, his eyes huge in his face, and then whooped, happy to have the bird back again.

'Oh don't worry, it's all for a bird.'

Vicky shrugged at that answer, in a blasé, worldly-wise way. But the girl still looked miserable and so Richard had to tell her. 'It's no big deal. You must fight for everything in this city, big or small. Else they will crush you.' He waved as they went past, the boy holding the bird up, and the girl so demurely that Richard was amused.

That night he walked all the way to the Sea Link, its lights over the still dark waters, reminding him of a plane flying low. He looked out toward Bandra Fort in the east. Below him the sea rolled against the pylons of the bridge, dashed against the rocks as the tide came in. The wind thudded against the tall columns of the bridge, the cables swayed and creaked, and Richard blinked, and he blinked again. A car had zoomed past but, instead of picking up speed, he saw it veer sharply to the right and then brake jerkily to a halt.

No one ever stopped in the middle of the Sea Link. The sea belonged to no one. But there was a man who now got out, slowly and very deliberately. He leaned against the car. The night wind was hard, and his kurta beat hard against him.

Richard's eyes followed the man, thin and balding, now walking to the very edge, towards the stone railings of the bridge. Richard picked up pace. He did not run, but he kept the man in sight, getting to him steadily and surely, till he was walking along the railing too, only a few steps behind. As he neared the other man, Richard fell to a deliberate step and whistled tunelessly. It was hard for the wind got into everything; still it got the man's attention who looked back startled.

'I am just out to get some air.' The incongruity of the situation did not make the explanation sound ridiculous, and now as the man bent to light a cigarette, Richard saw that his hands were trembling. He caught too the look of relief on the man's face.

'And I am just walking here,' Richard explained in turn. It made the man laugh. They did not want to admit the truth to themselves.

'There is something beautiful and innocent in how the

city looks now,' the man waved with his cigarette, his light sweeping over the old fort in the distance. Richard saw the tension leave the other man's face. Richard realized the other man had been terrified of himself, of his own intentions. 'Sir, you don't have to do what you are thinking about.'

The other man took his time to reply, 'What makes you think that?'

Richard did not explain. Then the man went on to speak about other things, almost as if he were bursting to tell someone. He spoke about wanting to write poetry, and giving all else up. 'I mean giving up the work I do.' And though he did not explain that either, somehow that did not matter.

Richard replied instead that poetry could strike anyone, at any age. He was saying things he had never thought before, and while it had been a long day, Richard felt refreshed. The day fell away from him. He understood how his mother felt then, and just as quickly, he drove all thoughts of her away. Not all things had to be understood. The man began humming some tunes, and so did Richard. The other man corrected him at some places, and Richard did not mind.

Then from the far end of the bridge, they heard a hum, one that grew louder, and the girders shook with a menacing intensity. The bridge was trembling, almost unwillingly. An ordered line of motorcyclists came by, they whistled and beeped as they saw the two of them on the bridge. Right at the centre, the motorcyclists parted in a neat manoeuvre and a gleaming yellow car came into view. Richard knew the kind instantly: a Mercedes-Benz, and not a very old model too. Richard saw its lights zoom up the bridge, the purring sound of its engine almost feline-like. The man next to Richard drew his breath in sharply.

'The only time of the night such a car can be driven,' said the man, 'it'd be hard on the city streets otherwise.' The motorcyclists veered and turned their bikes around. They positioned themselves by the roadside, almost as if they would salute the car as it drove past. Richard thought he saw someone like Ghatge at the wheel, but he couldn't be sure. Then it was all over in a jiffy.

The bikers were hooting and raising high fives at what had just happened. They waved at the two of them as they revved up their bikes and prepared to follow the sleek car into the city's now empty, sleeping streets. The spray rose below, and Richard saw its whiteness bared in a smile.

The man asked him if he'd like tea at a dhaba that stayed open all right. But Richard said he had to go home. 'I think my mother would be mad with worry by now.' He allowed himself a wry smile. The older man nodded and walked back to his car; the sound of their steps loud on that bridge. Far ahead they saw the last blinking lights of the motorcycles. The city had never looked so alone, so lovely and they had it to themselves, at that moment.

'Here's my business card,' said the man. 'And a short while ago, I thought I'd never have need of it.' But they didn't want to talk of such things now and Richard slipped it into his pocket. It struck him that the man had not looked at him strangely, neither had the girl nor even Vicky.

Suhel's Afternoon with Father

In the minutes that remained as the plane began its descent, Suhel heard the murmur of conversations closing, the clink of seat belts being fastened, and the stewardess's last announcements. It took him some time to figure out what 41 Celsius meant. Even in December, Mumbai was as hot and humid as he remembered. Surely, he told himself in half-admonishment, he had not expected the same air-conditioned atmosphere everywhere? There was only that one day in August that temperatures in Baltimore had touched the low 90s, and even that, as Suhel converted in a few seconds, was something around 32 degrees on the Celsius scale.

In the cab, leaning back into its comfortable faux-leather seat, Suhel thought over all his reasons for visiting Mumbai. He intended to accomplish something important this time; something he had left unattended for far too long. Every two years Suhel would visit to look up his father, sort out his own affairs, but this time he had to see Mohini again.

Perhaps it was already too late. Two months ago, he had learnt from Dr Joshi's email that Mohini was seriously ill. Suhel had tried asking Dr Joshi for more information but after an initial chattiness, the doctor had been veiled in his replies. Veiled and evasive, just like his own creations, Suhel thought glumly.

He remembered the doctor's painting that had first got Suhel's attention. That thumbnail image called 'The Woman at

Dawn'. Suhel had chanced upon it, and then Dr Joshi too, as he scoured the internet, looking to do up his new townhouse in an upscale Maryland suburb. He had wanted something by a Mumbai artist, the city of his childhood and youth, the city that would never leave him. He had admired how the early morning light played on the woman's face turned away in profile, and the way Dr Joshi had etched in detail the woman's striking bone structure, even the lashes that left a soft shadow on her cheek.

Suhel was too late with his inquiry, however. The painting had only just been sold. But for Suhel, that first email exchange had opened his past up. Dr Pankaj Joshi had indeed once known his father, and then him, Suhel, too. Two decades and more ago, a time Suhel didn't really want to remember. When he had skulked in the corridors of his hostel, hoping to get at the morning newspapers before anyone so he could tear out any mention of his father, Suhas Kolhatkar, a richly decorated soldier but then in controversy for wanting to marry a foreigner. It was something the laws did not allow for its military personnel.

A few more email exchanges had also established other connections. That Dr Joshi knew Mohini as well—but then, who didn't, for Mohini had married well, and had made a name for herself with her work in the arts and her charities. And soon, Suhel learnt too, that Mohini was dying of cancer.

Old memories rushed in and Suhel smiled absently as the young taxi-driver enthusiastically indicated all the conveniences in his vehicle, including a television. Suhel shook his head, explaining he was sleepy. He had to urgently work out a way to meet Mohini, but even after a long twenty-hour restful flight, he hadn't been able to figure anything out. And for this there was Dr Joshi's unpredictability to blame.

Twenty years ago, Suhel and Mohini had parted bitterly, or rather, not even that. He had left with no explanation.

Now Suhel had hoped Dr Joshi might help in securing a meeting with Mohini, but the doctor's email, telling Suhel of a sudden trip to Panchgani, had come just as Suhel waited to board his flight. Dr Joshi was an artist, more than a doctor, and artists did strange, and sudden, things, Suhel understood that, but what annoyed him was the email's brevity. The doctor, most times, offered information in small doses, and sometimes almost as an afterthought. Couldn't the doctor have told him about Mohini much before, and in more detail considering all the information, he, Suhel, had plied him with regarding Joyce? She was a local Maryland painter Dr Joshi had evinced a strange curiosity about. But life never offered a fair exchange, and it had taken the doctor several emails to offer him that vital information about Mohini.

Mohini Sahani Gupta—Suhel felt his eyes widen in shock as the words shaped themselves in Dr Joshi's message on Facebook—*the one who is supporting the avant-garde painting exhibition at the Taj Hotel, is a rare being. She has courage.* A pause before the doctor's last sentence appeared: *And she has cancer, or something serious, I think. I read something about her. A pity, she's quite young. She is. She is only forty-five or...*

Suhel moved his cursor toward the reply bar, but his eyes were drawn again to the doctor's words, and they now clutched at his heart. All these years, and though he was no longer his young immature self, he had imagined several things. That he would come back. That he would meet Mohini and, this time, things would work out between them, despite her being married to someone else. In more recent times, he had idly thought of Mohini, but with a somewhat lessening intensity. That had left Suhel disappointed in himself. He still thought love was the one emotion that lasted, at the expense of everything else. He knew what it had done to his mother.

The previous times he had visited Mumbai, something had always stopped him from seeking out Mohini. He still wasn't quite there, Suhel felt. Not as rich as her husband, nor as successful. Anil's was a success story every business magazine had written about a hundred times over. His 'Ready in Minutes', a range of instant foods, was even a case study in an American business school. Though he, Suhel, hadn't done too badly either. He had a doctorate in biochemistry and had moved into specialized medical systems. His firm, which had initially found funding difficult, was now being sought for collaborations. And the new lung cancer testing device he had patented, had recently secured the approval— for all that it was cautious—of a couple of reputable doctors at the National Institute of Health. He had clearly made an impression. He had people speaking for him. Then, there were the other accoutrements of his evident success: the apartment in Baltimore, the yacht, the flying lessons, his involvement in the restoration of Maryland's old lighthouses.

It still took Suhel, for all the advantages promised by the new Sea Link, an hour and a half to reach Napean Sea Road, and the building where, three years ago, he had invested in an apartment. He took the elevator to the fortieth floor, and the view took him, once again, by surprise. Through the floor-length windows, where the sunlight lit up the marble polished floors and made fleeting black shadows of the gulls overhead, he had a view of an entire stretch of the sea.

He walked around, and moved the furniture here and there deliberately. Now he drew the curtains aside, then pulled them back. He kicked over the beanbags, and touched the vase, hated the still life paintings in the kitchens, and the other empty walls that needed to be filled up. And he wondered about Dr Joshi.

This block of apartments had come up on a piece of land that a maharaja had once owned. It had then been auctioned for unimaginable sums and Suhel had been lucky, so everyone said, to snag an apartment here. But now his father did not want to live in it, for he said he was happy in his Borivali flat. How could anyone be happy in that faraway suburb, where even a train commute took two hours? I can reach Philadelphia in less than that time, Suhel thought.

He returned to the living room, and walked closer to the glass wall till there was only that thin frame between him and the sky. The city of his boyhood fell away at a dizzying pace.

Stepping closer, he looked down to where Naaz had been, a café with its red rails that was close to the Hanging Gardens. High above now, the sea fell away and he felt as if he was standing on the edge of an abyss. The world looked spread out but also diminished.

There was the winding Marine Drive, loping right by where the Air India building was, with the centaur on top. He saw the old hotel too and, straining to catch a glimpse of the plush theatre complex that lay just beyond it, he caught sight of himself in the glass. His hair, styled in a buzz, now rose abruptly over his forehead, reminding him of an old shoe brush. He hoped Mumbai had some good hairstylists. His face had shadows, perhaps from the long journey, and he remained just as skinny in his college days, something that had made him the butt of everyone's jokes. Now he wished he had that extra weight. Or even a double chin. At least that would make him look prosperous.

He walked through the rooms before he realized he had done it five times already. And then, with a mix of guilt and resignation, he finally called his father. The old resentments still hadn't gone, he still blamed his father for many things but now, Suhel thought as he heard his father's phone ring, he'd tell his father that his flight had been late. But it was a woman's voice he heard first in his ear; a woman who in turn seemed taken aback when he answered so very quickly.

'Where's my father?'

He looked at his phone, and had the sensation of the world sinking around him. He took in the apartment, the afternoon sun all ablaze and heard the woman now call for his father.

'Mr Kolhatkar?' she said, in the same even, soft tone she had greeted him with. The woman sounded familiar but Suhel couldn't, for the life of him, recollect her name. He sensed the tension in the silence before a tremulous male voice sounded. 'Suhel, when did you reach?'

'Baba, who was that?' Suhel asked instead, but there was a strange new meekness in his father's voice as he said, 'Rosie. Yes, it's him. Thank you.'

'Rosie, of course I remember now,' Suhel clapped a hand to his mouth. He remembered his calls and emails with the employment agency to work out Rosie D'Souza's recruitment as the housekeeper for his father's apartment, and now Suhel was annoyed. She hadn't been officious enough, or even grateful. He knew the straitened circumstances she had been in, a single mother with an unemployed son and the job had been a godsend for her. Her voice then, he remembered, had been soft, barely a whisper, and she seemed ideal for taking orders. Suhel frowned, wanting to ask his father more about her. Instead, he heard himself say, 'Baba. I am downtown. Could we meet for lunch?'

'Let me see.' His father had turned away again, and Suhel once again heard the two people at the other end in conversation, their low soft tones like the beginning of every morning.

'No, I am afraid,' Suhel heard Rosie's gentle firm voice, the one she had used on him only some moments ago. 'I do need to be off at seven today.' This was followed by his father's soft, indistinct cajoling voice. Looking out, Suhel saw the yachts, the island of Colaba far away and the voices at the other end dropped to an even lower murmur.

At long last, his father came on the line, laughing in soft relief. 'Yes, she's agreed to wait for me. I'll see you, son.'

His father looked the same, only a bit diminished. And he was still a natty dresser, in his short kurta and the carefully pressed churidar. Someone had evidently ironed it with care. He had called up Rosie soon as he reached Suhel's apartment. Suhel noted the laugh in his father's voice as he told Rosie about the bad traffic. It was the laughter of long companionship, shared between people who had things in common. Restless with his thoughts, Suhel rose, paced the floor, and then turned to his father.

'Let's go out.'

His father took his glasses off and wiped them on his short kurta.

'I now get very lost in the city, with what it's become.'

It struck Suhel then that his father's prevarications helped lengthen their conversation and perhaps, as he heard his father now say, imbued it with new meaning.

'Once when I was deep in the forests somewhere in Cambodia, the trees were high and blocked out the sky. There was a monkey overhead and it appeared to keep pace with me. Periodically it'd look down, and bare its teeth at me in mockery for not being able to keep up. I just feel these buildings will fall on my head.'

Suhel wanted to ask him about the woman from Cambodia his father had once loved but something about the way he sat, austere and resigned, on the designer sofa, stopped Suhel.

'We'll go out, Baba, I'll take care of things.'

Impatient now, he picked up the building's glossy directory, and leafed through it till he stopped at something that got his attention: the number for a private helicopter the apartment owners could avail at will. On his father's face, he saw the shock, and then it was replaced by a quiet uncertainty. 'Trust me,' Suhel said in that airy tone he used at times—it left things open-ended at least for a bit. The city had surprised him of late, with all its news; it was time he surprised himself.

Minutes later, they took the elevator up to the terrace, where the helicopter, a silver white AgustaWestland Koala, waited for them. Suhel helped his father up the few steps. For a moment, the sky was caught in his father's glasses and Mumbai became smaller than he had ever known it. And then something got into him. Perhaps it was the pilot's obsequiousness, the way he almost slid down, missing a step down the chopper's sleek white door. 'I will fly this, all right,' Suhel said, tossing his hair back, hands in his pockets and the accent that worked always. The look of the I'll-have-my-way American businessman. His father and the pilot wore the same startled expression before he shrugged, 'Come on, I have a licence.'

'This isn't the US, you know,' his father said, in that mild tone of his.

'Of course, and it's harder there to get a licence. The skies are clear so it's almost like being on the expressways. Come on, Baba.' The stewardess appeared, curtseying prettily, and then she folded her hands in a namaste as she noticed his father. Suhel touched his father's elbow gently, and then, as if he understood his father's nervousness, pointed somewhat roguishly at the stewardess' way, 'Don't worry, you are in safe hands.' This time she giggled and even blushed. The pilot only laughed in a bluff manner, a strange red look on his face. Suhel sensed his confusion, the fact that he knew he must protest, but wouldn't. Suhel felt bigger than he really was. Looking back, he saw his father, who strapped to his seat, now looked a shrunken creature.

It gave him a heady feeling, the minute he took off. The whirl and turn of the chopper, and the wind rushing past. The sea widening in moments with its myriad yachts, and the square oil rigs standing like Lego blocks. Suhel banked swiftly left, ignoring the startled whoop from the pilot. He was headed for the eastern section of the city. But his father was pulling down the sunshade, and half closing his eyes.

On the salt creek side were the old fishing boats, with their snout-like wooden ends, waiting out the afternoon. On the plain wooden docks, the fishing nets had been strung out to dry, the morning's catch had already been gathered and taken to the city's main markets. Then, almost whimsically, Suhel banked again and, this time, the chopper was hurtling toward Alibagh. The first time he had been here had been with his parents. A time when the two of them had constantly fought, though his father had kept his absent smile on every time Suhel returned with a report about his fishing. Some years later, in college, some of them, Mohini and Anil too, had sailed to Alibagh, taking one of the many boats plying from the Gateway. They had all waded into the distinctly murky-looking sea, but not Anil. He had stayed back, insisting that he would cook them lunch. The cartons were all from his father's restaurant, even the sachets of sauce had the logo they were already familiar with, two hands folded in a namaste, a logo that was almost everywhere now, from restaurants to readymade foods and to hotels.

They had snickered, teasing Mohini about Anil's true intentions, that he was trying to impress her. She had only smiled in a dismissive, regal way. Even then she had known something they hadn't grasped yet, for a year or so later, she would be married to Anil. Suhel smiled thinly and, looking back, he saw, like his father, the stewardess too, held onto her seat tightly. He still hadn't learnt the right way to impress a woman. 'Not scared, are you?' he asked, with a lightness he did not feel.

'Be careful, son,' his father said.

Suhel looked down to where the swamp and the patchy

green in places gave way to warehouses, a clump of slums, low stretching malls, and the chemical factory that had been there ever since he could remember. He flew across Vashi, the city's northeast suburb. Dreary apartment buildings rose, became higher, as he turned, and flew past the ribbon of the Mithi River.

He decided to cut through the city now. The western suburbs were taller than those in the east and one could still divide the city this way. The new expressway ran east to west, and the trains slithered out snail-like from the tin railway sheds. The clouds had divided up the city, thinner in the east and darker towards the sea. The sun now came through in fits, blazing between buildings, sometimes a blinding yellow spot, before it broke up into orange lines that slid past them, lighting up the chopper's panes. Suhel looked to his right, and the pilot who sat just behind gave him a reassuring wink, and did the thumbs-up, adding, 'You're doing fine, Sir.' The stewardess reached out to pat his father on the hand.

His father's eyes were half shut, he was still trying hard to keep the strain away from his face. When Suhel mentioned they were flying over Bandra, his father's face lightened for a moment. He asked Suhel if he remembered the time he had taken the three of them for a film at the Gaiety. Suhel had hated it for all the subterfuge he was put through. His mother had not wanted to tell his father that they had already seen the movie when he was away, and Suhel for his part, had tried hard to control his excitement, the urge to tell his father everything but, in the darkened hall, his mother had held him fast by the wrist.

He loved the movies screened at the Regal, Suhel said instead. They had to talk over the roar of the engine and that made it almost like an argument. 'It was near my college too, Baba,' he said smiling now, hoping to reassure the stewardess that this was no family quarrel. Those films, recent Hollywood hits, were what Mohini liked; she would talk him often into accompanying her.

Suhel saw the new buildings in Parel, outgrowing each other in a frenzied competition, and all around were the now closed mills and roads like narrow sewers. The light caught against the glass panes and struck his eyes. His father flinched, and pulled the blind down only to raise it again. 'Son, don't you think you're flying too low?'

The closer Suhel flew, he saw the unfinished top storeys of the new buildings, deliberately left incomplete in an obvious flouting of the government's mandated construction indices. A story already played out in the buildings already complete. As the builders illegally added more storeys, the matter would go to court, where the builders would make much of the fact that public money was already heavily invested in these buildings. And on that ground, the buildings would grow taller than before, unsafe in every way. Suhel moved the helicopter around slowly, the wind thudded hard against it. The helicopter lurched, and Suhel heard his father say, 'You need to go higher.'

Only Suhel knew his father was afraid. Suhel laughed, filled with an old recklessness again. 'You sound as afraid as you were when I asked about a motorcycle, Baba.'

'Yes,' his father said.

'And see what I can do now.' Suhel zoomed lower and this time, the stewardess let out a shrill cry before stopping herself. The clouds gathered and then appeared to dissipate of their own accord. He saw his father's iron will assert itself as he brushed his hair back, sat up straight, and replied in that mild voice of his, 'It's a good thing I said "no" that time. What would you have done? Isn't it all good, all that's happened to you since then?'

Far out in the sea, away from the city, the small islands of Janjira and Elephanta appeared. The sleek tourist boats were heading out, and the old Siddi fort stood etched out like a pinned insect fossil, looking like it had always been there. The light dappled across the waves, now slow and lulling. Suhel saw his father's face in profile. He was looking indifferent, too casual, with not a frown on his face. But there was that tensed jaw, a stoniness in the eye, his knuckles white and clenched tight.

The silence prevailed till, guided by the unseated pilot's quick instructions, he landed the copter at Dhule, some fifteen minutes to the east of the city. The runway was a narrow strip. The stewardess chirped up about some ice cream, and his father, laughing in some relief, refused. His diet made it impossible, he explained. The pilot lurched in his seat for the copter dipped as it landed. He managed a quick 'no' to the stewardness' offer, and a 'fine job, sir' for Suhel, at the same time. And so only the stewardess and Suhel had the ice cream. When she was done, he noticed how carelessly she threw it on the runway.

His father fiddled with his cell phone, sighing as he looked to catch a signal. Suhel caught the impatience on his father's face, the way he brushed his hair back carelessly. 'We will get back soon,' Suhel offered, pretending to look at his watch, wondering why he had made that reassurance. His father held out a hand for the stewardess who smiled in surprise. His father seemed relieved to be headed back. Suhel noticed too the stewardess' silly prettiness, and this time when he asked her if she was nervous, the flirtatious tone was all gone.

An hour and a half later, he had the reason for his father's anxiety. At the far end of the Juhu airport, a woman—whom Suhel knew at once as Rosie—waited. She was in a pink sari, and she was blinking nervously through her glasses, as she rushed towards his father. His father patted her on the shoulder and then, pointing to Suhel, told her that it had been quite a flight.

'You were gone longer,' she said. It was hard not to look away from her face. Relief had now given away to an almost translucent luminosity. 'I have to leave now.' His father touched Suhel briefly on the elbow, then his shoulder, and he said something else but Suhel did not notice. He felt flat, as if the flying had given him too much of a high.

He tried Mohini's number later that night. To his surprise, she did answer though it took them some time to establish that fact.

'Mohini?'

'Mohini,' she agreed. Friends should have no need to call each other by name, it struck him then, and the distance between them only grew at that thought.

'Mohini Gupta?' he said, in hope and despair. A newspaper piece about her flashed before his eyes and Suhel collected himself. 'Mohini Sahani Gupta.'

'Speaking.' She was answering in monosyllables and all his recent conversations, he realized, had begun the same way. Peoples' voices had changed. Had he been so long gone?

'This is Suhel Kolhatkar.'

'Suhel!' Just for a moment, there was a lilt in her voice and the old Mohini came back but she was gone the next second. She sounded weak. 'You've heard about me.'

What she said, how she had said it, might even have sounded pompous but Mohini had little time, Suhel understood that. His old love let him make these allowances. He brought in his light tone again. 'It's no big deal,' he said as he might have to the Mohini of old.

'I just wondered if we could meet.' His words were strangled, for her voice had already made him a stranger. He had the same sensation he did when he was flying. It wasn't to scare his father but that he hadn't wanted to descend.

'I could maybe see you tomorrow. Let me see.' He heard her soft sigh in his ears, and then her voice piped up again.

'You know, Suhel, there's an interview of me on television. In another fifteen minutes.'

'I'd love to see that,' he said, and his hand was reaching for the television remote as he heard her say, 'We'll talk tomorrow. It's so nice to hear from you, Suhel.' Then he lost her voice completely as the television came on, a burst of voices that came to him as some relief. Had he become no one to her? A compromise, she had said once when he asked her why she had chosen to marry Anil. It was something Mohini said often but what did one do with love then?

Mohini wore a purple kurta, and she was thinner than he remembered. She spoke in a low, modulated voice and she had shorter hair. Her skin was still flawless, but the fatigue, the jowls on her neck, and the downward curve of her lips were all too visible. She was talking of breast cancer awareness before she moved on to general health issues. She had a way of turning her head and it reminded Suhel of the way she'd often sit. She always liked to present her left profile. He felt she was still mocking everything in the way she had, even when she said that women had to help themselves. Her charity would provide everything: from counselling to medical help to rehabilitation. A one-stop shop, she said, and corrected herself: a one-stop solution.

He switched off the television. He switched off the lights too and for some moments sat in darkness. Suhel remembered he should have called to check on his father, to see if he had reached, but it was too late. Something about his father's face turned away from him, towards the window, had been remote and austere. It was the face he had seen in profile the time the rains had been once heavy in the city, and Acharya Donde Marg, the road leading to his grandmother's house, had flooded over. Quite by surprise, Suhel had seen his father on the other side of the road. He waved and laughed, mouthing the words that he had come to look for him. Suhel, had only stared back, unable to put a step forward.

His father had waded across, for the road had already turned into a stream, with a dangerous swift moving current, then pulled Suhel towards him. The narrow street he remembered was now harder to cross. One never knew if wires and open manholes waited below the swirling grey waters. But his father held his hand and every now and then, when he felt Suhel's eyes on him, he'd turn and smile, as if to ask, 'Are you okay?'

His father cautiously led the way ahead. Suhel could only follow, afraid of far worse things. What if snakes, and worse, crocodiles, swirled beneath the murky waters? But they finally reached the old steps that led away from the road. These led first to a row of shops and to his grandmother's house. As they walked, more relaxed now, his father began a story about how he had helped a woman in Cambodia through a dense forest path. He never finished the story and the next day his father left again.

Suhel wondered now about that woman in Cambodia, the woman his father had wanted to marry. He thought about his mother; alive one year, and dead the very next. More than malignant floodwaters and choppy copter rides, it was death that came unexpectedly, with too little warning. It struck him then that Mohini had sounded tired towards the end of their conversation. Suhel knew now what the luminous glow on Rosie's face, as she looked up at his father, meant. He found himself breathless, in the manner a desperate prayer forms in the mind.

There were more lights going out all over the city now. The city snoozed, never completely asleep. When he closed his eyes, he thought of a late evening he had found himself alone on the Turkey Point Lighthouse on Chesapeake Bay. There he was high on the tower, late that evening, with the surf moving in closer and then inching away. The fog descended slowly, eating up the cliffs in the distance. He felt the sea understood his need for companionship and yet his need to be alone. He wondered just before he fell asleep if there was someone like him in this city, at precisely this very moment, watching from a window somewhere, the city fall asleep, claimed in degrees by the slow darkness.

The next morning, he was jerked awake by the buzz of the intercom. Suhel heard the security man's hushed whisper, almost like a warning. *The police, Sir.* But there was already that ring on his door, expectant and not impatient in any way. An inspector, dazed with the slow ride up the elevator, still managed to be officious while serving Suhel the notice. He had to appear before the magistrate for breaking the law— privately flying an aircraft without authorization. It was, Suhel read on, a bailable offence.

It irritated Suhel that the first man he tried to reach for help was away in Panchgani. 'Just taking a break, man.' It was the first time they had spoken in over twenty years, and Dr Joshi's voice sounded reedy, almost as if he was singing in some relief. His chuckle unnerved Suhel—either Dr Joshi did not consider Suhel's offence a serious one, or that he had had a bit too much to drink. But it was, Suhel looked at his watch blearily, only nine in the morning.

He was not to worry, Dr Joshi quickly added, but Suhel wasn't convinced by that breezy reassurance. Was the doctor referring to himself? 'Come down here,' Dr Joshi said next, 'there's someone who can help. He has connections.'

But Suhel couldn't ask more for the doctor had begun chuckling again. 'He's here romancing, but we will see. He could be of help to you. Just come down here.'

The doctor made his last strange request just as Suhel was about to hang up. A high-pitched, strangling sound that made Suhel clap the cell phone back to his ear. He missed the doctor's first words but he clearly sounded nervous as he went on, 'It's an old building and I've never left it for long. The walls run damp, the pipes leak.'

He was taking his time. Suhel wondered if a plumber was what Dr Joshi was looking for. The suggestion set the doctor cackling again. 'No, am just worried. About the paintings, you know. I did push them into the room's centre, but there are a couple in the cupboard. Wait, you don't know how to reach that too.'

The cupboard, Dr Joshi explained—and Suhel noted how detailed he could be—was behind an old iron clotheshorse. There were two low stools and an armchair that were in the way. Suhel had but grudgingly agreed.

Only a day or so later, he would know of the painting, one of two hidden away in Dr Joshi's cupboard. The one that would make him draw in his breath. It would make him pull it out gently, shaking the canvas out from the old clothes that lay around, just so he could look at it more carefully. He'd move with it to the window, and then the realization would dawn on him that it was the woman he had seen first as a thumbnail image but now bigger and very life-like. It'd be the painting he'd want to ask the doctor about, because he had to know the woman in it. Suhel looked at her, this time not in profile but with the shadows on her face, her sea-green eyes, the hair around her forehead, escaping in loose tendrils. A face, he knew, that would glisten in the morning light and—he traced a finger along her cheek—a face whose delicacy would always remind him of night frost, how it crackled like winter silver under his feet; the sound like an echo in his heart.

Sneha Desai Has a Wasted Day

Dear Sir/Madam

The decision to call off the sex education programme for schoolgirls is deplorable. I condemn it in no uncertain terms. For the last one year that I conducted the programme, the response was encouraging. The decision to call it off has been arbitrary. It followed no debate, or discussion as would befit any democracy.

Our civil servants, who should know better, succumb easily to threats by obscurantists and fundamentalists, from those who would keep women in a state of ignorance. We cannot live in an atmosphere of threat, in a land where people are threatened with obscenities, and coerced into submission. Such a state of affairs is intolerable.

I make my protest known in the clearest terms,
Sincerely

She was breathing fast by the time she came to her name. *Sneha.* She typed it in full: Sneha Desai. And she added her qualifications and credentials, most of them, for it would take up too much space in one email. She was a leading radiologist with her own clinic at Parel, consultant to several leading hospitals and pharma companies, a columnist on women's health issues, and an occasional television commentator. Then Sneha had second thoughts and deleted the last. Television commentators were all over the place these days. It didn't take any special ability, apart from outshouting other fellow panellists to be one.

Sneha tapped the key with some emphasis, then lifted her finger to trace the beads of sweat dotting her forehead, the bridge of her nose. She leaned against the column, a flowerpot and an empty broken chair her only companions on the porch. The door behind her stayed locked, the notice firmly taped to its dirt brown panels. And there, right by the door, was the other bit of paper with the graffiti. She hadn't found the words to write about it in her email. A vulgar abstraction of petals and whorls and words and exclamations, complete with hearts and arrows, a mishmash of confused emotions and inexpressible rage. It mirrored what she saw all around her.

A city with its young out of control, a torrent of emotions and feelings swirling in them, just barely leashed. Sneha had tried her best to teach young teenage girls a few things: about choice, and control of their bodies, but, most of all, about awareness. But it was all gone now, barred and shut like that lock on the door, its rounded ends like the belly of a laughing Buddha, mocking her and her efforts. Nothing ever changed.

Sneha went to her 'Sent' folder, clicked the email she'd just sent, read, and then reread it. It sounded too formal, she thought and not angry enough. She changed a word here and there: *terminate* for *call off*, then *strongest* for *clearest*. And then looking over, she did it again, putting in *forced* for *coerced*. She almost attached the picture she had taken of the obscene graffiti, but then hesitated.

She had been first shocked but then she was made of stronger stuff. It was time she upset some people instead. Sneha pointed her cell phone, focused at the graffiti on the wall and took a picture of it again. On her camera frame, it looked just what it was. The vagina in all its curved complexities. There was no mistaking it for anything else, a flower or something decorous. Though the vagina was this too and complex. She, a radiologist of twenty years standing, knew this better than anyone else.

She resent the email. The same people would get a second, more forceful version of the first one. She clenched her fists, now imagining the lock cranking open, and the door presenting its old self to her, the one she had got used to, its frame creaking, the faint lines on its panels visible on catching the sunlight, and the girls in the front row, smiling in the shy way they had. Remembering that made her relax. That was the first thing she had told them. *Laugh. Laugh your heart out and loud. Not just smile.*

They had put hands to their mouths and giggled. Sex education was a serious matter, but it only made them giggle, as if they all shared a guilty secret. These classes offered them freedom of a kind, where they could ask the unthinkable and then giggle at their own audacity.

What could she do to change things? Had she done the right thing in sending the letter? The girls, for whom she was fighting, would not care one bit. They would move on to other things, accepting whatever was in their lot. But just accepting things was not right. And Sneha knew she could not just sit here, with such thoughts drumming inside her. The letters were all sent, but there were always other places she could send to—television channels, websites and even diasporic magazines who could be relied on to get agitated on controversial matters like these—but she wondered what to do next? A protest, but who would join her, who would she lead? She could not imagine her patients, her clients, rich though most of them were, marching in the heat, out of their air-conditioned cars, chanting slogans, raising their arms simply to display their new diamond bracelets. She had heard that gentle monotonous clink of jewellery in her chambers so many times, it sent her into a deep fatigue now.

No, she decided she'd wait for the newspapers to do their

work. They were the only ones who stood for modern ideas, for choice, freedom and awareness. There was no one else on her side otherwise. She stamped hard on the porch, biting fiercely to stop her tears. She wasn't weak, she wasn't the kind to go scrounging for support. She sneezed as the dust rose. The leaves scattered under the neem tree and the grey cat bounced on the slanting roof. This municipal school building too had been slated for demolition. Everywhere tall high-rises were going up, the city's new modernity held in place by the scaffolds visible all around her. The clock sounded loud, it was the new addition in the mall just across N.M. Joshi Marg. It stood high on the roof of the chalet-like building that housed the latest Western brands. Sneha remembered the coat she had left behind at Zara's a week ago. She hoped the alterations were done by now. If only this country would speed up a bit.

Sneha got to her feet, slung her backpack over her shoulder. All those charts and clippings were of little use now. Her strident march slowed, faltered, as she neared the gate, then she lurched over scattered pebbles, and hurriedly righted herself. The world outside remained as unmoved and unmoving as she had always perceived it. But within the usual unhurried crowds were interspersed distinct circles of waiting curious onlookers, who must know what had happened, who waited now in expectation and anticipation. They were waiting for her, for a reaction, an outburst, a tantrum, something to liven up their afternoon. Sneha's steps died completely away. The wall behind her was a curtain that now dropped, and she stood before them, a defenceless performer who had forgotten her lines. Their glances strayed towards her and moved away, too deliberate. The crowds of shopkeepers, delivery boys, idling cabs and even her driver among them, who now catching her eye, hurriedly walked towards her. But she did not want to perform, she did not want their pity, or even their righteous anger. He dawdled as he neared, an anxious, eager to please look coming over his face.

'What were you doing there?' she snapped, loud enough for those around to hear.

'Nothing...' He shuffled his feet, smiled and then pulled his shirt even lower. 'I went for a cigarette.' He pointed to the building behind her. 'No classes, today?'

'No. Did you want to attend?' She stopped, and then made sure her voice carried. 'You people just stand here and watch the fun.'

No one noticed the tremulous note in her voice. The driver scratched his hair, the other people shrugged, and she heard some of them say, *what's Madam's problem? Why taking anger out on us?*

In the car, she was careful not to call anyone. The driver staring rigidly ahead, his unseeing eyes on the traffic, was all ears. She'd follow up, once she had some privacy. She had an hour or so till her evening appointments.

Sneha sent the email to more magazines and websites she had googled for. It took her more time than she imagined. Already a few hours had elapsed since she had sent it the first time and yet she had had no acknowledgment, let alone a response.

She checked, rechecked, logged out, logged in again but no one emailed. Her heart bursting with her lonely indignation, she rose several times to stand by the window, where the last remnants of a breeze came in. She had deliberately switched off the air conditioner for an hour or so. Somewhere miles away, she knew of the farmers who were denied electricity simply so cities could be supplied with twenty-four-hour power. She wasn't simple, or even Gandhian, she just had her empathy, she believed in doing something meaningful. She checked her watch, by evening, she would switch on the air conditioner again.

An hour later, for all her terrible wanting, there was still no response to her email. Her patients entered, lay themselves down, prepared their bodies for her intrusive administrations and questions, taking her absentness to be something that came routinely to a doctor. Sneha would have even cancelled her appointments, but she didn't want to disappoint a new patient who had booked a month in advance.

'Looks like benign cysts...' she mumbled, distractedly.

'Is it serious?' the patient asked instead. They all wanted easy explanations, quick-fix solutions. Sneha's work was to offer an opinion, most times open-ended. The next step was a recommendation to a specialist. In that sense her work was not hard. She might cause worry but not inflict devastation. Sneha turned back and looked at her computer screen. In her mind, she was running over the names of websites she had sent the letter to. Behind her, the lady fidgeted. 'You can get up now. I need to think this over.'

'Is it something incurable?'

'It isn't for me to say anything definitive. Your doctor will speak to you.'

Sneha sent the email to a place she had missed, a magazine for South Asians in Wilmington, Delaware. She frowned, was Delaware a Democrat state? She didn't know much about the state, but if it had a magazine for desis, it meant it was liberal enough to encourage all kinds of thought. Sneha thought over this, and over other websites. She snapped repeatedly at Vasudha, her assistant, for being so slow, and then at another patient, who was too fidgety as Sneha held her transducer ready.

It was late afternoon when she took a cab back to the school. She was not expected at this hour and so no one noticed her, no crowds gathered. The notice was still there, firmly taped as before. But the paper with its graffiti on, was already half-torn in the wind that ran like a strangled wail within the compound wall and along the corridor. Sneha tore the paper off the wall and wrote with a marker: *No defacing the walls. No Obscenery Obscenity.*

Despite the hurriedly corrected misspelling, Sneha was pleased. She looked around, there was silence. It was then she felt bereft. Without that paper on the wall, she felt her anger had not dissipated but had turned into chaos instead. Mingling with the wind that ran trapped everywhere, the wall blocking it from the road and the city outside. It raised high mounds of dust, like the cat that rummaged in the bin, time and again, and hissed at the stray mongrel that dared not come closer.

Sneha put the torn bit of paper into her bag, crumpled it with her fist. She had felt she was doing something useful, something enduring, for the country, for future generations, something that took her beyond the immediate, and now it had all been taken away. She bit back a sudden sob again.

She tried calling the principal of the school. He had never taken her calls and this time like before, the phone rang on. Perhaps she never had the right number. When she dialled again, someone sounding like a junior clerk from the school administration board—for he spoke in a mix of utter boredom and effrontery—answered.

'Yes, there was an order.'

'Yes, I do not know, Madam.'

To everything she asked, he had almost the same answer. He did not know. The 'Madam' bit made it sound even more insolent.

She sat, agitated, then wondered if she should write a letter about this too, the apathy of government servants. She sat on that porch till the shadows lengthened, bringing in a welcome darkness. Then at last her phone rang.

It was Neera Joshi. It had been ages since they had last seen each other and Sneha fumbled. A surge of wild new hope filled her. Neera always got to know things first. At one time, the days when Sneha first knew her, Neera had been a reporter. Sneha wasn't sure though if those skills had lasted.

'How are you, Sneha?'

Neera always began with that offhand gentle voice, as if she looked out at the sea, or from a great height. It made her sound god-like in an absent-minded way. Only Sneha knew how much it was a put on. Long ago, Neera would appear in the chawl where Sneha lived with her aunt and uncle, the trade union leader, Ramakrishna Desai. Neera always had that lofty gaze, and with that absent voice, she would ask Sneha how her studies were going. It was two or three questions later that she would ask Sneha where her uncle was. Sneha always noted how Neera's eyes continually strayed towards the poky curtain at the door in case Ramakrishna Desai appeared. It was for him, Sneha knew, that Neera was there.

'Such a drama queen,' she had sniffed to Mausi, Ramakrishna Desai's wife. The latter had overhead and only chuckled mildly.

The chawl was just a five-minute walk from where Sneha lived now. Neera had exerted a strange fascination for Sneha those days, in large part because everyone else hated Neera for her proximity to Ramakrishna Desai. He had been Neera's one great obsession and it had lasted, as most people believed, all her life.

'Haven't heard from you in a long time, Sneha,' Neera said in that voice that held the sea, the high-rises, and Mumbai past and present. She went on, her voice like the invisible breeze that came in from the sea, 'You hardly call these days.'

Neera was getting old, she had to be seventy plus. All of Sneha's experience, and she had little interests beyond her work, was now invested in women of a different age-group, yet she knew it was best to let old people talk. 'How is your work going?'

But before Sneha could begin, Neera broke in again, her voice wavering.

'But I've been hearing…'

Sneha held her breath. She now waited for the

commiseration, the sympathy, the shared anger but there was a silence. Neera looked for words, and then she finally found them. 'Oh yes, you saw the industrialist Gupta's wife recently, didn't you?'

Sneha sighed, she was a mass of disappointed exhalations. Her breath broke against the column, a small shower of red earth poured down on her feet. Trust Neera to have insider knowledge of most things. She would, of course, know what had happened to Mohini Gupta, whose art exhibition had to be cancelled after she had been suddenly taken sick. The papers had carried stories of her having some fatal form of cancer, but everyone close to her had been secretive about the entire thing.

'Yes, she came to me. And then I referred...'

She was cut short. Neera went on, with a certain unbecoming enthusiasm, 'Quite tragic it all is. To think of what she was. So what is the diagnosis?'

'I had to refer her immediately.' And then Sneha bit herself. She had given herself away after all—she had breached a patient's confidentiality, and allowed Neera to hoodwink her again.

'I can't tell you more, Tai.' The disappointment with herself, with Neera, with all that happened to her that day came back to her, upset her in double measure. It had always been that way. 'I had a bad day.' Her voice wobbled. She had to get it out first, before giving it all up. And Neera's voice was immediately concerned.

'What is it? Tell me all, Sneha.'

She had the tone of a god about to grant a boon.

They had a long familiarity with each other's lives, having known each other from a more vulnerable time. So despite the occasional unkindness and indifference, there was still tolerance. For some time Sneha had hated her. She knew what most people had disregarded till her uncle, Ramakrishna

Desai, had been gunned down that rain-filled afternoon: That his perpetually tormented gaze, his forced lightness of heart did not come from his agonizing over worker issues and his realization of imminent failure. It was always about Neera. After his death, they said she had used her black magic on him, to first interfere in his marriage and then to destroy him. But Neera had taken the insults and the humiliation and she had lasted. Perhaps love had something to do with it. A sharp pang of envy filled Sneha. It was something she had been denied, and could never claim.

Sneha remembered the showdown at the hospital where her uncle had been rushed. It was Neera who had taken him there but her aunt and all his supporters—and soon, there were more of them than she had ever seen—had pointedly cold-shouldered Neera. Neera had always made her feel insecure. She was so pretty, so in control, so capable of making her clever uncle laugh heartily. Even Sneha had watched in delight as Neera had been pushed off the truck carrying the funeral cortege. Everything that had been secret and hush hush was now in the open. They all hated Neera, the mistress, the interloper, the one who had distracted her uncle. He could have been a greater leader if only he had not been so besotted.

Sneha had heard the abuses hurled on Neera. The obscenities never changed, women who crossed lines were all marked. It was a lesson that had stayed in her subconscious mind, in some ways warning her never to cross the line, into behaviour most people would never accept. That one last moment, as the van carrying her uncle's cortege picked up speed, and Neera's face moved some distance away, their eyes had met. It was then Neera's expression crumpled. She looked a small, vulnerable and terribly frail woman, her sari end trailing on the road behind her. But it was only for one second. Neera's eyes met Sneha's and she arranged her hair, her sari and stood watching the van go.

'It's all right, Tai.' She felt disappointed about a whole lot of things.

'Sneha.'

And Sneha understood Neera wanted her to talk. Her words poured out then, half caught between her sobs and loud hiccups. 'The sex education classes were so different. And radical too. It was creating awareness, empowerment. It was for an equal world. But they stopped me. And in such humiliation too.

'There was just no reply, from them,' Sneha went on after a brief pause. 'All of them indifferent. Totally oblivious that the next generation is changing. Some old fuddy-duddy perhaps was offended. What we need is a protest. Something that would totally drive sense into them.'

She ended and the dog came up to her to sit next to her on the porch, tired after all its recent exertions with the cat over the garbage bin. And Neera's voice was fainter still, as if the effort to listen to Sneha had tired her out.

'Sneha, who understands such language now? People are so easily displeased these days.'

It was then that Sneha hung up. She could blame the dog, who came just a bit too close. Neera's words had set her head throbbing again. Didn't Neera sense the somnolence, the apathy everywhere?

'Shoo. Go away, dog. Nothing for you here.'

Looking up, she saw a crowd had gathered. They stood by the gate, a straggly bunch of half a dozen men and a woman among them too. They stood watching her, unblinking and silent. 'Give him some bread, Madam,' one shouted. The dog, mangy, with its brown skin peeling off around its neck, stood up and whined instead.

Sneha would give them the performance they wanted. She dialled Neera's number and this time it was engaged. But she yelled, holding her cell phone close to her lips. 'Those classes were important. Important. Important. What do you people understand? You'd rather remain mired in your ignorance, and apathy.' She stopped as they looked at her, blankly curious. The dog limped away behind the darkness of the bin. Didn't anyone know the meaning of apathy any more?

She stopped, and disconnected Neera's number. It was busy when she tried again. Ever busy woman, Sneha thought. With all her commitments and yet not there when one needed her. Some among the crowd were leaving, and new people came in to take their place. Some lounged against the wall. Some sat on their haunches.

'Damn you, all of you. You will take the city down with you.' She flipped her bag open, looked at the mirror embossed on the inside and hurriedly closed it. She needed to look angry, but not dementedly so. Her phone rang again and Neera's distant voice came on again. 'I forgot something. It was to ask a favour, Sneha. Would you have time?'

Sneha swallowed her anger and even her surprise. Her words tumbled out, hurriedly, as if she found them distasteful. Was Neera about to apologize, begin again?

'Favour? Yes, just a moment.'

She sat down on the porch, and waved the crowds away. That didn't work. Her hand muffling the phone, she hissed, 'This is an important call. Police. Go away.'

They began dispersing then, in ones, then twos and by the time, Neera's voice came again, Sneha was again all by herself. 'Sneha, are you all right?'

'Yes, just some idiot beggars.'

'Yes, aren't they a nuisance?' said Neera and then she began again. 'I know you are busy. You have some very important persons among your clients,' Neera laughed.

She must learn to be wary, she must, Sneha told herself. For a moment she had been stumped by that word, *favour*. She wished she had used that word—favour—when writing to the editors. The word had such hidden meanings, contained so much audacity and charm.

'There's this woman I know,' Neera was saying, You know, she's been married for some time and...'

'No children...' Sneha finished for her, dryly. Perhaps it was one of Neera's activist friends. Too busy with all the protests, all the marching and the hunger strikes. Their throats constantly parched, their voices prematurely raucous and cracked with all their shouting. But of course, they'd never take the advice Sneha might have given them. Go easy. Your eggs won't last long. Those frozen egg banks were too expensive, not easily affordable. Yet she could have done with their help in organizing some protests.

'She works for me,' Neera said. 'And I think she needs some...'

'Intervention?'

'Ah yes. All those medical words. Yes, intervention. And do pass on her bill to me.'

'That's all right, Neera Tai.' Intervention is not a medical word, Sneha wanted to say. But there was too much to say, and too little time. She never picked the right moment for anything.

'I will see. Who is she?'

'Pooja. She comes to help me at times.'

One of her research assistants then, Sneha thought. Someone with boyfriend problems. And her guess appeared to be confirmed when Neera went on, 'She's not very forthcoming but I can tell the matter bothers her. What time shall I tell her to come?'

Now Neera was sweeping her along, and Sneha was filled with a resentment. But she had missed her moment and now it would take her too much time.

'Nine tomorrow.'

A heavy thud of sorrow and disappointment hit her. That

was the time she had taught her girls at this same very rundown building. The thirty lively cheerful girls who had shared so much with her. 'That is the time I had my classes.' Her voice came out almost like a whine. 'Did you know a survey was actually done, and that most people think such...? '

'But that would automatically happen, my dear Sneha. Surveys are all doctored and manipulated. We don't discuss such things...in our culture.'

'But we should. We could...'

But she could not go on and when that conversation ended, Sneha put her hand in her bag. She found the paper she had torn off the wall. It was then her anger returned. It beat against her head all the way home, the paper clenched tight in her fist. Once home, she flung it against the paintings on the walls, picked it up before throwing it against the ceramic pots, the cushions that were never out of place, that never had a speck or a tear on them. The curled-up paper nestled on the low bed, as if it too, wanted to hide away. There was her computer on the table, and the files she carried home, the research she did. She straightened the paper and pinned it to the board. It could look like a child's doodle to the ignorant but otherwise it was daring, even glaringly offensive. She took it down and put it back in her bag. It was better to hold anger close than to have to look at it, pinned to a wall.

Everything else looked in place. But when she looked at herself in the mirror, she saw the dark shadows under her eyes, her ruffled wavy hair falling loose from her barrette. Her kurta was now crumpled and looked far too loose. She pulled one end away and saw her hollowed bones. For someone in her forties, she had maintained herself well. She would miss the classes and the girls. She stopped, thinking such thoughts didn't ever matter. No one understood. She had just sobbed out loud when the phone came again.

'Too many times I am...'

It was Neera's voice followed by Neera's laughter but it broke off, and then Sneha heard her say, 'Hello, Sneha, you are okay, right?'

'Yes, yes,' she was sniffling.

Neera didn't wait for an answer. Everyone, of course, expected her, Sneha, to be okay. The women who came to her, with all their stresses, their irritating—and at times put on— shyness, had to be reassured, comforted, their fears taken away, in return for assurances, recommendations, even promises, at times false. Sneha understood all this and followed the routine, but she wished they would think differently, and think ahead. Was having a baby that important in life? Couldn't they have careers too? Couldn't they do something else, just as worthwhile, with all the time and money they had?

But she heard Neera asking for the address. 'Sneha, Pooja will be alone, and she may not understand much.'

'What do you mean?'

'She's the one who helps me...' Neera laughed, 'And she's a very good cook.'

A cook. Sneha's mind swirled at a dizzying pace. A cook. She almost laughed. Oh dear, were cooks giving themselves airs too. Did this one cook know that she, Sneha, was the highest paid radiologist in the city? She looked at herself in the mirror, straightened herself, brushed hair away her forehead, and lifted her lips in a half-smile.

'Sneha, do see her.'

There was that cajoling tone again. Sneha stifled her chuckles, then almost as if she was humouring Neera, she said, 'Yes, I will.' 'See the cook,' she added in an undertone.

'Good girl,' Neera said. 'And now it must be late.'

It was ten. The news channels would never mention the incident, the closure of the city's sex education programme for its girl students; a prototype, and ahead of its time. She had only the next morning's newspapers to look forward to.

'Sneha, we must meet for coffee,' Neera had said at last, her voice wavering and falling till Sneha realized she was stifling a yawn, and then she hung up too. Later, having put out all the lights, all Sneha remembered of her day was her long unending conversations with Neera. Neera, the ever do-gooder, who had not been overly bothered about her.

Morning came but sleep had eluded Sneha all night. Hours later, as she looked at all the morning newspapers crumpled in a heap by her side, all she wanted was total oblivion. She took a deep breath, walked around the apartment, picked the papers up, riffled through them several times and then again.

But the shock of her letter not finding a mention at all did not ease. Sneha felt alone, even her anger couldn't help her now. The heat in her head diminished yet returned time and again. Her beating heart would quell somewhat and then act up again. She knew she had to somehow get through the day.

She was late by the time she reached her clinic. The cleaner had left already, but there was someone waiting. Sneha heard a low murmur from the corner sofa but she was looking at the newspapers that the cleaning woman had left on the table. The same set Sneha had seen at home yet something made her turn the pages over again. For some wild unbelieving moments, she thought she had had the date wrong, that these were the previous day's papers, but every other news item was there. Her letter had not merited a mention even in the local news pages. She folded the newspapers up in one careless pile and swept them to the floor.

Sneha went into the second chamber inside and checked the websites all over again. And then it was a mildly uttered 'excuse me' that made her look up. 'Are you looking for something?' the woman asked in Marathi. None among her clients ever spoke that way. Sneha was in a daze as a new thought struck her. Maybe a newspaper had indeed sent a reporter. The woman before her was young, slim and very pretty, like someone in television shows. But the salwar kameez she wore was too bright, and there was her hesitation that gave her away. The superciliousness then came easy to Sneha. She remembered this was the woman Neera had mentioned.

'Pooja?'

'Ji. But are you all right?' The young woman asked instead, in a high thin voice. The voice of nervousness, Sneha could tell her patients well.

'Can you fill up a form?'

Sneha thought she would make her fill two forms instead. Forms that were routine, and could be done later. Her patients hated filling out forms, but it gave them time to sort themselves out. Pooja looked at the papers and at Sneha who asked, in a deliberate mocking tone if she knew English. But Pooja didn't look away. 'I am learning. It will just take me a bit longer to fill it up right now.'

Sneha nodded, she wished she had slept for a bit and had never woken up. All her hopes had dulled, everything, even her niceness had been taken from her.

'I never anticipated that. The forms need to be filled before I can see you. And I have a long day ahead. Perhaps you will wait till my assistant comes.'

But the woman lifted a small hand to her forehead, ran it down her kurta and asked if she could come back again. 'I have work.' Sneha had had no patience with women who gave themselves airs. She snapped now, 'Don't we all?'

It was all a favour for Neera, and she wondered bitterly why no one did her a favour. She saw a shimmer of tears on the young woman's face and looked away. This country operated on a network of favours. Small favours moving onto bigger ones and it left no one with a sense of duty. She wanted to tell the woman to dry her tears. One working day gone would not matter.

But Pooja smiled then, quite surprising Sneha. 'I will wait, Madam. No problem.' She stumbled over the last word and blushed.

In her own chamber, Sneha could hear her out in the reception as they both waited for Vasudha. She held her head in her hands and listened to the other woman mouthing softly words from the newspaper. Pooja said the words slowly, uncertainly, sometimes giggling at herself, and it reminded Sneha of her girls. She had still so much to teach them. Half an hour later, Vasudha rushed in all flustered, complaining about the late trains and Sneha gave her a tongue-lashing too. Then they made Pooja wait some more.

'Do you know what all this entails?' Sneha asked Pooja once she was in. Vasudha had already done some explaining, had even had Pooja sign the confidentiality clause, but Sneha was still going to ask her. For a moment, the old uncertain look crossed the young woman's face, but Sneha was beyond caring. 'I need you to know what I am going to do. In detail, and it's somewhat complicated.' The woman smiled in apology, and asked if Sneha would speak a little slowly.

Sneha sighed. She would be damned if she was going to speak in Marathi. She was not going to make concessions for anyone. But it was all going to take longer than she thought.

Pooja listened to all that she said, with amazement of her own, and then as if she could not help it, she said, 'I had no idea all that was inside me. And that they had these names.'

'Yes. And these machines will tell me if there is a problem.'

'Problem?'

'Isn't that why Neera sent you?'

'Not about problem.'

'Look, I don't have time.

She was about to say how late she was getting for her other appointments. And then realized she had nothing waiting for her till late afternoon, for that was when, after her classes, her appointments usually began.

Pooja was shy, and uncomfortable as she examined her. Time and again, everything swam before Sneha, and she longed to disappear in the haze of coolness that came from the air-conditioned room. The screen shimmered in response to the faint sounds she heard, the nearby honking of a horn, and Pooja's sighs as she felt the cold gel of the transducer on her skin.

'I need you to come back again,' Sneha said finally, tired. She couldn't go on. Something was exhausting her beyond her will. Thank you, the young woman only said. And even mocking her ridiculous formality came hard to Sneha. She leaned against the window and then turned angrily as the door opened again.

It was Vasudha who came in to ask after the payment details.

'No, it's all right. Neera Joshi…'

'Madam, no, no. It's okay.' It was the young woman again who barged in behind Vasudha, her earlier shyness gone. 'I will pay.'

Sneha did not tell her how expensive it was. Her fees could be almost a month's salary for her. She made to dismiss her, but Pooja appeared adamant. 'I do mean it, I will pay. Maybe not now, but I will.'

Sneha smiled thinly, then saw Vasudha's pleading look. It begged Sneha not to be sarcastic. 'I don't know yet,' Sneha only said, turning away, 'It might take me some time to study. Now go.'

She'd meet Pooja later that night again. Sneha had just walked out of the lobby onto the dark road with its flickering lamp lights, when she first heard the shuffle of steps, before the shadow moved quickly out of the awning. Sneha felt her heart drum fearfully. She leaned against the wall, remembering then that she hadn't eaten anything the whole day. The woman smiled, then gestured with her hand, and Sneha tried hard to place her.

It was someone who had come to her clinic recently. *Blocked fallopian tube.* Sneha frowned. No no she was getting confused. It was Pooja, of course, but what was her problem? *Undecided stress?* Wasn't that what she had labelled her? Or was it the *cyst case?* No, she had put it down to *continued new bride syndrome.* Pooja had never gotten over her shyness. Maybe it was her husband who had to be talked to. But that wasn't quite it. Sneha stared at her, much the same way as she studied the fuzzy computer images on her screen. She knew she had never been so forgetful.

Sneha was about to give her customary vague superior smile to the younger woman when a soft humming purr filled the street and a yellow Mercedes-Benz of the latest make swished to a stop very close. The dust rose and settled as the car, with its smooth silkiness, went silent. Its headlights dimmed, and Sneha saw the car reflected in the old dust-encrusted glass windows, an incongruous graceful animal in that concrete forest of sooty old buildings. She knew the car, and who was in it. And with this one realization came others too. Inside the car was the one person she might have approached. Ghatge could have done her a favour. He could have helped her, her letter might have got the audience it deserved.

Across the road everything else fell silent, even the lamplight's flickers slowed as Ghatge descended. A long leg emerged and then the rest of Ghatge glided out of the Mercedes. He took off his dark glasses, ran quick fingers down his kurta and over his thin moustache. He was taller than he looked in his photos and thinner too—in a surprisingly fit, gym-toned way—but his hair was noticeably thinner. Sneha knew he was important these days. There had even been a couple of television appearances of late. Near her, Sneha heard the clink of bangles as Pooja rearranged her dupatta.

A man on a scooter cautiously circumvented his way. Some bystanders raised a slogan, calling out his name. Ghatge raised a lazy hand to silence them, and he was smiling as he walked up to them. He folded his hands in a namaste before Sneha, 'Already done for the day, Sneha Madam? I thought you worked longer hours,' and then placing those same hands in the pockets of his loose kurta, he turned to Pooja, 'What a surprise, Pooja.'

It was the other woman who showed more poise. Sneha heard Pooja's laughter, deliberately muted, before she replied, 'I didn't think my movements were of any interest, Ghatge Sahib.'

'Arre...it is my duty,' he bantered, and then, giving Pooja the lazy once over, he pointed to something she held. 'Something for Madam, nothing for me, Pooja.' That deliberately flirtatious tone made Sneha feel left out, even more alone than she felt. She leant against the old iron railing and replied in just the same easy and indifferent tone, one the city's rich often adopted. 'Yes, she came to me. But you don't want all the details, Ghatge Sahib, do you?'

Everyone called him that and he laughed, 'Arre, Madam, are we going to spend time standing here? Why not go somewhere else?'

There was the quick sound of anklets, and Pooja reached out, handing over a wrapped packet. 'Something for you, Madam.'

Sneha's hands closed over something soft, and then she was assailed by its fragrance. Ghatge stood apart, a knowing smile on. Holding that soft packet, done up with thin string, his smile now seemed the most benign thing Sneha had encountered. The fragrance drove away all the smells of her clinic, the unpleasant events of the day. When she had felt unimportant, unworthy, all her work of little use. Then she saw Pooja walking quickly away, and Sneha said quietly to her retreating back, 'I will talk to Neera Tai.'

Around her she saw people preparing for the night. There were still a few bystanders, but the women had brought their small stoves out on the sidewalk, and in some shacks, the televisions were on. Someone came and wiped the Mercedes, and saluted as Ghatge raised his hand in acknowledgement. They doted on this man, hoping he would make these shanties permanent. But the buildings allotted for them in the suburbs, in accordance with the government's slum redevelopment scheme, were really all fair game for the real estate dealers. She was sure Ghatge had a hand in this as well.

She pointed to them, speaking to Ghatge, 'Shouldn't you be worried about them? And not my hours?'

'Well, we could talk about this also. But somewhere else?'

His voice was soft yet forceful, and then he took in everyone around. An empty traffic podium stood a few metres away and he walked up to it, in determined easy steps, and then he launched into a quick impromptu speech. 'Dr Sneha is doing important, valuable work and I am doing my work, as your representative. And what are all of you doing? Just idling, trying to hope for some gossip. No wonder this country isn't going anywhere.'

Some of them pinched their ears in apology, others laughed guiltily, and a few nodded, folding their hands in apology. Sneha felt a brief flash of admiration. This is what she should have done. Stood on the podium and given her speech. And then the other truth hit her, bringing surprise tears to her face. He had, after all, said it, he had acknowledged her work openly, before a small crowd of people. He was the only one who had done so.

He must have seen the shine of tears on her eyes, then her face. She let him see it. By then, she was too tired. Too alone. And for the first time she was not afraid to cry. 'You can't cry here,' he said, his voice still soft, but now she thought she read a gentleness too. 'Besides, you look hungry.' Then he stretched his arm to where his car was.

'Fancy a ride?'

'In a Benz, and why not? But it's a fast car.'

'What do you think, Sneha Madam? Alas, the roads are not smooth everywhere but still you can trust me. I know how to control unruly things. And maybe we can stop somewhere and have the fragrant puran poli your admirer gave you.'

'She's not my...'

'But we all are...the rich and the famous drive up in their cars to consult you. It's for you to acknowledge it.' The last was said in such a soft tone that she knew she had to be very careful. But now she felt herself laugh. Ghatge could be funny and did not at all seem threatening.

They had the puran poli sitting on low stools outside the new Starbucks in Colaba. And then dinner in a small and secret restaurant up in Andheri's Saki Naka, where he drove past the Sea Link, down Linking Road, just as the sidewalk shops were just shutting down. The last buses were out, and autorickshaws were idling by the road. Some prostitutes too were out on the streets; unearthly figures when the neon street lights turned their lipstick and heavy jewellery into shiny greying plastic. The Mercedes-Benz covered the city in two hours. It was quiet, and seemingly peaceful.

The night soon claimed everything, the mall showrooms dimmed their lights, the sidewalk sleepers no longer fidgeted restlessly, but Sneha did not want to go home—not yet, she told Ghatge, with some laughter in her voice once and then again—and so they lingered by the sea front in Marine Drive. She still wanted something more from this day. Sometimes Ghatge's phone rang and he walked a little way away to answer. The film posters everywhere talked of happy lives, the commercials advertised the new boutique stores, and the hotel lights blinked down at them invitingly. When the night breeze felt cold on her shoulders, she moved towards him.

He pulled her close with one arm, as his other hand held the phone cradled against the shoulder. The feel of his hands on her shoulders felt cold and very new. She wanted this newness a bit more. That was when she reached up and snatched his phone. She let her hand glide by Ghatge's, and did not mind as his arm slid from her shoulder to grip her waist, very suggestively.

'You are too thin,' he said. And when she looked at him, he told her he knew what happened. 'No one stands by the one who is alone, Sneha Madam. Not your brave newspapers and fierce television channels. They will go where the money is.' He sat down on the low stone wall, drawing her down alongside him and together, they stared out at the sea. 'Do you think your ideas will work? For the politicians, your programme was something that would get attention quickly, away from what they really do. And why bother, when you have your clinic, where the city's rich and the baanj come?'

Having used that crude word for the infertile, he looked at her and smiled provocatively. 'Don't get angry.'

But she knew she wasn't, and he knew too. 'Then why?'

'Those who came for your classes, enjoyed the fun of it all. Our society is too repressed. I am not sure if something happens to these girls after this. That they turn immoral, enjoy the sex because they fear nothing. More knowledge sometimes leads to loose behaviour.'

'That's ridiculous.' She felt the hot flush of anger rise this time. She was going to defend her students though she knew the girls did not bother. They would be pulled into the dull routine of their lives. Anger had no point if it was to be wasted.

'Sneha?'

'Don't talk to me like that.' But the sea had lulled her anger, pulling it away like it did the city's refuse. She saw a plastic can bobbing on the waves, before it was pulled under.

'You will see I am right. There is a right time for everything, and there's just too much happening...' He turned to face her then, not looking away. 'Between you and me.' She was weeping then and had no idea. For he held her close and yet afraid as if she would resist. 'You are tired.'

The hotel across the road had a cosy, luxurious feel. Sneha heard happy laughter around her. Happiness was so easy to find. One had just to walk into a hotel.

He led her into a new boutique, a new twenty-four-hour one that had just opened in the hotel. The shop girls appeared and just as discreetly vanished when he waved a hand. 'Try it on,' he said as her fingers lingered on a kurti on display. And his eyes glinted when she emerged from the trial room. She felt a long-lost wave of desire then.

'It makes such a difference,' he said. He insisted on paying and she resisted. 'Pay me back later,' he said and they laughed. Secret romances are born of such innuendoes, of protests and false resistances that could be swept away with a wave of the hand.

From there in the corridor, he led to her back to the reception, then they took an elevator to the room. The next days and weeks were to be her happiest, as her life, and love too, became an open secret.

On one of her nights out with Ghatge, as she stood on the parapet between the sea and Marine Drive, Sneha realized she still had that graffiti-marked piece of paper she had torn off the school wall. She wanted first to fashion it into a plane or even a boat but then she crumpled it up, and flung it towards the waters. Ghatge stood apart, as always, texting. And just behind him, on the darkened parapet, she saw a dark blob suspended in air for a second, a shadow tripping over the ghastly looking tetrapods, and then falling, like an arrow into the water. The grey swirling water turned into a white waterfall, striking her on the face. It was one of the urchins who lived on the sidewalk and earned a living cleaning the cars parked there. Sneha saw a flash of white as he surfaced. He waved at her, at the other urchins, and dived in again. The piece of paper floated away, and he reached for it with fluid graceful strokes. She could only watch him, fascinated, not noticing when Ghatge returned to her.

The boy thrashed around. For a moment, it was quiet and nothing was seen, except for that blob of paper, still dancing. She called out, 'Someone save him.' But Ghatge bent to laugh softly into her ears, 'He will be fine.'

The boy plucked the paper up, and held it high. A couple of other boys still standing on the parapet, began cheering. He came up smiling, the paper a soggy mass. He held it out and as Sneha took it gingerly with shaking hands, he held out his other hand as well. She was stunned, she fiddled with her bag, stupefied at his desperation. She realized she didn't have the necessary change to reward him. It was Ghatge who rummaged in his pockets. His hands found some paper notes, and he pushed these into the boy's outstretched hand. 'Now go. Leave us.'

They walked along Marine Drive then. Other evenings they would walk on Carter Road, on the blue-tiled walkway along it, from where she would look at the once famous bungalow of a once famous film star and the other high-rises that had been among the first in the city. They would stop and turn back right at the point where the fish were hung out to dry, the stench overwhelming around them, but it was something she was used to. There were other things she got used to as well, more slowly.

Such as how the Bandra–Worli Sea Link loomed over them as they crossed it in his car. The sound of the car ricocheted to its ends and returned—the tall girders rose higher still and sometimes the silver on it flashed, as it caught the lights of the city. The moving shifting lights sometimes made her feel as if she was on a moving stage, the lights trained on her. Then there were those gangs of motorbike riders, who would sometimes appear to escort the Mercedes-Benz down the Sea Link. All along the bridge, the bikers would arrange themselves around his car and at the very end, they would take off their helmets, cheering and whistling.

She wondered if Ghatge feared being recognized but he didn't seem to mind. And that carelessness comforted her. Sometimes at a signal, late at night, while she saw sleeping bodies on the sidewalks, urchins would rush out from under the streetlights, eager to wipe the car and earn a pittance.

Ghatge and she always returned very late. If it was towards dawn, there was every chance Sneha would miss her appointments the next day. First, she took to rescheduling them, then she had Vasudha cancel them altogether. Sneha had no idea when she began living for the nights. It seemed to her she was grabbing life—all the things she had never tried nor had—when it threatened to pass her by totally. She scanned her face anxiously, several times over. She knew she looked younger than her age and yet she still worried. She painstakingly thumbed through her wardrobe, trying on something, mixing and matching dresses and then rescheduling her meals, missing them as well, for one could never have a romantic evening on a full stomach.

She began waiting for him right from the afternoon hours, before the evening trains that she could see from her window sped past, crowded with passengers hanging out from every door. Finally, the city that had earlier towered and crowded around her, leaving her empty, claimed her too. With him by her side, she felt snuggled by the city.

Sometimes he'd message to tell her when he would come by. Then he stopped doing it altogether. As if they both knew he would come anyway and he knew she would wait, though she hated it if he veered from his scheduled time by as much as a few minutes. She counted down the minutes, when looking out of her window, and she knew it was late when she saw the stoves in the shanties outside dimming their flames, the children eating by the roadside, their mothers sitting on their haunches, looking on, with their tired droopy faces.

They knew, like she did, that he came for her in different cars, though the yellow Mercedes-Benz remained his favourite. He would drive up in a swish, and the children would scatter in a yelp of frightened joy. They danced in that cloud of orange-yellow dust, lit up by his car headlights. It would take a while to settle down, and only then would they return, pick up their abandoned plates and resume eating.

Sometimes the waiting got too much, and she'd hate him, but she couldn't. She couldn't bear the thought of being left alone, or even discarded. So she'd lie when he'd find her in tears. She'd tell him she missed doing something useful. 'Those classes?' he'd guess, his hands in his pockets, looking up at the sky, pretending to be at an utter loss. Ordinarily this would have made her laugh, but she was still teary-eyed.

'Do you think anyone would be bothered in a class for sex education? Sneha…Sneha, you can't still be obsessed with that.' He continued in some irritated affection, 'All of it is of no use—all these modern ideas corrupting our people. Old people deciding to marry. Men cavorting with men, women with women, I hear. This will just not do.' His voice was soft and dream-like.

Days later, as she stood by another lake, she would realize that evil came in softly, even seductively.

But at that time, she had heard him detail the moral corruption he saw everywhere. 'There's a place in Gujarat where they pay women to have someone else's babies. Is this a factory? We hold sex sacred, something private, only between a man and woman. A child is born and that is a gift of God. It is not something commercial.'

Sneha had never said a word to refute him. For now, he was after all the only one on her side, who comforted her, who listened to her. She'd listened to everyone else for so long. She thought of all the women who came to her—full of hope, flashy and laughing, craving for a child and frightened by their inability to have one. She thought of the girls, her students. Their way of giggling and nudging each other every time she described something. They were so inattentive too. And some would drop out often, saying they had to watch a film, or catch up on chores. They did not seem to want to be themselves.

Sometimes she'd cry more noisily, confused by her own reasons. It was his gentleness, even his casual dismissal of what she had once loved. She sobbed at her failure, at her fear of facing up to it, and Ghatge held her, smoothed her hair, and patted her face.

'Why would you want to waste time? And waste yourself this way?'

His eyes were glinting, they roved over her in a way that made her feel desirable. Then he pulled her sari end over her shoulders and said in a mock scolding way. 'If you want to come for drives with me, you need to stay warm.'

It was on these drives, with his one hand on the wheel, he'd pull her hand to his crotch and insist it remain there. He'd press it down harder and then press on the gas too, and they'd race down the city, taking the road that ran right through it— from Bandra, to Andheri, Malad and beyond. Then, as they stopped by the fishing boats of Vasai, he'd tell her of the plans he had. 'We should do something for our city. You know, do something.'

Ghatge was fond of those two words. He would make speeches looking up at the sky, at the city arranged around him and always end with those words. *Do something.* His speech in a mix of Marathi and English but those two words at the end, always spoken in English, or else, to him, his own words made no sense.

Some nights when they drove farther than before, out of the city, past the last villages caught in the half-empty forests, where the earth had been hacked up in places and not been built over, it seemed there were just the two of them in this vast land. Enclosed by the last trees still bending down, and far behind, the road that had brought them here.

'There is just so much possibility here in this silence,' he said, bending down to her, like the trees around them. 'In this silence, you won't bother about the petty creatures who come in your way. The person who stops you being you is you.'

'You should make more speeches,' she said, light-headed now.

The smell of jasmine was in the air. Of other flowers that she could not place. She who had always been so orderly and composed, now felt like twirling around. 'I am trying to only impress you, Sneha.'

In that unbelievable light of the moon, filtering through the ancient trees, she liked that he was flirting with her. She couldn't recall if anyone ever had. Most of all, she liked the night drives, the coffee she had. And he did not seem to mind the coffee in her breath when he kissed her. 'It tastes like the earth,' he said.

It was early morning when they returned once. A grey dawn had appeared in the city, falling slowly on the high-rises. Under the flyovers, the darkness still lingered. Those who slept were fidgeting as they huddled under their sacks. 'It isn't physical poverty,' he told her before he left, 'Poverty of mind is the first thing that has to go. One shouldn't live always in depression. That is poverty. All this talk of sex, you get it, it gets us nowhere.'

He was probably as tired as she was. He was rubbing his eyes, and yawning, and then he smiled thinly, his eyes retaining a faint gleam still. 'You are a good doctor; you first use your skills. Work in a good hospital, with a sophisticated operation theatre.'

'I am a radiologist,' she had bristled.

It made Ghatge hit his head repeatedly, admitting he was an idiot. Sneha smiled, a little hesitantly. Did this mean he did not know the first thing about her? Did he even care?

In the dim streetlight, she saw herself in the tinted glass of his gleaming car. She knew one more day had gone by and the only thing that had changed was that she had gotten older.

It made her keener to shake off time's passing. The days following, she completely lost track of time. He was her only marker. When he couldn't come, he'd call and ask her how her day had been. She told him of her patients, the things they wanted done.

He must have taken her to Panchgani just when the monsoon broke. He drove fast down the hill roads, taking the curves with a flourish, laughing as she fell against him time and time again. On the edge of a hill, he showed her the low red-brick building. A driveway broke through the hills and it led to an immense portico, Greek or Roman, Sneha couldn't tell. 'Here I will build a fancy hospital. It will have a special place for you.' Ghatge was charming, especially when he wove his dreams to include her. Sneha loved this about him.

They did not return to Mumbai that day. The industrialist, Ghatge's friend, had invested a lot in this region. The hospital was his too, an act of charity, he said, his small framed glasses slipping off his cherubic face as he smiled at Sneha. He insisted they stay, and made the best room available for them.

It was at that party that she met Dr Joshi. His soft 'hello' made Sneha nearly lose her grip on her glass but she held on. Of course, she knew who he was. His realistic portrayals of Mumbai had made him fashionable—and as was rumoured, very rich—but he was also unpopular in some circles. He showed up the city's underclass, its unsavoury side. There had been recent vocal protests at his depictions—Sneha had read the letters to editors in almost every newspaper—especially at a time when attempts were being made to make the city investor friendly. It was to be India's answer to Shanghai, or even Singapore. No wonder, she thought, fighting off a sneer from her face, it had driven him into hiding. She had had no idea he was here in Panchgani.

He must have seen her half-scornful smile, for he said smiling somewhat vaguely, his eyes looking away from her, 'You should be careful you know, Sneha.' He didn't say more. She did not ask him to explain either. For he looked lovingly down at the whisky in his hand and then his eyes drifted towards Ghatge, who had moved over to them, his coat, with its faux-gold buttons, a size too small for him.

His eyes rested on the way Ghatge's hand rested briefly on her shoulder, before he again moved away. And though Ghatge might have believed that his hand on her waist, the way he squeezed her flesh were unnoticeable, Sneha knew the doctor had seen everything, for he said next, more softly. 'I might have painted you, but there's something in you now, Sneha…'

The way Dr Joshi had spoken filled her with horror. Her mood, so high moments ago, now fell at a dizzying speed, till she saw her happiness crumple, break into shards and fall to the floor. For everyone to stamp on, butt out unthinkingly. Some minutes later, she caught sight of herself in the restroom mirror. She laughed and couldn't stop herself, even when someone banged on her door in some concern. 'Am all right. Go away.' She cackled and went on laughing. She had, after all, let herself forget, not just herself, but her dreams too. Forgetting is a sin, or worse, a crime.

She had become like them, all the ladies she mocked, and

scoffed at. She was as plastic and brittle like them, throttled by society around them. There seemed nothing she believed in. For a while, it had been good to be airy, to make false promises, to stop thinking for a while that the responsibility to do good, and be good, rested on her shoulders no longer. But she had blanked herself out in the search for happiness.

Sneha walked out, through the big French windows, down the manicured lawns, past the iron railings, down the hill, to where the lake shimmered. She walked on, with unseeing eyes, the blood drumming in her head. The water felt gentle against her feet. Her eyes felt bloodshot, and the moon was bigger than it ever was. There were the heaving tent lanterns not too far away and they looked bigger now. The dark heads of the boulders around watched her like mocking furry creatures. She saw shadowy outlines of people, not too far away. They were rising as one and heading for the gate. They would protest right outside the industrialist's house, not let any of the guests out. And the thought made her run, stumble on the thick weeds and then run with no pause, with no further thought, right into the dark inviting waters of the lake.

The divers were called in the next morning and for hours they scoured the lake, plunging into its depths, or peering into it as they waded out in their rafts. It was in the afternoon that the local television channels announced the suicide of the city's well-known radiologist, Sneha Desai.

For Vasudha: A Room of Her Own

The doorbell rang in a series of loud bursts and Pooja knew she had never heard it ring that way before. She saw the transducer slip from Vasudha's hands. A moment ago, Vasudha had heaved herself up on the high chair. Her other arm stretched towards the bed where Pooja lay, her kurta pulled up, the drawstrings of her churidar loosened to expose her stomach.

As the sound stopped, Vasudha made an awkward lunge for the transducer. She caught it just as it threatened to slide down her knee before the bell rang again, loud and insistent. Pooja saw Vasudha's face turn a spectral white as she jumped down from the high chair, holding her distended stomach.

Hide. Under the bed. Vasudha gestured as the dim light turned the room purple and dark blue. Her arm moved, the vase on the table lurched and fell to the floor, its shattering coinciding with the doorbell. It was a shorter ring but repeated this time, once and then again. Whoever was there was determined to hang around.

Vasudha's grip was hard on Pooja's wrist as she urged her down. On the floor, shattered glass lay amidst small pools of water. Pooja's feet scrunched on them. She had just ducked under the bed when she heard the hard thumping on the door. The echo of the ring whirred in her ears and she heard Vasudha's warning again.

Stay there. And mind the glass.

Pooja's eyes followed Vasudha, who was now casting a wild quick glance around the room. Vasudha ineffectually kicked away a few glass pieces. Shifting position, Pooja pulled down the sheet where it hung from the bed, and through its translucence she could see Vasudha rearranging her dress, still gesturing, quickly and softly. Over her head, the bed moved once.

Vasudha half closed the door that led to the outer office. She checked herself in the mirror affixed to it, and then Pooja heard her urgent whisper hissed across the space between them. *Good. I can't see you. Stay that way.*

Pooja bunched herself even more tightly, flicking away a piece of glass. She wondered if she had been too awkward, too clumsy. If there was a foetus inside her, hanging onto all those cords and ropes, maybe it had loosened its grip, maybe it would soon dissolve into clots and float away, through and out of her. She would no longer be pregnant. Then a heavy, sad thought filled her head: she was not pregnant.

She heard Vasudha's loud, cheerful: *Coming, Coming.* Her heavy steps shook the floor near Pooja. Then the door chain slipped with a click and was followed by a piano somewhere bursting into a joyful *Happy Birthday*.

The voice that came next froze Pooja. *Ghatge.* He had to know Sneha was dead. And the next moment, the truth struck her with blinding clarity—of course, he was here because she was dead.

Pooja made herself go very still, even her breathing. The lamplight moved over the glass pieces, the bed sheet flapped, and the table fan whirred, moved away, before turning its face towards her again.

Whenever the fan turned away, snatches of the conversation outside came to her. Ghatge was asking Vasudha why she had taken so long and Pooja heard her reply, 'I was clearing Madam's files.'

Pooja knew he had stopped to ask this. Perhaps somewhere near the low table with its pile of magazines. She had been in this office, and this inner chamber, so many times she knew most things about it.

She could almost see Ghatge standing there in that outer office, his knee knocking against the glass table that faced the mounted television. There was the low couch against the wall, the beautiful paintings and the lush green carpet. The air-conditioning unit was next to the couch. Pooja never sat on the couch as she waited for Vasudha. Rather she sat on the steel, hard-backed chairs just adjacent to the front door. It was from here, on her first day to meet Sneha Desai, that she had seen the doctor cry with her face half hidden behind her computer. The doctor sat in her swivel chair, her head in her hands. She had then fallen forward on the table, her shoulders heaving.

After that day, Sneha had rarely been around. She forgets her appointments, Vasudha would say casually and fill in for her. Vasudha examined Pooja with more assurance, even with a gentleness Madam never had. And now Sneha Desai was dead.

That night, the phone in Sneha Desai's office had rung several times. Vasudha had finally shut the door in the other office before she continued her work of setting the machine up, getting Pooja ready. Vasudha had been Sneha's assistant for nearly three years and this, coupled with Vasudha's incomplete degree in radiology, meant she knew as much as Sneha did. Doctor, Pooja would call her, and Vasudha would laugh in a wobbly way as her old dreams resurfaced. 'More a pharmacist.'

Ghatge was speaking in low, urgent tones to Vasudha. Pooja knew the tone, it was one he adopted when he had to send Mahesh on an important errand. She could hear Vasudha's hard breathing. Then Pooja heard Vasudha explain in a nonchalant way, 'The files are too many and there's much to clear. Most have to be returned to patients. And then the outstanding claims.'

Pooja saw Ghatge's feet in strapped sandals, the swish of the curtains and Vasudha's warning. *Watch out.* Ghatge's startled hiss followed almost at once. He stepped away gingerly; a few glass pieces crackled under the leather of his sandals.

'Yes, so that's what I was doing,' Vasudha said coolly as she walked ponderously in, nudging away a shard or two with her sandalled foot.

'Vasudha, be careful, be very careful.'

'Sahib?'

Pooja could tell it wasn't the concern in Ghatge's voice that brought in that uncertain tone in Vasudha, but something else.

'I know your condition.' His feet moved closer to Vasudha's and Pooja heard her gasp, as his arms rose. She understood that Ghatge now held Vasudha by the shoulders. 'I know your condition.'

Vasudha's behind was pressed hard against the bed, and her voice was strangled. 'Yes, so?'

He let her go then, and Pooja felt the relief in the room, in the way the bed creaked. She saw the way Vasudha's fingers crunched over the translucent bed sheet, then relaxed, almost as if she were reassuring Pooja.

'You say nothing.'

'I don't want to.'

'You say nothing about me and Sneha. Madam was a good friend. You say nothing more. And keep looking. The file, you know...'

Ghatge's voice was steely and cold. Pooja went very still. All the stories were true, then. Sneha did have an affair with Ghatge. That confirmation sent several thoughts tripping through Pooja. How could she have? But how could Ghatge? He was married. She bit her lip to stop herself from gasping. Poor Gauri Tai.

He stepped back and his foot caught on a shard of glass. It broke, and a piece flicked off right towards Pooja's foot. She moved against the wall, knuckles on her mouth. She saw Vasudha bend low, moving the shards with her foot. They exchanged a quick look from under the bed, one of shared fear and something else too. Pooja felt a new nonchalance. She'd never be afraid of Ghatge any more. If her hiding place was discovered, she would stand up for Vasudha. Then she went colder still with a new realization: it was not her, but Vasudha, her friend, who was pregnant, and who was now speaking up, her voice deliberately light.

'Are you here to threaten me, Ghatge Sahib, late at night?' He laughed, low and soft. 'No. Just giving you advice. To help me. To not endanger yourself in your condition.

'Yes, I know,' Ghatge went on, his voice low and mellow, a tone when he was at his most sinister and Vasudha was only learning a truth Pooja knew already, 'Sneha did tell me.' The fan whirred all around, eating up his soft laughter. The papers in the open file on the table flapped over slowly. 'Yes, Sneha had a nice way of telling me your story. And the reason I am here is that I won't tell people your story, your being pregnant, if you don't say a word. And do as I say.'

'What do I have to say? You think...'

There was a strangled sound, she couldn't finish. 'Just telling you,' said Ghatge leaning over Vasudha. Pooja saw how their feet met under the bed, he was almost stamping on hers. His toes were curved inward; she knew then that he was very tense. 'I want the story to end. And the file to be found. I know it's there. Don't try anything smart.'

There was the sound of glass again as he stepped back. The bed was narrow, rising at the head in a rectangular recline.

Ghatge's feet were still lit up in the narrow circle of the lamp. He was looking around, taking in everything in the room.

On the table, next to where Sneha Desai had her ultrasound machine, was a photo of Ramakrishna Desai, the labour leader and his wife—Sneha's uncle and aunt. One portion of the wall overlooking the bed had Sneha's framed degrees and the vase had stood on a high stool just by it, flanked by a lamp.

'The vase broke,' she heard Vasudha say, when the silence got too long.

'This is such a mess. Did anyone hear?'

'No, there's no one around.'

There was a thin clinking noise and Pooja heard his key ring fall. For the briefest of seconds, she had a glimpse of him. His neat sideburns, the moustache curving down, and the square chin. If he turned around ever so slightly, she would be right in his line of vision. Then something else drooped down, slowly to the floor, and sighing heavily.

It was Vasudha's distended stomach. Everything else dissolved as the evidence registered itself again in Pooja's eyes. It was Vasudha who was pregnant and not she.

'All right, clear this up. And remember.'

'There is no point your threatening me, Sahib. She's dead, and I have to look for a job anyway.'

'And who will give you one, eh Vasudha?' Pooja saw through the translucent sheet the way his hand streaked across Vasudha's cheek, and the way his hand brushed her stomach.

'Take care.'

There was the swing of the door, the soft tread on the carpet, the occasional crunch of glass. And then the other door opening, the chirpy beginnings of *Happy Birthday* and then silence. Vasudha took a long time coming back; Pooja was already picking up the glass shards, using two ends of an old newspaper.

Vasudha did not look at her. Pooja waited for her to speak

but she let out an involuntary shriek as her hand scraped carelessly against an exposed glass shard. As Pooja lifted her fingers to suck in the blood, she saw Vasudha still stood looking uncertain, and her eyes had a glazed look.

'Why are you quiet? Couldn't you have told me?'

Pooja's tone was accusing. Then she saw the tears in Vasudha's glasses, and her trembling hand. Vasudha's eyes dropped and she reached for Pooja's hand. A spot of blood now showed on her loose half-green kurta. 'I had to hear it from him,' Pooja went on, her tone softer now.

'Yes...sorry.' Vasudha had lost her earlier insouciance.

She was crying in relief as they sat in the front room. As Vasudha rested with her head against the couch seat, Pooja gave her the food she had got her in two small stainless steel boxes. Pooja watched as Vasudha opened the box and, rolling up the appam, dipped it lavishly in the coriander chutney and ate in quick sharp bites.

'That man made me hungry,' Vasudha said finally.

It made Pooja laugh and then she couldn't stop. 'I never realized. Here you were getting fatter. And I thought it was my cooking you couldn't resist.'

'I can't. Everyone says that too.' Vasudha nodded, munching seriously. 'That's why you are getting so many orders. Soon your catering business will take off. And you will have no time at all. Maybe the stress is affecting ovulation. Tell me...?' she asked, sitting up straight as if reminded of something, 'Have you had your period on time?'

'It's not about me.' Pooja was careful to push her back gently.

'No, it's not all right. I don't know what to do now. Madam had promised to help but now she's gone.'

She began crying again. Pooja held her, not knowing what to say, for a thousand thoughts rushed through her. Vasudha wasn't married. Then, through her sobs, Vasudha told her more: how Sneha had known everything and had tried to dissuade her. And Vasudha, after vacillating for long, had finally made up her mind. 'I told her there are so many women who come to you. I've seen them long for a baby. I can't give this one up.'

Pooja knew a bit about desperation. She inwardly berated herself. She had been so immersed in her own work and worries that she had not cared much either. There was all the evidence of Vasudha's pregnancy she had missed. Vasudha had thrown up once, right at the station. She had retched over the platform while some other women watched in sympathy. Someone had offered her water, another her handkerchief. When Vasudha threw up again in the office, or claimed to be too tired, she was always dismissive of Pooja's worries about her. No other women would have missed such obvious signs but Pooja had, and she had only her motherless self to blame for her silly obliviousness. A girl usually learnt all this from her mother. In turn, Vasudha would look at Pooja and say breezily. 'You will be fine too. I can see nothing wrong with you. Maybe you need to spend some time with your husband.'

And Pooja knew that was precisely what she did not want to do. She followed every cookery show possible, looked up YouTube videos on her smartphone and read magazines, especially those that carried detailed recipes. It helped her English too. As for Mahesh, he came home late, they talked a bit, and he ate whatever she offered him and promptly fell asleep. She would watch him sleeping with a happy and sad face, before she returned to the window. Standing there for a long time always made her cry.

Mahesh wasn't the drinking kind either. Pooja sometimes rolled over and smelled his breath. Once he had even come awake, smiled, and patted her shoulder. 'Go to sleep. Tomorrow is another long day.' So, the times Vasudha would prod, ask her, Pooja usually had no answer. 'He comes home late,' she would mumble. Other times, seeing Pooja's lost look, Vasudha would be reassuring. 'Don't worry. There's always a right time.'

Now Vasudha reclined on the couch as Pooja cleaned up. The glass pieces were sharp and every so often she had to stop to pull out pieces that lodged in her kurta and suck her fingers when she nicked herself. Vasudha, now tired, mumbled her answers. The files? Yes, she'd sort them out and return them. There were some very old files too, some even from before Sneha Madam's time. Madam herself hadn't bothered, though she had told Vasudha that there were some important papers in them too. And this clinic? It was part of the mill building and the union was still fighting the builders over that. Sneha Madam hadn't been bothered.

'And you?' Pooja finally asked, watching the blood drip from a long cut on her index finger. 'And you?' She asked again. The clock ticked slowly, some of the glass pieces fell softly through the bin, the fan moved again, the pages shifted. She heard the low cheep of a mouse somewhere. If she turned, she might see it scurry under the carpet. She shook Vasudha by the knee, and at last she replied. 'I don't know. Perhaps move to a different city.'

'He won't marry you?'

'I won't marry him,' Vasudha said, looking up, a fierceness in her expression. After a silence, as she lay back again, Pooja prodded. 'Vasudha?'

'I'll be fine. I came to Mumbai to do well in life and it was okay. I don't want to go back to the village. I will find a place to stay.'

Then she stood up, pointed with a touch of disdain at Pooja's bleeding fingers. 'Let's get you some bandages.'

~

Neera still hadn't recovered from her shock. A month ago, Sneha's death had been all over the papers. No one would miss that: a few paras in the local pages mentioning how the well-known radiologist Sneha Desai had committed suicide. Her body had been fished out from the Dhom Dam Lake in Panchgani.

But Raina hadn't let her wallow in her shock. Now Neera saw Raina's number flash on her cell phone again and knew she would answer it. Minutes later, Raina herself would come over, flushed and excited like always. Raina would apologize in her high voice, but that evening Neera sensed no trace of the usual laughter in her voice. Neera then knew she'd be asked precisely the things, she, Neera never wanted to answer.

Neera sighed, keeping her thoughts to herself. Raina had been more talkative these days. It wasn't the excitement of working on a book with Neera that was doing it. The girl had all these mother problems. Mohini, useless woman that she was, and still not thankful that she had been granted a reprieve with that medical miracle, still refused to communicate with her daughter. There were all these things Raina couldn't ask her mother and so here she was, always with Neera.

Neera looked at the photo Raina had returned. It stood there on the mantelpiece as a reminder at times—it all depended on her mood—of her old foolishness. Most times, however, the photo made her feel nothing, it just made Neera resent Mohini less. So much so that she'd find herself often speaking up for Mohini, when Raina wallowed in self-pity.

'She never had time for my father too,' Raina had said soon enough, that evening.

'But the self-sufficiency you have comes from her, Raina,' Neera cajoled.

She said no more understanding now that Mohini had always wanted attention for herself. Neera glanced at the newspaper and a photo there reminded her of something. In Suhel Kolhatkar, perhaps, Mohini had indeed met her match and she had let herself forget it, forget him. And so Neera told

Raina the story from another time that had once amused them all.

'Suhel, he's recently come back I believe. His father's not been well. Once Suhel waited for long outside Mohini's house, the one your grandfather built in Bandra. Then finally, the police had to be called. His father was a decorated army officer, serving in the UN, so it was all hushed up, of course.'

'That sounds like a wonderful story.'

They were both looking at him now, in the newspaper. The court had granted Suhel a reprieve. It had also reprimanded the state government and the city for not framing rules in the case of airspace violation. 'If there are no laws, what did the defendant violate?' The court asked.

Raina stared at the picture, her eyes scanned over the story. The picture showed Suhel looking a trifle abashed at the television reporters pouring all over him, training a camera on his face. He had apologized before them again. He agreed there needed to be stricter laws. For him, it had been a memorable afternoon spent with his father. A real high, he had said, and this had apparently made everyone laugh. Raina lifted the paper up for a closer look. She murmured, 'My mother would have gotten bored of him in no time.'

But then she didn't look away, nor did she put away the paper. 'I wish they would report on serious things rather than something sensational. And just because the guy is good-looking.'

'Oh! Good-looking, you say?' Neera picked up her glasses and peered down at the photo again, before she confirmed. 'That's true. He is.'

'You didn't realize?' Raina asked, this time the breathless laughter was back in her voice.

'Maybe he's not my type,' Neera said. That made Raina giggle again.

She took the newspaper with her to the kitchen. Neera

had just mentioned that Pooja had cut her hands badly in a few places, and might need help. 'Though like always, she will refuse help...that girl can be stubborn,' Neera murmured.

Raina stared at the photo as she walked into the brightly lit kitchen. It overlooked the salt pans, and sometimes the smell of the sea far below drifted in. The way people could disagree about what made a person good-looking always intrigued her. It was easy enough to dismiss someone as ugly but appreciation about good looks always came grudgingly. Or perhaps Neera had old-fashioned ideas. These days—now that they were working on her memoirs—Neera laughed whenever the subject of Ramakrishna Desai came up, though there would be that wistful look as her eyes caught the photo. Then Raina would tell her she was lucky. Love vanished far too quickly otherwise.

Pooja had a cloth around her fingers as she gingerly lifted the pan of boiling water. 'Here, let me do it,' Raina said. As Pooja demurred, it was Raina who pulled her away with some mock irritation. And then to the sound of pouring tea, she noticed Pooja fingering the newspaper, flipping it over and then the way her eyes stilled on the photo.

'What do you think of him, Pooja?'

Raina placed the mugs on a tray, then called to Pooja over her shoulder. 'Come and join us and tell us if you think he's handsome. It took Neera Tai some time to admit it.'

And Raina laughed even more as she saw Pooja blush first before saying hesitatingly, 'True, he is. The photo's a bit blurry though, and he isn't like Shah Rukh Khan.'

And because Pooja took most things very seriously, she went on. 'He seems tall too.'

Then they were sitting around in Neera's small living room, and Suhel appeared on television again. The reporters asked him what he thought, what his plans were and it was Pooja who remained serious. She hadn't ever seen anyone quite like him. He had grey in his hair, a rather rugged face, and his eyes crinkled as he smiled down at a woman journalist.

'Do you think we are being too frivolous, Pooja?'

Raina had to ask her that twice before she turned her eyes slowly back towards them.

'No. I was just listening to him.'

'Yes, I am impressed at how much your English has picked up,' Neera smiled.

Then Pooja smiled. 'I guess I will never speak like him though. So polished, and with an accent.'

'You'd do better, my dear.' Neera was happy to see Pooja smiling. As with Raina, Pooja too had been on her mind for, since Sneha's death, Neera wasn't sure of what to do about Pooja. She had, after all, gone to Sneha's on Neera's suggestion. At least the catering business was keeping her happy. She worked long hours and much too hard. Then Neera's attention turned to Raina who had picked her bag up, ready to leave. She hugged Neera and even Pooja in the effusive way she had. 'It's so nice to be with you, Tai.'

'I wish you'd settle down, Raina.'

'There's time for her to do all that.' Pooja chided, smiling. 'And in any case, one doesn't need to be married. There's always some way of being happy.'

She saw Suhel was still on the television screen. Some agitating journalists were upset, screaming into their mikes about why he had been let off. Pooja stared at him as he smiled, shook his head, apologizing all over again. Neera, watching her, knew she'd have to find other ways of helping Pooja.

'Tell me, Pooja,' she spoke up now, 'has that room of yours been let yet?'

'No…' Pooja looked away from the television, and as the sun flashed on glass, leaving golden squares on the floor, an idea came to her. She intended to ask no one's permission for what she had in mind. Not Mahesh's, and not Ghatge Sahib's either.

~

They were so much like siblings. Vasudha felt a funny contraction in her heart, watching Pooja and Mahesh. It was a blessing to have them around, to arrange the memorial event for Sneha Madam. Vasudha found it strange to manage the funeral and then the memorial events. It made her feel Sneha Desai was still very much around.

If Sneha had known she had so many friends, perhaps she would never have committed suicide. But Vasudha blamed herself too. She had been too preoccupied with her own growing self. She was finding it hard to manage her own temper. Only a few minutes ago, she had snapped at Pooja for the flowerpots had not been arranged the way she wanted. And the poor girl still had some of her fingers bandaged, the ones she had cut from picking up the glass pieces.

Vasudha now hated herself for snapping at her. Her pregnancy had foisted another self upon her. She was relieved to have Pooja around, for things had turned busier for her. Pooja had just been offered a contract by an event management company; this was a way her small catering service could get established. Vasudha smiled in a conciliatory way at Pooja as their eyes met. Pooja scrimmaged in the wings, arranging the flowers and lighting up the incense sticks before placing them on the low table in front of Sneha Madam's garlanded photo. Mohini Gupta was scheduled to come any time but she was running late.

Mahesh hurried around, running an eye over everything. Goodness, Vasudha thought, the man was never still. He was the one who arranged the chairs in perfect order. He had got the bottling company to put up the drinking water unit, then he had also ensured that the fans were in working order. But the more the two of them did, the more there remained to be done. There were all the contingencies that no one could never account for.

Like George Mathew coming in, especially when he knew he was not wanted. He wiped the sweat from his brow, undid the first button on his shirt and pulled his collar down over his back to air himself. Then he saw Vasudha and came over, smiling in that weak manner he had. She longed to slap him then. It wasn't that she blamed him for this pregnancy but that she was irritated by the choice she had made. The man had a weak laugh, and he slouched. How on earth did he manage to sell those medicines for his company? These days they were arguing too much.

It was only minutes before the memorial meeting was to begin, and the first guests had begun drifting in, when Pooja caught them in a furious argument.

'We should get married. I am willing,' she heard the man wheedle.

'I don't want to get married. And to you? Do you think it will help living in a house in Vasai or somewhere far off? On your salary?'

Vasudha held her stomach. Pooja knew she probably felt the baby kick inside her. And then the reality hit her. Now that Sneha Madam was gone, she sensed Vasudha's desperation and understood her stubbornness. Sneha had written to Vasudha's landlord requesting an extension of her lease. But now that she was dead, that old man would soon hound her out. Even if she didn't want to be hooked into marriage, there was the baby.

George Mathew slammed his helmet down on the floor, picked it up and walked out. His shoulders resumed their automatic slouch as he faced the world. Vasudha was in tears when he left and Pooja squeezed her shoulders. 'We could do something. We will.'

'What?' That was when Vasudha snapped again. 'Things haven't happened in your life and you think...'

The very next moment Vasudha regretted what she said, but Pooja only smiled, 'Maybe you're a size too big for George now.' Vasudha's eyes widened at that before Pooja, slapping her gently on the shoulder said, 'It's all right. I am supposed to forgive you, the state you are in. But I do have a plan.'

The room next to theirs had been empty ever since Maria had left. It was Ghatge Sahib who had decided such things for them. Mahesh deferred to him and Pooja did too, by default. But she clearly remembered the scene in Sneha Desai's office, and now she felt a contempt for the man. She rubbed a hand over her face, as if erasing the scene. She was prepared. The room was ready for letting out.

She would, of course, ask Ghatge, but it would be a formality, she thought as she watched Mahesh escort someone in—she wished Mahesh wouldn't be so obsequious—and she knew she would bring him around as well. The next moment she saw why he had bent forward so, the way he reached forward with a hand to help someone up the steps to the auditorium. It was an elderly gentleman who looked oddly familiar in a way that made Pooja frown, and he was with Rosie, Richard's mother, who held him by the other elbow and pointed to some chairs.

The next moment, she saw the man behind them, a part of the group. Pooja felt her breath die away. As the realization slowly sank in, her lips turned dry and her heart slowed down as well. For he was the man in the newspaper. And on television too. It was him all right. She knew his peppered hair, crinkly eyed look, his way of dressing, with that vest inside a chequered shirt.

'Pooja?'

The voice called her so unexpectedly that she felt a total blankness first. She knew Ghatge's voice, even if for some weeks now he hadn't called her. She bent and touched his feet out of habit. When she looked up, she saw he looked tired, there were dark circles around his eyes. She knew the newspapers were giving him a hard time, all of them asking him about his relationship with Sneha. Every time he had spluttered that one explanation: 'It was a professional connection.'

'Nice to see you here, Ghatge Sahib. And on time too.'

'Yes, she was a professional colleague.' That word again, and yet she saw the tiredness, the emptiness in his face. Even if he professed not to have loved her, for some moments, for some time surely, there had been love. She felt she understood him and had not a moment to waste.

'I wanted to ask you something quickly. Vasudha...' and she pointed to where Vasudha was, among the audience, welcoming the guests in. Pooja also saw, from the corner of her eye through the wings, the man in the newspaper now helping seat his father, and they were smiling quietly at something. The curtains brushed against her arm, and behind her she could feel the low table with the photo. The flowers smelt good, and she was reassured.

'She needs this room urgently, and so she should have it.'

'The room?' Ghatge Sahib's head bent towards her. He had lost hair and there was new silver on his sideburns.

'Our room to rent in the chawl.'

His lips set in a stern line, but he couldn't hold on to it. 'She is being turned away by her landlord, and now...'

He stared and she looked up at him, then his eyes dropped and he asked, 'What happened to your fingers?'

She had not expected that, and looking down, past her fingers, at the floor and at his feet, she remembered the night again. 'The glass that broke, I helped clear it up.'

Their eyes met, and Ghatge knew what Pooja knew. She saw the strain in his eyes and how they widened for the merest fraction of a second. He nodded, then moved away, past her and stepped onto the stage. At the table, he paused, folded his hands before Sneha Desai's garlanded photo. Then his hands fidgeted for a moment with a kurta button, but his face still gave nothing away as he moved to sit among the audience, right in the front row.

Pooja peeked through the curtains and looked for the man again, Suhel Kolhatkar. They were all looking serious. Mohini Madam, in her light musical voice, was telling them about Sneha, and Pooja knew Neera would speak too and then others would follow.

She couldn't look away. She couldn't stop herself. There was no longer the habitual voice that always berated her to behave.

Suhel, who had come with his father and Rosie, was already bored. The hall's high ceiling was held up by impressive wooden beams. Suhel noticed its interesting pentagonal shape, the curved high windows with their old-fashioned grilles. It was his father who had wanted to attend the memorial, and Suhel had agreed to drive him and Rosie after Mohini had called and said he must. She always sounded excited these days, filling up the new lease of life given to her with too much chatter. Suhel felt the kind of happiness for her that one feels for old friends. His eyes drifted to Raina too, who sat some rows ahead. She had done up her hair in a French plait.

Suhel was just stifling a yawn when he saw her. She had stepped away from the wings and was exchanging a smile with a heavily pregnant woman. Suhel must have gasped for his father turned to look at him. He knew something strange had happened. Every day he had wondered about her, every day he had thought about the painting. It had just so happened that for some moments, the painting had slipped from his mind, and then he had finally seen her: the woman in Dr Joshi's painting.

Mahesh Takes a Joyride

The longest day of Mahesh's life began at the crack of dawn. Ghatge had called several times the night before to make sure that Mahesh had got the instructions right. Ghatge hadn't let him speak at all, pausing only once to ask if Gauri Tai had called. Not even to ask, Mahesh noted with bitterness, if he had been home, if he had had time to sleep. Ghatge had told him the words he must use, for it was to be made clear to Dr Joshi, in no uncertain terms, that he must stay quiet. 'The doctor first, and then the hotel. Sort it out. Get it?' Of course, Mahesh got it all right. Threatening people was what he was good at. Ghatge Sahib had said that he had had enough of the doctor; that Dr Joshi had a habit of always being where he was not wanted. Ghatge had not elaborated. All Mahesh knew was that Ghatge had forgotten his promise once again. The one thing Mahesh had his heart on—the yellow Mercedes-Benz that he longed to drive on his own, down the city's streets. Especially in the late hours of the night, when the streets were emptied of all cars and people. In one hour, Mahesh knew, he could easily drive from Vasai to Colaba. Faster than even Ghatge claimed to have done it.

Mahesh rode his motorbike towards the chawl. That early morning, it looked particularly grey, stained and ugly, older than the buildings around it and already an eyesore. Even if he called the chawl—a mishmash of buildings huddled close to each other—home, it deserved to be pulled down. It deserved a high-rise in its place, as tall as the other new ones—in Parel, Tardeo and Worli. But this decrepit building was also where Dr Joshi had his clinic and where he still lived on the third floor. The two doors at the very end were his, right where the corridor turned right. The wall which separated it from the old mill was now broken in places where the new mall had come up. Mahesh came down the sloping bridge that led away from the station, the boards of the high-end shops flashing at him every time he came up as the road rose again and became uphill. And closer still, on the sidewalks, he saw the people sleeping. He saw the stacks of newspapers bundled and lined up to be delivered, the dogs foraging in the bins, the trash scattered everywhere. Then, when he least expected it, he caught the whiff of jasmine, the fragrance like an invisible small cloud making a space for itself somewhere above the sidewalk. Mahesh drew in his breath deeply, like someone starving. He noticed the round cane baskets left by the road, the flowers strewn where a basket had tilted over on its side, its thin newspaper covering cracked open.

Mahesh slowed and as his growling motorcycle eased to a hum, he circled over a sidewalk crack and stooped under the awning to pick up some of the scattered jasmine flowers, holding them for seconds in his clenched fist. He wished once again for the yellow luxury car that Ghatge Sahib was so possessive about.

Minutes later, Mahesh parked near the gate, and felt the gun close to his heart. He could hear the drip of water from a leaking tap, and knew that soon his wife, Pooja, would be out to fill her buckets. His hands brushed the flowers in his pocket and he imagined himself leaving the flowers in a heart-shaped pattern just outside her door, in a line down the corridor outside, where the scratch marks left by Vasudha's old luggage stroller he had ferried up only a week ago, were still fresh. And Vasudha, all-knowing, prying woman that she was, would know then he had been there. He didn't want to run into her again.

Mahesh's eyes ran past the shuttered windows in every room, and when he saw a shadow flit in the darkness—the milk boy waiting for him—Mahesh knew he was on time. He ran a hand down his sweat-entangled hair, and at last he smiled, a thin grim smile that erased the silly grin on the milk boy's face. He held out his hand for the milk packets, the blue fluorescent colour on them gleaming over the white. On that floor, the doctor's rooms were the only ones occupied at all hours. 'Off you go.'

But the boy lingered, his eyes looked over Mahesh with a strange interest. Mahesh pulled him roughly by the sleeve, then pushed the gun hard against his waist.

'Get lost before...'

The boy looked frightened for the first time. His legs were trembling as he got on his bicycle but Mahesh leaned over the balcony, unrelenting, lifting a hand just once when his long scarf fell over his eye. The bicycle wobbled, the basket with other milk packets shook unsteadily before the boy righted himself, riding away fast as he could.

The doctor answered on the first knock, almost as if he had been waiting. Mahesh barged in, gun held chest high. But one milk packet that the boy had left by the doctor's door caught on the rusty door hinges. Mahesh cursed, tried to retrieve it, and the cold dew turned his hands clammy. He kicked the packets aside, and his other hand found the torch in his pocket. He gripped it tight, and as its light came on with a click, the doctor fell back.

Some jasmine flowers fell out as Mahesh advanced, taking his time. 'This is a warning.' In that still undecided early morning, the rasp in his tone sounded hesitant, broken by the fragrance of jasmine.

Dr Joshi, a small, thin man in old-fashioned gold-rimmed spectacles, was startled.

The light from the torch rose in a circle, sliding from one end of the wall to the floor, lighting up the doctor's paint-splotched shirt. He lifted a hand now to shield his eyes. His glasses had thick lenses, and one eye seemed bigger than the other.

'Ah yes, I remember. You came with your wife once.'

The doctor's voice was thin, and crackled like a short-wave radio station. Mahesh took in the oblong table, strewn with papers. He heard the flutter of pigeons, and it was then that he saw the canvases. Some hanging on walls, others stacked in various stages of disarrangement, lined on a table, or against a cupboard, a couple on a low divan at the other end. And Mahesh knew nothing had changed since the time of his last visit, in vastly different circumstances.

The doctor's paintings had become even harder to understand. Faces in macabre, bright colours, twisted in odd shapes. Buildings he had once known but now changed. Mahesh saw windows stuffed with skeletal faces, he saw flowers with gargoyle faces on them, insects that roamed the streets ape-like. It was just like the time he had come with Pooja, and he took an involuntary step back.

But the faces found him everywhere. And caught in a circle of golden light, he saw two faces, instantly familiar. The two canvases were next to each other, placed against the wooden legs of an old rocking chair, its arms half-broken and he knew them both. Even in shadow, his wife made him draw in a breath. Looking at her had always made Mahesh conscious of his own self. He knew he was ugly, his hands more like hairy paws, and his breath reeked hot and grimy. Even now, her face turned to him, she looked miles away. *Talk to me. Say something*, he'd said at these times and she had only looked at him, the expression on her face hard to understand.

'A painting,' the doctor laughed nervously, and Mahesh cocked his gun and turned a grim red-eyed gaze to the other painting. The face of a man that had never looked more alive as it did now, the left socket emptied of an eye that dangled on his cheek, but there was something about the scar that made Mahesh forget himself. 'Don't move,' he snarled and half-whispered to the doctor. Picking up the canvas, Mahesh took it towards the window where the thin golden light of a new morning came in. He peered for a closer look, brushing away his tangled hair in some impatience, and now he recognized the face.

Gerard D'Souza had been Mahesh's hero. The man who took on any dare, made him feel that anything was possible. It was Gerard who had given Mahesh his first earnings, the one who had taught him to use a knife, and dagger, whose every bidding he had once blindly followed, who gave him the most exciting jobs to do.

'This is the most important thing I ask you to do for me. Keep watch on this man.' Gerard had pointed to someone, a man whose photos were in every newspaper. And it was he, Mahesh, who had tailed the man, had seen him leave the chawl, and only then had he called Gerard up. Mahesh had been so fulsomely complimented then. There had been none of that abuse Ghatge now showered him with.

After the strike that killed the union leader, Gerard had gone underground. Every time Mahesh had spotted him, leaving a café all covered up or emerging secretly at night, he had tried to reach him, but Gerard would turn that scarred cheek towards him, point a menacing finger and warn him. 'Boy, don't ever tell anyone. Not if you value your life.'

Then, one night, Gerard had vanished.

Mahesh now heard the doctor's nervous laugh and he whirled around, gun in hand. The doctor raised both arms high and Mahesh said, irritated, 'I am not going to shoot you. But I will if you talk to any media guys.'

'Why...'

Mahesh screamed, 'Don't talk, don't talk.' The doctor winced, dropped his hands and waited. Mahesh looked around, his eyes found Gerard's empty and cruel face again, and he felt miserable and angry. Ghatge was trying to cover up his tracks. Like everyone, Mahesh too knew Ghatge had been in Panchgani, with his lady doctor friend, when she had committed suicide. Now the newspaperwalas were getting to Ghatge and he was getting Mahesh to help cover up his own tracks. All who knew of Ghatge's movements that day had to be silenced, or warned, and the doctor was on the list.

Mahesh tightened his fingers around the gun then fired at one of the milk packets lying forgotten on the floor. It made an odd pulpy noise, and a shower of purple and white rose like a fountain. Mahesh growled, 'Stay where you are.'

But the doctor was stretching, making a superhuman effort to lift the painting of Gerard's face and shove it aside.

'You can take it.' The doctor's voice wobbled before breaking into uncontrollable laughter. 'You can take the painting. Just the other day, I promised the other one to that man who flew around the city and got arrested.'

He was helplessly laughing now, bent over double. He hiccupped, Mahesh stood looking at him, before he said, 'Even if I didn't shoot you, you'd sure die laughing.'

The doctor straightened up, wiped his glasses, and then Mahesh added in a low, dry tone, 'It's better that way, for if you talk, you are a dead man.'

He turned, almost slipped where a sliver of milk made a riverine path for itself, and walked away. Running down, he fell onto his motorcycle like some long-lost love. The milk stuck to him, and he heard the buzz of a fly or two around him, as he rode away.

The confrontation had left Mahesh spent and the day wasn't done yet. At the station, he waited, flipping through the newspaper again, to read about the exhibition that was next on his agenda. It was one he was to disrupt in such a way the news would make its way into every newspaper and television channel and dislodge the controversy over Ghatge altogether. The board overhead his bench flashed awake. The next train, Mahesh read, was a few minutes late. Once it came rattling in, everyone slouching on the platform would come half-awake, the columns, the benches, the beams, would shake with new-found life.

Sooner or later Ghatge would call, for a report of his visit to the doctor. All Mahesh knew was that Ghatge wouldn't ever thank him. For he never did that, just as he never kept his promises. Ghatge had broken his promise twelve times already, and Mahesh kept count of such things. He did so want to drive the fancy new car, that Benz; instead, he was always sent on another errand, always given other chores to complete. It was always Mahesh who had to do it. For he was trusted.

But now Mahesh hated being so trusted. It was making him a liar, and it was all Ghatge's fault. Ghatge had warned him not to say a word of what had happened with his doctor friend, Sneha Desai, and because Mahesh couldn't lie to Gauri Tai any more, he had not taken her calls for some days. But he missed talking to her. She was the only one he knew who still lived in the village he once called home. His father had always been in the city for he worked in the now closed Jupiter Mill, and Mahesh only had the two donkeys which carried the clothes he washed by the river. Then his two donkeys died, one after the other, and it was Gauri Tai who had taken him in. She had put in a word to her husband, Ghatge, a man who was then getting things done in Mumbai. And, after some years, Mahesh found himself in the city as well. He had always wanted an orderly life and the Ghatges, husband and wife, had given it to him. It left him with no questions to ask. He had been so grateful that there had been no place for anything else, not even a wife. It was Gauri Tai who had arranged that.

Pooja came from as straitened circumstances as he did; everything was equal between them, Gauri Tai had assured him. But only Mahesh had seen the disinterest in Pooja's eyes. Pooja listens, she is a good girl, Gauri Tai had said, but Mahesh knew now. It was something that made her seem docile and too quiet to others but instead it was a watchfulness that Mahesh couldn't quite describe. As if the world fitted into how closely and minutely she saw it. It sometimes made him afraid.

'It is for your happiness, but ask us something,' Gauri Tai had said, as she suggested the marriage, and looking bashful, he had agreed. He'd marry Pooja, look after her, make her happy.

The truth was: Mahesh just did not know how to ask anyone anything. Now he felt, as the afternoon sun danced on his drooping eyelids, and he saw the waving palm fronds of a tree taller than the slanting roof of the station, that Gauri Tai in her village home would understand why he wanted a ride in that shiny new yellow Benz. He'd tell her of driving it all the way to his village. Past the last factory chimneys of Chembur, down the sad apartment buildings at Panvel, then speeding up as the road opened onto the highway that curved and looped and straightened only to lose itself in the hills till in no time he could see Chiplun below him, its houses red-roofed, white-walled in the morning, all sprinkled jewels at night.

Mahesh was dreaming of the yellow Mercedes-Benz when the train thundered in. The bench on which he sat jolted, bits of paper flew up and Mahesh sighed. The haze of sleep cleared, and as the train disgorged its few passengers—it was afternoon after all—Mahesh saw George Mathew coming up, the heat sharp on his crisp starched shirt, and glazing off his sunglasses.

Mahesh eyed him warily, he hadn't yet had the time to

think over something George Mathew had proposed. Since the time of their acquaintance, George Mathew had had weird ideas, one plan or another to make money. His most recent one had been very detailed: it was about letting out flats to people when these were between occupants. The city was crowded with people seeking temporary refuge, George Mathew had elaborated, and one could always make money out of them. To Mahesh, it was downright dangerous. Suppose these itinerant tenants just refused to leave? But George insisted that he well knew the ways of the world.

'Those who are new, temporary in every way, have new fears. You can bend them to your will. Relax,' he had said, patting Mahesh on the shoulder. Now he settled down next to Mahesh, pulled out a thin comb and brushed his long hair back. Then he ran it over his moustache, patted his lean cheeks, and began talking in a soft desultory voice. George talked of the empty apartment homes lying everywhere. Those abandoned, those just completed, and his voice rose and fell around Mahesh like sweet temptation. The effect it had on Mahesh was to believe he was in the gleaming new Benz again. He stretched his foot, imagining the car revving down the quiet roads.

'Did you think it over? Besides, they are not going to be in the city for long too.' George Mathew jogged Mahesh with an elbow. Mahesh felt a lurch, his head lolled to the side and he grinned sheepishly. George wiped his face with a towel and, his voice muffled by it, asked, 'Or are going to stay on here and work with the crook?'

It was the Benz, otherwise this insinuation on George's part would have made Mahesh leap to Ghatge's defence. A buzz sounded in his pocket and Mahesh knew it was Ghatge calling once again, but he couldn't answer, not with George Mathew sitting by him, his soft murmurs against his ear. He stared morosely down at his square stubby feet, ugly in their sandals. He was wrongly dressed to drive a luxury car. Everything was wrong about him.

'It's me who is the right partner for you,' George Mathew said somewhat sadly, as if he couldn't quite understand Mahesh's indecision. But George was evidently made of sterner stuff for he went on, his voice taking on a more persuasive tone, 'I have another idea, a really good one. You know that American guy...yes, yes, I know he's Indian but American now. He got into trouble for flying a helicopter all over the city without security clearances. We could do that too. Advertise, take orders in advance and just disappear. We don't even need a helicopter. Just some papers, and some photos.'

He gave Mahesh a dazzling smile as he finished but Mahesh couldn't quite make the leap of thought George had just done. Of course, George wanted to make a criminal out of him. George Mathew even had a definition for the right kind of criminal: 'If you take someone's life, you're the wrong kind of criminal. The right kind is one who breaks rules and gets ahead. All heroes are criminals in the beginning.'

George Mathew then moved on to Vasudha. He was always gushing about how Vasudha broke rules. How she had landed a good job and excelled at it, though all her certificates had been fudged. 'Now, once we are back in Kerala, she is going to open a clinic.'

Mahesh let his eyelids droop in pretended fatigue. He knew Vasudha and her ways. She had moved, just as Pooja had wished, into the room next to theirs in the chawl and he had helped Vasudha with her luggage. The room had given them an added income, but Mahesh now despaired—it seemed the room was doomed to always having short-term occupants. People left or were otherwise forced to leave. There was something false in the room and Vasudha made it more so. In the last month, she had become unrecognizable. She was fatter than ever, thanks to Pooja's ministrations, and she was also demanding. After all, she had George Mathew who, when not thinking up wild schemes or selling fake medicines, was at her beck and call.

Mahesh swatted away a fly, wishing he could dismiss such thoughts and George Mathew's words just as easily, but the fly came back time and again. When the phone rang for the fifth time, Mahesh knew he had to answer it. It was a number Mahesh did not recognize but he knew it was Ghatge refusing to give up.

A barrage of abuses came at him just as the train thundered into the platform. George Mathew rose, ran a hand to smooth his hair, his shirt, shook hands with him as if Mahesh was an important business associate, and then limbered up gracefully to catch the train. Mahesh waved joyfully, glad to see him go as Ghatge barked into his ear.

'What were you doing?'

Mahesh cleared his throat, 'Gone to pee.'

'Were you looking for a fancy bathroom?'

'No, but some...privacy.'

Ghatge laughed, short and abrupt, as if he could not help himself. Then he changed tack. 'Did Tai call you up?'

And this time Mahesh did lie. After all his lies to Gauri Tai, it was time Ghatge had a taste of it. 'Yes, she did.'

'What did you tell her?' Ghatge screamed, making no attempt to hide his panic, 'What did she ask?'

'I told her,' Mahesh said, taking his time, 'that I had not seen Sahib in ages.' Then he went on, 'It's true. I haven't seen you, her, nor my wife in ages.'

He spoke the words and the silence descended into his heart like a bucket roiling into a dry well. Ghatge barked out his orders all over again, 'You fool. This isn't the time to get romantic. Now get on. You know what to do next. Yes?'

'Yes,' Mahesh replied dully, but Ghatge repeated it all over again. 'Get to the Taj Hotel, in time; disrupt the art exhibition, and make sure to do the right kind of damage. It must get good press attention. Get it?'

He could almost imagine Ghatge now: turning his head away, spitting into his waste bin as he finished. *The Taj Hotel, get to it fast.* Mahesh's forehead was wrinkled and he stared up at the sky. There was something else. Something about the hotel he should remember but he couldn't. As he heard the click against his ear, Mahesh knew he had well and truly forgotten and still he did not want to let the phone go. He did not want anyone to see how torn he was, how tired but he had to fill himself up with a new anger as he set off on yet another errand for Ghatge.

As Mahesh rode towards the Taj Hotel, he remembered to put his scarf back on. This time, with the afternoon sun beating bitterly down, he felt, ensconced in the scarf's woolliness, that he was being bitten by ants. He felt the hot metal of the gun against his chest. He let the anger build up and ran over in his mind the things that had to be done.

Mahesh had rounded up the boys and given them precise instructions. This, in turn, had been passed onto others. By the time Mahesh reached the hotel, he was certain the requisite numbers would be there, ready and waiting for him, the van loaded with sticks and bottles of black ink. His men's target: the obscene paintings that had to be obliterated, and in full attention of camera crews and reporters.

Mahesh was only a bit finicky. All his men had to be experienced and trusted troublemakers. They had to inflict damage responsibly. No woman was to be hurt. Especially if she was decently dressed. Not a word of abuse was to be directed at them, or at anyone. Only patriotic slogans were to be raised. It was the paintings that had to be singled out. Not a single obscene one was to be spared. Mahesh had also detailed what obscene meant: anything that revealed a woman's private parts, or showed something too romantic. Such paintings had to be destroyed. On some particularly vulgar ones, black ink was to be poured to ensure they were obliterated beyond repair. Mahesh repeated his instructions loud over the phone, felt the anger in responses he heard, and knew it reflected his own.

Unlike his morning ride to the doctor's clinic, Mahesh now rode more carefully, stopping at every signal, not sidling his way past cars as he liked to do. He must do nothing to get himself attention. But the scarf covering his face only made him feel stifled. Only a few minutes more, Mahesh told himself. Only a few more signals to endure. His hand found the gun, he shook back his mane of curls and kept riding, the task ahead filling him with new rage, new ambition. He'd do it well, so well that even the gods, whose dignity he'd protect, would be pleased. Even Ghatge couldn't come in the way. Ghatge would be forced to hand over the keys of the yellow Mercedes-Benz on a platter. He might even hook the key onto a gold chain and garland Mahesh to thunderous applause.

Stop, stop. Mahesh knew his thoughts were racing blindly ahead. He passed a car, then a cab after it, and a crowded bus that he had been following for too long. He raised his arm as he rode ahead and shouted the slogan out loud. *Jai Hind. Bharat Mata ki Jai. My country, my mother.* Around him a cacophony of horns sounded in wild appreciation. He felt a swelling of pride in himself, in what he was about to do—a glorious act to save his country and its culture. And when it was over, he would be cheered in the same way.

His phone rang again as he neared Apollo Bunder. He drifted by the arched corridors that lined the old financial houses and banks, he saw lovers melt away in the darkness, saw them necking in the garden facing the Town Hall and turned his head away in disgust. Everywhere he looked, there were people with loose morals. 'Hello!' he yelled into the phone.

The man at the other hand, one of his boys, who waited for him, laughed in surprise. 'No need to get angry, boss, we want you there soon.'

He grunted, 'Yes, not so long now. You will know when I am there.'

This part of town was lined by old leafy trees and old stodgy buildings. Mahesh had seen them in the dark night hours, whenever he had to deliver a threat to some businessman or the other. He had lurked by the colonnades at Ballard Estate, often slouched on the benches, and crept into the old Afghan Church, and felt the city dark and quiet. Far away, the tall lights of the Taj Hotel had always appeared remote and he felt an envy for those who could afford it. But today, his envy mingled with some contempt. The hotel hosted the rich and the spoilt, who would in a few minutes be frightened out of their lives. Mahesh felt the gun again. He breathed in deeply as he slowed, avoiding the crowds and the horse carriages around the Taj.

Mahesh saw the gates of the Taj Hotel ahead and fumbled in his pocket. The last of the jasmine flowers fell out and at last his hands closed around the false press card he used for occasions like these—a break in, a protest about something or whenever a recalcitrant author needed his face blackened.

'Ready?' he asked as someone he recognized came forward cautiously. They cast watchful looks around, as they waited for their forces to converge. It was a good thing the exhibition was right on the ground floor, close at hand. That made their work easier. His men emerged, some who lounged against the hotel's columns, others from behind the trees, others leapt up from around the cars parked haphazardly. They were all suitably dressed, in dark glasses, jeans and checked shirts, and all of them had a rough map of the hotel. His men now produced the sticks and short clubs they had hidden away against their trousers. Some held aloft placards and Mahesh ran his eyes over them approvingly. He gave a thumbs-up and as they were about to cheer, he raised his hands 'No, not now. But soon. And remember, no random damage. Only the right damage.'

He rolled up his sleeves, and then gave out orders, making the quick precise gestures with his hands his men were familiar with. His men spread out, orderly and in military precision. The chauffeurs who had been idling now stood up. Mahesh waited; he had to check with the television crews. But as he turned around, hoping his motorcycle was securely placed to help him make a quick getaway, he stopped short, almost falling over. His jaw fell open, for there, among all the cars parked randomly in the open courtyard, was the car of his dreams. There it stood, distinctly recognizable and parked in a somewhat askew manner between a white BMW and parrot-coloured Beetle. He knew Ghatge Sahib was there then, and he always was careless about parking. The only time Mahesh had driven the Benz was when Ghatge had wanted it properly and safely parked somewhere.

As Mahesh watched his men melt away into the hotel and beyond, he walked towards the car, in slow deliberate steps as if he was afraid it would disappear with every step he took. It was like a painting he had to touch. He peered through its window and stepped back with a start. The keys were right there, on the black leather driver's seat.

Mahesh rubbed his eyes, leaned down, saw his face in the window, with the lamplight just behind. His unwashed, unkempt hair swirled around. He saw the snot on his nose, the eyes bulging out. His face appeared fused to the window. He knew how he would look now as he sat in the driver's seat. He swivelled around as someone came up. It was another driver, who asked in a simpering voice, 'Something's happening?'

Mahesh straightened with a jerk. He waved away his sweat, his distractions. He raised his hand, the keys in the engine were a sign, and he believed that now. Mahesh pulled out his gun, and heard the hiss of alarm around. Moments later, he heard the shouts. The flippancy died away on every face, a silent tension spread. He saw a television van draw up and knew one of his men had obviously informed the stations. One channel assured of a scoop had in turn promised a favourable coverage of the event.

Now. Leaning against the Mercedes-Benz, Mahesh raised his arm and fired. A moment later, the lamp-lit driveway came alive with shouts and screams. *Save our culture. Down with Imperialists*. Mahesh saw some guests coming up the driveway—they noticeably shrank, then turned and made a run for it. He smiled a grim tight smile of satisfaction. He knew it was time for him to go in as well, but he did not want to leave the car, fearing it would vanish if he did so.

The drivers and chauffeurs around him had congregated somewhere ahead, where they could have a ringside view of events. Mahesh, running a fond hand over the car, heard his stomach growl and realized he was hungry. He skirted the crowds, often looking behind to check the car. He moved along the hedge, the car still clearly visible and then he turned a corner where he was assailed by something new altogether. It took him some time, then he threw his head back and took in the wondrous heady fusion of aromas and fragrances from the hotel kitchen. He moved quickly around the curved building, and realized he still remembered his way around it. Some two years ago, there had been protests over another American scholar who had dared write a book riddled with falsehoods on Shivaji. Mahesh touched his heart as he thought of that and then about his growling stomach.

Mahesh found the low blue and white awning and walked up the low steps where the sounds of the kitchen mingled with the shouts and screams that now reached him clearly. He heard the blows, the thuds, the whistles and the slogans. His men had begun the destruction too early. It was best if it was gradual. The television crews had more to film then. He'd wait before he made his own entry. He made out different smells: something like chicken, a cloying, sweet aroma quite like flowers and then the sauciness of pakoras being fried.

It was this that made a new thought tumble irrevocably into his mind: Pooja cooked like that. Perhaps she was near. With a jerk Mahesh came to a halt. All that he had forgotten came rushing back. Pooja *was* here. She intended to be here, at this hotel. She had texted him just the previous day and it had slipped his mind entirely. The errands he had to run for Ghatge Sahib, his own sleepless days and nights had ensured that. Pooja was one of the caterers engaged for the very same exhibition he had now come to disrupt. When he had read her message, he had not managed to get the word right in his response and so had given up. *A caterer? You mean a caretaker?*

But there had been a smiley in Pooja's text. Mahesh rarely saw her smile and this meant she was happy. His steps quickened as he walked along the portico. If he looked in through the glass, he could see things in the kitchen. Should he let Pooja see him? He inched closer, hoping to take a quick look in. He opened his mouth and took in the full sweet smell of something being baked; it mingled with the spicy, savoury smell of samosas. He hadn't eaten since morning, except for a rather crushed-looking vada pao, something he had snatched from a wayside vendor and he hadn't even paid the poor man for it.

Mahesh toyed with the idea of sneaking in, picking up a samosa or a muffin. He must remember to pull the scarf over himself again, he told himself. He bent closer towards the window and then moved sharply back as he saw two darkened figures, very close, on the other side of the glass. He knew he was peering into an alcove of some kind, one cut off from the rest of the kitchen. Evidently the two figures had chosen it for precisely that reason.

A smile twisted his lips. In the glass, Mahesh saw the smirk on his face and rubbed his moustache in some glee. He knew what he saw before him. Two people making out secretly, kissing each other, away from the bustle in the kitchen around. His hands closed over his gun wondering if he was meant to disrupt this section of the hotel.

A hotel van came around the driveway and its light flashed inside for a moment. It was the lift of the woman's face, the curve of her arm against the column that made Mahesh go very still. His hand dropped away from his gun. He knew then it was his wife, and she was kissing another man. Mahesh felt a roaring in his ears, but it was only the men shouting. The sound receded. His own heart beating fast overrode everything. The glass before him appeared to shiver, he blinked and realized he was drenched in perspiration.

Mahesh knew he should look away yet he looked on, and rubbed the glass pane to be sure. Then he leaned in. He looked till she, sensing something, turned around and saw him too.

She looked, to Mahesh, like someone he had never seen before. For that moment, as their eyes locked, he could not tell if it was his wife. And when she raised her hand to her mouth, he wanted to tell her something though he didn't know what. All he knew was that he had to leave before things changed, before the expression on her face told him something else.

Mahesh took a few steps back before the sounds of people running came to him. He would bide his time before finding his own way out. The break-in had been a success, of a kind. His men had created sufficient mayhem for the police to be called in. It was just enough material to keep everyone occupied, especially the television channels and the gossip magazines.

Some minutes later, he made his way to where the yellow Mercedes-Benz had been. It was still there. Mahesh knew he could not think of anything else. He remembered the shock on his wife's face. He realized he did not know who she had been with.

But there was the yellow gleaming, shiny car, and Mahesh sighed with pleasure as he pulled its door open. He sank into its cool dark interiors, leaning against its soft cushions that took away all his memories, erased the long hot day that had gone before. He revved up the engine, felt the gentle purr in his ears. In minutes, he was in the less crowded parts of the city, and heading out into the country, towards his village home.

An hour later, as he coasted down the hill road, he rolled down the window and switched on a radio station. It was just the way rich people drove, as if they owned everything.

Pooja: The Evening of the Immersion

The bulldozer moved over the uneven road, lurching over potholes, and scattering the broken stones. Pooja heard the sound fleetingly, muffled by the rain drumming outside. It was a bit after twelve.

Pooja stood in the darkness thinking over her recent conversation with Gauri Tai. Tai had been hesitating, as if she was trying to hide some anxiety.

'Pooja?'

'Tai.' The stove near Pooja sizzled.

'Do you know where Mahesh is, Pooja?'

'Mahesh?' Pooja felt a blankness descend on her. For some days now Mahesh had become someone she didn't know and now Pooja found she couldn't conjure up his face at all. All that came to her, almost with the force of the blinding sun, was her shock at seeing that gun under his pillow. There it lay, a neat brown-black thing, its imprint marked on the sheets and still warm from the pillow over it. The gun had seethed with menace and all those secrets she had never wanted to know about Mahesh.

'Do you know?' Gauri Tai's agitated voice sounded very close. Pooja hadn't known before about the gun, but there under his pillow, on the bed they shared, it looked as if belonged there, more than she did. Mahesh had caught her looking at the gun and then reached for it. For security, he said importantly, his eyes evading hers. Then he had flung the towel, the one he was using to wipe his tousled hair, aside, and rushed away. Moments later, she heard the rev of his motorcycle outside. Pooja had not seen him since then.

Barely weeks ago, she had heard the news of Sneha Desai's death. Suicide, it was said. And Vasudha had added more detail: Sneha Madam had been driven to it. Hadn't Pooja, of all people, seen Ghatge's Mercedes-Benz parked in the lane leading to her clinic, so often, at an odd hour too? To Pooja, the gun seemed a reminder of Mahesh's association with Ghatge. She did not want to know more.

'No, Tai. I thought he was with Ghatge Sahib.'

'With Sahib?' The cracked note in Gauri Tai's voice didn't come from a bad connection. Pooja knew Gauri Tai had not expected this.

'And Sahib, where is he?'

'Tai, I haven't seen him in a while.' Then she heard the phone click shut.

That had been two hours ago. Now behind Pooja was the door, and she saw the corridor lights on outside. Outside, beyond the unchanging rhythmic fall of rain, she thought she caught someone moving.

In the lane leading to the chawl, Vasudha was moving cautiously, negotiating every puddle, her umbrella held high, moving often whenever the rain became too forceful. Then the lone streetlight showed her up as she stepped over an overflowing gutter. Pooja recognized the zebra-striped umbrella and shook her head. All that business of clearing Sneha Desai's files had become, for Vasudha, a near obsession.

Soon she would turn into the gate. Her gait was heavier but she moved with a slow assurance. Pooja admired everything about Vasudha. All those times, all those years, and all those questions about her own childlessness, Pooja had never learnt a way to answer. Her childlessness had made her want to hide away. Vasudha, finding herself pregnant and unmarried, had stood up proudly to every question, even those unasked. 'So, I am not beholden to the world, am I?' she'd said.

Vasudha moved slowly, but the way she held the umbrella meant there was something else in her hands. Something she was holding onto tightly. As she took the first step into the chawl compound, and Pooja leaned closer, she heard voices. Richard too had been waiting outside. Now she heard Vasudha laughing, the swish of her squelchy slippers on the floor, and then the pause before her own door.

'Pooja, already asleep?'

Pooja opened the door so quickly that Vasudha fell back. Looking out, she saw Richard lounging against the column, wearing those crazily designed T-shirts he had taken to doing of late. But it was apparently getting him good money too. 'We are in business in strange ways, Pooja,' he'd said, half-proudly but even a little embarrassed by his showing-off.

'I've to tell both of you.' Vasudha held up a plastic blue folder covered by another plastic sheet. She brushed the rain off, and a drop caught Pooja in the eye. 'This is a prize catch. Now you two just see. Things may happen sooner than you expect.' Vasudha looked at them both, a wild feverish excitement in her eyes. Then she turned her head, listening intently to something.

'Can you hear it…? Hush, and you will.'

Pooja heard it more clearly then. Through the rain came the trundling and slow rolling sound of the advancing bulldozer. The rain had lessened but not relented. The three of them, standing by the veranda, heard the grunt and roll, the splash and crunch as wheels rolled over the unevenly tiled road and the rain-marked puddles. A few minutes later all became quiet, the rain gentled and then the wind picked up.

'There will be more of those in the morning. Bulldozers, I mean. So early that we will never know.' Vasudha was talking in her breathless quick voice, tripping over her words, and slapping her soaking wet sandals against the veranda. She tore off the loose scarf and ran her fingers through her tangled hair.

'What's the time?' Richard asked.

'Well past twelve,' and Pooja yawned in emphasis. Tomorrow she had to begin early. She had placed more buckets in line before the municipal tube well and hoped the other women wouldn't pick up a quarrel. She needed more water, for there was that school function she had to provide breakfast for. An enormous order of sabudana kichdi, shrikand and modak for an international school that wanted its exchange students to learn about the state and the city they were in. The nuns from the school had especially recommended her.

Now she wondered aloud about putting a couple of more buckets in the line, just at the end. Richard jumped in to offer his help, as if he knew Pooja would turn him down and he wanted to pre-empt her. Vasudha watched them both with an interested expression, before she gently chided Richard. 'You should help me out more, see my condition.'

'I have a long day tomorrow,' Pooja snapped, finally at the end of her tether. 'I must begin early.' Later she would remember this day, just as well as she would the one that came after it. It had rained so very heavily. Almost as if it had washed Mahesh away forever.

The rain's misty dampness was everywhere the next morning. The line of buckets rose in Pooja's vision as she took the first steps down. Richard sat at the very bottom of the stairs, his sharp knife scraping the coconut shells and scattered around him were shells he had already painted and stuck on poles to resemble puppets. Richard moved his stuff self-consciously as she walked down to the ground floor. There was a flurry of more scraping sounds, his embarrassed cough, and into this came other sounds. Looking around, Pooja saw someone familiar. It was Dr Joshi in a paint-splattered apron; he stood before his easel in place, his hands waving to her.

He was saying something but his movements, in rhythm to his words, were all disjointed. Across the lane and behind him, stretched under the awnings and the shuttered shops, Pooja saw more huddled figures. *Tai, you need to walk faster.* Dr Joshi ran fingers through his hair, and the thin elastic band holding it in, stretched and snapped.

He had barely finished when a different sound broke in. One that trampled over Dr Joshi's words and every other sound for some distance around. Someone rummaging utensils in a kitchen, a baby bawling, and not too far away, the bells clanging on a passing bicycle, a shop's shutters being raised and on the main road beyond, a car screeching to a halt. Over all this, came the ominous rumbling, half-familiar and yet alien. Someone yelled, as if rushing out of the way, and then came all the sounds of the night before, but this time the grating, the crushing, the squelching and crunching of things being smashed under, was ominously loud and very close.

A cloud of dust gushed out from the lane where Sneha Desai once had her clinic. The cloud grew quickly, as if a thick brown and grey curtain had dropped, erasing the clarity of moments before. Behind all this, slowly, imperiously, appeared the bulldozer of the night before.

The bulldozer advanced, its blade gleaming and shiny, a funnel of black smoke rising from above the glass cabin where someone sat, yellow-hatted. An odd whistling sound rose over the bulldozer's monotonous grating. It paused at the corner where the cell phone shop was. The cigarette and paan stall next to it, that had for long stood on rickety legs, now tottered. The blade lifted slowly, its rollers gritted, trundled, making that grating noise that lasted for seconds and then the bulldozer came to full life, like a huge creature that had just learnt to walk, and was taking its first steps across the cracked, potholed road. The cigarette stall fell first, its thin wooden planks cracked and splintered. For a few seconds, its insides were revealed; shelves packed with coloured cartons of cigarettes and candies that came crashing down only to be crushed under the ever-advancing rollers.

Splinters flew up. The blade lifted, hung in the air, looking for its next target. The earth was turned up and over, and a smell of rubble, decay and dust wafted over everything. The wheels moved, bringing the yellow looming hulk of the bulldozer closer into view, now filling up every available space. Pooja saw behind it a road roller. Everything else dwindled in comparison.

The buckets were right in the bulldozer's line of attack now. They formed a precarious thin wall of defence, as silent as the people now standing around—the doctor-painter, and the women who stood at the tube well every morning. They had appeared out of the last quietness, but their sullen, unsmiling everyday morning faces had now changed to disbelief and astonishment, as if all this was happening from the dream of the night before, one they hadn't quite shaken off. Pooja saw other sleeping figures rise from under the awning, some on the ground floor close to where the painter-doctor had his easel. A few held onto their blankets, some were mechanically folding them, by long habit. There was someone very tall, standing amongst them, running his fingers distractedly through his hair, and as many thoughts rushed through Pooja's head, she knew this too. That this was an unfamiliar figure and that she had seen him somewhere.

The upturned buckets stood in some obedient formation, looking to Pooja like figures marked out for a brutal public execution. Just at that moment, the municipal tube well came to life with a splutter and cough.

The bulldozer advanced, its sound rising over the water that fell on the damp cemented square surrounding the tube well. All at once Pooja's own set, two in yellow, and one, a rough aluminum pail, appeared the most vulnerable of all.

It was that moment when she did not have to turn her head, when the machine and the line of buckets and the horror-struck, still women were all in her vision that Pooja raced forward. First there were only four steps between her and the buckets, but there was that puddle whose depth she miscalculated. A wave of water rose and splattered her on the knees, and then her face too. She heard someone shout behind her, before this too was erased by the roar and grunt of the machine as it moved towards her, the blade not veering away at all.

She stood at the tube well, the cold water ran over her feet. The water had a soothing feel but Pooja could smell the machine, the rubble enmeshed in its rollers, the decay and rubbish caught in its upturned blade, and she could read on its side, the letters K O M a T S U. The machine huffed, a funnel of black smoke flew up again, quick before it was snuffed out.

No. Pooja screamed. She saw through the glass, the same yellow-hatted figure. A face with no eyes, she caught a glimpse of teeth as yellow as the hat, then someone waving a hand her way as if swatting a fly away. She stood on her toes, lost her balance momentarily and slipped, and the grin broadened. She lifted herself in no time, and stepped into a deeper puddle. The wet mud slid and squelched against her feet, and Pooja screamed again *No.* And then again. *No.* She bunched her hands into a fist and heard her voice cracking, her heart beating so loudly it would burst any time. Over her, the sky loomed down, almost gathering her in. Behind her, she heard more Nos. *No. No.* A wave of them. Her cries picked up by the other women. Afraid, almost faint at first, and then growing louder as they heard her, heard each other.

But the blade lifted, like the barred grin of a demented prehistoric monster. The blade was now closer than before, and smelt of dust, dried blood and leaves, abandoned wood, all the smells of a broken-down city. The blade hovered over

Pooja and she stood, immobilized, knowing it would descend any moment. Then she heard a shout, a different one. A figure leaped across the puddle and as she heard the first splash, it seemed to her as big as the sea before she was pushed aside. Then someone was holding her. She felt cold hands on her waist, and that someone yelled up at the driver too, his voice very close.

Get away. Stop. Stop.

There was another advancing roar. The rush of feet, screams and shouts, the clank of utensils and then against the machine, there was a wall of people, their hands on it, women mainly, screaming at the yellow-hatted man on it, his smile no longer visible.

Pooja lifted her head and looked up at someone familiar. The voices everywhere then dimmed, and faded, leaving a faint throbbing in her ears. It was the man she had seen in Neera's house, the man who had appeared on television, the man in the chopper, though he looked older, with lines on his cheek and a dark frown. The man she had glimpsed at Sneha Desai's memorial. His eyes looked down at her, and then he was urging her in Marathi, a whisper that blew a tendril across her forehead. *We must go.* His eyes looked red-rimmed with exhaustion and lack of sleep, and his voice was hoarse.

No. She shook her head, her fist. She turned towards what she knew had to be done. For the buckets had to be filled, but he stood by her—tall, too solid, and there was that damp smell on him too.

Come away.

Pooja heard the glass break. Something struck her forehead, the warm blood fell, its taste metallic on her lips, before everything darkened before her eyes. But someone had stood up on the wheels and was reaching for the man in the bulldozer in his glass cabin. Pooja took a step backward, and there was the man in the bulldozer, his hat now torn off his

head, being pulled down to a torrent of abuses and slaps that
rained down on him, unrestrained.

He said his name was Suhel, and Dr Joshi nodded his agreement,
running his fingers through his now sticky paintbrush—yes,
this was indeed Suhel Kolhatkar—then having said this, he
looked vaguely around. Almost on cue, Richard came running
up. 'Pooja, tu thik aahey?'

She had her hand on her forehead. It throbbed painfully,
and she heard the chatter of women around her. Some laughing
in their nervousness and relief, then Pooja heard her name.
She thought too of the man who had stood next to her, as the
bulldozer slowly advanced. She shivered, then felt a warmth
spread over on her face. How could anyone feel cold and
warm at the same time?

'We will fill up the buckets for you, Tai.'

And the tall man called Suhel said, 'We need to get you to
hospital.' He stood stiff by her side, still looking at her, one
hand in his pocket, before he shook his head ruefully. 'I don't
even have a clean hanky to give you.'

He spoke Marathi somewhat differently, and when trying
to sound reassuring, he looked considerably awkward. 'No
hospital,' Pooja said, firmly, putting up a hand to ward them
all away.

'Pooja, it's bleeding,' Rosie said.

'I need to get a lot of work done,' Pooja said. All this took
her an effort, even her voice seemed elusive. The faces around
her were becoming fuzzy, and Suhel looked at her, his eyes
crinkled with concern. Her hands felt clammy, and frayed, as
if the rope she held on to would soon give away. Rosie was
next to her now, offering her a dainty handkerchief that smelt
still of old perfume.

'We do need you to see…' Suhel sounded worried, but
his words now sounded faraway and ineffectual. He looked

around, and she missed how he and the doctor exchanged a quick look. 'Here, what good am I for then?' And Dr Joshi pushed away his absent-mindedness and elbowed his way in. He bit into his straggly long ponytail and peered up at her, his warm breath fanning her elbow for a few seconds. As he raised his fingers to where her forehead now throbbed painfully, Pooja saw how paint-splattered they were, and he grinned, 'Yes, quite a wrong day to paint.' And this made Suhel, standing still very near, say grimly, 'You never know. It may have been the right day after all.' It was Suhel who now lifted a gentle hand over her forehead and let his hand stay there. She noticed all this, only moments later, for she was still dazed at what had happened. The touch of pain first, when she had been hurt, and then this unfamiliar brush of someone else's fingers on her. All she felt then was the first prickle of tears, and his voice close against her, 'She does need to see a doctor and you, doc, are in no state.'

No no.

'Pooja, why make this fuss after all that...action. You were all filmi, no?'

There was Vasudha now, standing akimbo, and Pooja saw herself in her glasses, her hair falling out of its usual neat knot, and that line of blood right on her hairline. 'Listen to us. You do need to see a doctor.' Vasudha said, looking up and staring like the others at her forehead. Suhel's hand had fallen away, and she saw it resting against his jeans, the slow breeze making the hair on his wrist move ever so gently. Then Vasudha had taken her hand in hers, talking to her almost as if one were cajoling a child. 'Pooja, you are just too much. That machine could have...could have run over you.' Her hand gripped Pooja's a bit more tightly and they smiled shakily at each other.

Pooja had little idea of what followed, the sequence in which things happened. Her insistence, her mention of the school order that she had to fulfil at all costs, was overridden. There was Suhel assuring her familiarly that it would not take much time at the clinic. The doctor nodding, agreeing with him. And his voice overrun by Vasudha's as she hollered over them, at all the ladies still standing around, 'Come and help her out when you can.'

'Yes,' Vasudha said again, assuming the imposing stance she could so very easily. 'Otherwise this machine would have destroyed everything.'

'Go,' she said turning now, looking Pooja firmly in the eye, 'it will be okay, just go.'

It wasn't a long walk to the clinic Dr Joshi had pointed them to, but she remembered breaking into shaky laughter at the only thing Suhel had said on the way, when the pain had returned in double measure.

'I am Suhel Kolhatkar,' he'd said, and he had stammered, then almost stumbled as he led her down the sidewalk, 'I once saw your painting and you are more beautiful than...'

He frowned as he thought over what he had just said, and it was then she had laughed. It was how he said it, how he had told her his name twice, his mention of a painting and she felt it must be a mistake, he was confusing her for someone else. Then she felt the skin on her forehead pull and the warm blood fell now, over her eye, and he said, his hand gentle and yet firm on her elbow, 'Not too long now. Am sorry.'

Late that night, when the bulldozer stood still and abandoned, and she, relieved that she had still been able to fulfil the order, it was Mohini Gupta who called. *Raina's mother*, she identified herself and of course Pooja knew. She knew Raina from Neera's house. Like her, Raina was also a regular there. Talking, not just about the book she and Neera were working on, but about her mother, who as Raina always said, continued to ignore her. It was then Neera would look very disapproving, telling Raina she had to get over her American notions, where children, she said, blamed their parents for everything.

Pooja had been wary but all this had dissolved, for Mohini Gupta had been commiserating and so fulsome in her compliments. 'I heard, everyone's heard about it, though it won't get much coverage,' she said. 'But you were so brave.'

Pooja knew she hadn't been. It had all been sudden, and had left her with an injury and a strange meeting with a man called Suhel who had compared her to a painting. He wasn't strange, she was now thinking, he was nice, and had been gentle and in the silence as she held the phone to her ear, she knew Mohini had asked her something. Mohini repeated herself again, sounding almost apologetic. 'It's the twenty-fourth today, would something around the first work for you?'

Some seconds later, Mohini had explained it all over again, apologizing if she was rushing Pooja in any way. 'It's only some days from now. An art exhibition at the Taj Hotel. Would you be able to arrange some Maharashtrian stuff for us?'

That was how she had agreed to Mohini's suggestion. It would make Vasudha gush the next morning, her eyes turning into circles of delight, behind her glasses. 'It's a big thing, Pooja, you will be popular with these high-society people.'

Richard came up behind Vasudha too. Those days he seemed to be always at that place near the stairs, just hanging around, doing his customary carving and scraping work. But that day when Richard came right up to them, he had something different to say, a curious announcement. 'Those photos I took of that morning, I gave them to the newspaper lady.'

'Who?' Vasudha and Pooja asked simultaneously before looking at each other. Richard replied in a low grim voice, and it struck Pooja that he looked them straight in the eye as he spoke. His way of constantly blinking, something he had once explained as a psychological thing, that had once made him such a figure of fun, seemed to have gone now. Richard stretched his hand out, gripped the veranda rails hard and said, 'I did not dare go to the cybercafé to mail the photos, like she wanted. The ones of the bulldozer and your protest, Pooja. For everyone here is Ghatge's man, not just Mahesh. So I gave her my phone. And she has the photos. The ones I took in the morning.'

Pooja did not react to his mention of Mahesh, then. It brought up more forcefully for Pooja the image of the gun under his pillow, the hasty way he had grabbed it and left without a word to her. But the previous night, soon after Mohini's call, he'd called too.

Mahesh had begun with no preliminaries, he never had to. 'You think you are some heroine? That chawl is tottering, and Ghatge Sahib plans to set up a tall building there. For all of us. For all of us. Get it?'

She heard the low snarl in his voice, as if he was barely restraining himself from screaming. 'I wasn't thinking of that,' she had wanted to say, and then realized how laughable it did seem. What had she wanted? To save her buckets. And all because of the fancy order she had received?

'You keep out of this, understand? Let things happen as they will. I am his man, he trusts me. He trusts me.' He had repeated it almost to convince himself. 'And you better not do anything.'

She pressed her head to the window bars and felt the pain return in waves greater than before. She remembered the touch of a man on her skin, someone she had only just met. Suhel Kolhatkar. She remembered it all then. How he had pushed her aside as the bulldozer neared, her face close to his, and that strange thing he had said. It was funny, else why had he flushed, scratched his ear and then had said nothing else. But in that silence as he had walked her back, as the city awoke around them, everything seemed somehow different. Though she hadn't asked him why he had been there too. Dr Joshi and he somehow knew each other. There was the way they spoke to each other—an easy familiarity. All these questions came to her much later, and now they confused her, made her smile.

A month or so later, she learnt more about the painting, then Suhel himself texted her a picture. The painting hung in his apartment. In a second message, he told her he had positioned it so the changing light could catch her face in different ways, and he liked that. She was too embarrassed to follow up with a leading question. She would come back to it, later. Suhel, after all, was always a text message away.

The painting had been on her mind ever since Suhel had first mentioned it. It had taken her some days to work up her nerve and ask him, but the delay had been natural, even inadvertent. Ever since that momentous day by the tube well, she and Suhel had texted each other daily. There were the things that filled their thoughts, yet their words and messages had centred on other things. Deliberate and half-teasing. Innocuous and still urgent. Banal and yet meaningful. Playful but serious. And still, in this time, the first messages of concern, and her own hesitant responses also changed into something else altogether. The stiltedness gave way to a watchful familiarity, something jokey, almost affectionate had crept in.

It wasn't the timing of the messages and texts. These could come at any hour, at any moment, on his part and hers too. He would tell her of his meetings, of his plan to set up an office in Mumbai. She would tell him of her new orders. They would laugh over the articles that had appeared on her, especially in the Marathi papers. And he would be fulsome in his praise. Not flattering her, but being gently insistent. Then there was that hotel incident that she couldn't forget, and neither could he. Sometimes he alluded to it, and her silences were a kind of response. He asked her once if she was upset.

I don't know, she typed back. She couldn't lie. For since then, she hadn't seen Mahesh. She didn't want to tell Suhel that Mahesh's messages to her had been of a totally different kind, very unlike his. She had been called names, she had been threatened. And though Ghatge was lying low now, embarrassed by the wrong kind of media attention, she knew she had only a little time. She had to establish herself fast, to move away from the stranglehold he held over her life. And she was going to do it on her own, while her good fortune still ran.

I can't say sorry, he had texted. *I can't lie to myself.*

No, I just need time, she had texted. *I can't make out what to think.*

He had not texted for some hours after that, and she knew she had upset him. Then she had remembered that painting, and that had set off another exchange. But the kiss in the hotel. She would think of it often. Just as she thought of Suhel almost every minute now. It seemed to her that when she was not planning her day, looking to her new orders, he was there in her mind, in her thoughts, looming over her as he had done that first morning.

You must come and see the painting, he texted her once.

She sent him an emoji, followed with: *That makes me out to be someone very vain.*

She could almost hear him sigh then, as if a ruse on his part hadn't worked. *Pooja, can't we meet? Just meet as friends?* he asked.

What would everyone say?

Do you care?

Yes, I have to.

Everyone expected you to stay quiet when the bulldozers came, Pooja, he wrote back and she could tell he was typing fast and furious, perhaps looking out of his apartment window, as he had told her he often did. *But you didn't. You did as you wanted to, and you did something wonderful.*

Yes, but this is something else.

What is? he asked. *Pooja, if this is something else, please don't let it be just something else.*

That was the message he had sent her late one night, sending her a heart emoji soon after. The next morning, he had sent her a bouquet of yellow roses, carnations and dahlias. Vasudha's eyes had widened in wonder and Richard smiled thinly, reluctantly.

'Someone's lost his heart, Pooja,' Vasudha said.

'And I haven't lost my mind,' she snapped, and she saw Vasudha roll her eyes as she exchanged a look with Richard.

She was to meet him early in September, before she called it off. She was being practical and realistic, she told herself. And nervous. To Suhel, she said that her father was here on a visit. It was his first visit to the city, and she had to be there. Suhel hadn't texted after that. She couldn't text him too, knowing she had made him angry, hurt him, even led him on.

It was the time the Ganapati festival had the city in a fever grip. City squares, suburban town halls, school playgrounds, a corner of the railway station, every available public space was made over to the god, and statues of him were placed high on daises and pandals that stretched all around. For that fortnight everything, even the heat, seemed whipped up to a frenzy. It was intolerable, this weather, and everyone prayed to the god, Ganesha the giver, asking not for better weather but for money, a job, and even marriage.

Pooja felt the breeze warm and cajoling on her face, and it little eased the turmoil and confusion she felt. He didn't, she thought, stride through the world in an aggressive way, like so many others, claiming what wasn't his by right. But the world was a different thing altogether, and Suhel, rich and used to getting his own way, was still part of the world as they knew it. She knew how this romance could look to the world.

A rich man, and she a woman in a chawl with fancy dreams, that could come crashing down any moment. Ghatge would recover. He was the one whose words mattered in the chawl. And her own position was precarious in every way.

That afternoon was the last day of the festival, when the Ganapati idols would be taken out in procession for immersion. She had had no orders for that evening. The entire city had given itself to the elephant god. Even her father, on his first visit from the village, who had complained and whined incessantly about the weather and the noise in the city, had perked up. He watched her doing up the rooms, making a vividly colourful new rangoli pattern on the veranda and smaller ones inside, and then rolling out the aroma-filled modaks and basundis that she would offer to the god in her prayers. He'd watch the idols going by and would pick a good spot for the procession, he told Pooja then. 'And I don't need Richard to keep an eye on me,' he insisted.

'All right, Baba, I will be around with Vasudha. She needs her rest now with the baby due.'

She felt a fleeting guilt, and a sadness too, thinking about Suhel. She wondered if he had made other plans. The other day, he had had a big launch party at his house to celebrate his new office. He had hidden away her painting, he had texted her to tell this. She didn't ask why. He didn't elaborate, and they both knew he was still upset with her. She could think what she liked: that he was angry and wanted to forget her, or that she was his own special secret and he wasn't sharing her with anyone, not yet.

Up high in Suhel's apartment, she knew she would have had the best view—the Ganesha idols travelling in a crowded and orderly procession all through the city, and in perfect order, then carried to the shore on the shoulders of his many devotees, down to the beach, to be immersed.

She found herself praying again to the god, as she had

always done. The time of her mother's illness, the many occasions she had been upset by the taunts directed her way. Now she just wanted some measure of happiness: of what kind, how much, she had no idea. Nor could she bring herself to ask. For she had been happy in ways she hadn't expected. The catering orders, and then Suhel. Sometimes secrets that one couldn't share held a special happiness. One could always play back those moments of happiness, look back on them like a photograph hidden away in an old family album. Such memories never changed and coloured over every other moment, dark and sad.

She thought of Suhel as she knew him from the days just gone. All the messages they had texted, beginning from the day the bulldozer had struck, to their encounter at the hotel and then for days after that. Pooja invariably stopped herself as she always did, when she remembered again the evening at the hotel. There was always something new and different about a memory that had grown familiar, and lovingly old.

She had seen him come into the hotel kitchen as she stood with the junior chef and his assistants. Suhel had been hesitant at first, before he had come forward, his eyes on her, swallowing his nervousness and then he had asked after her injury. A few moments later, they were in the alcove, his finger tracing the faint line of the injury on her forehead, running down her face, as if he had longed to do this, and then at last his head had bent to hers.

Every night, at her small altar, she had asked Ganesha, her own small idol of the elephant god, if she could think about him, and especially those moments in the hotel, more often. The feel of Suhel kissing her, his lips on hers, his arm on her shoulder, how his heart had beat under her hand—all this came rushing up to her, at almost every moment, when she willed the memories back, and she knew even Ganesha could not mind. The gods had compassion, they understood, their sense of what was right and wrong was different.

When she remembered it all, she wondered if she would experience such heaven again, and if she would be allowed it.

For she had stepped out of line, and she had to be careful, especially in her happiness. She knew her father had been sent by Gauri Tai in the hope that things between Mahesh and her could be patched up. The Ghatges didn't want their minions to ever step out of line. Mahesh and she were to be forever indebted to the Ghatges for their generosity. There would be a price to pay for any infringement or recalcitrance. She felt her heart torn as she realized Mahesh was caught on the grindstone of loyalty, forever trapped, always trying. But a minion would always remain one.

Her father, for his part, would do nothing. It was beyond him to manage his daughter's life.

On that last auspicious day of the Ganesha festival, Pooja decided to deck up. She took trouble over herself. It made her forget that Suhel was upset. It made her imagine how he would look at her, how his eyes might run over her, and how his eyes would crinkle up in a smile. It made her think of the evening at the hotel again. She pinned her hair up, and wore the expensive sari she had. Then Pooja had done her eyes up too. The first time the kohl seemed overdone, and smudging it away left a shadowed look, and then Pooja had redone her eyes, applying in a blue shade, then a gentler black.

~

'We have to figure things out,' said Vasudha, long after the revelry outside had died down. Pooja had made her comfortable. Vasudha's pregnancy had advanced but she still wouldn't take the extra rest the doctor had recommended. 'We will have all the time to rest in peace, I assure you,' she told Pooja when she became a bit too insistent, 'but we need to think.'

Looking across at Pooja's troubled gaze, she went on,

'Being a hero is good, but not for long. The attention will not last long. Neera Tai is doing all she can, but the builder guys never give up.'

Pooja knew the bulldozer had not left the place since the first day it had come, nearly a month ago now. A story had appeared in the international press, thanks to Raina. It was about Neera's speech, when she had revealed the letter found in Sneha Desai's lost, and now found, file, thanks to Vasudha. Ramakrishna Desai, as the labour union leader and the representative of the workers those many years ago, had signed an acceptance of a ninety-nine-year lease on the chawl, in return for the union agreeing to a voluntary retirement scheme. So the chawl could not be pulled down arbitrarily. Neera had looked wistful when she had seen Ramakrishna Desai's signature. She had held up the old letter, fraying at the edges, as the television cameras zoomed in. The letter had been authenticated by legal officials.

'The attention helps, the crowds that a television camera draws, is all necessary. We need to just keep at it.' Neera's eyes gleamed. It was a long time since Pooja had seen her this way. She was perhaps getting over Raina and her surprise decision to leave.

The letter, and the doctor's painting, the one he had sketched the day the bulldozer had come in, had drawn a lot of attention. He still refused to sell it. 'The third of my paintings that will stay with me for a while,' he had said meaningfully, looking Pooja's way. She had blushed and then wondered how much Dr Joshi really knew. But he had to know quite a bit. It wasn't just that the painting was now Suhel's—unless he had discarded it, for she must have irritated him beyond measure, but Suhel had been there that morning, and she knew his presence had to be intentional. It was again another thing she had never asked him about, and suddenly she wanted to text him. Looking at her phone, she saw there still wasn't a message from him and her spirits sank low.

And now when Vasudha made these statements almost casually, of imminent doom, of disaster that could hit them any moment, her finger quick with the remote, Pooja wanted to stuff her fingers in her ears. Vasudha looked at her, her glasses hazy in the dim neon light of the room. Pooja reached for her diary. She flipped over the pages, and knew her days were full. There were orders from many other places in the city, and Vasudha, for all her warnings, was drawing up plans for Pooja to have a proper establishment somewhere, some rooms they could rent for a catering office, even sell stuff and a small staff to manage it. 'Somewhere in a mall,' Vasudha had said. 'There are too many, and they will rent us some space.' When she was this way, Pooja was filled with optimism. They couldn't evict her from the chawl, Pooja thought, not yet, and not so easily. She would always find herself something. She would even sleep in her bakery if it came to that. Though she would have to look for a small enough bakery first.

She listened to Vasudha with half an ear, and found herself doodling and then she was writing Suhel's name, all across one page, drawing flowers around the letters that made his name, splicing the letters diagonally, breaking them up, and scrambling them around till she wrote them again to form the name she could never have enough of.

Suhel. She didn't know all of him yet. She just waited for his texts, longed for them. She found herself checking her phone often and did so again. There was nothing from him, and this time a heavy stone set in her heart, making her sigh, making Vasudha look at her and ask if she was hungry. Though she shook her head, Vasudha still got up and rummaging on her table, returned with a packet of chocolate biscuits. They smiled at each other, both looking absent in the way old friends could be with each other. Vasudha flopped down heavily on the low divan and Pooja felt herself sink into the deep mirrored cushions. The diary slid towards Vasudha, and Suhel's name, written, done up in different ways caught her eye. She patted her stomach, arched one eyebrow, and looking Pooja firmly in the eye, said, 'Do something.'

And that was so reminiscent of Ghatge that they broke into helpless laughter. They were almost hysterical, as if the laughter helped cover up the worries they had had only some moments ago.

'Do something. Really, Pooja, you must do something.'

'Oh yes, I must,' she said in the same bantering way. But Suhel hadn't texted and half the evening had already gone. She thought of calling him to explain, but it would be so ineffectual. She knew and he knew. They were skirting around things, and she was refusing to look the truth in the face. Then she was afraid. He could well refuse to answer. He could be with someone else. Someone of his class, his background, someone with his kind of money. Once she let in a doubt or two, she now drowned in an avalanche of despair.

Suhel had money, a lot of it, and that was what frightened her too. Money never made you happy, it caused trouble instead: like that between Mohini and her daughter, Raina; Ghatge's flirtation with it, and his affair—when he had used Sneha Desai and embarrassed himself no end. As for herself: she was forgetting who she really was. Giving herself airs. A woman from the chawl, a childless woman—who had had, till now, no friends—and who fancied herself as a good cook.

You smelt nice. Of roses and chocolate.

She remembered Suhel's message then, referring to the evening in the hotel and that made her smile.

On his return after watching the procession of idols headed for immersion, her father looked happy. It was the first time the city had made him smile and Pooja told him so. He said he had seen all there was to see now, and he wanted to go home. 'A few more days, Baba,' she said.

'Tomorrow,' he said, tiredly. 'I spoke to that boy, Richard. He will take me to Dadar. You have work.'

He turned to the wall, pre-empting further conversation. It was perhaps an omen of sorts that he chose not to bring up Mahesh's name at all.

She did not tell him what Vasudha had explained to her in some detail. That soon she would have nowhere to live. The rooms were Mahesh's, after all, to do with as he wished. Her phone rang then, and her father murmured in his sleep. She rushed out as noiselessly as she could, not wanting to wake him, biting on her tongue as the old door creaked annoyingly and its bolt let out a soft screech. She held onto to the veranda rails, afraid to look at the luminous dial of her screen. She wanted it to be Suhel but some of Vasudha's realism had rubbed off on her. It had to be Ghatge, or even Gauri Tai. As for Mahesh, she knew it had been nearly a month since they had last spoken.

But it was his 'hello' she heard first, and her voice wavered in reply.

'You...' she said, dully, half-fearfully. He was her husband and as habits go, she still couldn't call him by name.

'Yes,' he snarled and she remembered he hadn't called despite her injury, 'and while you're having a nice time, let me tell you it won't last. I've signed those rooms over.'

'You had told me you would,' she said dully. A floor below was lit up in streaks, as the light through Richard's window made patterns on the old grey tiles. She heard Mahesh abuse her at the other end. He called her a traitor, for letting down someone who had done so much for them. He called her all the names she knew she deserved, and she kept quiet, and then when he did not relent, she finally hung up. It was a bit later that she read his text message. He wanted a divorce. *Talak,* he texted. *I want one. I hate you.*

She lingered on in the veranda like she had done before.

The city was quieter today, than on other evenings. The revelries had left everyone spent, she thought, though the late-night bars, and restaurants were open. She heard the discreet swish of cars, the flashing lights of a high-end restaurant not far away. There had been a mill there too, some years ago. Somewhere beyond were the offices, their lobby lights still on. In two of those offices, she now delivered lunch boxes. And perhaps a third would work out soon. She lifted her head, blinked away her tears, and saw then what she had been waiting for. A message.

Suhel had sent her a video, telling her she had missed some good things. She heard his voice as he let his cell phone move in a broad sweep, letting its camera take in the purple and gold evening and below, trucks that looked like Lego objects, surrounded by moving, dancing figures, blobs of black with occasional flashes of colour. Then he had zoomed to take in more of the city, revealing neat squares, the city's tall towers, all of uneven height, juxtaposed against each other, looking like the coloured sound bars of a music system, and standing companionably next to a few older smaller houses.

She heard Suhel laugh as he showed her the frenzied dancing on the streets, the cacophonous drumming, the scenes of devotees wailing as the god was carried out to the sea and then immersed at some depth.

He had zoomed still lower, picking up the terrace of another building crowded with onlookers. She saw the women in their black burqas, some clicking photos with their cell phones, shifting positions, running over the parapet for a better view. Some held children too, who clapped every time an idol was held up high and bounced lovingly as it was passed on, hand to hand, before a last group of people ran with it to the sea. Over the loudspeakers, the announcements rang out every few minutes, interspersed by the loud clashing of cymbals and the beating of drums. As the sun sank, its golden rays racing across the water like several slanting arrows, the biggest idol in the city, the one the city knew as the Raja of Lalbagh, moved in a stately manner to the sea. A loud wail resounded, for this was the god, who remained the most popular, who was the most visited, the one who had the most gifts showered on it, and the children held high up in their mothers' arms, bent their heads, folded their hands to their chest in their own way of saying farewell.

Suhel must have been suddenly lost in thought for the camera picked him up then, and he was looking at something in his apartment. Behind him, the skies had darkened, and she picked out the silence. The last of the devotees had dispersed, and they were alone again, separate and yet together. Then she saw him, the phone stuck on a shelf somewhere, and the camera still running—perhaps he had forgotten—showed his face in profile. She held her breath, looking at the drummer tattoo on his upper arm, a mark on his neck, and the grey edges in his hair.

The video ended abruptly and as she typed out a thank you to him, her phone rang again. It was him.

'Er sorry…' he began in the offhanded, casual way he had, 'never realized the video picked up some crazy stuff.'

'It was nice,' she said, stumbling over her words, nervous, and teary. She was relieved to hear his voice.

'I did miss you, you know,' he said, 'and I put up your painting again. Here, you can see it again.' She lifted the phone away to look at what he was showing her. She looked at herself, at the painting, and it made her cry. It wasn't her, she told Suhel tearfully. It wasn't who she was, she insisted. It wasn't the entire reason for her crying, she said. The woman in the painting, she stumbled, more nervous now as she explained, she felt it was someone she had lost; someone she had left forever behind. And she was sad because becoming someone else seemed necessary and so inevitable.

'I like you as you are, Pooja,' he said. She went still.

And he laughed, in the manner she had become familiar with, 'Seems like I shocked you. And you mustn't cry. I hid away that painting, not wanting anyone to see it…I wish you had been here today to see it yourself.'

She slept happy, and a few hours later, as she returned to her routine—preparing, arranging and cooking up meals to fit half a dozen different menus, and then seeing that all the lunch boxes and carriers, labelled and numbered, were efficiently despatched to the offices around, she received a message from him again.

Pooja, off to the hills, sweetie. Don't worry too much. All his secret endearments, written almost innocuously, that he perhaps thought little about, had stamped themselves on her skin, attached themselves to her heart. She'd come to depend on such words more than anything else. Sometimes she would read his words several times, knowing they belonged to her.

'About what?' she texted him back, wishing she could put a teasing note into her words. And he replied almost instantly. *You worry about so much, and I worry about my age, and how much older I am to you. And we will forget our own lives in all this. Think about it, Pooja.*

All these conversations would return to her at random moments, which made her wonder if Suhel replayed them too, in his own mind, in his aloneness. But men were different and perhaps they were busier, or had other things to think about in their spare moments.

Do you have children? She must have texted him in a moment of preoccupation. It was a thing that, of course, bothered her a lot, though of late, there had been other things, or just someone, just one thing, one person, on her mind. She hadn't given this message much thought till much later, after her day's work was done. It embarrassed her profusely when she checked her messages later, and she alternately berated herself or else blushed, hands on her cheeks.

He texted her late at night.

Children? No.

Then he texted again:

If you asked me that, Pooja, for some reason, I have to tell you I can think of nothing else but you. Nothing matters but this, that I love you, Pooja.

How Raina Lost and Won Love Again

www.mumbaidaily.com/2015/08/25/attack-on-hotel-yields-second-victim

From our local bureau: In the attack on the art exhibition at the Taj Hotel, reports of two injured victims have now emerged. The security guard injured in the fracas with protestors is recovering at Nair Hospital. It is now confirmed that a second victim, a woman, was found unconscious in the bathroom a few hours later. She had been fleeing the attack and had locked herself in it.

The victim has been identified as Ms Raina Gupta, daughter of the well-known foods business and now real-estate baron, Anil Gupta, and his wife, the philanthropist Mohini Gupta. Raina Gupta was found with injuries to her head. Doctors at the new Jaswantibehn Hospital, where Ms Gupta is recuperating, have now described her condition as stable.

The attack on the art exhibition has been condemned. Academics and scholars have labelled it as part of the ongoing onslaught on freedom of expression seen elsewhere in the country. Hotel groups have stepped up demands for security. Following the attack on her daughter, Ms Mohini Gupta gave a statement to the police. This included a description of the attacker. An alert has been issued and the police are confident of nabbing the assailant soon. They will comb through the

CCTV records and interview the hotel's security. The local inspector refused to divulge more details at this stage.

Even before he left for the television studio, Ghatge was in a foul mood. There were still unresolved matters that took up too much of his time. It seemed now that the Jupiter Mills chawl, grey, dampened with decades of rain, and close to collapse, would stand forever. This followed the discovery of an age-old agreement in a file that, as everyone had believed, had long gone missing or had been made to disappear.

Still Ghatge worked on his smile and hoped it would stay on. He had made his conditions clear to the lady from the television channel when she had called. He was going to be asked only about the event at the hotel, and nothing else.

'You know, nothing about the other stuff on me. All that gossip...'

'Yes, the speculation.' Her offhanded manner made Ghatge self-conscious. He found himself fumbling. 'Yes, there is no reason to bring up personal matters.'

He knew right away he had made a mistake. The silence that followed the young woman's intake of breath told him so.

'Sir, you mean that it is deeply personal for you?'

She had perhaps even grabbed a notebook and now held a pen ready. 'No, that is just none of...' he stopped himself. He could not be rude to these people with elections so near.

'I'll not talk of anything but this matter of the art exhibition, which is being misunderstood. All our bleeding-heart liberals are upset, but can you disregard our two-thousand-year-old culture? That you can get away insulting it?'

'Yes, Sir, I know your feelings have been hurt.' There was a bored pause, as if she knew she couldn't expect anything more from him. Then she said she hoped he would be there by seven. Ghatge pressed his fingers to his forehead, stretching the skin, erasing the frown. He practised his smile again and he spent ages choosing before settling on a checked blue kurta so it wouldn't glare under the harsh studio lighting. And then he was all set.

But the sight of the white Toyota van sent by the television studio was like a slap on the face. A wave of humiliation swept over Ghatge at the memory of his lost Benz. He wanted to turn around and rant—at its strange inexplicable disappearance and how no one seemed to understand.

Ghatge could not understand why the police were taking so long. The car had still not been traced. And what was more, he had had no idea where Mahesh was, for Mahesh had the details Ghatge had never bothered about—the car number, or where the insurance papers were, for instance. The inspector had dared ask Ghatge for these and all he had wanted to do then was punch the man's face. The inspector was most reassuring. 'We will find it, Sahib.' Holding out his pad, and pulling a pen from his ear, he had mumbled a sheepish apology, 'We do have to ask for these details, else how we will know what we are looking for?'

Ghatge wanted to give in to his rage. Once he found his beloved Benz, he promised to hunt Mahesh down. He couldn't afford to talk to his wife, Gauri, just yet; not before this Sneha issue was cleared up. He hoped Mahesh hadn't got to her first and filled her ears with nonsense about Sneha. He had to bring Mahesh in line first.

Things had always gone as Ghatge had willed them to. He assumed this would be so at the television studio as well. To any question the anchor asked him, he was going to reply in the negative, to deny everything. Attack was always the best verbal offensive. But things didn't go as he had planned. Later, seeing himself on prime-time TV, he knew he had let down his guard a bit too early.

'Some of your men had been arrested. What do you have

to say to that?' the anchor, his eyes straying to the clock, had asked. A patch of his gelled hair glinted purple in the light and he smoothed his chequered tie with his ring—it had a ruby on it, Ghatge noted. It was almost over then, Ghatge surmised, and he was prepared to be somewhat more loquacious. 'The arrests were a mistake. It was a peaceful protest.' His face darkened. He remembered his warnings to his men, now out on bail. They had to lie low for a while, it was for the best.

'Are you saying then that there was no violence?'

'Yes.' Then Ghatge said forcefully, 'Yes. Some miscreants were responsible for the violence. True, they got offended.' The anchor looked quizzical. He nodded at the producer and the cameraman so Ghatge couldn't be sure of his intentions. 'But we do know of the critical, even…' he looked at a page before him, 'life-threatening injuries on one, as the newspapers report?'

'In a bathroom,' Ghatge scoffed. 'And no one saw her or her attacker. Where are all the CCTVs, as the police say?'

But the anchor, it seemed, couldn't have enough. He leaned forward and spoke in low, deliberate tones. 'It is believed that a car was also stolen. Your car, Sir?'

A deep sense of anguish tore through Ghatge. But he held on and responded through gritted teeth. 'The hotel security has been most lax. There were no security men, no CCTVs in place. If there had been, my car would not have been stolen.'

'Then…' Ghatge added as an afterthought, 'no one would have been injured either.'

'Are you suggesting that because of a car…?'

Ghatge could not pre-empt the look of deep satisfaction that spread over the anchor's face. He could, however, decide not to answer and that is precisely what he chose to do. He did manage a hissed *no comment* before he rose from his chair.

www.mumbaidaily.com/2015/08/29/missing-car-spotted

A yellow Mercedes-Benz was spotted going above the speed limit on the highway to Chiplun. The police, just as they claim to be monitoring safe driving on our highways, have also been on the lookout for this car. Presumably they are so busy doing the latter, that they cannot possibly keep track of other errant, overspeeding drivers. This photo was sent to us by college students of the local medical college. The students, who had then no idea about the antecedents of the car, said it had presented a magnificent sight to them, its colour caught against the ghats and the trees. The driver had plainly been racing against the Konkan railway train scheduled to reach Chiplun station in around two hours.

www.mumbaidaily.com/2015/09/02/hotel-attack-victim-remains-critical

Sources at the Jaswantibehn Hospital say Raina Gupta, injured in the protest attack at the Taj Hotel, is recovering but her condition still needs to be monitored. Sources have mentioned some clarifications relating to Mohini Gupta's (the victim's mother) earlier statement to the police. It was dark in the hotel corridor and Raina couldn't see her attacker clearly. So far, we have been told it was a tall bearded man, who was armed. But Raina Gupta is still not talking to the press. Mohini Gupta, who has been interacting with the media and the police on her daughter's behalf, pointed to Raina's bravery. 'Raina's making a special effort to cooperate with the investigations and should be applauded,' she said. An entire section on the fourth floor, where Raina Gupta is recovering, has been cordoned off. Mrs Gupta also hoped that well-wishers would leave a donation to the charity she was actively associated with.

http://mumbai-social-butterfly.blogpost.com/2015/08/a-historical-and-social-rivalry.html

Raina Gupta, victim of the mob attack on the Taj Hotel, has now been in hospital for three weeks. The other victim is the security guard, a poor migrant worker from Bihar but it'd be so uncool to talk of that here. Who bothers about them anyway? Raina is the daughter of Anil Gupta, the industrialist who has promised to transform Mumbai into a new Shanghai or even Singapore. A rising city of a billion and more. Gone will be the grey tenements, the barely functional water taps, and the common toilets. Instead, Mr Gupta, in his own housing projects has promised self-sufficiency in every way (read gated communities), with every facility the resident might wish for, including elevators in garages. Of course, to make these sustaining, residents would have to pool in (read high rents). Those who cannot afford to do so will be relocated to apartments in upcoming suburbs of the city. Is this a city for the elite?

Is the attack on Raina Gupta then, one on Mr Gupta's plans, and not really an attack on freedom of expression? Are the two things linked? In raising these questions, we could be guilty of obfuscation, but we ask questions the newspapers are afraid to.

We must now ask about the woman, Dr Sneha Desai, who committed suicide in a posh Panchgani resort that belonged, as we understand, to an associate of Anil Gupta.

Sneha Desai was the niece of Ramakrishna Desai, noted labour leader killed in the 1970s. The chawl she lived and worked in has been the cynosure of all eyes, ever since an old agreement was subsequently recovered in Dr Desai's office. Mohini Gupta, now married to Anil Gupta, once had an affair with Ramakrishna Desai. She was rumoured to be close to Suhel Kolhatkar, the current sensation who is in hot water for flying over the city in a chopper with no permission. Watch for updates: it is believed that Mohini Gupta may hyperventilate on this matter and issue a customary denial, as is the practice.

www.mumbaidaily.com/2015/09/07/citywide-freedom-protests-planned

A peaceful protest for freedom of expression is to be organized tomorrow at the Azad Maidan. The organizers of Save Our City (SOC) are requesting all peace-loving citizens to participate. This will be the second in the series of peaceful marches planned, ever since the disruption of the art exhibition at the Taj Mahal.

The organizers are confident their march will draw a big response. An earlier protest at Bandra's Carter Road had been peaceful and had drawn a big crowd (see accompanying photo). A line of people had walked silently down the road, holding up blank placards to signify the clamping down on expression the city has seen of late.

Neera and Pooja saw Vasudha first. She was waiting for them, at the hospital's foyer, peering into every vehicle that drew up. When Vasudha spotted them, she came up waddling, setting quite a fast pace. She looked too big for seven months and catching each other's eye, Neera and Pooja realized they were thinking the same thing.

'You are here, finally. There's been no more word from Mahesh?' Vasudha made no effort to lower her tone. Neera gave the two of them a quick look of incomprehension. It made Vasudha move deliberately back, to keep pace with Pooja, who looked around, somewhat confused at the methodical orderliness of the hospital and its constant busyness. People moved with a robotic urgency, everywhere there was that smell of phenol and disinfectant. But Vasudha did not wait for a reply. Instead she rushed ahead, like a small bulldozer in that neatly packed lobby, where attendants bearing gurneys cried for room, babies wailed and a television played loudly in a corner. 'Neeraji,' she hissed urgently as the older woman went up to the reception desk.

There was a hurried exchange between them that Pooja caught as she walked up. Vasudha hissed, 'Raina's not being allowed visitors, they won't let us in.' And even as Neera looked nonplussed, Vasudha put on a deliberate nonchalant air. 'Just follow me, you both,' she said. She was going to lead them to Raina, as only Vasudha could.

Vasudha indeed took charge, and they embarked on a circuitous route to the fourth floor, where Raina's room was. First, past a long corridor, where they rode on a travellator for some time, then up an elevator to the sixth floor, then the descent to a children's ward, up a spiral staircase, which was the special fire escape, said Vasudha, panting and sweating. Every time Neera got a few paces ahead, Vasudha would slow down, turn to Pooja, grip her hand tight in hers, and ask in a quick low whisper, so her words, half-swallowed up, would mingle with the lime-scented talcum powder she used, the mint she had been sucking, and her stale perspiration.

'Have you heard from Mahesh? The news is he has gone to Chiplun. Ghatge has sent his men to find out.'

Then they came to a long corridor, 'The last one,' Vasudha said laughing. 'The doc said I need the exercise at my stage, it will do the baby good.' The three of them walked quietly now, in single file, past the nurses' room, quickly sweeping past the reception counter, then down a soft-carpeted narrow corridor that led to the VIP suites.

'It's now believed he has taken the car…Ghatge's fancy car to Chiplun and Ghatge daren't go there. Because his wife is most upset. About his affair, you know.'

Vasudha giggled and then they stepped into the coolness

of the room. Pooja did not have the heart to tell her about Mahesh's decision, for Neera's long heartfelt sigh of relief came to them, and Raina's startled 'oh' followed by her smile, both strained and happy, as she lowered her tablet onto her lap. Pooja heard the click as Vasudha closed the door behind them. Raina leant back on her pillow, her tablet half-open and a gentle sun blazed through the linen curtains. It registered on Pooja that Raina's face looked thinner than before, and her eyes behind their glasses had an intensity she had not seen before.

Neera placed a thin shrivelled hand on the bed, and pulled the chair closer to the bed. Her sandals scraped against the smooth polished floor, where the carpet ended, and the chair's steel ends made a high, screeching sound. 'It's so good to see you, my dear.'

Over Neera's head, Raina smiled, closing her eyes briefly. Pooja swallowed hard, and took in the bed, the way Raina reclined with its end raised up, and the bottle of glucose dripping into her. Raina looked more ill now than in the first moments they had seen her. The tablet she had been working on lay heavy on her lap and Neera sat on the low chair, and it was Raina's low murmured responses that they heard, that she was well, though she was weak and she would be better soon.

Neera held Raina's hand. 'I missed you, dear.' She sat there stroking Raina's slender fingers and after a while, when Rana no longer responded, Neera bent down and something in Raina's hand caught Pooja's eye. She did not miss the thin tube injected into her hand, the red spots and Raina's swollen finger knobs. That was when Neera broke down, and wept. Raina's eyes flashed open at the sound of Neera's quiet sobbing before it was all interrupted by a hissing matron who swept through the door, her wide eyes full of horror.

In the split second before Pooja turned to face the matron, she saw Raina's eyes—sharp, with some curiosity—trained on her, and Pooja read in them, a resentment Raina couldn't quite disguise. Then Pooja knew why. Mahesh had been at the window but she had seen Raina turning too, fleeing in that one moment when Suhel had lifted his face away from hers in the hotel. In their own minds, the two women held that one moment differently, and Pooja felt in herself a new surge of welcome power.

http://mumbai-social-butterfly.blogpost.com/2015/08-9/ hospital-secret-visitors.html

Despite warnings that any visits and meetings would endanger her health, it does seem Raina Gupta in hospital had a surprise visitor. It is unclear how Neera Joshi managed to find her way through the hospital security (like hotels, it seems such places can be easily breached) with two companions. Apparently, their presence was soon noticed by an alert hospital staff and they were asked to leave.

Later Neera Joshi did speak about her meeting with Raina. At the lobby, we had our representative, though her two companions tried to hush her up. One of them, evidently pregnant, was more belligerent. It is Raina, the patient, who is being held prisoner, she said. But she was silenced by a stern glance from Neera, whose looks at one time did set a thousand workers' hearts aflutter, especially Ramakrishna Desai's who led the labour union for decades till his death. Neera mentioned she was relieved to see Raina, though the meeting was short. They were working on her memoirs together.

Neera Joshi was once a much-respected labour leader. It is believed her memoirs will contain details of a time that needs to be preserved. The book will have other details of people now prominent in public life, and will have much to reveal about what happened when the textile mill unions were suppressed. And also about the last chawl that remains standing—the Jupiter Mills Chawl, that will fight all this out.

Neera, however, would not answer when we asked her if her secret visit had something to do with her wish to avoid Mohini, Raina's mother and who had for a short while, been Neera's rival in love. 'I have nothing against Mohini,' Neera only said. 'Why would she disallow it?'

But we know better don't we, Neera? There are stories in the past, and how some of these never truly die. Stories linked to Ramakrishna Desai and now as it appears, it is his dead niece, Sneha Desai, who held the key to the chawl—eyed by real-estate hawks like Anil Gupta—and its future. There's more to it than meets the eye, but a blog can't do the investigative journalism that newspapers simply refuse to do. A blog sees the truth and reports it.

www.mumbaidaily.com/2015/09/10/citywide-freedom-protests-planned

The City Hospital Nurses Union has threatened to go on strike. This follows the sacking of a nurse in Jaswantibehn Hospital at the behest of Mohini Gupta. Mrs Gupta, whose daughter Raina, remains in a critical state, had expressly forbidden any visitors. But the union has protested at this arbitrary suspension. The hospital, one of the city's biggest and private hospitals, sees over a million patients, several from abroad. It has set records in heart and liver transplants, having treated thousand transplant cases in the last six months alone.

We do know Raina Gupta had visitors and that they reported seeing Ms Gupta in a cheerful mood. According to sources, Neera Joshi, writer and former labour activist, and two others had visited Raina. When asked if there had been visitors, Mohini gave a rather clipped confirmation. The visitors, she revealed, came with their own interests in mind. 'They should have let my daughter recover.'

http://mumbai-social-butterfly.blogpost.com/2015/09/
hospital-secret-visitors.html

New truths are emerging about the fracas at the hospital, where Raina Gupta has been for a month now. There is now war again between Neera Joshi and Mohini Gupta, two aging stars who at one time shone, though we exaggerate, over the city's firmament. A time when the city was not in thrall to film stars or celebrity writers. The present developments are related to events at the Jaswantibehn Hospital, where a nurse has been suspended for a 'security lapse'.

The nurse claims to having been made a victim. She said 'Madam (Mrs Gupta) did not want visitors because she has been hiding the truth behind her daughter's illness.' She wouldn't elaborate further. But we are given to believe that Raina Gupta's injuries were not inflicted by an 'unknown attacker still on the loose', as the police have it. The nurse only indicated that it was a 'rich people's disease'. According to her, 'too much money, too much tension', she said before hanging up.

The Gupta family insists that Raina's head injuries are more severe than expected and a neurologist from the UK is expected to visit. She is cooperating with the police every way but any disturbance and rumours could affect her frail health. The family pleads for understanding. Our sources tell us this is obfuscation, that there is some truth to the nurse's story. The reason for Mohini Gupta's ire, her tirade against the nurses and the hospital's administration is her wish to conceal that Raina Gupta has been anorexic-bulimic for a long time. Her illness forms part of the reason she had been sent away for rehab in the US and where she is now studying. It is not quite clear why a relapse happened.

The City Hospital Nurses Union is up in arms. The nurses emphasize that they provide much needed and valuable humane service. 'Providing security to VIP isn't our concern,' said the head of the union. But when the police commissioner was asked about the incidence of lax security again, this time in one of the city's most sought-after hospitals, he pleaded helplessness. 'There is just no way can we provide security to everyone. There are too many important people in this city, politicians and film stars and even cricketers; always too many important things happening in the city.' Then he came up with a bizarre statement. 'While we do stand for freedoms guaranteed to us, policemen just can't rush from protecting one freedom to another, freedom of expression is fine and so is freedom of movement. Both simply can't be handled together.' When we tried to contact him later, he said he had been misquoted.

www.mumbaidaily.com/2015/09/20/citywide-freedom-protests-planned

The city pages of *The Mumbai Daily* carried more photos of the missing yellow Mercedes-Benz. There it was parked in front of the State Transport Depot in Chiplun, ogled by hundreds of passengers, vendors and others. And again, there it was, taking up pride of place before the primary school in Khed and again, in the wholesale market where Mrs Gauri Ghatge loaded sacks of vegetables onto its nice leather back seat. According to the paper's local reporter, the Benz is being used extensively in the civic elections since Mrs Ghatge announced her candidature as an independent. She plans to bring about immense changes and fiercely opposes the development of hotels and resorts planned there.

Mrs Ghatge apparently loves the Benz as it allows for faster communication and draws attention like nothing else. In a statement, she said she was happy she had her husband's support. There were absolutely no differences between her and Ghatge Sahib. He would come to campaign for her.

~

Raina's article in TheAtlantic.com appeared on the very day of her departure from Mumbai. She sat at the very end of a cushy reclining seat at the airport lounge, feeling it vibrate every time someone else plopped farther down, giving her a polite embarrassed smile. She looked around aimless, fretting. The boarding time was still an hour away. She had been assured her piece would appear and seeing it now, on her phone, she felt some karmic coincidence was at work.

She hadn't slept the night before and it was dawn when the driver had rushed her to the airport. But it wasn't just her impatience, she knew, it was her mother's tears that always confused her. The night before Raina had imagined precisely such a scenario. Her mother would weep, throw herself at her, and plead once again. 'Raina, you're leaving. You can't.'

'I did tell you about it, Ma.' She bit her tongue on the words that threatened to come automatically. 'But you were too busy...'

'Raina, I wish you would not be so complicated.'

She knew her mother had stood at the window and they had waved to each other long after the car had turned the gate, past the creepers on the walls and climbed the Pedder Road flyover. That morning, her mother had made a pitiful figure, in her loose shirt, her hair awry, and the tears that stained the kohl around her eyes. It struck Raina then that Mohini wasn't fully recovered yet. Where were her people—her secretary, her make-up person? Somehow, they had added to her mother's presence, and now without them her mother seemed nothing, wraith-like, and very vulnerable.

Raina held herself rigid all the way as she was driven to the airport. She had refused breakfast as well. From now on, her life would begin anew. Back in New York, she would resume a rigorous schedule, diet carefully, visit the gym and take up swimming too. Her father had patted her mother and said it was all right. They would soon plan a trip to the US. 'It's no big deal,' he had put an arm around his wife, in a bluff and hearty way and they had nodded in unison, in the manner of false animated figures. Raina was glad when she could finally turn away.

Raina saw her piece the fifth time she refreshed the webpage. She fell back on the seat, feeling the rods creak under her. The man at the other end shifted too, she straightened herself, the man awkwardly moved again before Raina got a grip on herself, wiped the smile off her face. The man was smiling in an overfriendly way. In another moment, he would sidle up, ask her for coffee.

Raina got up, her eyes fixed on her phone. There was no doubt now that her piece had been featured. She liked the cover photo, it made her smile. The artist, Dr Joshi, serenely painting, oblivious to the happenings around him. Her photo had caught the chawl on his canvas, a loving reflection of the ugly, much-loved building, as it rose behind him. It had taken some nerve for the protestors to stand tall before the builders, as they moved in with their cranes and bulldozers. And there was Neera at one end, bespectacled and in her starched cotton sari, holding onto a megaphone, reading aloud the old agreement.

It had been recovered from Sneha Desai's files after all. A valued piece of paper, one dated to 1973 and signed by the mill management handing over the chawl and the land around it to the workers, as a Diwali bonus, in return for their acceptance of the voluntary retirement conditions put forward by the textile company. So it was the workers who were the rightful owners of the chawl land, and they could do with it what they wanted. The piece of paper Ramakrishna Desai had signed, almost as a betrayal of all the causes he had fought for: a piece of land in place of their jobs.

Life, Raina thought, was made of betrayals like these, but now after all the protests, it seemed like a complete victory— the chawl and its people, as David-like figures, standing up to the Goliath-like real-estate barons.

Raina liked the title her editor had given it. *Lone Chawl Standing*. They had included most of Richard's pictures too. The one of the bulldozers, trampling over the plastic buckets at the municipal tap. There was also a picture she had taken of the yellow Mercedes-Benz, the one that was in the news, with the man who loved it, standing tall and glowering next to it.

Within minutes of her sharing the article on Facebook, Raina counted several likes. In a few hours, news of the piece would reach her parents, enraging and embarrassing them in turn. Her father would be furious. While unnamed, it was clear he was the businessman mentioned with real-estate interests and close links with politicians, while her mother would be miffed, even angry at Neera upstaging her once again.

A month or so after her return to New York, Raina finally decided to write the letter she had long put off. Email wouldn't do, nor even phone calls. These were just perfunctory in nature. Her parents and she listened to each other, made promises, and then longed to hang up. There was always something calling them away. But then once in New York, Raina too had thrown herself into a frenzy of activity. The gym, the yoga sessions, the walks home from the station, the pristine diet, except for the occasional indulgence. It was working and helping her get over many things.

The long postal way, Raina decided, was the best way to write to her mother. She thought over it as she wrote out the letter once, twice and several times, before she was ready to do so one final time. In some senses, it was easier than emailing. She would not begin worrying the moment she hit 'send'. She'd never even know when the letter reached her mother, or if it really did.

Ma,

You must be surprised why I have written. I am surprised too, but I guess I must answer things for myself. This is about something I've been meaning to write. They say your own can be full of mystery. But you, Ma, have deliberately and always been so.

There were so many things you never talked about. For instance, your jealousy of Neera first made me curious. Why was she never invited to your parties? I mean why did you not even ask her? Why did you walk out that time she spoke at Sneha Desai's memorial? All that had an answer in this old photo. I have attached a copy here. It's while working on a piece about Neera Joshi, that I found it. And so found out about your affair with Ramakrishna Desai.

I came back to know you better. It was part guilt. It's what everyone here does all the time. It's dinned into every non-fiction class you attend: 'get into yourself, ask yourself things, find your past selves' and I came back to do that. And found more than I bargained for, at the cost of myself.

For the past caught me in strange ways. You were just the same. Papa said it was the Portugal method, the magic cancer cure by the genius surgeon there. I was amazed. Those first days were a whirligig of so much happenings and events and one day when I looked in the mirror I found I had bloated terribly. It was me who had changed. I felt as fat as I had been before, the sad neglected Raina of old.

It was almost as if I had willed back my bulimia. Within a month, I found it was so easy to be pulled back into the past. One day I was stuffing myself, with Malini, cooking up all that heavenly stuff for every meal that none of us ate together and the very next hour I'd be throwing it all up. I hated the contrast between me and you. Did you ever notice me? The only time you did was when you swished into my room to ask how you looked, or when you wanted something from my wardrobe. You would never look at me. And when I saw you busy with that art exhibition, I could almost see you with pity and contempt. There you were, ready to become a favourite of

all those liberal television channels, and to foist on them and
for yourself—yes, for yourself—some no-good painters who
just knew how to draw attention (pun intended, if at all).
    I did come to know you a fair bit, and it makes me your
admirer. And what confuses me is this: you can never love
or even like someone you admire, can you? And admiration
always is a first step, never something that happens later. So,
I am puzzled with that, about myself. And this is where I am
actually smiling as I end this letter.

~

Days after she had sent the letter, Raina still thought over her
lines. She had read bits of it out in a late-night reading at her
college, and everyone had been amazed at 'My Mother's Brave
Struggle'. Raina had made them laugh, in places where she
referred to her mother's rigorous timetable, specifying to the
exact minute, how much time her mother gave to anything on
her schedule. They chuckled at her mother's silly perfection
that had made her often run into Raina's room to ask how she
looked, how she preferred the mirror in Raina's room to any
other in the house. 'But it wasn't like the Snow White story,
my mother never looked at me.' Then the chuckles dissolved
to a quiet silence.
    She made them laugh sympathetically, reading the parts
about their cook Malini, who was the only one who spoiled
her. All the lavish breakfasts, multicourse lunches and the
rich suppers. The clarified butter (for she had to explain to
her American audience what 'ghee' was) swelled up in your
tongue, glazed your eyes and ran quickly through your veins,
till you were too heavy to move. She had made them weep and
was secretly pleased when she caught a sniffle or two as she
described her own traipsing to her mother's empty room, left
unchanged since her childhood, trying to find her mother of
old. Raina told them last about her bulimia, a cry to a mother

who never noticed, how it was a way to fill herself when there was nothing else. Her mother filled with life, emptied of much else.

Looking out over the city, from her apartment at Remsen Street, with the sun low over the Brooklyn Bridge, Raina had that sensation of peace and a welcome emptiness. All around her were people, and she could see no one. The lights everywhere, in every apartment house, felt more human than anything else. It was a day she found herself alone. She would have to get herself together soon, she told herself. Find a roommate. Or even get a cat.

The sun caught on the silver steel blades of the bridge. There were some things you could never tell anyone for all one tried. Suhel Kolhatkar, for instance. A man who had once been infatuated with her own mother and then had finally given it up, for it was all one-sided. And that was long ago too. She knew then she had also been harsh to her mother.

Suhel Kolhatkar. A man so near her mother's age, but it was she, Raina, who was besotted with him. She took a swig from her beer can, munched her chips and laughed heartily. He was perhaps in his early fifties now, and would be sixty, when she was thirty. Worse, when she was forty, the swinging years, he would be an old doddering seventy, no matter how much he rejuvenated himself or pumped himself with Viagra.

Raina cried and then laughed. She munched on the chips, opened a new packet when it was done, and had more beer. But she still could not get the humiliation out of her mind.

The one afternoon, she had gone to meet him, bringing with her, her mother's invite to the art exhibition at the Taj Hotel. It was Raina's excuse to invite Suhel. There was a chance she would run into him at Gymkhana Club. The club was right in the city's genteel south, standing in all its secluded greenery, away from the crowds, and its sullen heat. Its bamboo curtains and wooden corridors dulled the sound of traffic. Occasionally, there would be a rugby match in the grounds outside and the shouts of the players, the sound of feet hitting the ball, the scrunch of figures falling over each other would filter through the curtains, rustle the newspapers, and arouse memories of a distant age. The old colonial presence was everywhere, in the liveried servants, the gramophone playing Percy Grainger, the clinking of glasses, and murmured conversations.

Suhel had been so very gallant, rising to his feet as Raina came up, and the quizzical look he had in his eyes as she held out the card. She should have understood his responses then. But all she was conscious of was how she looked. The way he bent down to her, making her feel light and very feminine, the frown and the amused glint in his eyes.

'You know, perhaps your mom might not want me there?' He looked at her, hoping she would understand but she liked the way his eyes crinkled with amusement, or was it worry? He added, shrugging, 'She perhaps knows it's not quite my taste.'

'It'll be quite...avant-garde, the exhibition,' Raina said, hoping her accent came through. He lived in Maryland and he'd guess her accent too.

'Yes...I see,' and then he indicated to her that she join him for coffee.

He poured coffee for her, then flipped open the envelope. Raina saw his neat, square hands, the thin hair on his wrists, the watch with the plain leather band he wore. There was a gentle frown on his face as he read, and then he went very still, his voice strayed off in mid-conversation and she was forced to ask him twice.

'It'd be nice if you came. Will you?'

'Yes...yes, I'd like to,' his voice had a cracked edge to it, and there was a strange brilliance in his eyes, as if a light had entered it. It had given her a thrill then. 'I'd be glad too. Thank you.'

They were talking of other things and she remembered how distracted he had been, checking his phone, looking past her at the window and now she knew why. He had come to the hotel, to the exhibition, because of Pooja. He had seen her name on the invite. *Catering from Pooja's,* it said, and everyone by then, Raina thought a little bitterly now, knew who Pooja was. Everyone in posh south Mumbai, that is. But she, Raina thought, had more likes for her piece in *The Atlantic* than Pooja would ever have for her Facebook page, if she ever decided to have one.

When Raina had looked for Suhel at the exhibition, he was nowhere to be seen. She had searched for him in some desperation. Someone said he had been seen heading out, perhaps he had received a call. Raina had been blinded to everything else but the thought that she must find him. She had taken trouble over herself, as she dressed herself for the event. Her mother's beautician had done her hair too, and she wore a sari, though running around the grey stone façade of the hotel, she wished she hadn't. Her sari end caught against a creeper and when she cursed, she heard the muffled laughter of the waiting chauffeurs around.

That had made Raina pull open the door closest to her and she found herself amidst the hot pipes and tanks of the generator room. But there were other smells around, stray whiffs and inviting aromas and she knew she had only to take a corridor that led out to find herself close to the kitchen. But she was soon quite lost, and all Raina felt then was a panic. For she still hadn't found Suhel. All her plans to impress him, to make him fall in love with her, were failing. The French baker had smiled at her in some surprise but all the others— the cooks, the assistants, the stewards—had barely had time for her. All she could do was plunge into another corridor and she saw it lead to a small door further away.

Even now the memory made her heart catch. For they had

looked heartbreakingly beautiful. Suhel leaning over Pooja gently, a hand on the wall, and another on her shoulder, and she, her face lifted, her hands on his shirt, and they were lost to the world as they kissed each other. Suhel and Pooja.

Raina must have stood there for some moments. But all she remembered was how she had run away, blinded by the smoke, the shouts that came from the busy kitchen and elsewhere. She wanted to rid herself of that image, of all that was around her, she wanted to abandon herself as well. Her ugly, always unwanted, forever unloved self. It was with some relief that she found the restroom, but she hadn't liked how she looked. That was what made her bend over the commode, after which she remembered nothing.

She wondered now if she should tell Pooja what she knew. But Suhel wasn't a cad, he hadn't strung her, Raina, along at all. He had behaved just like a man in love. She was tempted to tell Pooja this too but she couldn't, not now. Maybe something more scandalous later, she told herself, something that was more her, Raina's style. She picked up her tablet, and toyed with the words she'd use for her new post on her blogpost: Mumbai-social-butterfly.blogpost.com. A plane flew over the bridge; she knew the last of her chips was over. Raina pushed away her tablet, looked at the clock. The gym, she knew, was open. It was always time for new beginnings. A thousand and more Facebook likes for her piece could perhaps translate into one small like for herself, from herself.

Suhel's Lists for Life

Waiting for his father as the bar filled up around him, Suhel made a list all over again. Like everything with him, it wasn't straightforward in any measure. No neat, numbered sentences, instead his fingers made a 'v' at the corner of the papery serviette as he wrote randomly, then stretched his pen to form balloons and arrows to show his abbreviated thoughts and half-sentences.

My life:

1 Broken the law—five times, including very recently for overspeeding.

2. One failed marriage: Though it was doomed from the start. He wrote the word 'marriage' and circled it once and then again. Helen and he had propped each other up socially, and it felt good for a while. They had been unfaithful to each other right from the first year. But it was his hotel bill that had given away the entire thing. Now Suhel did not even remember who he had been with.

3. Two, or maybe three, failed relationships. And he felt guilty about none.

4. Named by *Fortune* as an entrepreneur to watch out for.

This was after he had worked on a patent that would, via an examination of saliva, enable an easy and cheap identification of certain kinds of cancer. Suhel was proud of this; it would prove a boon especially in rural India, despite the time it had taken him to secure government permissions.

He ran a line underscoring what he had written. This was what mattered; work defined one. In the end, when one was betrayed, slighted by hurts, offences, grudges, no matter how imagined these could be, there was always one's work, one's passion that stood faithfully by one. But...and Suhel wrote the word again—But...and put a question mark, before he pushed the serviette away.

Such lists, for all improvisations, missed out the shadows, the in-between things, the almost-happened, the stuff that truly mattered and made up things still undefined. Things that made you look for reasons not to leave, to stay on.

Like the painting, he had seen at Dr Joshi's: the woman's face caught in the dawn light. She looked lost in herself, as a crowded city arranged itself around her. It had intrigued him at first, and weeks later there had been that surprise encounter with Pooja at the memorial. The resemblance had taken his breath away. It wasn't the painting, it was how she had been, looking through the wings at the memorial gathering, that had made his heart move in inexplicable ways. He had been unable to look away, to tell if she saw him too, if her flustered look as her head turned and caught him, indicated anything.

On that fateful rain-drenched morning, Suhel had been outside, under an awning below Dr Joshi's rooms. He had been sleepless, and as soon as the day broke, he had left Dr Joshi's small apartment and walked down. All around him were huddled, sleeping figures. Suhel wasn't sure what he had been thinking. He felt like a stalker, and it was all so ridiculous at his age. A man almost fifty; no forty-nine, he corrected, holding himself straighter. Perhaps he had wanted to catch Pooja in the clear light of day, as she filled her buckets up at the municipal tube well. The wait had left him tired and drained. But all he remembered now was how soft her skin had felt against his own when he pushed her aside, away from the advancing bulldozer.

She had smelt of some herbal soap he couldn't place then, though now he knew it was jasmine, and her hair had a fresh, washed feel. When they had walked together to the clinic, he was afraid she'd wrinkle her nose up at the grimy smell that lay all over him. Later, she had fingered the bandage on her head and asked no one in particular, 'Does it look big?'

Then had followed the evening of the art exhibition when he had inveigled to meet Pooja in the hotel, once he had seen her name in the invite. He had wanted to see her again, feel the sensation of her skin against his. Then had followed the messages and the calls, the inevitable disappointments as had happened on the day of the immersion. That evening and then others since then that he had to keep thinking over. For since then, Pooja had been somewhat elusive, more teasing, wilful and hard to reach. It'd have made him angry. But he calmed himself. He was getting old, was already too cynical and the list-making helped. Had he misread all her responses?

Suhel scrunched up the serviette as he heard his father come up. This was something his therapist had advised. He rubbed his eyes, where a hazy redness had appeared at the corner of his vision. He seemed to be doing more of this often. Just before he had left Maryland, he had nicked his eye rushing to catch Luke, his neighbour's son, when he had nearly fallen from the swing. A shrapnel or a stray twig had bothered him a bit, but of late the irritation had returned in some measure. A redness appeared often at the corner of his right eye which made him rub it often. Sometimes, owing to this, he did not trust quite what he saw.

When Suhel's phone rang for the third time, his father across the table had just begun talking about Rosie. It took Suhel a moment to realize whom his father meant. Oh yes, his housekeeper. The phone rang, insistent for a while, like phones were at such moments, before shutting off abruptly. Again, it wasn't a number Suhel recognized and he assumed it was Ghatge. The man, hounded by the press, had been calling from different numbers. He wanted to make a deal with Suhel about investing in a hotel project in Panchgani. A big investment, Ghatge evidently thought, would make people forget the scandal of Sneha Desai's death, scotch rumours of his affair with her. His father looking around, his eyes stopping at the clock, only said wryly, 'You might get another call any minute. But yes, it's about Rosie. We intend to get married.'

Suhel had been looking at his phone, and now he looked up startled at what his father said. His father who, in the aftermath of those words, now sat in a glow all his own, or perhaps it was the chandelier that shimmered and glowed, and its light flashed golden on the table, then became hazy and Suhel knew it was his eyes. He blinked the haziness away again rapidly, remembered he hadn't eaten, and the wine had gone to his head.

'Suhel?' His father looked anxious and then amused. 'Is the news such a shock?'

He made to say 'no', and his father was explaining in his reasonable, assured voice. 'One does feel old, and I am afraid of being left alone.'

His father laughed, almost embarrassed and toyed with his glass. It reminded Suhel of something long ago. His father had been sitting just this way and there was something he had said then. Then Suhel corrected himself: it hadn't been a restaurant like this one but his father had been speaking in the same measured tones.

Suhel frowned, looked down at the table. He tried not to think of other things that intruded. His mother's voice loud and shrill in his head. Telling him about his father, her voice raised in anger and then wilfully calming herself down, before she began again. She circled around his room as he tried to study, casting a furtive glance around in case she spotted his old copies of *Playboy* and *Debonair*.

'Are you okay, Suhel?' he heard his father's voice over the din, sweeping into the rush of his memories. He was irritated with himself. He seemed quite the older, sicker man sitting across his father.

'Rosie wants you to do something for Richard.'

His father had moved onto talking about Rosie's son. 'He's younger than you. The only one who wants to remain in that chawl.'

His father paused as he caught Suhel's eye. He knew then he had Suhel's attention. 'The one in the news, yes.'

Suhel's disinterest vanished in a moment. That was Pooja's world. He knew it quite well. 'Richard lives in that chawl?' he now said, forcing a calmness into his voice. The image of an awkward young man stepping forward to help Pooja with an easy familiarity came to his mind. In turn, Suhel felt stiff and heavy-footed and it had made him intervene more forcefully, with his American swagger. He had insisted, firmly and quite forcefully, that he would take Pooja to the clinic.

'Yes, and the chawl is going to be broken up, no matter what these activists do, there's too much against them.' His father's lips set in a grim line, as he looked to the waitress for another drink.

His father turned his glass this way and that, as Suhel grasped a sudden truth, one he hadn't acknowledged so far. Suhel hadn't been bothered much about Pooja's chawl. In fact, he had been indifferent to Pooja's insistence, her loyalty to it. For him, it was all about her, and now from her prevarications, her excuses, it was clear the chawl was something important for her. Her heroism had been necessary. His lips lifted in a rueful smile as he acknowledged it all, and his father's practicality. 'I wish it would stay though,' Suhel said quietly.

'It's just some sentimental attachment. When the chawl is indeed falling apart,' said his father.

Suhel glanced at his father and then an unexpected new

thought took his breath away, brought about a constriction in his throat. He coughed, harshly and then repetitively and when he looked up, all he saw around for some moments, was the redness like a swiftly dissipating cloud. If Pooja couldn't live in the chawl, if she had nowhere to go, then he could persuade her to marry him. He blinked his eyes again, as if that thought had brought with it a welcome pain. It was almost like shrapnel locked in his eye.

He held his head in his hands. It wasn't the way he wanted things to work out. Not as a way out for Pooja and she'd never agree. His father touched him on the shoulder, 'Son, maybe you're tired. Do you need to see a doctor?'

'No, I am fine.'

His father looked at him and then moved on. As if he couldn't help but speak of his own plans. Suhel had seen it with the old and aging. They either rambled or were self-obsessed to a point; it happened with those who had given up on time, and the others who having realized there wasn't much left, thought only of themselves.

'Richard, he's funny, or so Rosie says,' his father said, his lips moving in disapproval. 'He doesn't want to give up the place. He can stay with us, but...' Then his father paused, looked at his own folded hands on the table, and then looked straight at Suhel.

'He'd need a regular job,' his father finished. 'Can you help?'

Now he sounded quite like the businessmen Suhel was used to. One could prevaricate, be watchful, indulge in generalities but sooner or later one did get to the point. Even his father. Suhel could see it in his pleading eyes.

'It'd give Rosie immense relief. She's seen the heroine...'

'Heroine...' Suhel now looked genuinely puzzled, his eyes locking into his father's questioningly. 'You mean Neera?' He asked in all seriousness. For Neera had amazed him; Raina's piece that had appeared in *The Atlantic* had been so detailed. The protests in the chawl, its drawing together of residents, activists and scholars of the city had required dedication and thought, and he admired Neera's energy, for all her frailty and age. She had been giving speech after speech, talking to the journalists, circulating that long-lost agreement. His father had meant it in jest, but Neera truly was quite the heroine.

'No...the other one,' his father sounded dismissive. 'She's pretty though. That picture of hers that came in the papers.'

Suhel felt something catch at his heart again—Pooja's mention by someone else. He hoped his father hadn't caught the flush on his face, the way Dr Joshi had. Suhel was deliberately nonchalant in what he said next. 'It does matter to them. It should to us too.'

'Yes, but they don't have the money to maintain it. The chawls are run-down, they need upgrading. Instead they should let the builders make something better, and sturdier. You know the chawls themselves weren't made in any long-lasting way.'

'True, but it's an entire lifestyle there. And it's important for the history of the city. You do know, Dad, what has come up in their place? Eyesores...' Suhel coughed again, stared with some distaste at his drink, before going on. 'And all over the place. They look so cramped, as if they are meant to bottle up the city's people...'

His father looked amused, and pushed his glass away. Then he refused another drink, smiling distractedly at the pretty waitress who came up. His eyes moved over Suhel's quickly, and this time his words were rushed.

'We will be getting married at the registrar's. Do come...' he said brusquely, somewhat embarrassed.

Suhel nodded in vague agreement. Around him, there was a new commotion. On the giant screen, a cricket match was on, and all he could see then were the wild surging heads everywhere, grey and black flashing against silver. His father was saying something, his lips moving and Suhel couldn't hear a word. Then his father put his hand on his shoulder, almost drawing Suhel closer.

'I am also afraid. This time I may lose her, like I did Phuong. And time doesn't forgive.'

Suhel looked down at his drink and realized his mind had fallen perfectly blank. He knew he should think about someone, but all he heard were the sounds circling around him, drawing him in: the tinkle of glass, the scrape of wood on floor, the hum of conversation and then Pooja's face came into view again. Pooja, her name appeared in his mind and like a drowning man, he breathed in gulps of air. He wanted to think of her and wondered why it had been an effort. It had happened before, he was thinking, and then his phone flashed again.

'I need to go,' he snatched it in some desperation. 'A meeting.' He said his last words in a rush. He would think over Richard too. But he had for some time been planning to go up north, take the trekking routes beyond Rishikesh to the hills.

He breathed in the hot musty air of Mumbai outside, the din behind immediately snuffed out. They waited in the heat, as his father's car was driven up. Suhel peered in to look at the driver. Sometimes there were these unemployed youths who loitered outside his father's apartment complex and made some ready money offering themselves as chauffeurs. Only the young and brash could negotiate the city's chaotic traffic and it got worse every passing day, Suhel thought. The man at the wheel looked nervous, did a quick namaste and blurted out his details when Suhel asked for them. He had to clearly give the impression that his elderly father had someone after all. He wasn't just another lonely man spending an afternoon at the bar.

'Call me when you reach home,' he told his father.

'Are you okay?' It was the second time his father had asked him that, and now the concern embarrassed them both. 'Yes, I just think it's the drink when I've not eaten much either. And I will take a cab.'

'Suhel...' his father called again, as he stood, his hand on the door. He hesitated, clearly looking for his words, 'You live too much on your own. You need to get married.'

Then his father realized the incongruity of it all and they were laughing as he was driven away.

In the taxi, some of what his father had said came back to Suhel. He rubbed his hands over his eyes again, then stretched out on the rubbery seat. He rolled the window down and then up. The city held the smell of rain, but it wasn't raining yet. He noted the dark clouds over Parel and for no reason, changed his mind about going home. Instead he asked the driver to head to Acharya Donde Marg, where Dr Joshi lived.

'Some music, Sir?' asked the driver and Suhel looked away too quickly as their eyes met in the driver's mirror. He did not want to make conversation with anyone, not just yet.

'No, thank you' he said, and then yawned, indicating he was tired. His father had mentioned Phuong, and now Suhel remembered the girlfriend his father had once had. The woman bedazzled by Mumbai and then apparently hurt and shocked by it. Suhel did not have the full story, for his father had never married her. And now his father had indeed said something about her, and that he did not want to make the same mistake again.

Suhel still thought his father's biggest mistake had been his indifference towards his wife, Suhel's mother. His father just hadn't been bothered, and it was an attitude that had turned them both, mother and son, against him. And now Suhel did not feel any anger for either parent. As for his mother, long dead now and so unmourned, she only invited his pity.

Looking out, as the cab moved over the Lower Parel flyover, Suhel saw with some delight that the rain had just started falling. A late monsoon rain. It was already October and he had stayed longer than he had planned for. He smiled, put a hand out to catch the rain, the way he had always done when returning from school in a bus, then rubbed the dampness over his forehead, closing his eyes briefly. As his hand fell away, his eyes fell on his cell phone.

There was a message, and it looked all blurred to him. He had hoped to catch the rain on his face, the way Pooja did too, as she had texted him only the previous evening, and with thoughts of her silencing things for a moment, Suhel keyed in a message. *I need to see you before I go.*

On the road, the rain now fell in a frenzy. Boys came out from under shop awnings, and bus shelters, and danced; odd little moves and steps made popular by the films. Some came up and cleaned the drenched cars' windows. A line of umbrellas bobbed, and jostled down the streets. Some matronly women waded and wended their way through traffic.

He wasn't going anywhere, not yet. But then like Pooja, he too could play difficult, and why not? He felt a guilty satisfaction, leaning back watching the dark clouds caught against the high-rises. He understood now she was worried about her chawl and about her husband. But Suhel didn't want to think of another man. His thoughts only lingered on how Pooja had responded. He could tell that, recognizing his own arrogance in this thought. She had her hand on his heart. And her eyes had that wild, glazed look and her cheeks were flushed. The confusion, the busyness in the hotel kitchen had not made sense to either of them.

Since then, the messages they had exchanged had been— and he was experienced at this—veiled, at times revealing, but always flirtatious. Sometimes he wondered at the odd moments in which they corresponded; if she was, at these moments, with her husband or with anyone. Now his father's news about the chawl, though he should have realized it himself, had filled him with new thoughts, new ideas. Almost as if he were close to pulling off a business deal.

He wished Pooja would see things his way too. Sometimes he felt he had no time left. His friends at their college reunion spoke of their children in college, and how quickly time passed. Suhel wanted at these occasions to bend his head so it rested on Pooja's shoulder and breathe in again that fragrance of jasmine. Or to hold her against him, so his beating heart could somehow convince her, when his words evidently couldn't.

Dr Joshi, his hair dangling loose, opened the door with paint-streaked hands. 'No, patients today, come right in.' He stopped, then looked back at Suhel's tousled hair, his sleep-ravaged eyes and nodded, ushering him in. Suhel stepped in with relief and something else he did not recognize. Being here was different from being alone, high up in his own apartment. Here he breathed in the city, and felt himself part of something. He also felt Pooja was nearer and somehow attainable, though he had not the foggiest idea how.

Despite the lateness of the hour, the doctor on his part was clearly glad to see Suhel. He gave it away by some unrestrained garrulousness. 'It's too early, I know but I can't drink alone,' he said, extending a bottle of Old Monk, and Suhel first shook his head and then nodded. It wasn't every day he let himself get drunk.

Some weeks ago, and it seemed only yesterday, in those days of early infatuation with Pooja or rather her painting—the memory made him laugh now—he had spent a sleepless night in the doctor's apartment, something that still amused the doctor considerably. The doctor recollected it again now, chortling at Suhel's feigned casualness. Minutes later, Suhel, his eyes half-closed, stretched out on one of the doctor's old cane chairs, feeling it creak with his every move, heard the doctor recount another story, one from his, Suhel's, past.

Dr Joshi, at work on the painting he had begun the day of the first bulldozer strike—as it had come to be called—turned around often, as if to remind himself of Suhel's presence. He talked desultorily, breaking into his strange shrill, whispery laughter now and then, telling Suhel of an event, the doctor was sure, Suhel had long forgotten about. The occasion, and Suhel had been much younger then, when some similar vagabond-like behaviour on Suhel's part had taken him right from outside Mohini's house, to the police station. And it was the doctor who had gotten him back home, after several hours.

'You were quite a sight, young man,' he said. 'Bruised but thankfully, no broken bones. You can well imagine how they would treat those even worse off...'

The doctor laughed as he spoke, and this time a bit of the drink spilled over on the table and onto the floor. The doctor looked at the puddle with some drunken dismay, trying to mop it with one sock-clad foot before he realized this wouldn't work.

'Age doesn't necessarily make one wiser,' said the doctor.

'One worries about wasting time,' said Suhel. They spoke in half-sentences, even elliptically, sometimes full of allusion. For his part the doctor's early discomfort with Suhel had long gone. He had known Suhel as a boy once and in their email exchanges he had appeared to have become a too suave, smooth American businessman, but he felt an ease with Suhel now, just as he felt a greater intimacy with the world around him and some of its people too. Dr Joshi saw everyone, himself too, like blundering, vulnerable objects, all of them flailing around with ambition while life itself seemed like someone else's huge joke. Perhaps it was Neera who made him think so. Her arrogance had all been a veneer, but now her very vulnerability had made her a hero. And in this way, she constantly and unthinkingly challenged him, and he was, like old times, always having to measure up to her. He could not understand himself or his reactions, but he did understand Suhel. Or perhaps because Suhel was younger, the doctor wanted to spare Suhel some pain, or even some unnecessary waiting, especially when he heard Suhel's next words, 'All things do is just take more time...'

'What things?' he asked curiously.

Suhel did not, could not answer. Saying things out loud even to someone you trusted, took away so much of their intensity. He wanted Pooja, sometimes the longing made him catch his breath, but he wondered about differences between them. Her unease and embarrassment. Even the errors she made when she spoke. It made him laugh, it was all kind of cute, but what about later? When people he knew back there would perhaps look away from her superciliously, even make fun of her? And would he remain so understanding too?

'Why not do one of those social experiments these researchers are always doing? Stuff like going without your favourite stuff, or spending time alone in a cave and all that,' Dr Joshi was not looking at him as he spoke, instead he was throwing smoke rings up in the air, as he tossed up one idea and then another. They were on his small trellised balcony now, the kind one didn't see in the city any more, watching the traffic die away below them and the sidewalk sleepers floating in from the shadows. 'Yes, they do it all the time, you know, these researchers. You need to do it. You've been by yourself too long and need to see...'

Suhel made to contradict the doctor, but Dr Joshi waved his hand instead. 'I mean not like me, a bachelor. But you are used to your own self and so it's different.'

'I'd write a book on that,' the doctor said later, looking at Suhel lost in his thoughts. It was the third time that evening, the idea of going to the hills, now as an experiment, had inveigled itself into Suhel's mind. And though he wasn't superstitious, he knew he must consider it then. Then Dr Joshi, tapping the rails with some finality, changed the subject abruptly. 'There is something of yours I do have.'

By the time he returned with what he had been looking for, having rummaged through his closet, his bookshelves, and even attempted a clearing of his crowded table, Suhel had fallen asleep, his legs stretched out, in the cane chair that looked far too small for him. The doctor stood watching him and walked away, knowing that his small apartment would never look so filled again. Then he returned, sighing in some irritation at his own forgetfulness. On the small table with its curved legs that stood by Suhel, the doctor gently dropped the stack of cards with the photographs of cricketers that schoolboys had once collected.

That afternoon, when his father turned up at his school, Suhel was surprised. Hadn't he been somewhere in Cambodia as part of the UN army? For that was what his mother had told him. Every day she prayed for his father, for his long life, good health, his safety and for his early return and yet obviously, she had had no inkling that he was back. Perhaps his father meant to surprise her, but while Suhel didn't know his father well, he knew too, that his father never did things like this.

'Have you just come back?'

'Yes,' his father looked sheepish before he drew himself up to his full height. All the previous occasions he had returned, they would measure themselves against the other, and now as they stood stiffly looking at each other, it struck Suhel that he was as tall as his father, or even taller.

He looked around for his father's car, a momentary excitement filling his eyes. Whenever his father returned to India on official work, he would come home in one of those forest green cars, that marked it out as an army vehicle, complete with military insignia. Now next to the tea stall, Suhel saw instead a long sleek Contessa. It drew eyes but Suhel wasn't impressed.

'We could have tea, maybe?' His father had never done that. And though his father's hesitation surprised Suhel, he did not question it. Instead, Suhel struggled to remember his father's preferences before he called out with some false cheer to the tea stall boy. 'One cutting chai, and some of that rusk too.'

As they sat on the low wooden benches by the open tea stall under the pipal tree, his father, brushing a finger across his moustache, told Suhel, 'I am here with...Phuong.' It was Suhel who looked away first. The name had brought a softness to his father's face; her name came to him, as light as the breeze, but Suhel only felt a strangeness. It was the age they talked about girlfriends and no one had any. That didn't stop them from boasting about their experiences, their boldness in chatting up girls. And all of them, without exception, eyed Mohini, with her easy confidence, her elusive ways. Some visited movies on the sly, the English matinee shows that were bolder than anything else shown on boring television. Suhel read the magazines at the American Centre, *Life* and *Time* and sometimes illicit old copies of *Playboy* that were circulated among some friends. And here was his father, sipping his tea and talking about his girlfriend as if it was quite the most natural thing in the world.

'Did you get bombed there?' Suhel asked in reply. It was the sight of his father laughing in his sophisticated way that embarrassed him.

'We are just there to maintain the peace. Call village councils, make them sign peace agreements. It's a nice, quiet place, far too green and rainy. And the temples appear like something magical. Out of *Phantom*.' He spoke desultorily and in pauses. Then he ran a finger around the cusp of his cup, and said, 'It was in Hanoi, for a stopover in Vietnam where I met her.'

'Her?'

'Phuong. You will meet her,' said his father in some impatience, as if Suhel's forgetting the name irritated him. 'I am here on urgent leave, and no, your mother doesn't know. I'd rather you didn't tell her anything.'

Then they were in the car and Suhel felt blissful, trying to forget the conversation, letting the car fan blow through his hair and on his face. The car stopped often at traffic signals and despite it being afternoon, the jams stretched on forever, as did the silence between them. They travelled from Matunga, where his college was, with the smell of coffee and spices wafting in, and half hour later, he recognized the older, cleaner parts of Mumbai—Dadar and Worli, and then the noisier, more chaotic Mahalakshmi area. Even now he liked how the city moved from old to new, from quiet to crowded in moments.

'I will tell your mother at a suitable time,' his father said, looking out of the window, as the road curved into Chowpatty. 'Things may or may not work out. The army doesn't allow its officers to marry foreigners. One needs special permits. I came for that, and to see you. And she wanted to see Mumbai.'

At the hotel, where they waited for Phuong to join them, his father spoke up again, looking around the lobby, rarely meeting his eyes. As if he found this meeting with his son all forced, but necessary. It was a spacious, luxurious lobby, with a few white foreigners lounging around at the bar, ladies in fine silk saris swishing past, and it helped drown the import of his father's words.

'Your mother and I don't get on, you must have realized that.'

His father did not see Suhel's stunned expression, not at the revelation but that it had come at all. No matter what parents felt about each other, they stayed together. It happened in all families and there was his father, with his distant voice, talking of things Suhel didn't want to understand. His father tapped his finger against the soft leather of the sofa and Suhel noted he still had on his wedding ring with the blue stone in it. His father grimaced, he was trying to smile and then he said in a lighter tone. 'I met her in a hotel and things happened.' His father looked down at his own hand and Suhel saw how his fingers bit hard into the leather, before he smoothed it out.

Phuong came down soon enough, smiling distantly at Suhel who did not smile back. He nodded, when he noted his father's discomfort, the slight tic on his forehead. Phuong was slim and had her hair done up in the manner of stewardesses in advertisements. It was the redness of her lips, and her quiet smile Suhel always remembered. This and the fact that she hardly said much, and his father leaning forward, solicitous and far too concerned, and then understanding her silence as well.

'I'd like to take her shopping.' It was then he, and Suhel too, knew they were in a hurry to get away from all this. His father had then walked away, his hand on Phuong's elbow, patting her on the shoulder as she obviously sought reassurance. When Phuong looked back once through the revolving glass door, Suhel attempted a smile, reassuring in turn. But she waved to someone, a bell boy, and was gone.

Suhel stood up and walked to the door. He stared at their retreating backs, watched them get into a car and that entire evening, he sat outside the hotel, by the parapet on the Marine Drive. He saw the sea move in time and time again, felt the salty sea air in his hair, heard the cars rushing by, and the city's rich jogging past, and everything then—the fat on their bodies and their sleek cars—seemed unnecessary and overdone. It reinforced their indifference to the shoeshine boys at the shop fronts, the hijras walking up, stretching their hands out for baksheesh. Suhel sat there till he was jolted into awareness by the sharp hiss of the petromax lamps, as the peanut vendors set up their carts. One vendor came up close, and he saw the bobbing reflection of his lamp on the waves, turning from grey to white in the surf.

Suhel had quite forgotten the whole thing by the time he returned home to his mother, who sat in front of the television. There was a music contest on, something she always liked and perhaps that was what had put her in a good mood. But things weren't this way several afternoons later. It was the day he was late home, for he had gone to watch the cricket match, with some of his classmates: Rajiv who now worked for Microsoft, and Kelkar who had his own leather export business. But there was Mohini too, and she had waved at them from her seat right in the pavilion and asked them to join her. They had not needed any prodding. It was, after all, a chance to watch their favourite cricketers from up close.

India had lost to the powerful West Indies, but greater excitement lay in store as Mohini assured them she would get them the players' autographs. It was crowded in the dressing room, as Mohini pushed her way in. It felt strange to Suhel how possessively she held his arm, just in the manner of the other women around, who were all crowded around the cricketers, laughing up at them, rushing at them to engulf them in tight hugs, swinging their arms through theirs, and behaving in what Suhel considered was quite outrageous behaviour. The sensation of Mohini's hand on his elbow, she, leaning with her head on his shoulder was strange to him as well. Perhaps it was all mandated by the air of abandonment everywhere. Suhel stood dazzled, not knowing where to look yet maintaining his calm, serious look, something he prided himself on, as men he had worshipped from afar appeared close, smiled at him in a general, friendly way, before moving on.

When Mohini drifted off to the restroom, Suhel had wandered around, narrowly missing a waiter with his tray held high, then boldly picking up a canapé from another passing waiter, and turning around he found himself looking at the man he had idolized all his life. Sunil Gavaskar. Short and cherubic, the great man had come by him, and Suhel found himself rooted to the spot, the canapé half raised to his lips. The great man stood for a moment in equal confusion and it was his one quirked eyebrow that left Suhel all flustered. He extended a hand, moving the canapé quickly to the other before slipping it embarrassedly into his mouth. Then with his left hand, he self-consciously took off his cap and asked Gavaskar to sign it. 'I have nothing else, Sir, and I'd be honoured.' But Gavaskar only smiled, stopped someone else, perhaps it was Shastri, grabbed a pen from him and did the needful. Shastri wore a pair of shorts with Puma written on it in zany, glittery colours, and Gavaskar was still smiling as he handed Suhel back his cap. This was what made Suhel babble a bit more. About his playing for his college team, his shots especially the hook and the square cut, and Gavaskar had only listened.

All the rest of that evening, Suhel had relived that sensation of the great man's hand on his. With that same hand, Gavaskar had scored so many centuries. He had hit those magnificent cover drives, his hand gripping the bat in that loose grip. Later, Suhel had not seen Mohini and taken the last bus home. The great man had left with his family, his young son held high in his arms. His wife had Mohini's easy sophistication, her careful lack of self-consciousness, and Suhel had not realized why he felt that sudden pang as the club nearly emptied. It was a longing for a life he never had, and perhaps would never have.

He did not want the bus journey to stop. He saw life around him dwindling to a halt, though there was always someone awake even in the darkest hours. People readying themselves to sleep, a half-open window where someone played the violin, a girl and a boy at the traffic signal counting their last flower garlands, men at a roadside dhaba, and an old man still waiting at the bus stop.

It had been 11.30 when he reached home, and having knocked with the latch hard on the door several times, he knew his mother would not let him in. A long while later, he had heard her voice, raised in a scream through the closed door. *Go away. Just get lost. You and your father have ruined me.* The merchant navy man who lived as a paying guest in the apartment next door had come over and only smiled, smarmily. 'She's been this way all evening,' he offered helpfully. Suhel turned away from him deliberately. He tried banging on the door but it was futile. He debated kicking it open, but he did not want a scene. Besides he was still a bit dazed after that evening. But he heard only his mother scream, though she sounded farther away now, having retreated to her bedroom, *Go. Go to your father.*

That was the first time he had stayed over at Dr Joshi's house. The next morning, she had opened the door, her thin face swollen with anger and her tears, her hair, loose from the usual tidy bun she bundled it in, made her look different, someone quite young, Suhel always thought later. She had leaned out, saw the merchant navy man opening his own door to study the situation for himself, and scowling fiercely at him, she had pulled Suhel in and slammed the door shut.

Suhel stood there in the hallway, hoping to talk, wanting his mother to explain herself, but she had walked away. Moments later in the kitchen, he could hear her talking to herself. And then as if she could not help things, she had thrown the dishes to the floor, one after the other, carefully and very deliberately. He heard the shatter of glass, the thunderclap sound of stainless steel plates hitting the floor. Then she emerged, tying her hair up again in a loose knot. 'Go wash your hands. You're smelling, wherever you've come from.'

As he washed his hands by the kitchen sink, he felt he was erasing all memories of what had happened the last evening. He remembered as the last soapsuds vanished down the drain, how firmly Gavaskar had shaken his hand, and the last pat on his shoulder as he encouraged Suhel to 'keep at it'. Now his mother stood close, making him wash his hands twice over. 'Scrub right under your nails. Rub the soap over your hands and up to your elbows, come now.'

She was in his room as he emerged from his bath. He caught her in the act of rummaging through his rucksack. But she did not look guiltily away. Instead, rising with some majesty, she spread out her hand and Suhel saw her scattering his collection of player cards—the glossy, even gauzy photos of cricket stars he had built up from his middle-school days, his collection growing in exchange for his marbles, or help in homework or in lieu of small change from the tea stall boy. But his mother now stamped on these and Suhel saw how some were already torn. And then she screamed. He heard the window rattle, his ears hurt and it was from the echoes around, that he sensed his mother's words.

'Your father was with that woman. Your father just cannot live without a woman.'

From then on, what he'd come to know later as her obsessive-compulsive behaviour manifested itself more regularly, though his father would tell him later that her finicky ways had simply got on his nerves. It was then Suhel wanted to tell his father that it was perhaps her endless fussing, her prayers and fasts that had in some way kept him safe year after year, in all those military deputations he was part of— but by then, the struggle between his parents, with him as a clear wager, had got to him. And when she made Suhel clean up rigorously every time he came home from college and especially from a well-played game of cricket, it seemed to Suhel that his mother too was determined to erase him from her life.

He took to staying over more and more, sometimes with his friends, or shacking out in the school tea stall itself with the two boys from Bihar who managed it. One night there had been a party in Mohini's house; it was her eighteenth birthday. That night, leaving her home, he felt the breeze come in from the sea that lay past the marshes on Carter Road, and when he lifted his head, its mustiness and dampness had an easy familiarity. The lights of the tall buildings behind him lay like dots on the quiet sea, and every so often he would catch a movement behind, telling him that there were happy families after all, quite unlike his own.

He stretched himself out on the bench, and must have dozed off for he did not hear the policemen driving up. He was yanked awake, and Suhel had looked up in a sleepy haze to see black-hooded figures converge on him and the stick blows that had followed. If anyone later asked Suhel if he knew what the homeless, abandoned people lived in fear of, he would always tell them, slowly, his face darkening at memories he had never truly forgotten, that he knew. It turned you into stone, or a helpless rag doll. You looked about, tried hard to make sense but your abilities in these unguarded moments had already abandoned you. So Suhel was kicked, shoved, cuffed, and cursed and placed in a jeep. And it was as the first smell of the sea reached him through his bleeding nose that he asked the police. 'Where are you taking me? What have I done?'

They kicked him again and one prodded his chest with a lathi. In front, he heard a snigger. 'Thought you were quite the hero, were you? Stalking a girl, night and day?'

They drove up to the Hill Road police station. Suhel recognized its high yellow walls and once inside the gate, the low, red-thatched building. He remembered having come there before to complain about the stray dog menace on the roads, as dogs often bit pedestrians out for a walk. But the inspector made him wait, on a hard bench against the wall, already stained red and oil-marked from several heads having rested against it, during equally long waits. Suhel was conscious of his stench mingling with the smell of old files, the overfilled trash bin, the cane chairs and their cushions with a sat-on look. He must have dozed before they again prodded him awake. The inspector picked his teeth, rubbed his face with a towel before he looked at Suhel, managing to sneer and commiserate at the same time.

'Your parents do not want to come. I tried calling them.' The inspector looked at the phone and shrugged. Then he took pity on him and said almost in a brotherly way, 'Don't you know better than to trouble a woman?' Suhel kept quiet. He would from now on always suspect the kindness that came too easily.

In the end, it was Dr Joshi who came by. Suhel had not realized how long he had been inside till he was surprised by the brightness and the noise outside. 'It was your father who called me,' the doctor told him once he had flagged down a taxi. Suhel found he could not even lift his arm to open the door. He knew his father wasn't there, but perhaps they had located him somewhere—in Phnom Penh or Bangkok. 'And I am sorry,' the doctor brushed his shoulder. 'Your mother was in no state to be here.'

When he returned to college, he noticed the security guards who now accompanied Mohini everywhere. The time she walked up to meet him, one of them lingered and at the end delivered a polite warning, as they both looked at Mohini's departing back. 'Keep away. You know what happened right? Her parents don't like it.'

He had been forbidden to see Mohini, but he did not mind this in the least. Mohini for her part, brushed it off;

she was amused, evidently reading into Suhel's behaviour or whatever she had been told about it, some evidence of his devotion, and unrequited ardour. She arranged to meet him secretly. For her, it was an elaborate game, simply to throw off the guards constantly tailing her. She loved the attention and evading it gave her some thrill. Sometimes Suhel and she saw an English movie together at the Regal, and kissed just when the actors did too, sitting as they did at the very back in the dark hall. There were the afternoons they spent in an old house in Colaba, hearing the crows perch and patter over the old tiled roof. Often, she would be more daring. She'd come right up to his table in the canteen, or turn up at the bus stop, a borrowed dupatta over her head, making an ineffectual disguise, and always with that teasing smile. It was she who wanted to get away from her rich, cloistered existence. And for some time, till she had that affair with that labour leader, a much older man and who would be killed too soon (her father's involvement was always suspected and never proved), it amused Suhel to see her thrilled for all the wrong reasons.

'No, I might have hurt her.' This was what Suhel had told the therapist when talking about his mother. And so he had lied to his mother often, insisting when she had asked, that he had not heard from his father. Or that he knew anything about Phuong.

'But that is a manipulation of sorts too,' his therapist had said instead.

Now walking on the hills of Ranikhet, Suhel felt again a great sorrow for his mother, one greater because he felt it anew. He had never said anything to his mother, for at the end, even he had deserted her. She had been sick, throwing up blood, when the merchant navy guy called him at his college hostel. By the time, they got her to hospital, it was too late.

He wasn't bitter, or even sad then. In fact, at the time he

longed to return to his studies. Like some of his classmates, the toppers, he was studying for his GRE, and his first scores had been good. The universities he had applied to had offered a full scholarship or most of it. And in the days before he left, he had been too excited to mourn his mother. His cursory goodbyes had even upset Mohini.

'I thought you'd understand.' Mohini's words came back to him much later, as they reconnected many years later. As he told the therapist, in the days just before leaving for Mumbai, it took so much time to understand yourself, that you had no time to understand others. But this time he was trying. It was a business visit, but he would try and patch up with his father. Over the last year, they had spoken often, though the conversation had been easier on email.

To his father, when he had turned up for his mother's funeral, Suhel hadn't been able to stop himself making one last accusation, 'You did take your time...'

His father had apologized and as everyone came up, offered their sympathies, asked Suhel if he had time for tea. 'No,' and Suhel had been brusque. 'You need to go to Phuong, don't you?' It was surprising how easily the name had then come to him.

'No, we never married.'

Suhel shrugged much like his father, 'Then I feel sorry for you,' and that last time, it was he who had walked away, in the manner his father had done some years before. And it would be twenty years later when he'd see his father again.

'You need to realize your parents have lives, had lives of their own,' the therapist only said.

Yes, he had noticed this more in the US since he had come. Everyone said that—your life was yours, not to be given up easily to someone else, for someone else's happiness. He wished his mother had known this. Instead, she had wasted away. Now he understood Pooja's reasons for not wanting to give it all up, her life as she knew it, the life that was now hers since she came to Mumbai and her beloved catering business. They hadn't talked over anything yet. Perhaps they never would. He had often held a hand to his chest, letting the old sensations of welcome pain and a strange grief grip him, especially the moments he felt Pooja had again been difficult or too stubborn. Almost a tease, he would think half-angrily before he calmed himself down.

Couldn't she find something to do in the US? He imagined a life for them in the future and couldn't. He only saw himself getting very old.

From Ranikhet to Lansdowne, it wasn't a long journey, but Suhel took breaks often. He was glad the connectivity wasn't good in some of these places, as this gave him a ready excuse. And the photos of his father's wedding came to him much later, courtesy the good doctor.

At Lansdowne, Suhel basked in the flush of bitter neem leaves, breathed in the sharp nippy air, heard the call of the birds, the slow rustling of branches, and rubbed in the dampness that struck one on the face. He lay on the grass and at last let himself think about Pooja, the messages and the photos she had sent him of late.

'When you coming back?' He read that message again and again, indulging her the error, looking at it instead for signs of wistfulness, longing and plaintiveness. He heard the sweeping waterfall somewhere close, the smell of cattle dung and fires burning, and it lulled him momentarily. The photos had come a few hours later: one of the baby, Vasudha's he understood, and the other one, of her, holding the baby up and they were looking right at the camera.

He saw instantly that Pooja had cut her hair. It lay now like a black cloud on her neck, and there was the baby, serious and pouting for the camera. Seeing Pooja in a different way made him feel lost for words. He remembered his own thoughts, seeing himself undoing her braid, running his fingers through the tangles and then leaning forward to cover his face with all of it. Abruptly rising, Suhel returned to the car, and headed for the river rafting office.

He had made up his mind to go kayaking that morning. There had been a storm earlier in the night and there were fewer people than he remembered at the pier. There were two men in the office, one dressed more nattily in cheap jeans and a shirt, and the other in a torn sweater. They put away their teacups and looked at him, glanced at each other, and nodded, clearly satisfied with what they saw. Suhel had called earlier about his intentions.

'We'd have told you not to go, but you're okay.'

'Okay?' Suhel asked, bringing a superior note into his voice. His cynical mind ticked away—was it because they knew he was a Non-Resident Indian, and so could be milked suitably for his dollars. Perhaps they were already charging him too much.

'No, no you are...decent,' said the nattier one, the yogic bracelet jangling as he reassured Suhel 'The younger folk here just come and drink. They pollute the holy waters. This river, our mother Ganga, is indeed holy, you know.'

'Oh I see. You can be sure I will do no such thing.'

The spray hit Suhel cold and hard on the face. At first it was a smooth sail, almost a glide. He rowed the kayak deeper in, down the bridge at Rudraprayag, and then as he became more adventurous, he turned it around, twirled it, careful now of the rocks that came dangerously close. But this was nothing to what he had done before. He liked pitting his strength against the elements. A few drops of rain hit him and he looked up to find the rain advancing over the water. He knew also not to get alarmed. The clouds didn't look dark or even ominous.

Although he was strapped well onto the boat, he knew he had to be careful.

Then he heard the ping of his cell phone and glanced down to note the message from his father. He and Rosie were in Panchgani, where they had run into Ghatge, who, his father added, had once again asked after Suhel.

He shook his head. But the inattention of a few moments had cost him; his kayak was now firm in the river's grip. It swept him away at a fast pace. Suhel strived for a calmness, he breathed in deep, as the waves rushed over him. He knew he had to keep the boat upright, and row against the water. But a strong cold wave of water now dashed over him, tossing his kayak, bringing him closer to the rocks that lay very near, deceptively hidden by the waters. He fought hard to regain control. All around him the blue-grey waters rose high and swirled greedily around. Far in the misty distance, he saw the smaller boats dashing repeatedly against the high banks, making a thudding sound that came back to him repeatedly, mixed with the rising swell of the water, and the flush of the rain. No one could see him nor even hear him if he needed help.

Steeling himself against such thoughts, Suhel pushed his oar in. He turned his kayak around with swift strokes, feeling the sting of cold water on his skin. The kayak instead caught against some rocks, and he kept his grip as a wave nearly upturned it. But he knew this wasn't the last one. Narrowing his eyes against the ever-hardening rain, he saw an overhang, a rock surface higher than the immediate water level, and lunged for it, in some desperation. It was slippery, and sharp, and farther away than he expected. Or perhaps it took him longer now to do such things. There was a gash on his palm almost instantly. But he gritted his teeth and held on tight, feeling the strain run along his arms, stretch his shoulders.

He gripped it hard, his head against the rock face, gulping in deep breaths. He knew this kind of storm, though dangerous in every way, would not last. Then he felt something slip, a certain looseness in his pocket. Looking down, he saw his cell phone slip out and as he reached out a hand, he felt himself almost fall, before he regained his hold again in some desperation. The cell phone was lost in the deep murky waters. A jet of spray came and hit him on the cheek in mockery.

No one would ever know, or even assume, that he was indeed battling for life. His hands hurt now. He could do nothing more for a while. He thought then of the photos Pooja had sent him. He remembered the way his heart had first caught seeing her. It was jealousy. He did not know why—that he not been the first to see her this way, with a new hairdo? That he did not know how her hair would now feel, curled in his fingers, and bunched up in his hands, brushing his mouth?

He imagined then what he might write back. *You look pretty.* But then he was always telling her things such as this. It made him wince later, the things he wrote: *Love that half-smile on your face.* Or, *I like your face in profile.*

She had asked him once what that last word meant. It made her seem childishly vulnerable. This time he told himself, he could be more teasing about the photo, texting her to say: *You look different.* Deliberately he would not mention her new hairdo. *How?* she might reply. Would she have that serious look on her face as she texted? Would she with one hand push her hair away? The way he had done at the hotel on the pretext of checking her injury.

Love makes you that way. Different. His message would have a clear hint.

And you said Amrika could. She might text back.

Bombay too.

Even Bombai. This time she would correct him. He smiled

to himself as he pulled himself up the ledge, noticing with despair the trail of blood on the rock, the gash on his arm. She would write of her city, the way she pronounced it. And he would hold her, place his head on the crook of her neck and smell her in. So that she would fill his world. He wanted nothing else.

Vasudha: Waiting for Luck

The Burj Khalifa offered a truly breathtaking view of Dubai. That was obvious even from a Facebook photo. Vasudha looked at a kidney-shaped swimming pool and at the towers rising from a sandy desert, like so many silver pins stuck onto a board. The planned neatness of it all, amidst the monotony, stunned Vasudha.

She clicked a like on Allison's photo and added: 'Wow, I'd be scared.'

'Isn't it scary?' Allison commented. 'And baby Matt wasn't bothered a bit.'

Allison's baby was only a few months older than Vasudha's own daughter. And he was already experiencing such wonders. The resentment caught at Vasudha's heart then, fierce and unlike anything she had ever experienced.

Things had been this way since George Mathew had left town just a day after his scheme had been exposed. The television news now showed his raided office, how the police had found the place emptied but for the sheaves of paper, the forms he had had people fill out, the scanner, the photocopying machine, even the printer. Outside the door, the board hung askew. Vasudha saw it on television, as the camera zoomed in, and she recognized her own artwork. The F had fallen off, and the anchor in the television studio had commented that the name indeed sounded apt: *ly by Night.*

Vasudha thought he had a terrible sense of humour.

Kiran, her daughter of three months, kicked out as she lay on the low couch. There was just space for the two of them, the rest of it taken over by baby clothes. Spittle rolled down the baby's chin and a drop fell on Vasudha's keyboard. *Stop doing that.* She bent to wipe it off with a quick harsh movement, then glared at her daughter, who blinked, as if startled by Vasudha's nearness. *How dare you?* She saw baby eyes darken, she saw her own self in her baby's eyes, a looming shadowy hulk, but there was no fear. Vasudha wanted her to be afraid. But the baby only looked back mesmerized. A moment later, her face puckered up. Vasudha placed her hand over the baby's mouth, trying not to hurt her.

It seemed a pity that the first person her baby would learn to fear was her own mother. But she had work to do, always there was more work to do, and babies just wanted more and more attention.

On the screen, an advertisement page had opened quite by accident. It showed a hotel in the Maldives, waitresses holding up trays offering coconut juice. Vasudha felt frazzled and, worse, thirsty. She could have screamed but she knew Pooja and the girls, her helpers, were next door. Vasudha smelt fresh coriander leaves, the bittersweet kokum as it was ground into paste. Work was on to prepare the afternoon lunch boxes that would be delivered to the offices. Pooja had so much work that the imminent disaster looming—of being turned out of the only home she had known so far—no longer mattered. Pooja had a blithe confidence, an insouciant assurance about herself these days. Vasudha wondered if her newly minted celebrity status had something to do with it. There were journalists traipsing up to meet her, occasions when Vasudha had to lie low, look for a job, hidden away in her room, conscious only of her heavy breathing, the baby's gurgling, afraid of attention all because of George Mathew. She cursed him now—an idiot, a self-centred coward.

Vasudha surprised herself by the sharp pangs of envy she felt towards Pooja at times, for she was a friend. One twist of luck was all they, George and she, had needed. If only the scheme of offering helicopter rides had taken off, they would have minted a large sum of money and disappeared, baby in tow. But the police had somehow got wind. Someone must have snitched—the photocopier, or it could have been the printer, both wanting more than had been bargained for. She bent her head very close to her daughter and hissed. *Listen, listen. You must let me work. Baby or no baby, I must get on with life.*

She wondered now at her own madness. She should have had that abortion after all. What had got into her? Maybe she had let herself feel pity for those desperate women in Sneha Desai's clinic, even Pooja. All of them, always hoping for encouraging news, all longing for a baby. She had seen their hopelessness up close. She had comforted them, felt herself in those moments ensconced by a warm sisterhood.

But the baby wailed. *Stop. Stop.* Vasudha pulled her close to her chest, and the baby thrashed wildly. Vasudha pushed her away, and wondered about shaking her. What did the books say? Did a good shake drive some sense in, or did it do permanent damage? Then she heard the door being pulled open and a girl ran in, wiping her hands on her dupatta.

'Tai wants the baby if you have work, Vasudha.'

Vasudha hid her relief. The girl smiled reassuringly at the look of concern Vasudha now put on. 'She will be safe with us.'

Vasudha held up her baby for the girl, just asking off-hand, 'Hope you wiped your hands now. You know babies are prone to infections.' Baby Kiran fidgeted in the girl's arms. Vasudha felt a surprise unhappiness at being parted from her. 'Now you be good. Okay. Don't trouble all your big sisters.' She leaned forward, planted a kiss on her daughter's forehead.

She saw the tiny face squelch up, and a wrinkle appear. George always said she kissed too noisily.

For a few moments, there was peace. Without the baby, with her attention on nothing, Vasudha could let herself get angry with George. The scoundrel. She checked her phone. He would call, he had to. Perhaps he would use a different number. She quickly liked a photo one of her friends had shared.

She had to sort out her own life. Get on with things. If George wasn't dead, he wasn't the kind to commit suicide either. He had that hunger, that greedy look in his eyes that went beyond just keeping the body together. Hunger for the illicit, the quick gotten, for luck, to be oneself, because this city conspired to barely let one survive. One was always running to catch the last train, to pay bills, to match accounts, but one could never catch up on time.

A less crazy scheme might have worked. Like drawing proposals for a building in one of those newly dereserved plots in the city's outskirts. But George had said, the few times he did disagree with her, that people were suspicious of such common con tricks now. They had had such a fight over it. And what he had opted for had been totally crazy, unworkable from the start: a venture that introduced chopper rides for the public over the city, beginning from Essel World and offering a complete sight-seeing tour of the city. But she had let herself be duped. The first time she had let him do things on his own. But those days she couldn't even think straight, with the baby heavy and restless inside her and the heat sapping her of all energy.

Now she was alone with the baby. Vasudha had thought, despite the scheme failing, they might have still managed to get away. Take the train to the north somewhere or even to the northeast. But the raid had been a surprise, George had rung to tell her this, that he would come and meet her once the police were off his trail. But a week had gone by, and he had not turned up. Nor had there been any word from him.

Her hand now trembled with anger. Allison had put up a photo, a party for her son's first birthday. An internationally known comedian was performing. Oh bother, Vasudha muttered, and scrolled down after a quick like. She couldn't bear any more of Allison now. Allison had once been a pen-pal. In their high-school days, they had written to each other almost every month, though Allison had been more regular.

Vasudha would look forward to the neat white checked envelopes and to news of Allison's father who had fought in the first Gulf War and was left traumatized. All those oil flares burning day in and out, Allison once wrote about her father, and that sometimes he had even seen them sprouting all over the desert as he drove his tank across the unending sandy expanse. Then about her mother's job as a librarian. Vasudha, on her part, would make up stories, for in Thekkady where she lived, nothing ever happened. She wrote about the new hotel, the elephant herds in the forests, and the scandal when a German tourist ran away with a Kathakali dancer. It excited Allison but Vasudha offered no more details. Things in her immediate vicinity then little concerned her. All her dreams even then had been about when she would leave the place and really begin living.

It was only the last month that she had recently gotten back in touch with Allison on Facebook. Now Allison no longer lived in Dorset but in Dubai, in those very sandy, albeit luxurious, wastes, Vasudha recollected with surprise, her father had been so troubled by.

Allison's profile picture showed her in a huge apartment in Dubai on the sixteenth floor. As they messaged, Allison greeted her as if they had parted only the other day. 'I remember you,' Allison said instantly. 'I have no other friend called Vasudha.' And then with the gush that was, as Vasudha would soon realize, typical of her, Allison added, 'Gosh, you must be one of my oldest friends. Indeed, you are!!'

'You've come a long way from Dorset, Allison,' Vasudha wrote, trying to mask her curiosity.

'Oh it's nothing. Peter is a banker, and so here we are.'

'And your dad?'

'Oh, he committed suicide. It was the year Mom left him. You see, she couldn't take it any more. His drinking, his bouts of violence.'

It was evident Allison was typing in a rush, and holding her breath, Vasudha stared as the words formed in her message box. Allison was letting it all out, these Western women usually did that. Maybe it was their loneliness or their self-absorption, but Vasudha waited for some moments of suitable silence before she wrote her words of condolence. RIP.

'Yes, that was sad. I was quite done up. Oh, one second...'

She vanished and then returned seconds later to tell Vasudha about Matt. That was the baby in the photo with her, and Vasudha mentioned she had one too.

Allison gushed even more. She asked for suggestions on parenting and barely had Vasudha gotten started on her complaining—after all, it was her turn now, having listened to Allison for so long, she burst in with a hurried *I need to go. A meeting.*

Vasudha suspected it could be a social gathering, perhaps Allison was meeting someone over coffee. For Allison soon enough put up a photo of herself in a new outfit bought at a Zara's sale (*a steal*, as her caption indicated). Vasudha saw the long Mexican skirt, the fancy hat and the string of pearls. Surely no one could go to a meeting dressed that way. She should have said 'meet' instead, Vasudha thought. She wouldn't have thought badly of Alison if she had.

As Vasudha moved her cursor to the right, hoping to log out, she noticed something new. Someone—and it was Ghatge, she realized with a start—had accepted her friend request. She had sent the friend request at random, and now she couldn't resist writing him a message.

Thank you Ghatge Sahib. You are so busy, and it's kind of you to accept my request.

Seconds later when she looked back again, there was a reply. *Arre, no problem, Vasudhaji. How are you, how's baby?*

It was the odd abbreviated manner in which he spoke that often intrigued her. One couldn't tell if he was being menacing or it was just a practised drawl. He had sounded just this way when he had barged in that midnight when she had Pooja in the doctor's clinic. Pooja had wanted her cycle checked and Vasudha was looking over Sneha Madam's files and had been afraid. Only a few nights later she would find in an old file, the old agreement, yellowing and frayed, punched up at one end, and tied with string. The stamps and the signatures at the bottom, stylistic, curved and extended, told her it was an important document. No one signed that way any more.

He is not giving you tension. I hope?

She, not he, she typed in automatically.

Sorry Vasudhaji. Sorry

An image of Ghatge flashed into her mind. In the beginning, those late evenings, he would come into the waiting room as she finished up for Sneha Madam. It was his lazy look, his way of striding around the small room, the way he had his hands in his pockets, and Sneha Desai's own flustered look, that told Vasudha of their affair. The speculation about them began only later. Then Vasudha too had learnt to flirt with him the few occasions he had come and now she wanted to continue the conversation with him.

You're busy always, Ghatge Sahib, election time?

Arre yes, Vasudhaji you do know about things.

She could imagine him, lifting a lazy, yet intentional, hand, scratching the thin bald spot on his forehead. *Helping the Mrs You see? We are here to help the women, see.*

You should stand for elections too.

She wondered at her audacity as she said this, but was gratified to see Ghatge's quick response: A series of *hahahaha.*

Then there was silence and she was afraid he had indeed logged off. She would be left with nothing but her own company, her worry and anger. The narrowness of her world would then throttle her. So she went on: *All women would vote for you. You are quite the hero.*

Ok, Ok, he wrote. *Vasudhaji, you make me happy. I thought you were not on my side. Working against me. Hurting me.*

Hurting you. No am sorry.

She knew he was referring to the agreement. The one that Raina had written about, that Neera Joshi had read out in her slow, precise way before the television cameras. But it was she, Vasudha, who had found it among Sneha Madam's old files, at the very bottom of the cupboard. One Vasudha was sure her employer had quite forgotten about. Sneha had been so full of plans, her thoughts on the present, that she hadn't bothered about the past, especially the cupboard, stuffed with things that needed clearing up, things whose belated discovery now came as a bombshell to many. Especially the agreement dated to nearly thirty years ago that Ramakrishna Desai had signed with the mill owners.

You say sorry now? Tell me, did it help anyone? That building will fall down any moment.

He sounded agitated. Vasudha was anxious, she had to keep him talking. If he logged off with anger, their conversation would never resume. She would be left looking for new ways to cheer herself up, to take her away from the immediate moment and all its attendant worries. Already she heard the girls outside, one making silly baby-talk to her daughter, the dull metallic clunk of tiffins being arranged for delivery, running footsteps everywhere, and then Pooja's calm voice telling someone: 'Just make a note on the register. Don't forget, okay?'

All that had happened had not made her a heroine, Vasudha thought, in fact she had brought disaster on herself. Instead, it was Raina who had got famous. Pooja had had her photos in the papers and Neera's speech had won her many admirers, but no one had bothered to think of her, Vasudha, or even thank her.

Yes you're right, I was just doing what Sneha Madam wanted.

She had typed that in blindly but there was his reply almost instantly.

Is there anything else you found?

Like?

She knew then he was worried and afraid, and she parried for time. He had been in quite a spot after Sneha Madam's suspicious death, when details of their affair threatened to go public. After all, that was why he was now in Chiplun, away from the scandal.

If I find anything, Sahib, you will be the first person I tell.

Yes. You know, she was trying to trap me.

Even reading such words against her former employer, someone who had shown her nothing but generosity and kindness, was a betrayal. But Vasudha thought of Ghatge's fancy yellow car, the trips he took Sneha Madam on, and his lazy, long-drawn-out way of talking. That he was now revealing himself to her in some way made her feel part of another world, far removed from her own, at least for a while.

The first meeting with Ghatge turned into something of a disaster. They had arranged to meet in an apartment complex on Yari Road in Versova. Vasudha had picked the keys up from the office of the owner, a well-known photographer. It was Ghatge who had advised that she do so around seven, when the office had closed, and other employees wouldn't be around to pry. The secrecy had oddly thrilled her, her mind had something else to think about. But she had been embarrassed at the way the photographer had looked at her. It had taken her everything to look him squarely in the eye, after which the man had said mildly enough, as if the matter wasn't of much concern, 'If Sahib wants it, what can I say?' Then it was the way he last said—enjoy yourself—that made her almost abandon the whole thing.

When Ghatge turned up, wearing jeans and a striped T-shirt, her eyes widened in amazement, before she quickly masked it with what she hoped was appropriate appreciation. 'You look different.' He looked down at himself, ran a hand down his T-shirt. It was a little too loose for him, and she noticed the price tag sticking out from his neck.

She had just been about to point that out, and he had been looking around the room expectantly, both evidently trying to hide their embarrassment in some way, when the intercom rang. A scratchy, long-drawn-out crackling sound that made them look at each other guiltily. Ghatge's face gave nothing away as his long arm reached snake-like for the phone. His hello was polite, even husky before Vasudha realized he was disguising his voice. A moment later he was laughing. A half-hearted laugh that turned into something full-throated. 'Sorry, sorry, I asked him to wait.'

He listened again before putting the phone down abruptly. Vasudha saw his clenched jaw, the rigidity with which he stood. His explanation, when it came, was broken and far too hearty. He had come by taxi, he said, scratching his head in the manner she knew, and had asked the driver to wait. 'Till I was done. But he doesn't have the time, it seems.' He paused then, looked at her, 'We'll go down. Else the bastard will...'

He did not finish, instead, he strode towards the window and they both looked out together. The cab, with its clear yellowing roof and a luggage rack, was parked under a tree and the driver paced impatiently by it. He stopped, gestured then to the guard at the gate, presumably the one who had called Ghatge on the intercom. The guard gesticulated in turn, evidently with some rudeness, for the driver ran up to him, and something of what he said carried up to them. Vasudha saw then how roughly the guard was jostled by the shoulders.

Behind her, Ghatge leaned closer, his hand clasping the bar. She was conscious of his nearness, his breathing on her neck. 'See, the bastard, so anxious, about his money. In another minute, he will be shouting to everyone about his poor family. How he is cheated, how everyone is out to get him? Who asked them to come to Mumbai then? All these poor people taking up the city, spoiling it.'

She laughed nervously at his tone and he smiled grimly, his hand dropping off from the window, briefly brushing her shoulder. 'We have to meet again,' she said lamely, as they travelled quietly down the elevator. The guard watched them in some sullenness as they appeared, and she and Ghatge were now even more careful not to give anything away. They walked apart, more formally. Ghatge lowered his cap's visor and adjusted his sunglasses. With one hand, he waved away the guard, and then laughed, briefly, yet loud enough to get the taxi-driver's attention.

The man stopped dusting his car with a rust brown dirt rag and glared at them. 'Hello, my friend,' said Ghatge, advancing with a friendly smile. What happened next was so sudden that later Vasudha never quite remembered the sequence of events. She knew then that Ghatge's mood changes were not something deliberate, it was just who he was. It made him unpredictable, dangerous and exciting.

When he was barely a foot or two away from the driver, Ghatge said in a voice full of hiss and menace, 'Trying to be a hero, eh? Do you know who I am?'

The driver's face froze in horror. Ghatge bent towards the cab, his hand coming to rest on the car roof. His other hand moved to the man's collar as he pulled him up close. Now he spoke so slowly and so deliberately that the guard at the gate had no inkling of what was happening; the few who had drifted up to watch the proceedings kept their distance, looking uncertain. 'Yes, it's me,' Ghatge said. 'Look close. When I tell you to wait, you do as you're told.'

'I didn't know, Sahib,' the man was trembling. 'Please forgive me.'

'Don't make a scene,' Ghatge replied, turning away to spit on the road. Vasudha stepped back just in time. 'You are all leeches, sucking up our city.'

'I am sorry, Sahib,' said the man again, with folded hands.

Ghatge's hand clasped over the other man's hands and he laughed again, a harsh forced laugh. 'No need to do that. Just remember the lesson.' Vasudha understood then that he was just as wary of drawing attention. She was only too glad to get away that time and wondered late into the night, as her baby slept content by her, just what had got into her. Versova was far enough and that flat by the sea was anonymous in its exclusivity. But she already knew there was no place safe from him.

Allison had shared a photo of the Archipelago, a replica of islands representing the world's continents created out of sand, right by the sea around Dubai. *Europe just a sea-ride away from where I am*, Allison put in a lot of smileys after that. Dubai—it was where Vasudha had always wanted to go. With Allison's photos, it all seemed so near.

Vasudha knew she had to get away. Every time this thought came into her head, she was filled with a wild, inexplicable desperation. She imagined herself at the very top of the world. On the highest floor of the world, looking down at everyone.

Vasudha looked at the employment agencies, but the vacancies listed did nothing to lift her spirits. On the Burj Khalifa website, she checked for careers. But these were largely for porters and the one she might have preferred—a concierge—was only open to men. And in the middle of this, there was always Ghatge and his messages: he cursed the taxi-driver again, blaming him for everything and he wanted to meet her again. *This time Vasudhaji,* he had texted, *we talk very seriously.* She was flattered by his attention. It overrode her nervousness.

She met him a week later. Half the week she had told herself she wouldn't go. But then on Sunday she found a message from him: it was a number she didn't know. *We meet Wednesday?* She thought then of the lovely, sea-facing flat, the wonderfully done-up interiors and suddenly looked forward to being in it.

She remembered how the first time she had sunk into the plush sofa in the living room and looked up at the gigantic TV screen. The dining table, with its lotus-shaped chandelier, could seat twelve people. Vasudha knew she had to see the other rooms too, to step once into the balcony, with its stone seats and the carved iron railings. She had not even peeked into the bathroom. She now replied, taking her time but not too long for that would be obvious.

Sahib, have something of interest. Some papers.

He replied quickly enough. *Exciting news. Now my heart beats more madly.*

That had had her in chuckles. Vasudha leaned forward, tickled her baby on the soles and laughed more when the baby chortled in glee. The papers she had would have him eating out of her hand though Vasudha didn't quite like that analogy. Her dignity and quick wit would keep him enthralled. She had none of Sneha Madam's nervousness and intensity. He would laugh at her remarks just the way he did on Facebook.

She kept her appointment with the beauty parlour a careful secret, for she knew Pooja would disapprove. Pooja did not need her much any more. Vasudha felt a sick bitterness as she realized this and as her baby began wailing again. Poor thing, she wanted to be taken around, to be played with more, to be given attention and Vasudha couldn't. For she had her life to live, and so Vasudha hugged her baby gingerly.

Her blow-dried hair bounced on her shoulders; she no longer had on her usual bunched up ponytail. She had put on blue eye shadow to match her long blue tie-and-dyed kurta. The laundry girl had put in a bit too much starch. The kurta shone whenever it caught the light directly. Her jeans now fit just right. And for one day, she would not wear her glasses.

Vasudha kissed her baby fondly one last time and felt a quick sorrow clutch her heart. A truth had come to her so unexpectedly that she stood still. She did not have a mother's sense of responsibility, for it was these moments without her baby that she most looked forward to. Her assignations were simply a way to get away from not just the immediate but from her ever-demanding baby. The door creaked in the wind, the baby chortled in pure happiness as one of Pooja's helpers tickled her playfully and Vasudha steeled herself for what lay ahead.

Only in the cab did some of her old reassurance return. She wondered if Ghatge would be dressed the same way as the last time. She had joked about it during their last exchange on Facebook, and Ghatge had made her laugh. *I will look so different you will not recognize me, Vasudhaji.*

He arrived five minutes after she had, wearing a rather garish blazer and a cap set at a jaunty angle.

In the apartment, Ghatge had taken his time placing his cap on the hat stand, then opened the mirror to place his jacket in the locker behind. Then for long moments, he had stood looking at himself in the mirror, running his fingers through his thinning hair. Self-consciousness made one do that, she understood, and that new knowledge filled her with new confidence. Only then did he smile, 'Vasudhaji, last time we were rushed. Have you seen the flat? Have you been in any place like this before?

She resented the assumption in his tone. 'Of course I have, Sahib,' she said pretending a gaiety. They had both turned into different beings now, apart from their real selves. He was a more public person than she could ever be. Was he now his real self before her? It made her heart beat, and she felt elated at that thought.

He laughed, 'Oh yes, sure you must have. Come let's see this carefully then.'

In the inner hallway, they stopped before a photo of a famous film star, clad in a diaphanous gown that left nothing to the imagination. This was something she had missed before.

'It's by this photographer. He knew her at one time before she became...decent.' Ghatge said, haltingly. She dared not look at him then, and the next moment, Ghatge leaned closer, slapped her on the butt and turned her roughly to face him. 'You are a big tease, Vasudha. A big ripe tease.'

He wasn't even remotely respectful to her. George, for instance, had been obsequious, always asking for permission before he took liberties with her. But Ghatge stared at her, looking right through her and smiling as if he read her thoughts. 'That photo. Tell me your thoughts. Do women think dirty too?'

'We should talk,' she said, trying to keep the tremor away from her voice. She would not give anything away, even her own fear. She was determined to see this through.

'Oh yes, we should talk.' He had an amused look, and she saw the scar on his jawline. A thin line that vanished into his neck. 'Sure, we can talk inside. And then someone will call.' He wagged his finger in front of her face. 'We don't have time.'

The room he led her to had wide sea-facing windows, with free-fluttering lace curtains. She smelt the breeze laden with the stench of stale fish. He pressed a switch and the curtains closed, but the windows stayed open. 'Nature is there for us to enjoy,' he declaimed, almost god-like, pulling her to him.

'The switch takes away the smell, leaving us the pleasure,' he laughed and she hoped she hadn't looked too dazed at that revelation. He stared down at her as his hands cupped her breasts. She felt his fingers, long, cold and snaky and she shivered. Then with a neat movement of his fingers, he pulled the bag off from her shoulders and it slid to the floor with a dull clank.

'No need to get scared. Just enjoy yourself.'

'That was my phone,' she said shakily.

'You are beautiful,' he said. 'Forget all this, your phone too. Be the tease you have been.' He smiled in the way he had, a thin twisting of the lips, but there was no sneer on his face.

For that one moment, she regretted the fact that she was recording all this. She hoped nothing had happened to the phone, she had placed it right in her bag's front flap, its microphone turned on full. She smiled, staring behind him, at her bag, as he lifted her, surprising them both at how effortlessly he did it.

The breeze thudded against the window, like the sea itself had surged in with a warning.

'Did you bring her here?'

She turned away not knowing why she had asked that, nor wanting to hear his answer. He laughed against her throat, 'Arre, come on, don't bring anyone else into this.'

On the table, a newspaper turned its pages noisily, the curtains moved around, quieter than before.

'When I was in New York, it was even higher up than this,' he said, looking down at her, as he removed her clothes expertly. 'And I was nervous. What if those planes came by again...?'

It was her turn to laugh. 'They have increased security in those places. Even a drone doesn't get in without permission.' Another of her Facebook friends, Sidney, had photographed a drone right over Times Square and reported how the police had no difficulty tracking down its owner. 'They have cameras now all over the city.'

'Ooh that's scary.' He ran his fingers down her back. She had had no idea how long they talked. Ghatge moved from one subject to another quite freely and randomly. In the midst of talking dirty, he would tell her about a politician who would have meetings while he was being massaged. Every slap on the skin—and he slapped her none too gently on her backside—would sound sharp like a gunshot. He was easy to talk to. He made her laugh, even the times he was evasive, or when he looked out in the distance. As if he had only just realized what he was doing. It made her overeager in some way, to make the present matter in some way to him.

'When I was in Burj Khalifa,' she began, keen to get her own in, trying hard to remember every detail from Allison's pictures. 'It sometimes felt the clouds would come in. And we could see passing plane lights from very near.'

'I need to go,' he said, after having looked out into the distance for some time. He turned and looked at his gold-banded wrist watch, something discarded on the floor with all their clothes. His abruptness hurt her. But he rose, pulled a towel from the chair and vanished into the bathroom.

She was checking her phone as she heard the water running, the clink of the shower curtains drawn aside. But he emerged far too quickly, startling her.

'Anything the matter?'

'No, no, just my daughter.'

Then anxious to change the subject, she looked past him at the bathroom. 'Goodness, the tub's as big as a pool.'

'Yes, it is. Sometimes they have movie shootings here. Why don't you freshen up? Sorry, I have to go.'

The next time she met Ghatge, she had with her some of the letters, photocopied from Sneha Desai's office. It was strange how she had forgotten about these the last time, nor had he bothered to ask. She flushed, remembering again how wild that last encounter had been, the bed left all crumpled—he'd only said dismissively that someone would see to it—and the new phone he had sent her just the other day. *Sorry, in case I broke phone,* said the note.

In her bag, she had a list of all of Sneha's last clients, a photocopy of the agreement and then the love letters, dated to more than forty years ago. Neera Joshi's long, soulful ones to Ramakrishna Desai. She wondered if Desai had ever replied to her, but he must have valued them, for he had stored them in a secret file. He wasn't to know what would happen to him. That he would be felled by bullets barely a week after Neera's last tearful letter to him. Vasudha also had with her the photocopies Ghatge certainly did not expect—details of his stay with Sneha in a hotel in Bangalore, and another of their email about the trip to Panchgani. The one Sneha had agreed to, before she had committed suicide by walking into the cold waters of the lake at night.

When she pushed across the long Manila envelope to Ghatge, his glance flickered over it once before returning for a longer and harder gaze. It scared her then. But it was the love letters that made him laugh, long and hard. It was even more than he had asked for, he said, tossing them aside and pulling her towards him.

'This city has been given over to old people and their love,' he said. And after they were done, his hand rummaged over the letters and he read them out to her, looking at her from time to time. Stroking her breasts, slapping her on the backside again, if he found something particularly amusing. 'Good English eh?' he'd said. 'Why, Neeraji was quite passionate, wasn't she? Who would have thought?'

Oh my darling, my heart beats for you.

Write me, else this city will stifle me. All I breathe in are your words.

He snorted with laughter, clutching his stomach before doubling over again with some helplessness. She knew then that was the last time she would be with him.

That was the time he left her with the handsome Vuitton bag. 'Gift for you, Vasudhaji, you are smart and clever.' He tapped her on the nose, squeezed her breast one last time and left. She realized moments later as she heard through the door, the elevator door close behind him, that the bag had twenty thousand rupees in it.

It filled her with fright and then delight. She held the bag close to her heart, and felt her heart beat hard against the expensive soft leather.

That entire month, on two evenings, she took a cab to the apartment. The pretence gave her some pleasure, she could revel in its luxury, give herself up to it for a few hours. These were things she liked. A sense of space and the freedom to move in. Not jewellery and expensive clothes. She hated returning to the chawl, and only thoughts of her baby brought her back. There was the one time she had felt insulted when a guard, a different one in the evening, stopped her once. 'I have the keys,' Vasudha had said haughtily. 'It's my apartment.' As it would be for some days, before Ghatge asked for the keys. She would end it once she felt he had plied her with enough presents and money. Else it would end when he had lost interest in her, in these secret meetings, the wildness of the encounters, and in her breasts that he liked squeezing a bit too much. He would never pursue her once she had made up her mind: the threat of the recordings would always hang over him like a warning.

The times she had used her head had always served Vasudha well. The time, several years ago, when she had left her home early one morning, taking the early morning bus from Thekkady to Trichy. She did not miss the red-roofed houses, the quiet still boats on the quiet still river, though sometimes she wished she had had at least a photo of the place. It might have looked good on Facebook. But those days, the picture postcard scenes that tourists marvelled about, suffocated her. The longer she stayed, Vasudha felt, she would be framed into a still existence too.

Her father had been a canteen manager in Kuwait. All he talked about was of building another storey to their house, making it the biggest in the area. 'Then what?' she had asked him during one of his weekly long-distance calls. He had laughed. 'When it is made, ours will be the biggest house.'

'Then what?'

'There is no then what,' he had said, annoyed, and asked to speak to her brother instead. He, younger by five years, was clearly the favourite. He'd do well in his studies, study engineering, as their father had decided and then he would join him in Dubai as a contractor. Her father believed that was the best job possible. A good contractor had money to play with and men to boss around.

'Then what?' Happiness, Vasudha answered herself as she took the bus to college where she had enrolled on her own, using the money she had earned from tutoring some kids in English. She would train as a nurse. That was where the jobs where, the work that would take her out of Kerala.

But the crowded rooms, the cramped teaching room smelling of phenyl, the doctors who treated them like servants, the patients and their families and their never-ending litany of demands and complaints depressed her.

One of the nursing supervisors, a plump dark woman, had passed on a book Vasudha immediately recognized as a romance novel, a Mills and Boons. 'I've been reading it,' said the supervisor, and Vasudha saw the thin moustache on her lips and the way embarrassment left two blotchy purple patches on her face. 'It's much better than the Bible, I tell you.' Vasudha had thanked her in surprise when the supervisor had leaned forward and squeezed her upper arm. 'I like you. Your English is very good.'

Vasudha smiled as she disentangled herself. 'I will read, sister. I will.' She had felt the supervisor's eyes on her till she turned the corner. She read it on the bus back to her hostel, to the dorm she shared with six others. It helped to keep away the stares, the brazen harassment from her fellow male passengers who would lean too close, jostle her but holding a book up, she could elbow people out. And a few pages into the book, she was hooked into its world, one totally different from her own, with handsome doctors, and lovely nurses who fell in love with each other and married. They lived in clean apartments and worked in well-functioning hospitals. She had decided she would apply to hospitals like these, perhaps in a place like Singapore or even in Europe. The supervisor said she had applied already but everything took time. Yet Vasudha refused to give in to despair. The happiness in those books filled her with a light-hearted wonder. Anything was possible. She hadn't anticipated falling in love but even that had happened.

When George Mathew came by, he was a visiting medical representative. There was something about the way he chatted her up. They had been talking about antibiotics and painkillers, when he said he had had something particularly effective for chikungunya. 'It's not patented yet but every effective. You could use it here,' he suggested.

'I cannot just sanction it, George, there is a procedure.'

He'd laughed at that. 'Things always never happen because of procedures involved.' He sounded bitter at the same time. Yet it became a joke with them. When he asked her out for coffee, and she hesitated, he had laughed, 'You mean there's a procedure for this too?'

She still smiled when she thought about it. When he reappeared in her hospital after several days, she read the tension on his face. Then it was she who had suggested they go out for coffee, despite the stares, the open curiosity this would invite.

'I had gone for this interview.' George was calm as he began but then had burst forth, spewing venom and anger. He blamed the system, the corruption of officials and how everything, all available jobs were reserved for some people or else it was all rigged. Vasudha listened, offered necessary words of comfort, and in all, felt very motherly.

It was she who had had the idea of forging papers, getting a letterhead drawn on the name of a reputed pharmacist who lived safely in Cochin. George basked in considerable false glory then, writing prescriptions whenever this was required and even peddling harmless medicines. Then barely a year later, they had left for Mumbai.

Vasudha remembered looking out of the bus often during their long journey. There were places on the way they might have stopped. Bangalore, even Goa, but it was Mumbai she had set her heart on. It was the only place that offered a chance.

It was there Vasudha found a job, and quite by accident. But that kind of luck no longer happened to her, though she longed for it. At the station, they had been intercepted by someone who appeared as a railway ticket-checker, but a chance look at his badge told Vasudha he was a fraud. It was she, a fraud herself, who read through his deception. 'That's an Automobile Association badge,' she hissed, a gleam in her eyes, feeling a thrill not because she had caught out someone but simply by the man's audacity.

'Don't give me away, sister,' he pleaded.

She yanked him by the tie and pulled him towards a tea stall. George followed with their bags, smiling his weak smile at the few bystanders. The ticket-checker looked dazed as she pushed them both down into chairs facing her. She felt she had now a renewed power, to make good, to give life.

'I am barely surviving in this city,' the ticket-checker explained.

'And we want to do that too,' she said insistently. 'Tell me do you make much money doing this?'

'Enough to feed myself. Forget about the soul.' He attempted a laugh but sobered when he saw her stern expression. Back then her heavy black-framed glasses had given people this impression about her and she was glad. At least it staved off harassment though it didn't get you the right job. George, tired from a sleepless, guilt-ridden journey, lay slumped across the table. The ticket-checker took off his coat, making sure the badge was hidden. Then he beckoned to the urchin who helped at the tea stall, and ordered tea for them. He looked around carefully as if reassuring himself that they were not observed, and then told them more about his ailing mother, the expensive prices for her medicines, how rents were rising everywhere in the city, and that their days in the chawl were numbered.

Then he had wiped his tears away and asked after them. And that was how she had gone to work for Sneha Desai and in a matter of weeks the city had seeped into her. It was a city given over to a hunger, a race between everyone to get ahead, and a desperation because they knew it was all over already. If you were always travelling by train, always keeping an imaginary account in your head, you didn't have the time or space to even think over your next step. Vasudha didn't know till recently that space meant something else, more than the obvious. Space for yourself. This city didn't give you that. And those who had even a modicum of space were the ones eager to stay ahead, greedy to always take more than their rightful necessary share. She thought of the empty apartment in Versova. An entire sidewalk full of people could sleep in it comfortably.

There had been times late at night, when she had listened to George Mathew's quiet breathing as the trains rumbled by just under their window. Perhaps she had seen in Pooja what the nursing supervisor too had once seen in her once. Someone who needed to be comforted. Vasudha had indeed been moved to pity. But the baby had been a mistake; making overtures to Ghatge had been another. She was just not in that league.

It took Vasudha considerable willpower but she emerged from her room after two days. She helped around with Pooja, even made some of the lunch deliveries herself. Ghatge didn't call. But she knew he wouldn't. The civil election results were out. His wife, as he had told her, would be elected the new chief of the municipality. It was all a foregone conclusion. Just some matters to be resolved, he had said in his airy manner. She knew what it meant: paying off rivals, threatening others.

She missed him in a way. He hadn't been all bad, and he had made her those gifts too, but she hated the thought of being used just for fun. She felt certain he was laughing at her. She felt mocked, humiliated and then angry. Always it was the anger that returned, giving her new reasons to live on.

It was the fifth day since her last visit to the apartment, a time when the baby was just beginning to sit up that she heard from Allison. Allison, who had just returned from her Australian holiday, and was already complaining of Dubai's dry desert heat. *I've to keep the air conditioner on almost freezing but just one look out the window will make you feel hot again,* she wrote.

But it was the second para that got Vasudha's attention. *Darling, there's something I'd like to share with you, and I hope you don't mind. You've told me before how you'd like to come here with a job. And I've been thinking I'd love to have you here. Baby Matt needs a competent, trustworthy and intelligent nanny. You'd not be a housekeeper but almost family. But the thing is, about the baby? That makes for certain complications, right?*

Vasudha stared hard at the words, unable to reply immediately. Allison was offering her a trip to Dubai, and a job to go with it. The apartment was huge, and it needed considerable maintenance, which meant hard, back-breaking work, Vasudha surmised. And Allison, moreover, appeared to trust her. The kind of trust that Vasudha found childish and flattering, even if she didn't trust it herself.

It's quite a shock I know, wrote Allison, a moment later, as she sensed Vasudha's hesitation. *I am sorry, maybe I should not have written in such hurry.* Vasudha had a feeling Allison was even laughing in some embarrassment now. It made her write back immediately. *Yes, I'd hate to leave baby Kiran behind. But I'd like to make enough money to come back and provide for her. She could be with my mother.*

The lie came easily to her. Vasudha had not seen her mother since leaving home those many years ago. Her mother, with her constant ill health, had frightened the life out of Vasudha. If she stayed on, she feared she would one day end up like her mother. And here was Allison, offering her just the right beginning.

But she couldn't bring herself to lie to Pooja. Not for the sake of their old friendship, nor for her baby. It was only Pooja she could turn to. 'I need to go,' she told Pooja, when she finally had a moment to spare from all her visits to the consulate, after all the check-ups had been done, and all the necessary documents had been obtained. This time the tears came willingly to Vasudha. The last few weeks of worry and humiliation now seemed too much. It was Ghatge who was making her life miserable, Vasudha added. 'He wanted me to give him the papers and then blackmailed me. To have sex.'

She stumbled over the words and Pooja's eyes widened in shock. She held her hands and Vasudha tried hard not to struggle to extricate herself. 'We can do something, even tell Raina on email. That's horrible.'

'No. This is my thing. I will get my revenge. I have it planned out.' She was rambling and breathless and she sobbed, taking in great big gulps of air that had Pooja genuinely concerned. 'I have to go. To better my prospects. And I can't be sure about the baby.'

Pooja had looked confused but only for a moment. Then she lifted her hand to her hair and said, in the quiet tone, Vasudha well knew. 'I am there for Kiran. And Suhel will understand, once he's back...'

Vasudha stared. Pooja was trying not to blush at the mention of Suhel, and it made her look lovely. Suhel was due to return from Maryland in two weeks. Vasudha felt a resentment then, at the unbelievable luck Pooja always seemed to draw, while her own came moth-eaten, always with conditions attached. She squeezed Pooja's hands, looked at her clear, unlined face. Someone had once told her that if you had a clear, unmarked brow, you'd have a nice secure future and Pooja deserved that. Her baby too would be safe with her. Vasudha had never been the maternal kind. Now she felt monstrous, as she realized the enormity of her decision. The look in Pooja's eyes seemed to only confirm that.

The day Vasudha left, her baby was still asleep in a cot that she had moved to Pooja's room the night before. 'We will manage, Vasudha,' Pooja told her with a sweet determination. 'We all will.' Vasudha looked at her sleeping baby, then turned around and left without a backward glance.

Acknowledgements

This novel began life as a short story. I worked on more stories as a student in Vermont College of Fine Arts' MFA Program in Writing. My advisors and workshop leaders helped me with their advice and critique, and my thanks are due to Lawrence (Larry) Sutin, my advisor for two semesters; Nance Van Winckel, Brian Leung, Ellen Lesser, David Jauss, Martha Southgate. I miss my father, Chinmay Chakrabarty, immensely; he passed away two years ago. My family in India: my mother, Uma Chakrabarty, my sister, Soma and brother, Dhruba, have always been supportive.

Rohan Chhetri asked me to write to Anurag Basnet at Speaking Tiger, who said yes to this manuscript and Anurag's inputs and suggestions helped me further. I am so grateful to both of them, and also to Radhika Shenoy for being so supportive and kind. A novel is largely an isolated act, so I feel fortunate that I had friends I could reach out to. Hansda Sowvendra Shekhar, Rajat Chaudhuri, Gauraang Pradhan, Arpita Das, Vatsala Kaul-Banerjee and Rumjhum Biswas (Shikhandin). My friends in VCFA continue to be inspiring and ever-encouraging: Tim Bridwell, Carolyn Ogburn, Donald Quist and Cristina DeSouza. I learnt a lot writing and researching other kinds of stuff for Scroll.in and *Economic and Political Weekly*, and other places, and my thanks are due to Naresh Fernandes, Aman Khanna, Nandini Ramnath, Arunava Sinha (even the rejections were encouraging!), and Lina Mathias and Lubna Duggal at the *EPW*. Ajay and Devyani have always been with me, in whatever I do, and am grateful they have been there, at all times, never asking too much in return.

www.ingramcontent.com/pod-product-compliance
Lightning Source LLC
Chambersburg PA
CBHW060530030726
47498CB00004B/1141